Davy touched Carla's arm and indicated that he wanted to talk to her. She felt her heart drop. Hadn't they said enough earlier?

Not tonight. Not on Christmas Eve, she wanted to say. But could she even pretend for one night that there wasn't a killer after her?

Davy pointed upward. When she looked up, she blinked at the sight of mistletoe hanging from one of the log rafters above them. Her gaze dropped to his.

"Carla, it's Christmas. Could we just enjoy this time together?" he asked as he brushed a lock of her hair back from her eyes. "Can we put our differences aside? We used to be good friends before we became..." He seemed to hesitate. Lovers? "More," he finished. His gaze met hers and practically burned her with its intensity.

Carla wanted that desperately—no matter how dangerous.

Davy Colt was a good, loving man. He'd dropped everything to protect her. One night without the past pushing its way between them sounded like heaven. She nodded and he pulled her to him.

B.J. Daniels is a *New York Times* and *USA TODAY* bestselling author. She wrote her first book after a career as an award-winning newspaper journalist and author of thirty-seven published short stories. She lives in Montana with her husband, Parker, and three springer spaniels. When not writing, she quilts, boats and plays tennis. Contact her at bjdaniels.com, on Facebook or on Twitter, @bjdanielsauthor.

Books by B.J. Daniels

Harlequin Intrigue

A Colt Brothers Investigation

Murder Gone Cold
Sticking to Her Guns
Christmas Ransom & Cardwell Ranch Trespasser

Cardwell Ranch: Montana Legacy

Steel Resolve
Iron Will
Ambush before Sunrise
Double Action Deputy
Trouble in Big Timber
Cold Case at Cardwell Ranch

Whitehorse, Montana: The Clementine Sisters

Hard Rustler
Rogue Gunslinger
Rugged Defender

Visit the Author Profile page at Harlequin.com.

B.J.
NEW YORK TIMES BESTSELLING AUTHOR
DANIELS

CHRISTMAS RANSOM & CARDWELL RANCH TRESPASSER

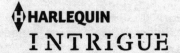

HARLEQUIN
INTRIGUE

Recycling programs for this product may not exist in your area.

ISBN-13: 978-1-335-44975-7

Christmas Ransom & Cardwell Ranch Trespasser

Copyright © 2022 by Harlequin Enterprises ULC

Christmas Ransom
Copyright © 2022 by Barbara Heinlein

Cardwell Ranch Trespasser
First published in 2013. This edition published in 2022.
Copyright © 2013 by Barbara Heinlein

Harlequin Enterprises ULC
22 Adelaide St. West, 41st Floor
Toronto, Ontario M5H 4E3, Canada
www.Harlequin.com

Printed in U.S.A.

CONTENTS

CHRISTMAS RANSOM

Chapter 1

The whole desperate plan began simply as a last-ditch attempt to save his life. He never intended for anyone to get hurt. That day, not long after Thanksgiving, he walked into the bank full of hope. It was the first time he'd ever asked for a loan. It was also the first time he'd ever seen executive loan officer Carla Richmond.

When he tapped at her open doorway, she looked up from that big desk of hers. He thought she was too young and pretty with her big blue eyes and all that curly chestnut-brown hair to make the decision as to whether he lived or died.

She had a great smile as she got to her feet to offer him a seat.

He felt so out of place in her plush office that he stood in the doorway nervously kneading the brim of his worn baseball cap for a moment before stepping in. As he did, her blue-eyed gaze took in his ill-fitting clothing hanging on his rangy body, his bad haircut, his large, weathered hands.

He told himself that she'd already made up her mind before he even sat down. She didn't give men like him a second look—let alone money. Like his father always said, bankers never gave dough to poor people who actually needed it. They just helped their rich friends.

Right away Carla Richmond made him feel small with her questions about his employment record, what he had for collateral, why he needed the money and how he planned to repay it. He'd recently lost one crappy job and was in the process of starting another temporary one, and all he had to show for the years he'd worked hard labor since high school was an old pickup and a pile of bills.

He took the forms she handed him and thanked her, knowing he wasn't going to bother filling them in. On the way out of her office, he balled them up and dropped them in the trash. All the way to his pickup, he mentally kicked himself for being such a fool. What had he expected?

No one was going to give him money, even to save his life—especially some woman in a suit behind a big desk in an air-conditioned office. It didn't matter that she didn't have a clue how desperate he really was. All she'd seen when she'd looked at him was a loser. To think that he'd bought a new pair of jeans with the last of his cash and borrowed a too-large button-down shirt from a former coworker for this meeting.

After climbing into his truck, he sat for a moment, too scared and sick at heart to start the engine. The worst part was the thought of going home and telling Jesse. The way his luck was going, she would walk out on him. Not that he could blame her, since his gambling had gotten them into this mess.

He thought about blowing off work since his new job was only temporary anyway and going straight to the bar. Then he reminded himself that he'd spent the last of his money on the jeans. He couldn't even afford a beer. His own fault, he reminded himself. He'd only made things worse when he'd gone to a loan shark for cash and then stupidly gambled the money, thinking he could make back what he owed and then some when he won. He'd been so sure his luck had changed for the better when he'd met Jesse.

Last time the two thugs had come to collect the interest on the loan, they'd left him bleeding in the dirt outside his rented house. They would be back any day.

With a curse, he started the pickup. A cloud of exhaust blew out the back as he headed home to face Jesse with the bad news. Asking for a loan had been a long shot, but still he couldn't help thinking about the disappointment he'd see in her eyes when he told her. They'd planned to go out tonight for an expensive dinner with the loan money to celebrate.

As he drove home, his humiliation began to fester like a sore that just wouldn't heal. Had he known even then how this was going to end? Or was he still telling himself he was just a nice guy who'd made some mistakes, had some bad luck and gotten involved with the wrong people?

Chapter 2

There was nothing worse than having to stop by work on her day off less than a week before Christmas. Or so Carla Richmond thought as she entered the bank to the sound of holiday tunes. She waved to her best friend, Amelia, then to one of the other tellers before she hurried into her office. She didn't bother closing the door since she wasn't staying long. They were having a true Montana winter, she thought as she shed her snow-covered coat, hat and gloves. She hoped she could purchase the rest of her Christmas gifts and make it home before the snowstorm got any worse.

That's why she hoped to make this quick. As executive loan officer, Carla took her job seriously, especially the privacy part. That's why she'd panicked this afternoon when she'd realized that she might not have secured a client file yesterday before leaving work. She was always so careful, but just before quitting time she'd been distracted.

Yesterday, she'd looked up to find Davy Colt leaning against her doorjamb wearing a sheepish grin and the latest rodeo belt buckle he'd won. It wasn't like she'd missed the way his Western shirt hugged those broad shoulders or the way his jeans ran the length of his muscled legs and cupped that perfect behind. He held his Stetson in the fingers of one hand. His blue gaze danced with mischief as he hid his other hand behind him.

She hadn't seen him in months, not even in passing, so being caught off guard like that had come as a shock, though a pleasant one. A while back, in a weak moment, she'd made the mistake of asking his brother Tommy about Davy. Was that why he was standing in her doorway? she'd wondered at the time.

Mentally kicking herself, Carla had wished she hadn't asked Tommy about his brother. Why hadn't she left well enough alone? She'd made a clean break from Davy and since nothing had changed…

"Hey," he'd said. "Bad time? I don't mean to bother you."

"You aren't bothering me." She'd closed the file she'd been working on and shoved it aside. "Is there something…" That's when he'd drawn his hand from behind him and she'd seen what he'd been hiding. "Is that—"

"Mistletoe," he'd said with a shy, almost nervous grin. He'd stepped into her office, bringing with him the scent of pine and the crisp Montana air. She'd breathed it in as if she'd never had oxygen before. "I got to thinking about you on my way into town. I pinched the mistletoe from the doorway of a shop down the street." He'd glanced at his boots. "It reminded me of our first Christmas together." When he'd looked up, he'd shrugged as if embarrassed. "Guess I was feeling a little nostalgic, the holidays and all. You get off work soon?"

Was he asking her out? Heart bumping erratically against her ribs, she'd checked the time. "In twenty minutes." That's when she'd remembered that she'd promised to meet a friend for an early dinner. She'd groaned because she'd already canceled on this friend the last time they'd had plans. "But I'm meeting a friend."

Had he looked as disappointed as she'd felt? "No problem. I'm home for a few days over the holidays." His denim-blue gaze had locked with hers for several breath-stealing moments. "Tommy mentioned something about seeing you, and I thought…"

Carla had nodded, although she'd had no idea what he'd thought since he hadn't finished whatever he was going to say.

He'd set the mistletoe on the corner of her desk. "Maybe another time."

She'd tried to smile around her disappointment as he'd settled his Stetson back on his thick dark hair. Every one of those Colt brothers was handsome as sin, but Davy… Well, he had always been her favorite.

He'd met her gaze and she'd felt the heartache of the past settle over her. "Merry Christmas, Carla." And he'd been gone, leaving her with a familiar ache that had gotten worse since their breakup.

Belatedly she'd realized she should have told him that she had the next day off. Not that any good would come from getting involved with Davy again.

But just seeing him and hearing that he remembered the two of them together way back when had her heart floating. Her brain meanwhile was digging in its heels, arguing that picking up where the two of them had left off would be a huge mistake that she would regret.

She'd had a crush on Davy Colt from as far back as she could remember. When he'd finally asked her out in high school, she'd felt as if she had filled with helium. Her feet hadn't touched the ground for weeks.

Her mother hadn't been as thrilled. "I've heard stories about those Colt boys," she'd said, but Carla had assured her that Davy wasn't like that. She'd believed in her heart that Davy was The One. She'd imagined them married with kids. She'd pictured a perfect happy-ever-after—until he'd told her that he wasn't going to college with her at Montana State University, even though he had a rodeo scholarship to attend. He was joining the rodeo circuit instead.

The romantic bubble had exploded with a loud *pop*. He'd rodeoed throughout high school, but she'd never imagined he planned to make it his occupation. Except she should have. Look at the rest of his family, all the way back to his great-grandfather who'd been a Hollywood Western movie star back in the 1940s and '50s. Ridin' and ropin' was in his blood, and being on the road following the rodeo circuit was the life all the Colt brothers had chosen as if it were their destiny as well as their legacy.

Carla, on the other hand, had been raised by a single mother who had barely finished high school. Because of that, Rosemary Richmond was determined Carla would get an education so she had options. Her mother hadn't wanted Carla to end up like her, in a low-paying job living from paycheck to paycheck. Rosemary had said from the time Carla could remember that her only daughter was going to college. Her mother had worked so hard to make that happen.

Carla had had no choice. While it had broken her heart, she'd ended the relationship with Davy and headed for college, where she'd majored in business and finance and graduated with honors. She'd had her pick of jobs.

But when her mother had gotten sick, Carla had taken a job at the local bank in Lonesome to help take care of her. And after she'd died from the cancer, the rest was history. She'd stayed in Lonesome, seeing Davy from time to time—but only in passing. She'd always wondered if she'd made a mistake choosing a career over the cowboy she'd loved. Still loved, if she was being honest.

That's why it had been such a shock when he'd come into the bank to see her. Was it possible he still felt the same way she did about him?

After he'd left, she'd sat at her desk fighting emotions until she'd grabbed her things and hurried to meet her friend. All the time, she'd kept reminding herself that Davy was only home for the holidays. His life was far from Lonesome. Who knew when he'd be back? She had to quit pining away for the rodeo cowboy.

Now as she looked around her desk, she realized that the file she'd thought she left there yesterday afternoon was nowhere to be seen. She took her key and unlocked the file drawer and was flipping through it when she saw that she *had* put the file away. But she had no memory of doing it. Her mind had been a million miles away—just like it was now. No, not quite a million miles. More like the distance from the bank to the Colt Brothers Investigation building down the street.

Davy Colt would be staying there in the apartment over the business, at least for a few days. Then he'd be riding in Texas after the holidays and who knew where after that, since she tried not to keep track of the rodeo circuit schedule anymore.

Her brain and heart were still at war since his visit yesterday. She told herself he would be busy with family. She might not even see him again before the holiday was over. She figured that, after yesterday, maybe he'd changed his mind about whatever thought had prompted him to stop by her office.

She picked up the mistletoe on the corner of her desk, but couldn't force herself to throw it away. She put it back down. Maybe he'd stop by work tomorrow or the next day. If he came in looking for her, she was sure that the other loan officer, Amelia Curtis, or one of the tellers would let him know that she'd be working right up through Christmas Eve, in case Davy wanted to stop back by.

Even as she wanted desperately to see him again, she knew how dangerous that could be. Davy was serious about only one thing—rodeo—and spending time with him would only lead to another heartbreak.

As she started to reach for her things to leave, someone in the lobby screamed and then the whole place broke out in what sounded like panicked alarm. Carla looked up. Standing in her doorway was a masked man in a Santa suit holding a semiautomatic rifle. The Santa mask—complete with big white beard and red hat—covered his entire head. The only thing visible was the shine of his dark eyes through two small holes and the ugly slash at his mouth as he rushed toward her.

Chapter 3

The plan had come to him in the darkest, most desperate hours of night. He hadn't been able to sleep in the weeks since going to the bank for the loan and realizing that there would be no Christmas miracle. No Hail Mary pass. No one to bail him out. And if he didn't do something soon, Jesse was going to leave him.

As he lay awake, he kept replaying the day he'd gone to the bank for the loan with so much hope, misplaced or not. Before he'd left that afternoon, his girlfriend, Jesse, had told him how handsome he looked in his borrowed button-down shirt and new jeans. It had made him smile despite how scared he'd been to ask a bank for money.

But like Jesse had said, what did he have to lose? A lot, he'd discovered, because when he'd returned home empty-handed, Jesse had run out onto the porch. She'd been wearing a new dress for the celebratory dinner they had planned. She'd looked so happy, so hopeful.

"Did you get the loan?" Her expression drooped as she must have seen the answer written all over his face. His shoulders slumped as she let out a choked sob and turned away as if she didn't want him to see her cry.

He'd rushed up the steps and taken her in his arms, holding her as if she was all that was keeping him rooted to earth.

"They're going to kill us!" she said between sobs. "Look what happened the last time they came for a payment." She felt stiff in his arms. When she pulled back to look at him, he saw her disappointment in him like poison in her eyes. She pushed him, then balled her hands into fists and pounded against his chest until he pulled her to him so tightly that she finally slumped in his arms and sobbed.

"I bet you didn't even go to the bank and ask," she cried.

"I did. I talked to Carla Richmond, the executive loan officer." Jesse had stopped crying and was listening, but he had no more to say. He wasn't about to tell her that he'd thrown the forms away without even filling them out. He shook his head. "Don't worry. They won't kill us. I'll take care of it."

He could feel the distance growing between them in the quaking of her body. She'd trusted him and look what a mess he'd made of it. They hadn't been together long. He still couldn't believe that a woman who looked like her had given him a second glance.

They'd met at a bar in another town. The next morning, in the light of day, he'd figured that would be the end of it. But when he'd asked her if she wanted to come home with him, she had. She'd only balked a little when he told her he lived in Lonesome. It had been her idea to move out of the trailer he was renting and into a house. She'd gotten a job right away. He'd really believed that Lady Luck was finally on his side.

That day after he'd been turned down at the bank, he'd held Jesse until she quit crying and he'd felt all the fight go out of her. His shirt had been wet with her tears. He'd wanted to be this woman's hero from the moment he'd met her and brought her back to Lonesome four months ago. He'd told himself he still could. He would think of something. He couldn't lose her.

"I need to go to work," she'd whispered, pulling back to look down in what could only be disgust at the new dress she'd bought.

"Call in sick," he'd said, afraid to let her go. All he had thought about was curling up naked in their bed, holding each other until they fell asleep.

Her job paid the rent and kept the lights on. His new temporary one would keep them fed and buy gas for their vehicles. With luck, they would have enough money at the end of the week to hold off the loan shark. Between the two of them they were slowly going broke because of the foolish mistakes he'd made. Worse, she was right. The last time the men had come for the money, they'd almost killed him and had threatened her. The next time they came would be worse.

Who was he kidding? There was no way he'd have enough money to hold them off. They would kill him, but his real terror was what they might do to Jesse if she were home. Probably the best thing she could do was leave him. He knew she'd thought about it. Maybe this would be the straw that broke the camel's back.

"I have to change," she'd said, pulling away. "I can't lose my job."

He'd watched her walk away, his gut cramping at the thought of her leaving him for good. He kept a pack of cigarettes that he'd swiped from one of the men he'd worked with. Jesse hated him smoking. But once she'd left…

She'd come out dressed for work. She'd fixed her face and pulled her long blond hair up into a ponytail. As with every time he'd looked at her, he was always stunned at how beautiful she was. How had he gotten so lucky? It still astounded him, and he knew he would do whatever it took to keep her.

"It's going to be all right, baby," he'd said as he'd quickly stepped to her and leaned down to kiss her. He'd thought she'd pull away, but instead, she'd looped her arms around his neck and pulled him down to her. The kiss had started a fire in his belly that slid lower. He'd thought of their bed just inside, thought of her naked.

"I'm going to be late," she'd said as she drew back. Their gazes had met for a long moment.

"Don't lose faith in me." He hated that his voice had broken.

She'd shaken her head and given him a weak smile. "I know you will think of something. You working tonight?"

He'd nodded. A lie. He'd quit the night stocking job at the grocery store in town when he'd realized it wasn't enough to get him out of trouble—and that Jesse was right. Maybe the simpliest answer had been to go to the bank for a loan. He'd picked up the temporary job through the rest of the holiday—one he had planned to quit once he'd gotten the bank loan.

The truth was that even the loan wouldn't have held off the goons for long. He was just as good as dead.

He'd been so down that day after going to the bank. He'd thought for sure that he'd lost Jesse. His words had felt like sawdust in his mouth. "I'd understand if you left me. I wouldn't blame you at all."

He couldn't have the men stopping by for the money and finding her home alone.

To his surprise, she'd said, "You aren't getting rid of me that easily. You'll think of something, Jud."

After she'd left, his throat parched from the cigarettes he'd smoked, he knew what he had to do. He'd been left no choice. But the plan hadn't come together until he'd talked it over with Jesse. It still amazed him how she'd known so much about robbing a bank. She'd been angrier with Carla Richmond than he'd been.

"She deserves this for not giving you the loan," Jesse had said. "She's probably had everything handed to her all of her life. How dare she. Someday she's going to get what's coming to her."

Before Carla could scream, the Santa-suited robber rushed around her desk to grab a handful of her long hair and drag her toward the lobby. She saw others already on the floor and felt the panic that seemed to suck all the air out of the room. Amelia was crying and so were the tellers. They all looked terrified where they lay.

"On the floor!" the man bellowed, using his hold on her hair to throw her down. Carla stumbled, landing hard on her side, pain shooting across her shoulder as the breath was knocked out of her. "Facedown!" he yelled and kicked her in the side.

She flattened herself facedown on the floor, fighting the pain as she gasped for breath. She tried to see if the others were all right. A teller was sobbing as she emptied out her till into a large bag, the kind Santa might carry toys in, and moved on to the next one. The bank had been about to close, so there were only a couple of customers on the floor, two older women frozen in fear. In all the racket, she could hear the bank manager trying to reason with one of the robbers.

There appeared to be three robbers, all in Santa suits and rubber masks. They wore white gloves on their hands and tall black boots, exposing no skin except for those holes where their eyes peered out—and that slit for their mouths.

One of the robbers had a gun to the bank manager's head as he led him back toward the vault. The other robber finished loading the money from the tills, then ordered the teller onto the floor to lie down with the others as he followed the bank manager toward the vault. Carla saw that the robber had an extra bag with him along with the one full of money from the tellers' tills.

She knew she must be in shock because her thoughts seemed to veer all over the place. Bank robberies were rare. The rule of thumb was that if a bank hadn't been robbed in a hundred years, then it was due. This bank hadn't been robbed in almost a hundred and twenty. She thought about how much money was in the vault and groaned inwardly. They had more money than usual because of the holidays. Had the robbers known that?

Stay calm, she chanted silently. *Stay calm*. She realized she was trembling. Her shoulder and side ached, and her scalp hurt from where he'd dragged her by her hair. She wanted to touch the spot on her head, to rub it, but was afraid to breathe, let alone move. Instead, she tried to concentrate on staying calm as she heard crying and praying, and the man yelling at everyone to stay down or die. No one wanted to die here today. Not right before Christmas.

Her gaze flicked up to the man who'd dragged her from her office. He'd moved off to the side, his semiautomatic rifle trained on those on the floor some distance away from her. He seemed nervous and kept shifting on his feet and pulling at the back of the mask.

She watched as he reached up under his fake white beard and scratched hard at his neck. She caught sight of what appeared to be a red rash and realized he must be allergic to whatever material the mask was made of.

But the rash wasn't the only thing she'd seen when he'd raised the mask. He had a tattoo low on his neck. There were two *J*'s with an odd-shaped heart between them. *J* loves *J*?

Even though she was sure that she hadn't made a sound, he quickly adjusted his mask and spun in her direction, leading with the business end of the rifle in his hand. She saw from his expression that he'd realized his mistake in lifting the bottom of the mask. Carla had quickly looked away, but she could feel his gaze boring into her. Did he know what she'd seen? Her heart pounded harder, her breath more ragged. She feared he knew as she heard him advance on her. "I told you to keep your head down!"

Chapter 4

Jud couldn't believe what had just happened. But the moment he'd seen her expression, he'd realized that she'd seen something when he'd lifted the Santa beard to scratch his neck. His tattoo! The foolish woman. She'd tell the cops. He tried to tell himself that the law wouldn't be able to track him down by some silly tattoo, but even as he was arguing the point, he knew he couldn't take the chance.

Jesse wouldn't wait for him if he went to prison. Hell, she was barely hanging on as it was. If he could pull off this bank job, they'd leave the country. Maybe go to someplace warm, sit on a beach and watch the sunset. Jesse would like that. He could finally make her happy. Maybe they'd even get married.

He'd asked her to marry him, but she'd put him off. He was no fool. He knew that she was hoping for something better. With his share of the money, he could be better.

He could give her more than some drunken sentimental gesture like a tattoo. He'd wanted her name embedded into his flesh, but hadn't had enough money according to the tattoo tech. Maybe if he hadn't spent so much on the booze before coming up with the idea…

Swearing under his breath, he tried not to scratch his neck again, but this mask and beard were making him hot and itchy. He wasn't sure how much longer he could stand having it on. He felt as if he couldn't breathe. All he wanted to do was rip it off and scratch his damned neck.

He glanced anxiously toward the short hallway to the vault. What was taking them so long? He quickly looked back at Carla Richmond. He thought about what Jesse had said about her. Worse, he figured Carla was smart. Too smart for her own good. But she'd made a mistake that was now going to cost her her life.

The thought made him a little sick. But how could he let her live now? Even if the cops couldn't track him down because of the tattoo, she might remember him from the day he'd come in for the loan. He swore under his breath again. If only he hadn't lifted his mask. If she'd done what he'd told her to do… It was her own fault. He hadn't wanted anyone to get hurt.

Glancing toward the vault again, he was about to yell back to see what was taking so long when two Santa-suited figures came out, pushing the bank manager ahead of them and forcing him down on the floor near the tellers.

The larger of the two looked up, signaling that it had gone well. "Let's go!" Buddy called and started toward Jud, carrying a bulging bag filled with money. Eli was right behind with a tote that looked just as full.

For a moment, Jud felt a surge of joy and relief and

pride. It had gone just as Jesse had said it would. His good mood didn't last though as he looked down at the executive loan officer at his feet. He couldn't leave her here alive.

Jud swung the end of the rifle at her head, his finger on the trigger. It wasn't like he had a choice. He hadn't had a choice his whole life.

Out of the corner of her eye, Carla saw him standing over her with his weapon pointed at her head. She could hear him breathing hard under the mask and she knew. He was going to kill her. She'd seen his tattoo. She squeezed her eyes shut and held her breath, but all she could think about was Davy. Hadn't she been holding out hope for years that somehow they would find a way to be together? She felt scalding tears behind her lashes.

"I said let's go!" She opened her eyes and could see that the other two robbers had joined them. "Whatever it is you're thinking about doing, don't," one man said. He was taller and broader than the one with the tattoo. She could feel the tension between the two. "We need to get out of here."

"I can't leave her here," he said, his finger still on the trigger. "Not alive."

"We said no one gets hurt."

"Then I'm taking her hostage."

"No. You're not."

Her arm was suddenly grabbed, fingers digging deep into her flesh as she was jerked to standing. He spun her around and locked his arm around her throat. Nearly lifting her off her feet, he said, "She's coming with us."

Carla heard the screech of tires. She saw a van pull up out front. The driver honked the horn. Somewhere in the distance, she thought she heard sirens. The larger of the men swore and said that someone had pushed an alarm and they had to get out of there.

The robber holding her began to drag her toward the door. She'd watched enough crime television shows to know the last thing she could let this man do was take her out of the bank and into that van. She tried to fight him, but his hold on her throat was cutting off her air supply.

The bank manager was yelling something at the men. One of the robbers was threatening him, telling him to stay down or he would shoot him. Someone on the floor was sobbing loudly now. Someone else began to scream. Then someone else screamed. She realized that the second scream was coming out of her mouth and her terror rose. The time for remaining calm was over.

Frantically she clawed at the arm clamped around her neck, but the Santa suit was thick and she found little purchase as the man dragged her toward the door and the waiting van.

Chapter 5

"Mistletoe?" James Colt laughed, and his brothers Tommy and Willie joined in.

"Hey, I was thinking fast on my feet, okay?" Davy said. He'd been taking a ribbing from his brothers for as long as he could remember. They'd always been close but had grown more so since their father's death. They had the classically handsome Colt features, dark hair and blue eyes, and the reputations to go with them—the wild Colt brothers, as they were known in Lonesome, Montana.

Even if they hadn't been rodeo cowboys like their father and grandfather, most mothers in town didn't want them dating their daughters. Davy didn't think it mattered that both James and Tommy had settled down recently, become private investigators and were now married.

"That is so cheesy," Tommy said of the mistletoe. "So what happened?"

"I hope you got the kiss," Willie said, eyeing him speculatively. "That was all you were after, right?"

His brothers knew how heartbroken he'd been when Carla had ended their relationship years ago. "Like I said, spur-of-the-moment. I'm not sure what I had in mind. Maybe to just say hello. Maybe I thought we could have a drink together, talk old times, I don't know."

They were all gathered in the Colt Brothers Investigation office. It had changed since his father, Del, had started the PI business almost ten years ago—before his death. James and Tommy had moved the office downstairs, keeping their father's desk and large leather office chair.

There were two bedrooms now upstairs for when Davy and Willie were home. They would have been welcome to stay with James or Tommy at their homes, but they preferred the upstairs apartment on Main Street, Lonesome. They all had memories of spending time in the office with their father.

"So did you get around to asking her out?" James had been the first to leave the rodeo circuit. After getting involved in one of their father's old cases, he'd decided he wanted to be in the PI business.

Davy looked down at his boots. "Just my luck she already had a date."

Willie shook his head. "You sure you want to go down that path again?"

He wasn't sure. That was the problem. It's why he'd stayed away today. "What's this about you joining the sheriff's department?" he asked, hoping to get the focus off him.

"Stop trying to change the subject," Willie said.

All of them looked toward Willie. "Davy's right,"

James said. "I distinctly remember you saying you were never going to become a private eye. Too dangerous, you said."

"You'd just spent a night in jail, as I remember," Tommy interjected. "So yeah, what's up with you joining the sheriff's department?"

"I needed a change and we have enough PIs in the family," Willie said with a laugh.

James narrowed his eyes at his brother. "This wouldn't have anything to do with Dad's death, would it?"

"Enough about me," Willie said, standing to walk over to the window that faced Main Street. Davy looked past his brother. Lonesome looked so picturesque with its quaint old brick buildings, Christmas decorations and snowflakes falling to the distant sound of holiday music.

"Willie's right," James said, letting Willie off easy, Davy thought. "I'd think long and hard about revisiting that love affair. As Dad used to say, there are a lot of Buckle Bunnies out there. It isn't like you have ever been short of female company."

Davy sighed and shook his head. There were always cowgirls who followed the circuit. True enough, he had no problem getting a date. But none of them were Carla.

"Remember, she was the one who broke up with you because she didn't want to be married to a rodeo cowboy," Tommy reminded him, as if he could ever forget.

"Can't blame her," James said. "What woman in her right mind would?"

"Unless something has changed?" Tommy said.

Davy shook his head. "There are too many broncs waiting to be ridden."

"Or bucked off of," Tommy said with a laugh.

"Well, I have a few more years." He was young, the

youngest of the brood. He wasn't ready to settle down, he kept telling himself. But he'd never gotten over Carla, and lately he'd been thinking about her more and more. When Tommy told him that she'd said to tell him hello, he'd gotten his hopes up that they might still have a chance.

"Did Carla at least seem glad to see you?" Tommy asked now.

Davy shrugged. "I was too nervous to notice."

Willie had grown quiet, almost reflective, for a few minutes. "Davy, you're ruining our bad reputations," he joked. "I'm getting the feeling that you're still hung up on this woman."

Davy groaned and got to his feet. "Maybe I'll go out for a while, do some Christmas shopping—"

"And maybe stop by the bank before it closes?" Tommy asked with a grin.

At the sound of distant sirens, Willie turned toward the front window again. "Speaking of the bank, it looks like something's happening down there."

Chapter 6

For a moment, Jud didn't know what hit him. He'd been dragging Carla Richmond toward the door, determined to take her hostage, when he heard the pop as one of his ribs cracked from the butt of Buddy's weapon. His own weapon was jerked from his free hand. Gasping for air, he was forced to loosen his leverage on the woman.

After that, everything went south. Carla, no doubt seeing her chance, elbowed him hard in the same spot Buddy had nailed him. The last of his air rushed from his lungs. He doubled over and the woman slipped from his hold to collapse on the floor.

He had only a few seconds as she hurried to scramble out of his reach. In that instant when she'd looked back from the floor, something had passed between them. She'd known he was going to kill her, and he'd known that she would tell the cops what she'd seen.

He kicked her, catching her temple with the toe of his boot. The blow flipped her from her hands and knees to her back. Her head struck the marble floor with a crack and she lay motionless. People began to scream and cry louder. There was shouting and he could hear some of the bank employees getting to their feet and scrambling for cover. If he'd still had his weapon, he would have turned it on all of them—starting with Carla Richmond.

But Buddy grabbed him, propelling him toward the front door of the bank before he could finish her off. The sound of sirens filled the air as the three of them stumbled across the snowy sidewalk to the diminishing sound of Christmas music and into the waiting van at the curb. Their getaway driver, Rick, sped off even before the van doors closed.

Jud looked back through the glass front of the bank. There were people kneeling next to Carla. From what he could tell, she still wasn't moving as the getaway vehicle roared down the road. All he could hope was that she never would again.

"You idiot," Buddy snapped as he pulled off his mask and threw it down on the floor of the van as they sped out of Lonesome—headed for the mountains. "What were you thinking?" he demanded as he struggled to shed his costume. Like the rest of them, he wore a T-shirt and jeans underneath. "The plan wasn't to take a hostage."

Jud glared at him, holding his side. He'd already ripped off his mask, each breath a torture as he scratched angrily at his neck. "Plans change."

Buddy swore, chucked his costume past Jud into the very back of the van and turned away to look out the side window. "I knew better than to get involved with this because you screw up everything you touch. You always have—ever since we were kids."

"We got the money, didn't we?" Jud insisted as he too shed his costume between fits of scratching at the rash breaking out everywhere the costume had touched bare skin.

"The money won't do us any good if we're locked up in prison, or worse, dead. You could have gotten us all killed back there," Buddy snapped.

"He still might," Eli said and pointed out the windshield.

Ahead of them, Jud could see the railroad crossing— and the approaching train. At their rates of speed, both the train and the van would reach the crossing at the same time. He swallowed back the bile that rose in his throat.

He and Jesse had researched their escape, knowing it was the only chance they had of getting out of Lonesome and evading the cops. They would hit the bank and head for the train crossing. He'd timed the robbery so they would get across the tracks before the train by a few minutes. Anyone following them would have to wait for the entire length of the train to pass before following them.

Because of that small window of time, he'd known how dangerous trying to beat the train was going to be. A thirty-car freight train hitting a vehicle would be the same force as a car crushing an aluminum soda can. It would take the train a mile before it came to a complete stop.

Add to that the fact that the train was about six feet wider than the rails. That meant an extra three feet on each side of the locomotive that could clip the van even after the back tires cleared the rails.

The timing had been crucial. Now he saw that trying to take Carla Richmond hostage had cost them critical time and might end up being the last reckless thing he'd ever do.

"Are we going to make it?" Eli asked, his voice breaking as Rick tried to get more speed out of the van as they raced toward the crossing. Lights were flashing, but there were no crossing barriers. The county had talked about adding them after Del Colt had been killed at this spot, but it hadn't happened.

The roar of the train and the locomotive horn was deafening in his ears. It was so close that Jud could see the panicked look on the engineer's face. The man had already hit the brakes, but there was no stopping the train in time to miss the van.

Rick had the gas pedal pressed to the floor. As the van bounced over the first rail, all Jud could see out the side window next to him was the massive front of the train's engine. They were all going to die. After an initial spike of panic, he felt almost relieved that his life would be over. Except for Jesse. He'd let her down, the one good thing in his life.

The van felt as if it were flying as the back wheels bucked over the second rail. Jud thought for sure the engine would catch the rear panel of the van, ripping it off and sending them cartwheeling through the air.

The train roared by behind them as the van kept going and Rick fought to keep the vehicle on the road at this speed. Jud realized he'd been holding his breath. He let it out, feeling shaky and sick to his stomach. He'd never come that close to dying. He sat back in his seat and tried to breathe. The pain in his chest was excruciating, and now that he was going to live, he was furious with Buddy.

Eli swore next to him, looking as shaken as Jud felt. "You sorry son of a—" Eli looked like he wanted to punch him. "You almost got us killed. If we hadn't beaten that train across the tracks…"

"I didn't get us caught or killed. Instead, I made you money. You knew the risk." He could feel Buddy's gaze on him again.

"You're right. I don't know what we were thinking. We definitely should have known dealing with you was more than a risk," Buddy said. "I still can't believe you were going to take that woman as a hostage." His gaze narrowed. "What were you going to do with her?"

Jud said nothing. He'd had to make a decision. Kill her where she lay or take her hostage. "I didn't have a choice. My mask slipped. I think she saw my tattoo. Once I realized she could make me…"

Buddy swore. "This just keeps getting better."

"Don't worry. If she's still alive, I know who she is. I'll take care of it."

He saw Eli and Rick exchange a look with Buddy as if he was the one who'd planned this. Buddy said, "You'd better hope she's still alive. Otherwise, they'll never stop looking for us for murder on top of armed robbery." Buddy swore. "What were you thinking? She can't ID you from that crappy *JJ* tattoo. Unless you've had your name and phone number tattooed on you since we last saw you. Or maybe your Social Security number."

Jud gritted his teeth. In a few minutes, he would see the last of these guys and he'd be rich. "Maybe I overreacted," he said sullenly, hating Buddy all the more for putting him in a position where he had to back down. "But Jesse watches this TV show where they find people with a whole lot less than an obvious tattoo."

Buddy shook his head and turned away to stare at the road ahead. Jud saw that they were almost to the spot where they would divide the loot and part company after one final step. He couldn't wait. He could feel his skin burning from wearing the ridiculous costume. At least one of his ribs felt broken. And Carla Richmond might still be alive. The only good news was that, with luck, he'd never see these men again. He regretted bringing them in for this. Once he had his share of the money, he and Jesse would leave the country.

As he shifted in his seat, he felt the pain in his side from Buddy's gun butt. It made him all the more furious that Buddy seemed to think he could tell him what to do.

"You don't know that she made you," Buddy was saying as the van came to a stop in the middle of the forest where an SUV and Rick's motorcycle waited for them. They would take the SUV to the spot where they'd left their vehicles. Except for Rick, who would stay behind and burn the van with the costumes and their weapons inside it. All the evidence would be gone, including any evidence on the unregistered weapons. While the rifles wouldn't burn, they couldn't be traced back to them.

If Carla Richmond hadn't seen his tattoo, the robbery would have gone off perfectly. Now he was going to have to deal with her. The thought made his stomach roil.

"Don't be a fool," Buddy said as if he could read his thoughts. The man opened the passenger-side door to climb out but hesitated to look back at Jud. "The cops can't prove anything. Just forget about the woman, take your share of the money and make a new life for yourself. If you're smart, you'll leave Jesse behind. You wouldn't have gotten this deep in trouble if you weren't trying to keep her. Let her go. Women are a dime a dozen. Especially ones like Jesse." As Buddy stepped out, Jud saw the bulge of a handgun stuffed in the back of his jeans.

The plan had been that no one would bring extra weapons. Were the others now carrying as well?

"Thanks for the advice," Jud said between gritted teeth as everyone climbed out of the van, taking the bags of money but leaving their weapons behind to go up in flames. He picked up his fully loaded semiautomatic rifle from the van floor where it had been dropped.

As his feet hit the dirt, he saw Buddy give a nod toward the others. They started to turn as Jud said, "Buddy, you should know that I've never been good at taking advice." As Buddy reached behind him for his weapon, Jud saw the others about to do the same thing.

He told himself that they'd given him no choice as he hit the trigger, opening fire on all of them before they could get off a shot.

Chapter 7

Carla woke confused, head aching. She blinked. The room seemed too bright, the light like an ice pick jammed between her eyes. She closed them again. Shifting in the bed, she realized that it wasn't just her head that hurt. Her whole body hurt. She pried her eyes open to slits. Where was she?

"Carla."

In that one word she heard so much relief and concern that she felt her pulse jump, and yet the moment came with more confusion. *"Davy?"*

As she opened her eyes, she turned her head and winced in pain. Davy was sitting in a chair next to her bed. The sight of him was as incongruous as the realization that she was in the hospital. She closed her eyes again.

She heard him rise from the chair and come to her side. With her eyes still closed, she asked, "What happened?" Her voice came out a whisper and suddenly she was aware of how weak she felt as he took her free hand.

When she opened her eyes again, she saw that her other hand was hooked up to tubes and machines that beeped noisily.

"You're safe now," he said, gently squeezing her hand in his two large ones. *Safe?* His hands felt warm and calloused, hands she remembered. She tried to sit up, but he urged her back down. "Just stay still. The doctor is on his way."

She closed her eyes again, trying to make sense out of all of it. She was in the hospital, she'd been hurt, Davy was here. The last was the most confusing. It was as if she'd been teleported back in time and she and Davy were still together.

Opening her eyes, she heard someone come into the room and felt Davy release her hand and say, "She just came to."

"How are you feeling?" asked a male voice. She focused on the sixtysomething doctor. Dr. Hull had delivered her his first year in Lonesome. He'd met the love of his life, a local woman, and had ended up staying all these years in their tiny Western town.

"I have a terrible headache," she whispered, as if speaking loudly would make it worse.

"We'll see what we can do about that," the doctor said.

"I don't understand what happened."

"You have a concussion and some minor bruises and swelling." He met her gaze. "You don't remember?" She shook her head and then wished she hadn't. "What's the last thing you remember?"

Her gaze shifted to Davy's concerned, handsome face.

She remembered him coming into her office. Or had that been a dream? She couldn't be sure.

"Do you remember me stopping by the bank to see you?" Davy asked.

So it had been true. "Yes."

Dr. Hull looked relieved, then nodded and smiled. "When was that?"

"Yesterday," Davy said, making her start with surprise.

"How long have I been in here?" she asked, feeling her fear rise. What had happened? Why couldn't she remember? Had there been a car accident? Had anyone else been hurt?

"Earlier today," the doctor said.

"Tell me what happened." She tried to sit up again, but the doctor placed a hand on her shoulder.

"Easy," he said. "You don't remember anything about the bank robbery?"

She lay back. *Bank robbery?* A flash of memory. Santa standing in her doorway. She frowned as the image blurred and disappeared. Her mind filled with questions that flew in and out like a flock of birds. She tried to grab hold of one, but it only made her headache worse. "Was anyone else hurt?"

"No," the doctor said.

"Did they get away with the money?"

He nodded. "But the FBI is on the case, so you need not worry. You just concentrate on feeling better."

"Why can't I remember?"

"The blow to your head," Dr. Hull said and patted her arm. "You just need rest so your brain can heal and your body as well." He started to turn away but stopped. "An FBI agent is here, wanting to ask you questions about the robbery." Of course. She knew the FBI investigated bank robberies and had since they became a federal crime in 1934 thanks to John Dillinger and his gang. "Don't worry, I'll send the agent away for now."

For now? She looked to Davy. "I can't help the FBI. I don't know anything. I can't remember any…" Her voice broke.

"Do what the doctor said. Get some rest. Your memory will come back. Or it won't." He must have seen her worried look. "Come on, I've landed on my head enough times that I know how this works. Worrying about it doesn't help, trust me. Just close those beautiful blue eyes. I'll be here if you need me."

She didn't want to close her eyes, but she could feel a strange kind of exhaustion trying to drag her under. "How…" She was going to ask how it was that he was here. But the thought whizzed past and was gone. "You're sure no one else was hurt?"

"Everyone is fine. You apparently got the worst of it."

"What if I can't remember?" Her words sounded slurred and took all of her energy.

"The feds will find them probably before you wake up, so you have nothing to worry about."

Nothing to worry about. Why didn't she believe that? A memory played at the edge of her consciousness. Dark eyes peering out at her from Santa's face. She shuddered as sleep dragged her under.

High in the mountains, Jud watched the van burn. There'd been several cans of gas in the back to use to start the blaze and make sure nothing was left but charred ashes. One can had been used inside the van. Another had been dumped on the three bodies. He'd been right. All of them had been carrying guns. All of them had been going for those guns when he stepped out of the van.

Was the plan to double-cross him? Or had they brought weapons because they didn't trust him?

Not that it mattered now. But it showed how little they thought of him. So much for former childhood friends. He kept thinking about the things Buddy had said about him. Worse, what he'd said about Jesse. The man couldn't have been more wrong. Jesse was the real deal. His stomach ached at the thought of how close he'd come to losing her. He'd known that he would do anything to keep that from happening. Look at what he'd already done. He and Buddy had known each other from the old neighborhood. It hurt that he'd been put in a position where he had to kill him. Sick at heart, his stomach roiling, his ribs making every move hurt, he pushed the thought away.

This hadn't been part of the plan, he thought as he watched the flames consume the bodies and the van and motorcycle. But now it was over. Time to move on. Any moment the gas tank on the van would blow. He feared that the smoke from the flames could be seen from miles away. He had to get going. He'd already loaded the bags of money in the SUV.

After climbing behind the wheel, he started the vehicle and drove to where his pickup was waiting for him. As part of the adjusted plan, he left the SUV with the keys in the ignition. With luck, someone would steal it—just as they had done.

He checked the time. Jesse should be getting ready for her night shift. He'd hoped to be back to the house before she left for work. She would be worried since he hadn't taken her call earlier. She would have heard about the bank robbery. By now, everyone in the county would know. He thought about calling her to let her know that he was fine. But he feared she would hear the truth in his voice. Better to head home, get cleaned up, calm down and then call her.

When she got off her shift, he would be waiting for her with the money. All of the money. They could make love in the middle of it if she wanted. There was enough to last them a very long time if they were careful.

Not that he'd taken the time to count it, but he knew it was a whole lot more than he'd been planning on since there was no splitting it. Now he didn't want to part with any of it. Once he tied up the one loose end, they could get out of town before anyone was the wiser. They could start a new life together. Jesse would like that. Or maybe they would just leave right away and forget about Carla Richmond. With blood already on his hands, the idea more than appealed to him.

From now on, only happy thoughts. The money would make sure of that. No wonder rich people always looked so pleased with themselves. The first thing he was going to do was buy Jesse an engagement ring with a huge diamond on it.

He remembered Buddy's voice from the day they got together to plan the robbery. "Don't do anything foolish like flashing the money around when this is over. It would be just like you, Jud, to go buy a sports car that you'd never be able to afford on your income and get the feds onto us."

Another reminder that Buddy thought he was smarter than him. But then again, Jud was still alive and rich and Buddy was toast. He turned on the radio to drown out his former friend's voice in his head, anxious to get home.

He thought about Jesse's face when she saw all the

money. He planned to make her smile for the rest of her life—even if he had to knock over another bank to do it.

Carla Richmond broke into his thoughts like a recurring toothache. He turned up the radio, hoping to catch the news.

When Carla opened her eyes again, Davy was asleep in the chair beside her bed. She had time to study him. She'd fallen in love with him not because of how drop-dead gorgeous he was. He was a good-hearted cowboy. Unfortunately, the rodeo had stolen his heart long before she'd come along.

He stirred as if sensing she was awake. Smiling, he pushed himself up, then winced and grabbed the back of his neck to rub it.

"What time is it?" she asked, her throat dry.

"Nine thirty." She looked past him to see darkness beyond the windows.

"You slept all this time in that chair?" she asked.

"I wasn't about to leave you until I knew you were all right."

"I'm fine. You should go home and get some sleep. You heard what Dr. Hull said." She smiled despite her headache. "All I need is rest and I'll be good as new." At least she hoped so. She saw his expression. "I appreciate you being here though. Thank you. But I won't have you sleeping in a chair anymore."

"I suppose I could use a shower," Davy said and took a whiff of himself. "That's really what you're telling me, huh?"

She shook her head, surprised that it didn't hurt as much. "Before you go, have you heard anything? Have they caught the robbers?" She saw from his expression they hadn't. "I'm still confused. Dr. Hull said no one was hurt? Just me?"

Davy seemed to hesitate before he stood and stepped closer, then said, "Apparently one of the robbers decided to take you as a hostage."

The memory came back like a bolt of lightning. Her hand went to her throat as she remembered being in a headlock, fighting for breath while the other robbers argued with him to let her go as he tried to drag her outside. "There was a van at the curb."

"So your memory is coming back. That's a good sign."

"But something happened, and he had to let me go. After that...there's nothing."

"Hey, that's progress," Davy said excitedly. "I can tell you feel better now that you can remember more."

Did she? He would know that not being able to remember would drive her crazy. She prided herself on being capable, self-reliant, independent. Having a dark hole in her memory and lying in a hospital bed made her feel vulnerable and afraid. Davy would know that about her. Unless he'd forgotten.

"When he let you go, he kicked you and you fell back, hitting the floor hard with your head. At least that's what I heard. One of the tellers saw the whole thing. She was terrified that they were going to take you hostage."

Not half as terrified as she'd been, she thought.

"But it's over and you're doing great," he said, still looking worried though. "Are you sure you don't want me to stay?"

"Yes." She needed to be alone, to try to piece the rest of it together. What had she been doing at the bank in the first place? Wasn't it her day off? "Go."

"Well, I'm coming back later to make sure you're

okay," he said as he picked up his Stetson. As he started for the door, it opened.

Carla saw Dr. Hull and two other men enter. FBI agents? They stopped for a moment to speak to Davy. She couldn't hear what was being said, but when Davy looked back toward her, there was worry in his expression.

"What's going on?" she asked the moment Davy left and the men came to her bedside.

"These are FBI agents Robert Grover and Hank Deeds," the doctor told her. "They'd like to ask you a few questions."

She didn't feel up to answering their questions right now. A lot of it had come back, but there were still holes in her memory that worried her. "You told him that I don't remember, didn't you?" she asked Dr. Hull before looking at the other men. Agent Deeds was younger with blond hair and blue eyes, Agent Grover had gray at his temples with dark eyes and bushy dark brows the color of his hair. She had another flash of memory of dark eyes peering at her from out of a mask and shivered. Pulling the blanket up, she said, "I doubt I can be much help."

"Well, let's see if that's true," Agent Grover said, and the doctor excused himself to take a call, saying he'd be right outside her door. "What were you doing at the bank? Wasn't it your day off?"

She frowned. "I must have forgotten something and stopped by." Wasn't there something about a file? Why did she suddenly have the image of mistletoe on her desk?

"Do you go into the bank on your day off normally?" Carla shook her head. He asked how long she'd worked at the bank, then how long she'd been the executive loan officer. She told him. "You worked your way up pretty fast," the agent commented. "You sound like you're ambitious."

His question made a hard knot rise in her chest because she was suddenly concerned about where he was headed with this. It also had been a bone of contention between her and Davy. Her need to make something of her life had been one of their problems, the rodeo the other. "I suppose I am."

He laughed. "Looking at your school records, I'd say you definitely are."

"Having ambition isn't—"

He didn't let her finish. "Were you aware of how much money was in the vault on the day of the robbery?"

The question disturbed her. "I'm the executive loan officer, so of course I know. It's part of my job."

He smiled and nodded. "You're single, no boyfriend?"

Her heart began to beat harder. She definitely knew where he was headed with this. "I've been busy—"

"With your career," he finished for her. "Is it everything you thought it would be?"

She couldn't help being defensive since she'd chosen this life over Davy. "I enjoy what I do."

"Really?" He studied her speculatively. "Don't you have to turn down a lot of people who want a loan?"

"Not always. We try to work with everyone."

He looked down at his notes. "Why do you think you were the only one hurt during the robbery?"

"I have no idea. Maybe if I could remember everything that happened…"

"How about you tell me everything that you do remember," the agent said.

She'd seen the exchange between the agents and Davy just inside her door and now realized that something new had happened. "Have you caught them?" The agents shared a look. "Please, I have to know what's happened."

Agent Grover was studying her closely. "We found the getaway vehicle some miles from here in the mountains. It had been torched, no doubt to try to get rid of any evidence. A motorcycle was also destroyed in the fire." His gaze bored into her as he said, "There were also three bodies found incinerated next to it. We're still trying to identify them. One of the robbers got away, the one I suspect you know. The one who tried to take you hostage?"

"Why would I know him?" Carla stared at him as her heart took off at a gallop. She could have been in that van. She would have been one of those incinerated bodies. If one of the robbers hadn't stopped the man... The angry man in the Santa suit who'd dragged her from her office. She saw him in her memory now standing over her, lifting the big white beard to scratch at his neck.

The tattoo. It flashed in her mind. *J* heart *J*. That's why he'd wanted to take her hostage. He'd been afraid she could identify him. He would have killed her. He'd gotten away? He was still out there?

The alarm on the machine next to her began to go off.

"That's enough for now," Dr. Hull said as he rushed back in. "Step outside the room, Agent Grover, Agent Deeds. Now." Then he turned to her. "You're having a panic attack. I need you to breathe, Carla." A nurse came racing into the room.

She closed her eyes, trying to blot out the memories that had suddenly rushed at her. That's why the man had wanted to take her hostage. He was going to kill her right there in the bank but changed his mind. He said as much to the others.

As frightening as that was, something else scared her

more. The way he'd treated her from the moment he'd appeared in her office doorway. It had felt personal. It hadn't been random. He'd known her.

The next thought came hard and fast. But didn't that mean that she knew him? That she'd known the killer?

Chapter 8

"How is Carla?" James asked when Davy walked into the office after showering and changing his clothing. He'd slept little after coming back to the office apartment. He'd waited until Carla was settled and safe—at least for now.

"She's in pain and doesn't remember what happened," Davy told him as Willie and Tommy came through the front door of the Colt Brothers Investigation building. "Also, she's scared. I just heard that they found the getaway van and three bodies. There's a chance that the man who wanted to take Carla hostage killed them and is now on the run. I spoke to a couple of bank employees who stopped by the hospital to check on Carla. They said the robbers were arguing over the man taking Carla before they left." He turned to his brother Willie, who shook his head.

"I was just at the sheriff's department," Willie said.

"No news, but there's a statewide manhunt that will probably be expanded before nightfall to the states around us. But so far, nothing."

"The feds are assuming that he's on the run," Davy said. "But what if he didn't run? What if he's local? What if he merely drove home?"

"Why would he stick around?" James asked, and they all shared a look. They'd all heard how the robber had been rough with Carla before trying to take her hostage.

"For some reason, he singled her out," Davy said.

"You think Carla's in danger?"

He nodded. "Everyone seems to think he might have known her, had some reason to treat her more roughly than the others."

"Is it possible she might have information that could lead to his arrest?" Tommy asked.

Davy swore. "Well, if she does, she doesn't know it. She says she can't remember a lot of it, but she was talking in her sleep. She saw something, something that has her scared. I think it's why he tried to take her hostage. I'm not going to leave her alone until he's caught." He saw his brothers exchange glances again. "What?"

"Maybe you can stay with her 24/7 at the hospital, but what happens when she's well enough to go home?" James asked. "Davy, you're already dead on your feet, not to mention you'll be leaving right after Christmas."

"You can't stay with her 24/7," Willie broke in. "We'll take turns. I'll go to the hospital now. Tommy?"

His brother nodded. "Just call me and I'll come relieve you."

"I'll help too, but it doesn't solve the problem," James said. "We can't do this indefinitely. We have no idea when or even if this man will be caught."

"Let's do what we can now and cross that bridge when we come to it," Willie told him. As the oldest, he'd always been the calmest in a disaster. It didn't surprise Davy that he was going into law enforcement. All three of his brothers had quit the rodeo now. It was only a matter of time before he hung up his spurs as well. He didn't want to think about any of that right now. All his concern was for Carla.

"The FBI agents were interviewing her when I left," he said. "Hopefully they'll find the robber quickly."

"Get some rest, Davy," Willie ordered as he left. "I'll stay with her until Tommy relieves me."

How could he rest knowing a killer was out there? One who had hurt Carla and might be back to finish the job? He realized he was exhausted. He'd gotten little sleep the night before because of thoughts of Carla, even before the robbery. All that time in the chair next to her bed had left his neck aching. Between that and worry, he hadn't slept much.

He went upstairs, knowing Willie wouldn't let anything happen to Carla. He'd drifted off for a while, then he'd spent some time talking to bank employees. Those who'd witnessed the robbery had been given the day off. Lonesome was such a small town it hadn't been hard to find out who to talk to and where to find them.

They all told the same story. It had looked as if Carla had been targeted by one of the robbers. The words *unnecessary roughness* and *seemed to single her out* had kept coming up.

"He was determined to take her as a hostage," a bank teller had told him. "I mean, he wasn't going to leave without her. If one of the other robbers hadn't hit him to make him let go of her..."

Davy knew there must have been a tie-in between Carla and the robber. What if she knew him? Why beat her up and want to take her hostage? Had she maybe recognized his voice or something about him and he'd realized it? If he'd taken her hostage... Then she would be dead right now.

Davy felt as if the clock were ticking. If the robber, now killer, thought she knew something about him, then he wasn't finished. He wouldn't know that she couldn't remember. Davy cautioned himself that this was all speculation.

Either way, Carla had to remember, he thought, feeling the urgency. She had to help the feds catch him. Until then, Davy couldn't shake the feeling that Carla was in danger. He quickly reminded himself that Willie was sitting outside her hospital room to make sure she was safe. He'd insisted. As long as she was in the hospital, one of them would be keeping an eye on her, but once she got out...

Davy told himself they'd cross that bridge when they came to it. In the meantime, he'd do whatever he could to help find the robber turned killer.

Jud was headed home after lying low until the time he usually came home since quitting his night job. He'd just started to turn down his street when he saw a vehicle he didn't recognize behind him. He made a quick turn and then another and another. When he looked back, there was no one following him, but his heart was pounding. He couldn't even imagine how many people were looking for him or what would happen if he were caught.

He took a long way to the house he and Jesse rented. He knew she'd be at work. He parked and realized he couldn't just carry two huge bags of money into the house. Not in this neighborhood. He covered the bags on his floorboard with an old blanket, then let himself into the house. It was almost dark. He'd wait. The truck was locked, and he figured in this neighborhood no one stole from each other since they were all piss-poor.

After showering, he pulled on a white T-shirt, some faded jeans and an old pair of sneakers. He wadded up his smoky, bloody clothing and picked up his boots and socks. He hated to part with the boots since they had sentimental value, but he knew he had to. Who knew what kind of evidence was on them?

In the backyard he put everything into the burn barrel and set it on fire. He quickly stepped away and went back into the house. The sneakers would have to do until he could buy new boots. He smiled as he remembered that he now had money. He could buy a good pair. Hell, he could buy two pairs.

He tried to call Jesse, but her phone went to voice mail. He checked the time. Her shift would have just started unless she'd been called in early. He decided he'd stop by her work, something he rarely did after she'd asked him not to.

But he had to see her to tell her that he'd gotten all the money and that everything was going to be all right. As he parked at the rear of the building in a spot for employees only, he saw her standing just outside with another employee, who was male. The man was smoking and laughing at something Jesse had said. They both wore scrubs. Jealousy reared its ugly head to see her laughing with another man, but he tamped it back down.

Jesse said something to the man, who stubbed out his cigarette and hurried back inside as Jud got out and sauntered toward her. He checked his expression before he reached her. If he acted jealous, they'd argue about it. He didn't want to fight with her. They had more important things to discuss.

On the way here, he'd heard on the radio that one of the bank employees had been taken to the hospital. He couldn't be sure it was Carla. The bank manager was old enough that he could have had a heart attack. But he had a bad feeling the patient upstairs was Carla Richmond. Which meant that she wasn't dead. Not yet anyway. He had to know her condition.

As he neared the employee entrance of the hospital, he caught a whiff of food coming from the cafeteria and realized the patients would be getting their meal trays soon.

Chapter 9

Jud walked toward the back steps where Jesse had been laughing with the man. He kept his head down until he got his emotions under control. He didn't want her to see that he was jealous, or worse, now that they had all this money, that he was uncertain what to do next. He was also scared that he hadn't covered his tracks well enough.

But the moment he lifted his head and his gaze met hers, he saw that she knew. Her eyes were wide, the words coming out on a breath. "You got it?"

He swallowed and nodded, hating that he was going to have to tell her everything. If he lied, she'd know it. It was like she had a sixth sense when it came to him. He didn't want to talk about killing Buddy and the others. She would see that it had gutted him. He quickly told her what was important.

When he got to the part about Carla Richmond seeing

his tattoo, the one he'd had done on a boys' trip to Butte, she'd sat down hard on the top step.

By the time he told her about trying to take the executive loan officer hostage and Buddy interfering and then later going for his gun, Jesse dropped her face into her hands.

He sat down beside her, wanting to take her in his arms, but he was half-afraid to touch her. This couldn't be the end of them. He had all this money. What if she decided to go to the cops? He started to tell her his plan for the two of them to leave the country and make a brand-new life for themselves, when she lifted her head.

Jud was surprised to see that she hadn't been crying. Instead, she was dry-eyed. Nor did she look angry. He felt confused and almost afraid. Maybe she would rise and march inside and tell someone to call the cops. Or maybe she would—

"Carla Richmond's on my floor," she said, so calmly he felt a chill wriggle up his backbone. "I'll take care of it. From what I've heard, she doesn't remember anything. You need to get the money off the floorboard of your pickup, Jud. Remember that hike we went on just outside of town? That little rock cave?"

He remembered the two of them naked as jaybirds before winter set in next to that cave as he screwed her against one of the rocks.

"Hide the bags in the cave. Then tomorrow you need to go to work."

He started to argue that neither of them ever had to work again, but she cut him off.

"We need to act as normal as possible. You go to work as if nothing has happened." She rose to her feet. "I got called in for a double today. They'll be serving dinner. I need to go. So do you."

"Jesse—"

"Don't worry. I'm going to help you. But those two bill collectors stopped by earlier. When you go back to the house, the men could be there. Before you put the money in the cave, take out just over fifteen hundred dollars from the bag with the money from the tellers' tills. Those will be the bills not banded. Tell your associates you hocked some stuff or sold your grandmother's knickknacks and that you can get more. That should hold them off for now."

"But Carla Richmond saw my tattoo. If she tells the feds… I think we should leave town now."

She cupped his face in her hands, forcing him to meet her eyes. "Like I said, I'll take care of it. Leave everything to me."

He stared at her. She wasn't upset with him. She wasn't going to leave him and never look back. She wasn't going to the cops. She was going to help him.

For the first time since the robbery, he felt as if he could breathe. He bent to quickly kiss her and headed for his pickup, his step lighter. Buddy had been wrong about Jesse, Jud thought with a grin. She was definitely the woman for him.

By the time a woman in scrubs brought her dinner, Carla knew she was getting some of her strength back because she was hungry. Her headache had lessened, and she was starting to feel more like her old self—until she remembered everything that had happened to her at the bank and how close she'd come to dying. Then she had to be careful not to have another anxiety attack.

Davy said she was safe now, but she didn't feel like it. Nor did she think he believed it. Why else did he think she needed either him or his brothers stationed outside her hospital room door?

The door opened and she got a glimpse of Willie Colt out in the hallway. He winked at her and gave her a thumbs-up as a young, attractive blonde in scrubs brought in her dinner tray.

"Hope you're hungry," the woman said cheerfully as she began to arrange the tray in front of Carla. "How are you feeling?"

"Better."

"That's good." The blonde finished with the service and seemed to hesitate. "I heard what happened. How awful." The aide took her hand and squeezed it quickly before letting go. "You must have been terrified."

"I was."

"Your memory of what happened has returned?"

Carla shook her head. "Just bits and pieces, but enough to be terrified all over again."

The blonde tsk-tsked and shook her head. "Well, it's over now and you can put it all behind you. Enjoy your dinner. I'll be back to pick up your tray." She smiled. "So you'd better eat everything."

Carla returned her smile, promising to do her best.

At the door, the young woman turned to look back at her. "There's an FBI agent outside and a friend of yours. I'm going to tell them that you're eating and that they need to leave you alone."

"Thank you," Carla said as the aide left.

Why was the FBI agent waiting to talk to her again? She'd told him that she didn't remember anything. Which wasn't quite true, she realized. But when she replayed their conversation in her head, she realized the agent suspected the robbery had been an inside job—and that she'd been a part of it. No wonder he'd rattled her.

Not that she couldn't see why he was suspicious. Why had the robber only hurt her? She recalled looking up and seeing him standing in her office doorway as if he'd come looking for her. His reaction to her seemed too aggressive even from the start. She couldn't shake the feeling that he knew her and had reason to dislike her. Had she turned him down for a loan? Could he be someone from town, someone who had a grudge against her for some reason? Someone she'd offended back in high school?

She'd just assumed the robbers weren't from around Lonesome. But what if they were? What if the man who'd attacked her lived in Lonesome? She thought of the tattoo on the man's neck. She was sure that she'd never seen it before. But most of the time it could be covered, she thought and frowned. She remembered greasy-looking longish dark hair that had escaped the mask covering his head.

So he could have a house down the street. He could be the man who waited on her at the grocery store or the one with the low ponytail who delivered her mail. He could be anyone and she wouldn't recognize him until it was too late. That made this situation all the more frightening.

But the FBI agent had it all wrong. She wished she knew how to convince him of that. He needed to be looking for the robber turned killer and not spend his time coming after her.

Her stomach growled. She realized that the last thing she'd eaten was Christmas sugar cookies a friend had dropped off that morning as she was headed for the bank and shopping. While she was feeling stronger, she knew if she hoped to feel like herself again she had to eat. More than anything, she wanted to feel strong and capable again—not vulnerable and scared like she was right now.

She began to uncover the small dishes on the tray.

The two goons who'd roughed him up the last time were waiting for Jud when he returned home—just as Jesse had warned him. Before he'd left the hospital parking lot, he'd taken Jesse's advice and had the fifteen hundred and sixty-five dollars from the bank tills ready. He'd left the rest of the money in the small cave and had driven home, prepared with the story about stealing his grandmother's jewelry and knickknacks. He must have looked like the kind of guy who would steal from his grandmother because they bought his story—just as Jesse had said they would.

One of the goons had cuffed him hard upside the head, warning him he'd better have the rest next week, before they drove away. By next week he planned to be miles from here, he thought as he rubbed the side of his head and went inside the house.

The past few days had exhausted him. He went to bed early, determined that when he arrived at his delivery job in the morning, no one would suspect anything.

Still, it would be hard pretending that nothing had happened. He'd planned the robbery around the two days he had off.

The moment he clocked in and headed to the loading area, he heard people talking about the bank job. He couldn't help feeling superior as he joined everyone and began loading boxes into his truck.

"I wonder how much money they got away with," one

of his coworkers was saying. "How much money does the Lonesome bank keep in the vault?"

He listened to them speculate and smiled to himself. He enjoyed this. He kept thinking, wouldn't they all have a cow if they knew just how much the score had landed— and that he had every dollar of it?

There were five of them busy loading the trucks this morning. Because of the upcoming holidays, there were more packages than usual, which was why he'd been hired. The only time he felt uncomfortable was when they talked about the deaths of the robbery accomplices.

"Pretty cold-blooded to kill them all like that," one of the men said.

"Greed. You know that's all it was," another said.

Jud bit his lip to keep from saying anything.

Their only female coworker added her two cents. "Bet he was the one who almost killed Carla Richmond. He was the kind who would kill his accomplices."

Jud had never liked the fiftysomething know-it-all Cheryl. "What makes you think it was a man? Could have been a woman."

That got a burst of laughter and put his female co-worker on the defensive.

"Well, now he has all the money," she said.

"Wonder what he'll do with it," someone said.

"Spend it," another said.

"If it was a woman, she'd be smart enough to hang on to it and bide her time," Cheryl said as she hefted a large box onto her truck.

The others scoffed and Jud joined in.

"Anyone heard how Carla is doing?" she asked.

One of the young men spoke up. "My girlfriend's cousin is an orderly at the hospital. He said she can't remember anything. She has a concussion. But that doesn't mean that her memory won't come back."

Jud hoped that wasn't true. "I had one of those. I never could remember what had happened to me." He glanced up. No one was paying him any mind. They seemed to think that his interest had been in the concussion part of the story.

"She probably can't help the feds catch the robbers anyway," one of the men said. "I heard they had on Santa suits that covered everything. Doubt they'll ever catch the one who's left." Jud could only hope.

"I heard the robber who hurt her had tried to take her hostage," Cheryl said. "Wonder what he had against her?"

"Or what he had against his accomplices," another added with a laugh.

"He might have just been having a bad day," Jud said and wished he hadn't, although that didn't stop him. "Or maybe they turned on him, pulling a gun with a plan to kill him. It could have been a double cross that ended with him being forced to defend himself."

Their boss had come out then and everyone fell silent and kept working. But he could feel Cheryl giving him the eye as if she knew more than she did. It was boring and repetitive manual labor. But it wasn't hard, and it paid the bills—just barely, and had he not been a temporary employee for the holidays, he would get an extra week's vacation after five years.

The thought made him laugh out loud, which only made Cheryl squint her eyes at him. He didn't care. He had a ton of money hidden outside town. He wouldn't be needing that extra week of vacation. Let these fools break their backs day after day here. Judson Bruckner was putting this hick town behind him soon.

The trucks were almost loaded. He was glad he'd come into work. It was interesting hearing what people were saying, especially about Carla Richmond and what she might—or might not—have told the feds.

"I won't feel safe until he's caught," a coworker said as they finished up and he slammed the rear door of his truck. There would be more to load tomorrow and a ton of packages to deliver. "Robbing the bank was one thing, but killing his accomplices?" The man shook his head. "If he's still around, I'd feel better if he was caught." The others agreed.

"But why would he stay around?" Cheryl asked.

"I agree," another said. "I'm sure he's long gone from here."

"I know I would be," one of the men added. "I'd be anxious to spend all that money."

"Which would get you caught," Cheryl said in that annoying tone of hers. "Some of that money is marked. I had a friend who worked in a bank. You know they keep marked money at every bank just in case they get robbed."

"I didn't know that," one of the men said. "So he can't spend that money? That would really suck."

"Couldn't he tell which bills were marked?" Jud asked as casually as he could over the sudden rush of his pulse. He'd heard about bank employees dropping into a robber's bag a container of ink that blew up. He'd checked the bags when he'd gotten the money out for the goons. All the bills were just fine.

"They're not marked like that. They keep bills that have consecutive serial numbers they watch for. Everyone will be looking for those bills," she said. "He'll have trouble spending the money—even years from now—and not getting caught."

Jud ground his teeth. Why hadn't he known that? Had Buddy? Had the others? He thought of the bags of money and swore silently. Carla Richmond would have known that. She would have known it the whole time they were robbing the bank. That woman.

Then he had a thought that stopped him dead. He'd just given over fifteen hundred dollars of the money to Wes and Fletch, the two goons who worked for the loan shark.

His blood ran cold at the thought of what would happen if they pocketed some of the money, tried to spend it, were arrested—and told their boss where they'd gotten the cash.

He reminded himself that Jesse had been specific about him taking the money that had come from the tellers' tills. He hadn't, but it was probably fine.

Carla was pleased to see that every lid she lifted on her food tray revealed something that looked and smelled delicious. She really was hungry. She hoped the aide was good to her word and kept the agent out of her room until she'd eaten. She'd already decided that because of the aide's promise, she would take her time.

Eventually, she would have to tell the FBI agent about the tattoo. She had her doubts whether he could find the man based on it though. But it was a clue. She'd bet that the man's name started with *J*. That had to be something, right?

She lifted the last lid to see what she had before she took her first bite and swallowed back a scream. On top of what smelled like a brownie lay a napkin. Someone had written in black marker TALK AND YOU DIE.

Chapter 10

Reflexively, Carla slammed the lid back down as she fought the tears that came on the heels of her shock—and terror. Past her initial alarm came a chilling thought: she wasn't safe here. Not even with an FBI agent and Willie Colt outside her door.

Worse, she knew why she'd been left the note. The man from the bank robbery. He knew that she'd seen his tattoo. He feared that she could identify him. That was why he had been so desperate to take her hostage. He'd wanted to kill her and would have if she'd gotten into that van.

But how did he get a note onto her food tray? Did he work here or did he know someone who did? Not that it mattered. She wasn't safe, and if she told anyone about what she'd seen—

Agent Robert Grover stuck his head into her hospital room doorway.

"Up for a few questions while you eat?" he asked as he stepped into the room, with his partner Deeds right behind him.

Carla made angry swipes at her wet cheeks and pushed away the food tray, her appetite gone. She tried to pull herself together and decide what to do.

As long as she was in the hospital, she wasn't safe. The robber knew what room she was in. How else would he have been able to sneak her the note? He could be a nurse. Or an orderly. Or work in food service. He could be so close that he had seen the agent enter her room just moments ago.

Her thoughts were immediately at war. Wouldn't the smart thing be to tell the agent everything and let him track down the man and put him behind bars? Maybe J, as she now thought of him, had left fingerprints on the dish or the food tray. If he had a record...

But even as she considered it, she reminded herself that Agent Grover thought it was an inside job. He was busy looking at her as a suspect. He might think the tattoo was just a stalling tactic on her part, something to keep him busy tracking down red herrings instead of looking more closely at her.

If she talked, J would know and he'd be coming for her right here at the hospital. Right when she would be at her most vulnerable.

She kept her mouth shut about the note out of terror. After FBI agents Robert Grover and Hank Deeds left, the blonde aide came in to take her tray as if she had been waiting outside in the hallway—as anxious for him to leave as Carla had been.

"You hardly touched your dinner. Is everything all right?" She didn't wait for an answer as she started to reach for the dessert dish lid with the note under it. "You sure you don't at least want your brownie?"

"No!" She'd said it a little too sharply, because the young woman looked at her with concern, but pulled back her hand without lifting the lid. "I'm just not hungry. Please take it and throw it all away."

"If you're sure," the blonde said before picking up the tray. "Maybe you'll be hungrier in the morning. Did I hear that you're going to be released tomorrow afternoon? At least you'll be with us for a while longer." The young woman smiled. "That's good news, even though I'm sure you're anxious to get out of here. Once you get home, maybe then your appetite will return."

Carla watched her go, feeling even sicker than she had been earlier. She wasn't being released until tomorrow afternoon. If she lived that long, she was going home to an empty house. Not only did she live alone, but also her house was outside town. Her closest neighbor was a half mile away.

She thought of her cozy little house, which had always been her sanctuary. Now it felt ominous, set back off the road, the home surrounded by dense pines on three sides and large boulders at the edge of the river on the other. How quickly the privacy and quiet turned into something else—a place where she wouldn't see the killer coming until it was too late.

How foolish she'd been to think it was over. She'd thought that she'd dodged a bullet when J hadn't taken her hostage, when she'd awakened in the hospital and realized it was only a concussion and she was going to live.

Then she'd read the note. It was a reminder that he not only hadn't forgotten about her, but that he could get to her at any time, even later when she was sleeping.

Carla could feel her pulse thumping hard just beneath her skin as the reality of her situation hit her. She had a killer worried that she might give him away to the feds. She had a federal agent who thought the robbery had been an inside job with her help. She wasn't safe. Not here in the hospital. Not anywhere until J was caught.

Maybe she should have told the agent. Maybe if she'd shown him the note… It was too late now. Worse, she doubted J would trust her to keep her mouth shut. Which meant he wasn't finished with her.

When Davy walked through her hospital door and rushed to her bedside, she threw her arms around him. She was so glad to see him.

"Hey," Davy said, unable not to grin as he held her. It felt good having her in his arms again. He told himself not to make more of it than it probably was. Carla was scared after her ordeal at the bank. Who wouldn't be?

"I wasn't expecting that kind of reception, but I liked it," he joked as he pulled back to look at her and sobered. "What's happened?" He could feel her trembling and swore he could hear her heart pounding it was beating so hard.

She looked toward the door. She was biting at her lower lip, tears welling in her blue eyes, and all the color had leached from her face.

"Talk to me," he said, drawing her attention back to him. He'd never seen her like this in all the years he'd known her, including the intimate ones. "You're scaring me."

She let out a strangled bark of a laugh. "*You're* scared? No one's threatening to kill you."

He stared at her in confusion. He'd talked to Willie

before coming into her room. His brother had sworn that the only people who'd come into her room were two FBI agents and a food server. "You were threatened here at the hospital?"

As she nodded, she brushed at her tears. "There was a note on my dinner tray."

"You still have it?" he asked and looked around. The tray was gone. When he met her eyes again, he knew that so was the note. "How long ago was this? Maybe I can still—"

"No, I don't want you getting involved," she cried.

He shook his head. "Carla, I am involved. You're in trouble and I'm here for you. Tell me. What was on the note?" He listened as she described it. TALK AND YOU DIE.

"He's here in the hospital," she cried. "He can get to me at any time."

"No, he can't," Davy assured her, angry with himself for leaving her room. Not that it would have kept someone from getting the note to her. But at least they would have the note to give to the feds. "I'm not leaving you alone again."

She groaned, but no longer appeared to be trembling. "You can't protect me. Not from a killer. Or the FBI."

"What are you talking about?"

"The FBI agent who questioned me? I can tell he thinks the robbery was an inside job and that I was involved." She buried her face in her hands. "If only I hadn't stopped by my office on my day off…"

"Don't." He took her hands in both of his. They felt cold. He rubbed a little heat back into them and thought about the winter they were together. She had always had cold hands and feet. He'd been more than happy to warm them up for her. "You can't rewrite history. I've done some of that and all it does is make you feel worse." He frowned. TALK AND YOU DIE. "Carla, why would the robber think you know something he doesn't want you telling the law?"

She looked away for a moment, swallowed and then met his gaze as if making up her mind. "I remembered something about the robbery. He had a tattoo, the man who tried to abduct me." She described it. "I'm assuming his name starts with *J*. Maybe so does his partner's."

"Did you tell the agent?"

Carla shook her head. "I was too afraid."

"Tell me about the tattoo."

"It was on his neck close to his shoulder. It was fairly crude. A *J*, then a heart and another *J*. The heart was a little sloppy and the ink had settled in the bottom of it."

"You need to tell the FBI agent."

She looked close to tears. "How is it going to help?"

"I'm not sure," Davy said. "But it's something. What about his voice? Would you recognize it if you heard it again?"

She shook her head. "It was muffled because of the mask and beard."

He questioned her about the size of the man. Average in every way. She hadn't gotten a good look at the other men. She thought one of them, the one who acted like the boss, had been larger, stockier.

"Who do you know whose name begins with *J*—other than my brother?"

She shook her head and winced. He could tell her headache had come back and was starting to hurt again.

"Try not to worry about it," he said. "I'm staying right

here to make sure you're safe. No one is going to get to you."

She met his gaze and tears again flooded her eyes. "Davy, I'm being released from the hospital tomorrow."

He didn't have time to react before there was a knock at the door and a blonde in scrubs stuck her head in. She had an armful of flowers. So did the candy striper behind her.

"I'm sorry—you have company," the blonde said as she put down two vases of flowers and took three more from the young candy striper behind her. She placed them around the room. "Seems you have a lot of friends."

He watched the aide fuss with one of the bouquets. "Is this the woman who brought your dinner tray?" he whispered to Carla, who nodded. "Excuse me," he said to the blonde. "Were you in charge of her dinner tray?"

The woman looked surprised. She carefully straightened one of the vases before she said, "The patient said she wasn't hungry and asked me to take it away. If she's changed her mind, I'd be happy to get her another tray."

He shook his head. "Where is that original tray?"

She seemed confused. "I took it down to the kitchen. By now the dishes have been scraped clean and loaded in the dishwasher." She looked past him to Carla. "Did you leave something on the tray that you didn't mean to?"

"Never mind," Davy said and felt the woman's gaze turn to him. Something like anger flickered in those blue eyes before she dropped her lashes.

"I'm sorry, but visiting hours are over," she said to him.

"I'm not visiting. I'll be staying as long as Carla remains in the hospital."

The blonde aide raised a brow. "Sure? I can't imagine you would be comfortable—"

"No problem."

It wasn't until she'd left that he saw Carla frowning at him as if surprised by his reaction to the attendant. "At this point, we have to suspect everyone," he said. "She had access to your dinner tray." Carla's eyes widened in alarm. "I didn't see a name tag, did you?" She shook her head. "I'll get James and Tommy to find out who she is."

He moved to the side of her bed. "In the meantime, I'm not going anywhere. Don't worry." But even as he said it, he was more than worried. He had feared that her life might be in danger. Now they knew it was.

Chapter 11

Carla told herself that she couldn't do this as she listened to Davy inform the doctor that he would be sleeping in the reclining chair next to Carla's bed. The last thing she wanted was for him to spend his Christmas holidays here in this hospital. But she couldn't send him away either. His being here made her feel safe and less afraid.

Her head ached and she felt sick to her stomach. She hated feeling so vulnerable. She was the one who helped others—not the other way around. She didn't like asking for help. Especially from Davy Colt, the man she'd given an ultimatum to all those years ago.

But she'd never had a killer after her before. Was this going to be her life until the masked man was caught—if he was ever caught? Running scared and being afraid of everyone who crossed her path? "I can't do this," she said when Davy got off the phone. "I can't ask you to either."

She was so grateful to him, but what if the killer wasn't caught? Davy couldn't put his life on hold. She wouldn't allow that. He didn't have that many more years to rodeo. She knew what it meant to him and felt sick at how she'd demanded he give it up if he loved her. She'd forced him to choose—and he had, breaking both of their hearts. He'd begged her to come on the road with him, calling it an adventure they would talk about when they were old.

But she'd refused, telling him he needed to grow up and quit being so selfish. She cringed now at the memory. Given the way she'd treated him, she had no right to ask him to keep her safe now.

"Hey, you didn't ask," he said as he moved to the bed. He brushed a lock of her hair back from her forehead, his fingertips gliding over her skin and sending a shiver through her. "I'm here for you. Don't worry. The feds are looking for him and my brothers are beating the bushes for information on him. We've got this."

She couldn't help the relief that welled inside her. "Thank you, Davy."

His gaze softened. "Just try to get some rest. I'll be here."

As silly as it seemed, she was exhausted. She closed her eyes. Davy was here. He was the only man who'd ever made her feel completely safe. Within seconds, she drifted off into a deep, dreamless sleep.

While Carla slept, Davy placed a call to the Colt Brothers Investigation office and filled James in on the latest information, including the tattoo and note.

"She needs to tell the FBI agent about both," James said.

"I agree, but not until she's out of the hospital. We

can't take the chance that J will find out. We know he has access to her here. Better for her to tell the agent after she's at home. Not that I suspect the feds are going to like it."

James agreed. "The agent is definitely going to be skeptical about this new information. She just now remembered the tattoo? As for the note, because she didn't keep it, there is no evidence that she's telling the truth. If he already suspects she's involved, he's going to think she's lying to cover up something. But don't worry, if the feds don't follow up on this, we will."

"Think you can get information on hospital employees with names that begin with *J*?"

"I'll do what I can," his brother said. "As for the tattoo clue, it could be an old girlfriend, so don't hang too much hope on the second *J*. The first *J* could be a nickname. Unfortunately, Tommy and I are both working other cases too and Willie is training over at the sheriff's department. Do you think you can hit the tattoo shops?"

It would give him something to do besides worry. The problem was, he couldn't leave Carla. He'd have to take her with him.

"The tattoo doesn't sound all that memorable," James was saying. "Have Carla sketch out what she remembers. I'll let you know if I get the hospital employee list."

Davy knew James was right. Neither lead might be all that helpful, another reason the feds would suspect her. "She's getting released from the hospital tomorrow."

"What are you going to do then?" his brother asked.

"I'm not sure," he said, looking toward the hospital bed where she was sleeping peacefully for the moment. "I'm not sure what she'll *allow* me to do. She's scared right now and still healing. Once she is strong again…

Well, you know how she is, and given our history, well, it's not like we've ever agreed on the future."

"Don't you have a ride coming up in the New Year?"

"I can't leave knowing she's in danger."

James sighed. "Davy, have you considered what you're going to do if this case isn't solved for months or maybe ever?"

"I guess I'll cross that bridge when I get to it."

He could hear his brother's concern in the silence that followed.

"Well, we'll all do what we can to help. Keep us in the loop."

A silence fell between them but neither disconnected. "I suppose you heard," Davy said. "The reason the robbers were able to get away from the cops was because of the train crossing where Dad was killed."

"I heard. Sounds like at least one of the robbers was familiar with that unregulated crossing and maybe even knew its history," James said.

"Which could mean he's a local."

"Yeah." His brother was silent for a moment before he said, "The two cases aren't tied together."

Davy didn't answer for a moment. "I know. It just brings it all back. You still working on Dad's case?"

"You know I am. Tommy's helping. We're trying to get the file on the case now that we have a new sheriff. Our lawyer thinks we should be able to since Dad's death was ruled an accident."

"Except that we don't believe that."

"No, we don't."

Jud had tried to call Jesse numerous times during work, but the calls had always gone to voice mail. He'd left messages. "Call back. I need to know what's going on." Each message had sounded more frantic, but still she hadn't returned his calls.

He was thinking the worst had happened when he finally finished his shift and drove home. As he came down the street, he looked for any vehicles he didn't recognize. Maybe the feds had already made him. He knew that was a long shot. They couldn't have this quickly. Not based on a tattoo—and that was if Carla Richmond had told them what she'd seen.

Even if Carla remembered him coming into the bank for a loan weeks ago, she didn't know his name. He'd never given it to her. Nor did they travel in the same circles. He also hadn't left any fingerprints or DNA at the bank. Or in the getaway car.

Knowing all this still didn't give him any peace of mind. Too much was at stake. He hated loose ends. That's why he was glad that he'd parted ways with Buddy, Rick and Eli. He'd learned a long time ago not to trust anyone. Like his old man used to say, two people can keep a secret—if one of them is dead.

No one even knew that he'd robbed the bank.

Except Jesse.

The thought made his pulse spike. She wouldn't turn on him. He trusted her with his life, didn't he? He thought about how well she'd taken the news earlier. But what if she'd just been pretending?

His breath came out in a rush of both relief and worry when he saw her sedan parked by the house. The curtains were closed in the front window, a light glowing behind them. There were no other vehicles around. He thought about driving around the block to make sure none were idling in the alley. But if he had, he'd feel guilty about not trusting her, so he pulled in next to her car.

He and Jesse were cut from the same cloth, his mother would have said. From what little she'd told him about herself, he knew that neither of them had ever colored inside the lines. They'd always taken the easiest way, no matter how many rules they had to break. Some people would have thought that dishonest, but he knew that he and Jesse just thought of it as surviving in a world that was against them since birth. His mother would have said he was making an excuse for his despicable behavior. But then his mother was no saint herself, was she?

Jud cut his pickup's engine and sat for a moment, staring at the front door. He wouldn't know if she'd betrayed him until he got out and went inside. If she had… Well, then he'd be going to prison. That's if he got lucky and didn't get the chair. Fortunately, Montana hadn't executed anyone in a long time. He didn't want to be the one they fired up Old Sparky for.

On what felt like a long walk to the house, he realized electric chairs were a thing of the past—at least in Montana. They'd gone to lethal injection a long time ago, he now remembered hearing. That didn't relieve him much as he opened the front door of his house expecting to see Jesse sitting in the living room with the feds—after making a deal.

Chapter 12

Jesse came out of the kitchen bringing the smell of fried chicken like a cloud around her. He could hear music playing at the back of the house. It could have been any other day. Except that Jesse hadn't brought home take-out. She was apparently *cooking* dinner.

Not just that. She looked happy.

Jud frowned as he glanced past her, still expecting the feds to come bursting out, weapons drawn and a SWAT team hiding in the alley.

"I hope you're hungry," she said, smiling as she leaned in to kiss him. "I made us a special meal to celebrate. Smarter than going out for dinner."

They were celebrating? He wondered if this was his last meal before he ended up behind bars. It dawned on him that making a deal with the feds was just one way she could have betrayed him. There was also Leon Trainer, the loan shark who'd sent the goons to collect his debt. She could nark him out to Leon.

He realized that Jesse had all kinds of ways to come out of this on top. He thought of the other women he'd known. None of them would have given a thought to double-crossing him. Did he really believe this one was different?

"What are we celebrating?" he asked, the words coming out slow and awkward.

"Are you kidding?" She laughed, making him feel as if he should go out and come in again. Had she forgotten how much trouble they were in? Leon's goons wouldn't hesitate to refresh her memory. Good luck convincing the feds that she wasn't involved from the beginning.

"Carla Richmond didn't tell the feds."

He shook his head as if to clear it. "How do you know that?"

Jesse grinned. "I know because I took care of it."

He suddenly had a vision of her holding a pillow down on Carla Richmond's face at the hospital. "How did you—"

"I'll tell you over dinner. Come on, I don't want the chicken to burn."

Like a sleepwalker, he followed her into the kitchen. She had the table set and candles burning. She wasn't kidding. This was a celebratory dinner. He just wished he felt like celebrating after the day he'd had.

But he wasn't in handcuffs. Yet. And Jesse was cooking. His stomach growled as she put a bowl of real mashed potatoes on the table and motioned him into his chair. He couldn't remember the last time he'd had anything but instant potatoes from some drive-through.

She plated the fried chicken, put it down next to the

mountain of potatoes and then she brought out a bowl of corn. He could see the can still sitting on the counter, but he wasn't about to complain that it wasn't fresh from the cob.

"Eat," she said as she joined him.

He began to load his plate, not sure how much longer he could wait to hear what was going on. "Jesse—"

"Not until you take a bite of my chicken. My grandma used to make the best fried chicken. She taught me how. I'd thought I'd forgotten." She loaded her own plate while humming along with the song on the radio.

He took a bite out of a drumstick. It was delicious and he said as much. She beamed at the compliment. He took another bite and asked around it, "Come on, Jesse, what did you do?"

"I made sure she got the message."

He listened while she explained how she'd gotten a note onto Carla Richmond's dinner tray and been the one to bring the woman's tray to her hospital room.

"You should have seen her face when I went back in to get the tray," Jesse said and laughed. "She was scared spitless. Couldn't eat any of her meal." She took a big bite of the mashed potatoes, still grinning.

"How do you know she didn't tell the feds?"

Jesse gave him an impatient look. "Because the note was still on top of the brownie. Don't you see? If she was going to tell, she would have taken the note and shown it to the federal agent. He was right outside her door waiting for her to finish her meal." She shrugged as if all this was child's play for her. "When I came in to take her tray, the lid was still on, the note under it. She could have given it to the feds, but she didn't. She got the message." She laughed, then sobered. "There's one problem though."

He had to wait as she took a bite of her dinner. He wondered if she'd heard about some of the money being marked.

"There's a long, lanky cowboy with her," Jesse said as she chewed. "Davy Colt? You know him?"

Jud swore. "Everyone in four counties around us knows about the Colt brothers. They're wild rodeo cowboys." At least they used to be, he realized. He'd lived in Lonesome long enough to know who they were—not that he'd ever met any of them. But he'd heard about them. "Two of them took over their father's old private-investigation business on Main Street. I think another was just hired as a deputy sheriff."

"Should we be worried?"

He gave it a moment's thought. "Naw. I doubt bronc riders know what they're doing out of the arena."

She gave him the eye for a moment as if trying to tell whether he was being truthful or just trying to mollify her. "Well, Davy Colt seems to think that Carla might be in danger. He's staying the night with her at the hospital." She blew out a puff of air, lifting her blond bangs from her forehead. The kitchen was small and hot. They usually ate takeout in front of the television in the living room.

"You think she told Davy Colt about the note?"

Jesse shrugged. "Depends on how much she trusts him. They seem close but not like they're involved. There's something between them though. He's way too protective. You sure he and his brothers won't be a problem?"

"They don't have anything because she doesn't have anything. If she knew who I was, she would have already told and I'd be behind bars."

"What about that tattoo?"

He shrugged, playing it down. "So she knows our names start with *J*. Good luck finding us—even if she does talk to the feds."

"She'd better not or she'll regret it," Jesse said.

He was beginning to think that Buddy had been right. "The only way they'll catch us is if I make a move on her."

Jesse didn't seem to be listening. Instead, she had a strange look on her face, her eyes narrowed, her lip caught in her teeth. "Carla's being released from the hospital today. I'll know if she talks."

Carla opened her eyes to sunshine streaming in the hospital room window. She couldn't believe that she'd slept through the whole night. For a moment she forgot where she was. When it all came back in a rush, she sat up abruptly.

"Easy, Sleeping Beauty," Davy said as he approached. He'd been standing on the far side of the room by the window. She hadn't seen him until he spoke. Her expression must have given her away. "You thought I'd left."

She started to deny it but stopped herself. "I was just startled for a few moments."

"Have I ever given you reason not to trust me?" he asked, frowning.

"No." She chastised herself. If anyone wasn't trustworthy, it was her. Davy had trusted her, thinking they had a future all those years ago. Then she'd given him the ultimatum—her or the rodeo. She'd known it was a mistake the moment the demand left her lips, but there had been no taking it back.

She'd never forgotten the hurt she'd seen in his eyes.

He'd pleaded with her not to make their relationship an either-or. But she'd been adamant, determined to make him choose. When he hadn't, she'd broken up with him and started dating Levi Johnson. She'd known about the animosity between Davy and Levi. It was one of the reasons she'd jumped at going out with him when he'd called. News of her breakup with Davy had spread fast and Levi had moved quickly.

Carla realized fast that she and Levi had both wanted to hurt Davy. After a few dates, she'd told Levi that she couldn't see him anymore. By then Davy had gone back to the rodeo circuit, so he probably hadn't even known anyway.

That she'd purposely tried to hurt him was one of her deepest regrets. That he had now slept in her hospital room on the visitor's chair to protect her only made her feel worse about the past.

"I've given you reason not to trust me though," she said quietly.

Davy shook his head and gave her a smile. "All water under the bridge."

She felt tears sting her eyes and had to look away as the doctor came in to tell her she could get dressed to go home. It was no surprise Davy had had one of his brothers get her clothes from her house.

"I'm going to step out into the hall while you change," Davy said, pretending he didn't see how close she was to crying.

Carla changed in the bathroom once he was gone. The clothing she'd been wearing the day of the robbery was now in the hands of the feds. Davy had picked up her coat, hat and scarf from her office at the bank.

As she came out of the bathroom, she saw an aide

waiting with a wheelchair. Not the same aide who'd brought her food and flowers yesterday.

"We can have your flowers sent to your house if you like," the woman said.

Carla felt ashamed because she didn't want to take the flowers. She'd hardly acknowledged the ones from her boss and coworkers. Her life had been so much about her work that she'd let other friendships go, hardly ever seeing old friends who'd stayed in town. How had her life become so small? And now there was a killer threatening to destroy it?

"Could you share the flowers with other patients?" she asked the aide, who quickly nodded.

"I have some elderly patients who would love them," the woman said, pulling all the cards from the bouquets and handing them to her. "I'll take care of it."

As the aide wheeled her from the hospital room, Carla saw Davy waiting for her just outside the door. Sometimes she forgot how handsome he was with his longish dark hair and those incredible blue eyes. But what struck her most was how genuine he was. It made her heart ache for what could have been and the lost years between them.

Davy helped Carla into his pickup and hurried around to slide behind the wheel. He knew this woman, so he could tell that she was uncomfortable being dependent on him. And yet she was scared and didn't want to be alone.

He knew she would balk when he suggested he stay at her house—at least for a while. James was right. It could take months for J to be found. Worse, he might never be caught. If so, Carla would have to look over her shoulder the rest of her life. She would never feel safe. Davy couldn't bear that for her, knowing how she prided herself on her independence.

"This isn't the way to my house," she said after he'd driven only a few blocks.

"Nope." He turned down the alley and came to a stop behind the Colt Brothers Investigation building. Shutting off the motor, he turned toward her. "I want you to stay here for just a little while. James and Tommy redid the upstairs apartment. There's now two bedrooms and two baths." He was talking fast, hoping he could get out his plan before she stopped him. "I'm staying up there, but I'll give you all the space you want. Please say you'll at least stay here until you're cleared to go back to work."

He took a breath. He could see her fighting the idea. "Or at least through the holidays. You'd be doing me a huge favor. You know how my brothers are. They'll cut me some slack with you around."

She sighed and looked over at him. Her expression said that he wasn't fooling her. She knew why he wanted her to stay here—in a place that he would find easier to protect her.

"Just until I'm cleared to go back to work," she said. "I had some time off coming anyway. After that, you go back to the rodeo, and I go home. Agreed?"

Davy saw that he had no choice but to agree, so he nodded. The truth was, if the killer wasn't caught, he couldn't see how he could ever leave her.

Chapter 13

Jud felt as if he was being watched—and had since the robbery. He especially hated doing any shopping in Lonesome, but Jesse had asked him to pick up a few things on his way home. How could he say no to a quick stop at the local grocery store?

Fortunately, it wasn't very busy. Maybe if he hurried… He brushed a lock of hair back from his face as he glanced through the frosty glass of the ice-cream freezer in front of him and tried to remember what kind of ice cream she'd asked for. There were dark circles under his eyes. He hadn't slept well. Last night, he'd awakened to find Jesse lying next to him, staring at him. When he'd started to ask if something was wrong, she'd closed her eyes and rolled over.

He studied his reflection. He looked older too, he thought, as if he'd aged ten years since the robbery. Out of the corner of his eye, he saw a figure standing a little off to one side behind him. His breath rushed out of him and he half turned to reach for the pistol at his back, but then he saw who it was. Not Davy Colt or any of his brothers. Not the local sheriff or his deputies. Not the feds.

Just an annoying old woman.

He silently cursed her for scaring him. His heart ping-ponged around in his chest as he released his hold on his weapon and said, "You need something, Mrs. Brooks?"

"I need to know why you have a gun stuck in the back of your jeans," she snapped.

"Keep your voice down." He glared at her. She was old and frail and a little more hunched over than he remembered, but that tongue of hers was sharp and lethal. The worst busybody in the entire county had just seen him staring at himself in a freezer glass door before going for his gun. She seemed to be waiting impatiently for an answer as if it was any of her business.

"These are dangerous times," he said. He'd started carrying the gun, except at work. "I'm sure you heard about the bank being robbed."

"Not to mention the robber's accomplices being murdered," she said, still eyeing him suspiciously.

"Exactly." He turned back to the freezer, opened the door and took out a quart of vanilla ice cream. "Jesse's making peach cobbler. Got to have ice cream," he said, hoping to change the subject. "Better get this home before it melts." He started to step past her, but she grabbed his arm in her clawlike fingers.

"Jesse Watney?" She spat the name out like a mouthful of dirt. "I heard a rumor that she was back here. So you've hooked up with her. Guess you've lost your mind. She ever mention that family of hers, who used to live not far from here? No? Suppose she wouldn't want to scare you away. Bet she hasn't mentioned her sister, who went missing, either." Cora Brooks chuckled. "Wonder why she kept that from you."

"I think you have her confused with someone else. Jesse isn't from around here. All her kin are down in Idaho."

"That what she told you?"

He wanted to wipe that knowing smile off her face. "My ice cream is melting." He stepped past her.

"Best watch your back," Cora called after him. "You have no idea who you're living with." She let out a cackle that raised the hair on the back of his neck. "I'd keep that gun handy if I were you."

"What was that about?" the checkout woman asked.

"Just Cora. You know how she is," he said, more shaken than he wanted to admit.

"She seems to have nothing to do but butt in to other people's business," the checker said. "Half the time I don't think she knows what she's talking about."

Jud wondered about that. "You've lived here your whole life. You ever know anyone named Watney?"

The woman thought for a moment before she counted out his change and handed it to him. "You sure it was Watney? I remember a family that lived back in the mountains. But I thought their name was Welsh. Or maybe they were Welsh. I just remember my grandmother talking about them. I think one of them was murdered or disappeared. There was something everyone was whispering about." She shrugged. "That what Cora was giving you a hard time about?"

"Like you said, she probably doesn't know what she's talking about."

* * *

It hadn't taken Agent Grover long to find her. Carla had just gotten settled into one of the bedrooms over the Colt Brothers Investigation office when he and Agent Deeds had shown up downstairs demanding to see her.

Not long before that, she'd made a list of clothing and other items she needed from her house. Willie had gone to take care of that while Tommy had asked her to draw the tattoo as close to the size, shape and design as she could remember.

"I'm no artist, but I'll try." She'd been glad to do it. They were trying so hard to find J, she'd do whatever she could to help them. Carla knew the only chance she had of getting her life back was for the killer to be caught and locked up.

She'd just finished the drawing when James called to say the agents were waiting downstairs.

"James and I talked about this. I think you should tell him everything," Davy said. "It doesn't matter if he's skeptical or suspicious. The feds' best chance of catching this man is with all the information. But maybe you should have a lawyer present."

Carla shook her head. Although not looking forward to another interrogation by Agent Grover, she wasn't ready to lawyer up. She felt it would only make her look guiltier. She said as much to Davy.

"Well, at any point during the questioning that you change your mind, ask for your lawyer. Give me your phone." He put in his cell number. "All you have to do is hit this button, and I'll come in and make sure the next time he talks to you will be with your lawyer present."

"Thank you."

"You don't have to thank me."

But she did, she thought even as she knew she'd never be able to thank him enough.

The agents were sitting in the office downstairs when she and Davy came through the door. James suggested they talk in the conference room at the back.

"We'll speak with Ms. Richmond alone," Grover said.

"You might want this," Tommy said and stepped toward the copy machine. He handed the agent the copy he'd made.

"What is this?"

"A tattoo. Carla will fill you in," Davy said.

The agent scowled at them before ushering her back into the conference room and closing the door. He tossed the copy of the tattoo she'd drawn onto the large table and pulled out his phone as Agent Deeds pulled up a chair.

Carla took a seat some distance from them, waiting for Grover to ask his first question. His expression had her on edge. She wasn't used to anyone not trusting her—let alone not liking her for no apparent reason other than a false belief that she was a liar and a crook and in league with a killer.

"What's this?" he asked, indicating the paper with the drawing on it.

"It's the man's tattoo—at least the only one I saw," she said.

He shoved the drawing over to Deeds. "So you're starting to remember, huh?" he asked after he had his phone recording their conversation. "Now you remember a tattoo. How is that possible, since as I understand it, the men were completely covered in their Santa costumes?"

She told him about the robber scratching at his neck and exposing the tattoo.

When she finished, he said, "That's it? That's all you remember?"

"I remember the robbery, but I didn't see the man who tried to take me hostage other than the slash in the mask for his mouth and the holes for his eyes." She hesitated, already knowing how this was going to look. "His eyes were dark. I saw the tattoo when he lifted his false beard to scratch his neck."

"That's it?" Grover said as he looked again at her drawing.

She swallowed, seeing that he thought she was making all of this up. What would he say when she told him about the note? "Something happened while I was in the hospital."

The agent looked up in surprise. Even Deeds seemed interested.

"Someone put a message on my dinner tray last night. It read 'Talk and You Die.'"

"Where is the note?" Grover asked, just as she knew he would.

She mentally kicked herself for not keeping the note, but at the time she'd been so shocked and terrified knowing that the killer could get to her even in the hospital that she'd just wanted it gone.

When she told him that he nodded, his mouth twisting in a smirk. "So you didn't keep the evidence that might help us find the person who robbed your bank and killed three of his associates."

Carla bit her lip. "I was scared. I'm still scared. I'm the one he almost killed. If he'd taken me hostage the way he'd wanted to…" Her voice broke.

"When's the best time to rob a bank?" Agent Grover asked.

The question was so out of the blue that she stared at him. "I beg your pardon?"

"Isn't there more money in the vault at Christmastime than any other time because a lot of businesses like to give cash bonuses?"

"I don't know where you heard that," she said, but she could see that he already knew the answer. It was true. As one of the top financial officers, she knew there had been more money in the vault than usual. Had the robbers hit the bank any other day, it wouldn't have been the case. Was that why he thought someone employed by the bank had given the robbers this information, making it an inside job?

"But it's true, isn't it," he said, eyeing her. "The day those men walked armed into your bank was the perfect time to rob a bank that hasn't been robbed in more than a hundred years."

She pushed back her chair and rose.

"We aren't finished here," Grover snapped. "Let's stop playing games, Ms. Richmond. You know exactly who robbed the bank. Isn't that what you were doing in the bank on your day off? Isn't that why you were the only one who ended up in the hospital? Make it look good. Isn't that what you told him? You saw the perfect way to—"

"You couldn't be more wrong. I'm going to say this one more time. I had nothing to do with the robbery. From now on, I won't be talking to you unless my lawyer is present." She had her hand in her pocket, gripping her phone, and she pushed the button as the agent started to argue the point. Davy's phone rang in the other room and an instant later he came through the door.

Davy looked at her face and turned to Grover. "I think we're done here."

Grover rose slowly, his gaze locked on her. Deeds got to his feet. He gave her a "what did you expect" look before they started out of the room. "I wouldn't leave town if I was you, Ms. Richmond," Grover said over his shoulder. "I suggest you get yourself a lawyer, because we'll be back."

"I thought you said we didn't have to worry about the Colt brothers," Jesse demanded the moment Jud picked up the call later that night after she'd gone to work.

He could tell from the background noise that she was standing outside on the back steps at the hospital and that she was smoking and not even trying to hide it from him. "What's going on?"

"The administrator's assistant told me that James Colt asked for the names of all the hospital employees. Why would he want those unless she talked?"

"He's just fishing. He's looking for someone whose name begins with *J*." He laughed, relieved that's all it was. "So there's no problem. They aren't looking for Debra Watney."

She lowered her voice. "But if the feds get involved, they could find out that I'm not who I say I am." Jesse had used her twin sister's name and nurse's aide experience to get the job at the hospital.

Jud had questioned her at the time, asking, "What happens if your sister shows up or applies for a job somewhere else?"

"We don't have to worry about Deb," Jesse had said. "It's all good."

Now he thought about what Cora Brooks had said. Was Debra the missing sister?

"The last thing I need is the feds snooping around here," Jesse was saying.

He told himself that the fear he heard in Jesse's voice had nothing to do with a missing sister. Cora Brooks didn't know what she was talking about. "You're not going to be working there much longer anyway."

Did he have to remind her that they had a ton of money in a cave? Or that she was the one who'd insisted they continue working at their jobs as if nothing had happened? She'd made a good argument, even though he couldn't wait to blow this town, this county, this state, maybe even this country.

But she was right. If she quit now, she'd look guilty and the hospital might dig deeper. Same with his boring job. He hadn't been completely truthful on his application either.

"Did you drive by her house?" Jesse asked.

They'd discussed this and she'd warned him to stay clear of Carla Richmond and her house. "You told me not to." He'd driven past earlier. The sidewalk hadn't been shoveled since the latest snowstorm. There was a fresh set of tracks where someone had driven in, gotten out and gone inside the house. Large prints, like a man's boot size. The tracks had gone in and come back out.

"Well, if you did drive by there, you'd realize that she isn't there," Jesse said as if knowing he'd lied. "She's staying with the Colts for the holidays above that office of theirs." He wondered how she knew this. "So there is no getting to her until she returns home."

"I think it's a sign that we shouldn't wait," he said. "We should get the money and leave. She told the feds everything she knows and nothing has really happened. We're in the clear. Why press our luck?"

He waited for her to agree or put up an argument. All he got was a cold, dead silence. "Jesse?" He thought maybe she'd already disconnected, before he heard her let out an angry sigh.

"I've got to go." This time she did disconnect.

Jud swore under his breath. He knew that sigh. Jesse was in this now up to her neck. He'd told himself the Colt brothers weren't going to be a problem and now they were. In the meantime, he needed to find out just how hot the bank money might be. If he'd given marked bills to the loan shark, he should hear about it soon. This day just kept getting better.

Before work, he'd spent some time on the computer at the town library. He'd quickly learned what a fool he was. Marked bills, he'd discovered, were often not really "marked." Instead, banks kept bills with sequential serial numbers—in the tills of the tellers. Once those bills were mixed with those from the main vault, there was no telling which bills were marked and which weren't. Apparently a countrywide bulletin was issued to all retailers to watch out for those serial numbers.

So now he realized he may have given the wrong people marked bills.

Jud hated feeling so asinine. It made him angry and that anger found itself aimed at Carla Richmond. She knew all of this. She'd known it the day of the robbery. That's why he'd driven by her house. He hadn't known what he was going to do. He knew he'd be smart to just let it go. But it made him angrier that he couldn't get to Carla even if he wanted to.

So he'd passed her house and gone to work feeling out

of sorts long before his conversation with Jesse. He felt worse after her second call.

"I was right. Your bank girl talked," Jesse said without preamble. "The feds know about the note. They're interviewing everyone with access to her food tray. I'll be called in at any moment."

"Lie." It was the best advice he had to give. "Tell them you didn't know anything about it. You can handle this."

"It just makes me so angry that she talked to the feds after I warned her not to," Jesse was saying. "She can't get away with this."

Alarmed by her tone as well as her words, Jud tried to calm her down.

"Easy. We don't want to do anything rash, right? You're the one who said we had to keep our heads and play it cool."

"I'm getting paged. I have to go." She disconnected, leaving him still alarmed and worried. Jesse could handle this, he assured himself. Unless she let her anger get the better of her, and he knew from experience how dangerous that could be. He'd almost blown the bank job because he'd wanted to punish Carla Richmond for not giving him a loan he hadn't even applied for. At least now he had a good reason to hate her and want to harm her.

He didn't even make an excuse this time for driving past her house.

Chapter 14

"Are you feeling all right?" Davy asked when Carla said she was going upstairs to lie down. "Maybe you checked out of the hospital too soon."

She scoffed at that. "I couldn't get out of there soon enough. I'm fine, really. I just tire quickly." He offered to go with her to make sure she made it upstairs.

"Davy, I can climb stairs by myself. Please, I feel helpless enough."

"Sorry." He let her go and went back to the office.

"Everything okay?" James asked when he walked in.

"She's still weak from her injuries." But he knew that wasn't the real cause. Like him, she was worried. The feds seemed to think the robbery had been an inside job. Agent Grover especially thought it was Carla. "She needs a good lawyer. You know one?"

"Slim pickings in Lonesome," his brother said. "You

might want to try Missoula. I'll ask around. How soon do you need one?"

"Yesterday," Davy said. "What about the lawyer helping us with Dad's case?"

"Carla needs someone who specializes in defense cases," James said. "Especially with the FBI involved."

Davy was worried about her, and he knew that his brother saw it.

"Might have trouble finding one over the holidays," James said. "Could be a problem."

That wasn't the biggest problem, Davy thought. After giving Carla some time alone, he climbed the stairs, hoping she'd gotten some sleep and was feeling better. At least he hoped she was upstairs and hadn't sneaked out. It would be just like her to feel like she was too much trouble and go home, scared or not.

As he entered the apartment, he saw that she was up and awake. He also saw that she looked anxious. She'd always been so independent. Not like other girls at high school who had to be with their boyfriends 24/7.

Before he could speak, she said, "I'm sorry I snapped at you earlier." He started to wave it off, but she continued. "You know me. I can't stay locked up here like a princess hiding in her castle."

"This space is nice, but it's no castle."

"You know what I mean. I'll stay for a few more days until I'm more myself, but I'd at least like to go over to the house and pick up a few more things. Willie brought everything on my list, but if I'm staying longer…"

"Sure. I'll take you." He realized that she was going to make it harder for him to keep her safe, but he was surprised that she'd agreed to come here to begin with. Not that he'd given her much choice. He and his brother

Tommy had picked up her car from where she'd parked it downtown and taken it back to her house. He hoped she wouldn't want it yet. "Whatever you need."

"I'm not trying to be difficult."

"You're not. I would feel the same way." Their gazes held for a few moments. He did know her, intimately. Or at least he had a long time ago. Had either of them really changed all that much? He didn't think so. She looked more rested. He could see that she was feeling better, getting stronger and more like her old self. So it would surprise him if she stayed even a few more days.

"Then I want to be part of the investigation," she said. "I overheard you and James talking about tattoo shops. I want to come along."

Davy's first thought was to argue all the reasons she would be safer not to, but he could see that she'd made up her mind and he didn't like leaving her here alone with everyone out of the office. "Sure, if you're up to it."

He saw her visibly relax. He knew she would feel better being involved, but still he worried. The killer was out there. He could be anyone on the street. They wouldn't know until it was too late.

She was quiet on the drive to the small house she'd bought outside Lonesome. Covered in snow, it looked like a fairy-tale cottage in a snow globe. Davy parked in the unplowed driveway and took in his surroundings. Dark shadows hunkered in the snow-laden pines that sheltered the house on three sides. He was glad he'd talked her into coming back to the office, even though he wasn't sure how long he could keep her there. But out here at the house, it would be hard to keep her safe unless he moved in, something he really doubted she would allow him to do.

After getting out, they walked through the fresh snow to the front door. *No tracks*, he thought. But that didn't mean that someone hadn't been here, hadn't checked out the place for when they planned to come back.

Carla unlocked the door and they entered the foyer. They left their snowy boots on the mat by the door, and he followed her through the house. It struck him how much this place reflected her personality. Everything was neat and clean, the colors bright and sunny. There was no clutter. It appeared every furnishing had been handpicked over time to give the place a warm and welcoming feel.

It drew him in more than he wanted to admit. He'd been living out of a camper in his horse trailer all this time. He couldn't help but feel a sense of pride and admiration for Carla. She'd done what she'd set out to do. She'd made a good life for herself.

And yet he knew this wasn't what she had planned. She'd had higher aspirations, but had to put those on hold to come home to Lonesome and take care of her mother. She'd wanted to make something of herself, while he had just wanted adventure—and her to share in it as his wife.

Davy felt that old ache. He'd wanted her more than his next breath. But he couldn't give up his dreams any more than she could hers. Still, he found himself wondering what their lives could have been if they'd married in these past ten years. Couldn't they both have had what they wanted and still found a way to be together?

He scoffed silently at that as he looked around the house. Could he not see that Carla had wanted permanency, security, a place to call home? She'd never wanted his transient lifestyle. For her it wouldn't have been an adventure at all.

Like she'd said back then, they wanted different things.

This house stood as an example of how true that was. Except for one thing. They had wanted each other. Did they still?

She came out of the bedroom with a small bag that warned him she wouldn't be staying long with him at the office.

"Got everything you need?" He watched her glance around the house before she nodded. She had roots, a home she clearly loved, a career. He would have taken that all from her had she come with him on the road. They'd chosen the trajectory of their lives back then based on what they wanted out of life. Thanks to a robbery and a killer on the loose, those lives had intersected again. But for how long?

Once the killer was caught, Carla would be going back to her life and he'd be going back to his. Even as he thought it, he knew that he wouldn't come out of this experience unchanged though. But changed enough to find a way to be together? Or again brokenhearted and alone?

He turned his thoughts to finding the killer. With James and Tommy both busy on cases and Willie down at the sheriff's department as part of his training as deputy, he and Carla would hit tattoo shops with the sketch she'd made.

"I thought we'd start with the local tattoo shop," he told her once they were back in his pickup. "And if no luck there, branch out."

Carla said nothing. She was looking in her side mirror as if she thought someone might be following them.

Davy glanced back. All he saw was a delivery truck behind them.

Carla leaned back and closed her eyes as they drove back into Lonesome. She hadn't been able to sleep at first when she'd gone upstairs at the agency earlier. She'd felt restless and had found herself moving around the apartment, studying the posters and photographs.

She'd seen them as a teenager when she and Davy had been together. The movie poster was of his great-grandfather Ransom Del Colt, an old Hollywood Westerns star. There were flyers from Davy's grandfather's Wild West shows. RD Colt Jr. had traveled the globe ridin' and ropin' until late in his life.

Del Colt, the brothers' father, had only stopped rodeoing because of an injury. He was the one who had started the investigation business. He was also the one who had taught his four sons to ride a horse when they were probably still in diapers.

As she'd moved around the room, she'd seen the Colt family legacy on the walls. Each generation had passed on that love to the next. Rodeo and horses and competition were embedded deep in the brothers' genes. Had she really thought she could get Davy to give that up? What had made her think she had the right?

Well, he'd made his choice all those years ago and it hadn't been her. That's what made this so hard. The past was almost palpable between them. She knew it was why he felt he had to protect her. It wasn't because of any residual feelings for her, she told herself. Yet she kept thinking about the day he'd come into the bank. Had he wanted to ask her out? If only he had. If only they could have started over then.

Feeling the weight of everything after she'd looked over the posters in the room, she'd finally lain down. As she'd drifted off, her last thought had been how desperately they both needed to get back to their lives before they tried to rewrite history—and got their hearts broken all over again.

* * *

Jud found Jesse waiting for him when he got home from work the next day. She'd traded schedules with a friend, apparently, so wasn't working her late shift. She seemed calm after being questioned by the feds about the note on the food tray.

"You think they believed you?" he asked as he joined her on the couch. He didn't smell anything cooking and wondered if she'd gotten takeout or if he'd misunderstood and had been expected to pick something up.

She shot him a look. "Why wouldn't they? Do I look like someone who would lie?"

He wasn't about to touch that. At first glance, no. But he'd gotten to know her. He'd seen below the sweet, shy, blond exterior.

She got right down to business. "We have to assume that they know about the tattoo and will start looking for the person who inked it." He'd never told her where he'd gone. He'd just come home with a tattoo. She might have thought a friend had done it because the tattoo was so simple. "The question is, how long before they track it back to you?"

Jud scoffed. "How would they do that? I didn't have it done around here." He could feel her gaze boring into him. "As many tattoo artists as there are in the state…" He shrugged. "Maybe if it were a unique design…"

She'd been sitting cross-legged at the end of the couch, but now she rolled up onto her knees and crawled toward him. He tried not to flinch when she jerked back the collar of his shirt to expose the tattoo.

"Why is your neck all red?" she asked, as if afraid to touch it.

"I told you—the Santa costume gave me a rash. I was itchy. I had to scratch or go crazy."

She made no comment, simply ran the tip of her finger over one *J*, then the heart. He was waiting for her to finish by tracing the other *J* when she said, "What's that at the bottom of the heart?" as if she'd never paid much attention to the tattoo before.

He'd gotten the painful tattoo for *her* as a symbol of his love. He bit back the bitter taste in his mouth that urged his tongue to lash out at her. "It's another, smaller heart."

"It looks black, but it has something in it. Something squiggly. Maybe it's just a mistake, but it looks like a snake."

"What is your point?" he snapped and pulled away from her, buttoning up his collar as he tried to tamp down his growing impatience with her. He'd gotten the tattoo for her, he'd robbed the bank for her, he'd gone back to work instead of taking the money and leaving—all for her. So things hadn't gone as planned. That was life. Learn to live with it. He had.

"Who did your tattoo?" she asked, after going back to the other end of the couch and picking up her wineglass. Even that annoyed him. She couldn't drink beer with him and had to have wine like she was someone he really doubted she was. But even as he thought it, he realized he didn't know much about her.

He couldn't help but think about what Cora Brooks had said. Was it possible her family had lived up in the mountains around here? Cora had made them sound like survivalists or criminals or squatters. Nothing good. Jesse had never wanted to talk about her family.

Then again, maybe Cora didn't know what she was

talking about. Maybe Jesse came from money. Maybe all her relatives drank wine. She could have been royalty for all he knew.

Except that she was with him, which told him she didn't come from money any more than he did and there wasn't a royal bone in her body.

"It was just a shop on the street in Butte. I don't even remember its name." There was no reason not to tell her. Then again, she didn't have to know everything, especially about that night.

"You don't remember which shop." Clearly she didn't believe him. She turned to glare down the length of the couch at him. "You might not remember the shop, but there will be paperwork. Paperwork with your name on it."

He wondered how she knew so much about tattoos, since as far as he knew, she'd never had one. But now she had him worried. He tried to remember what information he'd given the tattooist. He vaguely recalled signing something. A consent form? Had he shown his driver's license? Maybe—he wasn't sure. He'd had way too much to drink, and his friend had plied him with more as he'd egged him on. Jud had been feeling no pain—at first—and had been glad that he hadn't had enough money for Jesse's whole name. He'd gotten what he could afford. Something simple and quick. So who cared what was at the bottom of the heart?

"Maybe you should try to remember and get to the artist before the feds do, don't you think?" Jesse said.

Only if the feds find out where I got the tattoo, he thought. What were the chances?

Jesse sighed and asked as if reading his mind, "Haven't you taken enough chances?"

He didn't bother to answer. He could tell that nothing he could say would make a difference. Only one thing would appease her. He shook his head, even as he knew he would do whatever she asked. Worse, she knew it.

Chapter 15

Davy had little hope that they could track down the person who'd given the man the tattoo, but they had to try. The tattoo was simple, nothing unique about it that he could tell from the sketch Carla had drawn.

He'd had to park off Main Street because of the lack of parking with Christmas so close. Even the sidewalk was fairly crowded as they headed to Lonesome's only tattoo shop. He found himself looking at everyone they passed and trying to keep himself between them and Carla. Earlier, he'd considered just emailing all the tattoo parlors within a hundred-mile radius with an accompanying shot of the tattoo, but he'd learned that people were more forthcoming in person.

The shop wasn't much more than a hole-in-the-wall with one chair and one artist. The sign in the window read only Tattoos. The owner's name was Big John, a

burly former state-champion wrestler who'd done time
in Deer Lodge for check fraud. It was in prison that he'd
apparently gotten hooked on injecting ink under other
people's skin, where it stayed forever.

"Davy Colt!" Big John bellowed when he saw him.
"You finally decided to get a tattoo." He laughed up-
roariously and slapped him on the back before saying
hello to Carla. It was a small town and Big John had gotten his start-up loan at her bank, she'd told Davy before
they entered the shop. "Not afraid of an angry bull, but
a little needle…"

Davy had heard all of this before. Big John had been
trying to get him and his brothers tatted for years. He
hoped to get this over with as quickly as possible. He
pulled the sketch from his pocket and held it out to the
tattooist.

"This is what you want?" Big John asked with a chor-
tle.

"No, I need to know if you did this design."

The man looked insulted. "A child could have done
that."

"So I'm taking it that you didn't. Who might have
done it?"

The tattoo artist was shaking his head when Carla
spoke up. "I know it's really basic, but I think that little
squiggle at the bottom inside the tiny black heart could
be a trademark or just a slip of the needle."

Davy shot her a look, surprised she knew something
about tattoos.

"I did a little research on my phone," she said without looking at him.

Big John considered the two of them before he took
the sketch and held it up to the light. Stepping over to a

tray next to his chair, he picked up a large magnifying glass and studied the sketch more closely. He nodded and handed the paper back.

"You're right. It could be a trademark sign. If so, then I know the so-called artist. An embarrassment to our craft. Bad for business, you know," he said, giving Carla a nod.

"What's inside the tiny black heart?" Davy asked.

"Up close with a magnifying glass on the tattoo itself it could be a tiny broken heart with an *S* in it," Big John said. "Some artists put a little of themselves into every tattoo they do, kind of like a signature at the bottom of a canvas."

He handed back the sketch. "So let's talk about a tattoo for you, Davy Colt. I could do a bucking horse."

"I see enough of those, but thanks."

"Still afraid of needles, huh? Your girlfriend here wasn't afraid."

Davy didn't think Carla could surprise him more. "You got a tattoo?" Her face flamed.

"You haven't seen it yet, huh?" Big John laughed and winked at Carla. "He's in for a surprise, huh."

"Can you tell us where we can find the tattoo artist who might have done the tattoo?" she asked, clearly anxious to change the subject.

"If I'm right, Butte," Big John said with a sigh. "The name of the shop is Sam's Pit. Get it?"

"After the Berkeley Pit," Davy said. A former open-pit copper mine, The Pit, as it was known, was a mile long and a half mile wide and held fifty billion gallons of toxic water. It was a lasting symbol of mining gone wrong. Only 19 percent of cities were more dangerous as a place to live because of the toxic pit.

"Sam is really Samantha Elliot," Big John said with

a chuckle. "You'll find her rather interesting. You might want to take a sidearm just in case she doesn't like the looks of you. Or take Carla here with you." His belly laugh followed them out the door.

"I don't want to talk about it," Carla said the moment they were outside Big John's tattoo parlor.

Davy glanced over at her as they walked back to where he'd parked the pickup. She knew that grin. She also recognized the curiosity in those blue eyes of his. He was dying to know about the tattoo along with what and where it was. She should have known Big John would say something.

Holding up both hands in surrender, Davy said, "I won't mention your tattoo again." But that wouldn't stop him from thinking about it, she thought, feeling her cheeks redden again.

"So when do we go to Butte?" she asked, hating that he could get under her skin so easily.

"We can go today. I need to stop by the office and see if James is back. He might have heard something from the hospital," Davy said as they climbed into his pickup. "I'm anxious to find out the name of the blonde aide who brought you your dinner tray—and then took it away."

Carla knew she'd messed up by not keeping the note. She wanted to blame her concussion and that she hadn't been thinking clearly. That probably had played a part in it since she'd been feeling so vulnerable. But she knew it had also been fear. Just the thought that the person who'd hurt her could get to her even in the hospital…

"It's not your fault," Davy said as they drove the few blocks to the Colt Brothers Investigation building. Fortunately, there was parking in the back alley. "You were recovering from a head injury and you were scared."

She wished he would stop reading her mind. It had always been like this between them. She had thought it would have changed in all the time they'd been apart. "Maybe the feds could have gotten fingerprints or—"

"Not likely."

"But it would have been proof," she cried.

Davy glanced at her. "Or the agent would have suspected you wrote it yourself."

She groaned. He was right. She had to let it go. They now had a lead on the tattoo. Once they had J's full name…

After Davy left Carla's overnight bag upstairs in her room, they went down to the office to find James sitting behind the large desk. "Good news," he announced when he saw them. "I just got the list of hospital personnel and information about who's nearing retirement and vacation schedules."

Davy quickly moved to look over his brother's shoulder at the computer screen. It didn't take long to sort the names by the initial *J*. Carla joined him.

There was one Jennifer and one Jane. Jane worked in medical records and was about to retire. Jennifer was a young nurse's aide who was on Christmas vacation all week in Mexico.

Disappointed, Davy said, "Did you get the name of the blonde aide? She not only brought Carla's dinner tray, but also took it away."

"I thought you might be onto something when you first mentioned her," James said. "When I asked who had delivered Carla's tray, it turned out that one of the aides had volunteered to take it to her, saying she felt sorry for Carla after what had happened at the bank."

"Sounds like a red flag to me," Davy said.

"Her name is Debra Anne Watney. She's been there more than two months now and is a model employee," James said. "Apparently it's not unusual for her to help out in any department, and she's very compassionate with patients."

"She seemed *nice*," Carla said.

"And her name doesn't start with *J*," James pointed out unnecessarily. "But like I said, the tattoo could be about an old girlfriend."

Davy shook his head. "I felt like there was something off about her. I'd like to find out more about her." He told him about what they'd learned at the local tattoo parlor. "Big John thinks it might have been inked by a woman named Samantha Elliot at Sam's Pit in Butte."

"The tiny heart at the bottom might be her trademark," Carla said.

"I think you need to tell the feds," James said.

"We wanted to talk to her first," Davy said.

"Might be better to let them follow the lead. If it came from Carla and it pans out…"

"You think it might get Grover off my back," she said and James nodded.

"And if they don't take it seriously?" Davy demanded. "I think we should make sure and then tell the feds. If it turns out to be another dead end, Agent Grover is going to be even more suspicious of Carla."

"You make a good point," James said. "Still, I'd call up there and make sure the tattooist hasn't taken off for the holidays. Hopefully the woman will be able to help you. In the meantime, Willie said he'd help, but he had a ride-along down at the sheriff's department. Tommy's on a stakeout. I'll see what I can find out about Debra Anne Watney."

"Willie really is going to become a deputy sheriff?" Davy said, shaking his head.

James nodded thoughtfully. "I hope he knows what he's doing." He quickly changed the subject. "Lori called earlier. She and Bella are asking about our plans for the holidays. They were thinking Christmas Eve out at the Worthington Ranch and New Year's Eve to at least begin at our place," James said. "They're delighted Carla will be coming. But we'd also like to have you guys out to our house for dinner one night as well."

Davy looked over at Carla. "You game?" He hoped he didn't have to remind her that she'd promised to stay with him for a while.

She hesitated only a moment before she nodded. "Sure. Thank you."

"Definitely Christmas Eve at Bella's," Davy said and smiled, thinking of their last Christmas together. Now he and Carla would be spending Christmas together again— just not the way he'd often dreamed.

Carla couldn't help being disappointed that the hospital employee list hadn't been fruitful. But it had been a long shot. J could have a friend who worked there, although she couldn't imagine the sort of person who'd agree to put a note like that on her tray. Surely that person would know through Lonesome's grapevine that she'd been through enough trauma with the bank robbery. No way would anyone think the note was funny or just a harmless prank.

James was going to check out Debra Anne Watney, but Carla thought that too would be a dead end. She didn't see it leading anywhere since there had been nothing threatening about the blonde aide. Nor did the woman's name begin with *J*. Carla would have been much happier if they had more of a lead on J.

She'd been thinking about another possible way to find him. She stepped into the conference room and called her boss, president and manager of the bank, Larry Baxter. After he'd asked how she was and said how glad he was that she was out of the hospital, she asked him for the favor she'd been thinking about.

"I know it's against bank privacy rules, but I have a feeling that the man who attacked me at the bank might have come in recently for a loan," she told him. "If I could go through the latest requests that I've had to deny…" She could hear her boss trying to let her down easy. "If not all of them, then any whose names start with the letter *J*."

"Why *J*?"

"I saw the man's tattoo. I believe his name begins with *J*. I know this request is unorthodox but—"

"I'll tell you what," Larry said. "I'll go through your files and pull out all the ones starting with *J*, first and last name. I'm sure you told the federal agents this so they'll be asking for the same information at some point. But," he said, lowering his voice. "Because of the circumstances, I'm allowing it for your eyes only, and this stays between the two of us."

"I think it would be best if you let me know when you have the list ready," she said. "No need to send it by email. I could meet you at the coffee shop down from the bank."

"You're beginning to think like a criminal," he joked.

"I wish that were true. Then maybe I'd know what the man will do next."

"How about coffee this afternoon? Two?" Larry asked and she quickly agreed. They wished each other well before he disconnected.

"I need to do some Christmas shopping" she told Davy, knowing he was going to try to stop her. "I don't have anything for your family."

"My family doesn't expect gifts from you, especially under the circumstances." She merely looked at him until he said, "I suppose it won't do any good to mention how dangerous it is with all those last-minute shoppers crowding the stores and us not knowing which of them is a killer?" He must have seen that it didn't.

She knew she couldn't keep the truth from him. "I'm also meeting my boss at the coffee shop down from the bank at two. He'd prefer I come alone since it's bank business." Davy groaned. "You could drop me off, watch the shop from across the street in the bar and I could text you when I'm done. It shouldn't take long." She gave him a broad smile and saw him weaken.

"You're not an easy woman to keep alive, Carla Richmond."

"I appreciate you trying though," she said. "But you aren't always going to be around. Maybe it would be best if you changed your mind and walked away now so—"

"Not happening." He met her gaze. "Just to be clear, I'm not changing my mind. I don't want to see anything happen to you if I can prevent it."

She sighed. "Davy, I know this isn't how you planned to spend your holiday."

His blue eyes darkened. "Plans change, Carla. You should know that. Ten years ago I planned to marry you. If I'd had my way, we would be married right now. It wouldn't have been the life you had planned though, but I'd be just as determined to keep you safe as I am now."

She couldn't speak around the lump in her throat.

"Now that we have that settled, let me try to reach Sam's Pit tattoo shop again. I know that the shop is open. I left her a message to say we were coming. If I can't reach her, we'll have to drive to Butte tomorrow. She could be busy doing a tattoo and not taking calls. But I'd feel better if I could reach her before we take the drive."

It was no coincidence that Samantha "Sam" Elliot's mother named her after the baritone heartthrob who just happened to be in a Western on the hospital room television the night Sam came into the world.

Over the years though, Sam had done everything possible to erase that Hollywood image when it came to her appearance. The truth was, her body was the direct result of her love of food, alcohol and tattoos. A massive woman, she had a deep voice and a laugh that carried for at least four blocks. She loved life and she lived as if there were no tomorrow.

As for the tattoos, Sam had once thought that she'd become a famous artist. She could laugh about that now, but it had hurt when critics called her talentless. That, however, turned out to be true. It was after her first tattoo that she realized she'd found her calling. Since then she'd covered almost every square inch of her body with her art and others'.

That's how she'd found her career path. With her robust personality, her decorative flesh and her limited talent, she'd made a name for herself in the regional world of tattoo artists. She'd even put her own stamp on it with the tiny black hearts she put in every tattoo she inked. Inside that black heart was a tiny *S*. It was her trademark.

She never forgot a tattoo. So she recognized Jud the moment he walked in, right after her last customer had left and she was about to close for the rest of the holidays. She had a great memory. It would take her a minute or two to recall his last name though, without looking it up in her file. But she remembered that, when he'd come in originally, he'd been drunk and so had his friend with him. He'd wanted something for his girlfriend and asked what he could get for... He'd dug some crumpled bills from his pocket and shoved them at her.

She'd almost turned him away. But there was something pathetic about Jud. So, feeling sorry for him, she'd told him what she could do. It wasn't much, but then again his money didn't even cover her time.

She'd have wagered that he wouldn't be a return customer even before she'd sat him down in her chair that first time. He'd had trouble sitting still, so it hadn't been her best work. Some people couldn't take the pain. But Jud was in lust with someone named Jesse. He was merely trying to make a statement, so Sam had helped him out.

When he walked in now though, she got the feeling that things hadn't worked out. He looked so unhappy she thought he'd come to ask about redesigning the tattoo or covering it up since Jesse was now nothing more than a bad memory.

That's why she was surprised when he said, "That form I signed? I need it back." He glanced toward the adjoining room where the file cabinets were kept.

Her cell phone began to ring. She looked toward it resting on the table off to her right. It had rung earlier, but she'd let it go to voice mail because she'd been busy with a customer.

"Your consent form?" she asked, wondering why he would want it and if she could even find it as she took a step toward her ringing cell phone.

Before she could reach it, she saw the gun he'd pulled from behind him. "The consent form, *now*."

She saw then that he wasn't just unhappy. He was clearly agitated. Was he on something? Her phone rang again. He snatched it up and threw it across the room, where it landed on the chairs used for those waiting their turn. Fortunately, it had quit ringing.

"Jud, I'll be happy to give you your form. I file them by last name. You'll have to remind me—" She saw his surprise that she knew his first name. That's probably why she hadn't seen the blow coming, when in retrospect she should have, she thought. The butt of his gun broke her cheekbone and cut her nose, which began to bleed profusely.

She stumbled back, crashing into her table of tools. They scattered noisily across the floor. She was trying to get to the chairs and her cell phone when he hit her again. The room dimmed. She tried to speak, but nothing came out. As she began to slump to the floor, she saw him coming at her again. He appeared to be crying, his face flushed, spittle flying from his lips as he attacked. She felt nothing after the fourth blow.

Chapter 16

Jud had been home for hours pacing the floor as he waited to hear from Jesse. He'd tried calling her, but all his calls had gone straight to voice mail. The last time he'd talked to her, she'd been about to be called in to be questioned by the feds again. He was losing his mind and was about to go look for her when he heard her come in through the front door.

"Where the hell—" He caught himself even though he wanted to strangle her. Instead, he rushed to her, taking her in his arms. She smelled of booze, answering his question about where she'd been. But why hadn't she called him? She had to have known how worried he was.

He wondered who she'd had drinks with. Some other man? He held her tighter and realized that she was trembling. Letting go, he stepped back to study her face. At first he'd thought she was scared. But he quickly realized that she was furious. For a moment, he thought it was with him. It wouldn't be the first time. But he tried hard to keep Jesse happy. He'd dated a lot of women, most of them walking out on him once they really got to know him.

Jesse was different. She was worth keeping. It was one reason he'd taken the mind-numbing delivery job even temporarily. It was another reason he'd decided to pull off the bank job. He'd promised himself he would do whatever it took to make this one stay.

"Want to tell me what happened?" he asked as he followed her into the kitchen.

She opened the refrigerator and took out the wine bottle. As she poured herself a glass, she finally looked at him again. "I got grilled by the feds. They already knew I was the one who took in the dinner tray and picked it up from the first time they talked to me. Again, they wanted to know what I did with it. What they really wanted to know was if there was a note with it."

"What did you tell them?" he asked as he followed her into the living room.

She kicked off her shoes and sprawled on the couch, leaving him just enough room to sit, if he didn't mind her feet in his lap. "What do you think I told them? That I wrote the note?" She shook her head. "I said like I did the first time that I didn't see any note. At least one of the feds believes me. He asked what Carla had said to me. I told him again that she said she wasn't hungry and to get rid of the tray." Jesse smiled. "I could tell that they suspect she lied about there being a note."

"So it's all good," he said, sighing in relief. So why was she so upset? She looked angrier than when she'd come home.

"No, it's not all good, Jud." She bit off each word.

"Carla Richmond drew them a sketch of your tattoo. They were showing it around to everyone, asking if they knew anyone who had a tattoo like that."

"No one did, right?"

"That's not the point. The point is I warned her to keep her trap shut." She shifted on the couch, her expression going dark. "That woman is as good as dead. She should have done what I told her."

He was no fan of Carla Richmond either, but all he really wanted was for this to be over. "I think we should take the money and leave." He'd been thinking about it all the way home from Butte. It was time to get the hell out of Dodge. Not that he thought anyone could connect him to what had happened at the tattoo parlor. He'd gotten his forms and destroyed them on the way home. At least for this, he was home free.

He didn't want to wait around until the loan goons got arrested in case the money he'd given them was marked. Mostly, he was ready to start spending some of that cash—the unmarked cash. "We can go anywhere we want. I was thinking—"

"We're not going anywhere, not yet," she said, sitting up. She pulled her legs into her and wrapped her arms around them. She wasn't as angry now. Somehow it made her scarier. "I'm not leaving until she's dead."

He hoped she was merely venting. "That's not going to happen as long as she's staying with Davy Colt."

Jesse nodded. "Eventually she'll have to go back to her place. No one crosses me. No one." Her gaze met his, and he had to fight hard not to flinch. "I'm going to make something to eat." She got up and left the room.

He sat for a moment listening to her bang around in

the kitchen before he got up and followed her. He couldn't let her go off half-cocked. She'd get them both arrested.

"Jesse, you're making me nervous," Jud said as he watched her chopping up carrots. She was angry and waving the knife around as she cursed and fumed. "I can't let you do something you'll regret," he said.

"Then cut up the carrots yourself," she snapped, throwing down the knife.

"That's not what I was talking about," he said, quickly pulling the knife and then sliding the cutting board and the rest of the carrots across the counter out of her reach. "You can't kill Carla Richmond."

She glared at him, and he was glad he now had their only decent knife. "That's your problem, Jud. You don't stand up for yourself. You would have never robbed the bank if I hadn't put the idea into your head." Was that true? She had been nagging him relentlessly. "Just once, don't you want to prove to people that you have a backbone?"

He thought of what he'd done in Butte and grimaced. "I can't see how killing that woman would help matters," he said, only to have her turn toward him with a look in her eyes that chilled him to his very core. "I'm not saying we can't kill her," he amended quickly. "But we have to plan. We don't want to get caught, right?"

Her mouth was set in a stubborn line. "What are you suggesting?"

"That you let me take care of it." He thought of the day he'd had—all the blood—and tried not to gag. "You didn't ask me about my day."

"You have blood on your shoes," she said and met his gaze. "What is there to ask?"

He looked down, shocked to see that while he'd stripped out of his bloody clothing, tossed it into the wash and changed as soon as he got home, he'd put on the same shoes. He swallowed back the bile that rose in his throat. With the other bank robbers, it had been self-defense. They would have killed him for the money if he hadn't killed them first. But the woman at the tattoo shop…

"All I'm saying is that I have more experience with this than you do," he said.

Jesse laughed and cocked a brow at him. "You sure about that?"

He wasn't. He thought her more than capable of murder though, especially when she was angry. He could hear Cora Brooks again warning him about Jesse. Buddy too.

"Then you're going to handle this before we leave?" she asked, crossing her arms over her chest and glaring at him as she waited.

At this stage, he thought it unnecessary to kill Carla. It was risky and foolish, but right then he would have said anything to mollify Jesse. "You know she can't hurt either of us since she's already told the feds everything she knows." Jesse's eyes narrowed to slits. He could see that there was no talking her out of this. "I'll take care of her, though I don't think it's necessary." Jesse began to tap her foot. "I'll kill her, okay?" The tapping stopped.

Jesse took the knife, cutting board and carrots from him. She carefully chopped up the rest and dumped them into the pot. "When? When will you do it?" she asked, still holding the knife.

It wasn't until Carla came back downstairs after getting ready for her meeting with the bank manager that she heard. As she walked into the office, she saw Davy on the phone. From his expression, she knew something had happened—and it wasn't good.

"What?" she asked the moment he disconnected from the call.

"That was the Butte Police Department. They heard the message I left on Samantha Elliot's voice mail," Davy said. She felt her eyes widen in alarm and tried to swallow. "She was attacked and her office destroyed. When I told them why we'd been anxious to talk to her…" He met Carla's gaze. "They think her attack might be related to the robbery and murders. She's in serious condition in the hospital. They don't think she'll make it."

She lowered herself into a chair as her legs threatened to give out under her. "This is his doing." The shock of the horrifying reality of this situation ricocheted through her. "He's covering his trail." She felt her eyes widen as her pulse thundered in her ears. "He knows that I told the federal agents about the tattoo." She felt tears burn her eyes. She'd drawn a picture of the man's tattoo and now the woman who'd inked it could die. "This is all my fault."

Davy moved to her, kneeling down in front of her to grasp her shoulders. "None of this is your fault."

"I told the agents about the tattoo. He knows I told. That's why that woman—"

"There's only one way he would know that you told the agents," James said. "J either works at the hospital or he knows someone who does."

"Which means he's local," Davy said as he rose.

"There was no one with a *J* name on the list though that fit the description," Carla pointed out. She felt as if she were trapped in a nightmare and couldn't wake up. But somehow she had to. They had to figure this out. They had to find him and stop him before… She shook off the rest of that thought as a tremor moved through her.

"Then more than likely he knows someone who does.

Someone close to him. Just not with a name that starts with *J*," Davy said.

"I have to find him," she said as she pushed herself up from the chair. "If he applied for a loan at the bank and I turned him down…" His name had to be there. It was the only hope she had right now. She glanced at the time and wondered if her boss had those names. She felt as if the clock were ticking. She quickly made the call. He had the names and would meet her in ten minutes. "I need to go."

"I'm taking you in my truck," Davy said.

She started to point out that it was just a few blocks, but she saved her breath. He wasn't going to let her even walk down the street until the man was caught.

That's why she had to do everything possible to make that happen for both her sake and Davy's.

Davy was surprised that the meeting at the coffee shop was so short. Carla had gone in, ordered coffee and was joined only minutes later by an older man. They'd spoken for a few moments before he'd slipped her a manila envelope and she'd gotten up and left. Davy had been waiting for her parked at the curb, after earlier going in a few shops with her as she finished her Christmas shopping as if there wasn't a killer after her.

"I need to go by my house again," she said as she climbed into his pickup now. "If we're going to your brother's, I need more clothes. Sorry."

"You don't have to apologize. I'm happy to take you." He started the engine, just grateful that there was no talk of going back to her house to stay.

She snapped on her seat belt and without another word opened the envelope and began to go through what looked like copies of loan forms. She made sure he couldn't read them, but he thought he already knew.

"People you turned down for a loan?" he asked.

She shot him a look, and for a moment, he thought she might not answer. "This is highly irregular."

"So is a bank robbery and you almost dying and having a killer after you," he said.

Carla rolled her eyes. "Well, when you put it that way. Still, it would be best if you didn't know." She glanced at the sheets of paper she'd been given. "I thought maybe one of them might jog my memory. Only a couple have names that begin with a *J*. My boss gave me all of the requests over the past month. They're people I remember. He's not in here," she said and pushed the copies back into the envelope. "Neither are their spouses."

He could see how disappointed she was. She'd been counting on the man's name being in there. He hated that it was another dead end.

She sighed. "Also I need to go by the gift store. I have to do a little more Christmas shopping since my plans have changed."

"Under the circumstances, the last thing you need to do is go shopping for my family."

She shot him a look.

"Fine, but know I'll be at your side the entire time."

"Have you always been this stubborn?"

"Yes, but I think you already know that." Their gazes met and he could feel the chemistry sparking between them. He knew her as well as she knew him. They'd both been each other's firsts. They'd reveled in each other and the sex and had basically been crazy in love their entire last year of high school.

Then everything had gone south when he'd told her that he wasn't following her to college. He was joining the rodeo circuit. That had been the end for her. The end for them.

They'd parted, but so much of that passion was still simmering between them. He could feel it, stronger than ever. If she felt it, she didn't let on. But then, neither did he. He was home only for Christmas and then it was on the back of a bronco. They'd be fools to start up anything again. Letting her go way back then had been hard enough. He didn't want to do that to himself again—let alone to her.

"Stubbornness is something we have in common, among other things." He was no longer talking about stubbornness, and from her expression, she knew it.

"Davy—"

"Clothes first, then shopping? I will say again that my family isn't expecting gifts."

She looked away. "It's Christmas. Sometimes you get something you didn't ask for or expect."

He smiled at that, wondering if this time with her was just that.

Her gaze was on the snow-filled pines as he headed down the narrow two-lane road toward her house. There was fresh color in her cheeks. He smiled to himself. She felt the chemistry too. He'd bet his horse on it.

As they neared her house, he was again aware of how isolated her place was. Somehow he had to keep her from returning there until the killer was caught. He glanced over at her and shook his head. Ten years ago he'd tried to convince her that they belonged together and would find a way. Ten years ago they'd been in love. Did he really think he stood a chance of convincing her of anything now that they were no longer together?

Jud walked up to Carla Richmond's house through the deep snow blanketing her sidewalk. He could see that she hadn't been here for a while. There were recent tire tracks in her driveway, so she'd at least stopped by. Or someone had.

But from the looks of the place, what he'd heard was true. She was staying with Davy Colt at the Colt Brothers Investigation building on Main. Apparently, the two had been tight in high school.

Still, he needed to scout out the place for when she returned. The rodeo cowboy would be leaving again soon. Right after Christmas probably, since from what Jud knew about the Colt brothers, Davy made his money on the rodeo circuit. Carla would have no choice then but to come home.

He trudged through the snow, carrying an empty box like it was a delivery just in case someone drove by and saw him. He knocked on the door and waited. While he did, he looked for any indication of an alarm system. This was Montana—hardly anyone had security systems unless they'd moved here from somewhere else and brought their paranoia with them.

Jud still didn't want to do this, he thought, as he peered in the window through a crack in the curtains. The best thing he and Jesse could do was get the hidden money and skip the country. He didn't understand why they were still in Lonesome as it was. The longer they stayed, the more worried he was that they would get caught—especially if he did something stupid like kill Carla Richmond.

But he worried that if he didn't, Jesse might take matters into her own hands. He was still hoping that he could talk her out of it. He couldn't wait to put this hick town in his rearview mirror.

He was about to put the box down and walk around the house to check the back door lock when he heard a pickup turn into the drive. The last thing he'd wanted to do was be seen here. Fortunately, he was wearing his large company winter jacket and hat with earflaps even though the day wasn't that cold.

As Davy drove up, he saw a delivery man standing on Carla's front porch—and a delivery truck parked at the edge of the road. The man, seemingly startled, turned at the sound of the truck's engine. Davy parked in the driveway and he and Carla climbed out.

"Do you have a package for me?" Carla called as the man started to retrace his steps back down the sidewalk toward his truck—carrying the package.

Davy could see where the man had left tracks in the deep snow of the sidewalk to the front door. He made a mental note to shovel her walk before he left. It was supposed to snow again tonight. Davy wanted to be able to tell who'd been here after they were gone.

The delivery man looked down at the package in his arms and shook his head. "Wrong address," he said over his shoulder as he headed for his truck.

Davy started across the yard toward the man. "What address are you looking for?" The man didn't answer, as if he hadn't heard. He disappeared inside his truck. A moment later, the engine revved and he took off.

"That wasn't weird at all," Carla said next to him.

"Yes, it was." He tried to see the plate number on the truck, but it was covered in snow and ice.

"It's a busy time of year," Carla said. "That's probably all it was."

Maybe, Davy thought. Yet when he'd driven up, he'd thought the man had been trying to see inside the house. Not necessarily suspicious, unless the homeowner had recently crossed paths with a killer.

"Tell me where your snow shovel is and I'll take care

of your walk while you get what you need," he said, putting the delivery man out of his thoughts for the moment.

She smiled. "What is the point? It's supposed to snow again tonight and I'm not staying here."

Davy saw her eye him with suspicion. "A clean walk makes it look like someone's home. Just safer." That too was true. But he had a bad feeling that the delivery man would come back. He wanted to be able to check the tracks when they returned.

Carla shook her head. "You think that man was checking out the place to steal my silverware?" When he didn't answer right away, she said, "No, you think he might be…" She shivered and looked down the road where the delivery truck had disappeared. "If he comes back—"

"There will be fresh tracks in the snow. Snow shovel?" he asked.

She swallowed. "Garage."

Carla let herself into the house. She'd left the heat on, but still it felt cold inside. She flipped on lights as she went, hating how easily she'd been spooked. She wanted to blame Davy for scaring her. Was she going to have to be afraid of every delivery man who came to her door?

She had just started to gather more clothing for the rest of the holidays when her cell phone rang, and she saw it was her boss. "Hello?"

"Carla." The way he said that one word had her heart battering her rib cage.

"Has something happened?"

He cleared his voice. "Sorry, no, that is… I know you mentioned earlier how anxious you are to come back to work, but unfortunately, until the FBI's investigation is finished, I have to put you on administrative leave. You'll still be paid."

Unless I'm found guilty of being involved in the robbery, she thought. Then she would have to pay all of that back. That was the least of her problems, since she hadn't been involved. But could she prove it?

"I understand," she said, her voice breaking. She'd already lost so much, and yet her credibility and now her job hung in the balance? Not to mention her life.

"Also, I'd appreciate it if you shred those copies I gave you," he said, dropping his voice. "I'd just as soon no one knew about that."

"Of course. I didn't find anything anyway. But thank you for trying to help me." She disconnected and fought the sudden rush of tears. She'd almost lost her life and now she'd lost her independence. She would never feel safe again if the man wasn't caught. What if the federal agents felt they had enough evidence to charge her as an accomplice to the robbery and subsequent murders?

Fighting her growing fear, she finished packing. How was she going to get through the holidays? The FBI suspected her, Davy thought she was still in danger and, if that wasn't enough, how could she spend so much time with the man she'd almost married ten years ago and not fall in love with him all over again?

As if on cue, Davy came through the door smelling of the wintry outdoors. There were snowflakes in his hair and his dark eyelashes. He was flushed, his blue eyes sparkling. He stole her breath—just as he'd stolen her heart all those years ago. It wasn't as if she'd ever gotten it back.

Chapter 17

Back at the office, while Carla unpacked upstairs, Davy called the delivery company with a fictional story about wanting to give their usual driver a Christmas gift. He asked for the names of the drivers who covered her neighborhood, and the woman said she'd have to get back to him.

As he hung up, James came in and he filled him in. His brother fell silent for a moment. "Are you that sure Carla is still in danger?" he asked.

Davy turned to look at his brother. He'd heard something in his tone, making the question more loaded than it might have sounded to someone else. "What are you asking?"

James raised his hands in surrender. "Has there been another threat made against her?" Obviously aware of the answer, he quickly continued. "So the killer could be miles from here by now."

"Or only as far as Butte," Davy snapped.

"I'm just asking about your endgame because I care about you. It's great that you want to protect her, but for how long can you do this?"

"If you're saying that I'm using this situation to be with her…" He saw that it was exactly what his brother was saying. He shook his head, feeling his anger flare inside him. "Why would I do that? Carla made her feelings clear ten years ago. Nothing has changed."

"Exactly," James said. "That's why we're worried about you."

"*We're?* So you've *all* been discussing my life?" he demanded as he raked a hand through his hair and angrily began to pace the room.

"Davy, we love you. You're like a brother to us." James's attempt to lighten the mood fell flat. "Come on, we just don't want to see you get hurt again. We never want to see you that brokenhearted. We're concerned that being thrown together like this… You aren't falling for her again, are you?"

Davy stopped pacing and laughed as he turned to face his brother. "There's no need to fall for her again. I've never stopped loving her," he said and left the office before his brother could ask how Carla felt about him.

Christmas Eve was busier than usual. Jud knew that the time he'd spent driving out to Carla Richmond's house and screwing around had been part of it. Mostly it had been all the packages that just had to get delivered before Christmas morning—which meant he had to work until his truck was empty.

He hated the holidays. Did people really need all this stuff? His mother would have said he was jealous. He

didn't even want to think about his Christmas mornings
as a boy. A sad-looking store-bought tree with several
branches missing because his mom had gotten a deal on
it. Under the tree was always worse.

The year he was eight, she'd gotten him a can of black
olives. When he'd cried, she'd said, "But I thought you
liked them."

It was dark by the time he returned his truck, left behind his hooded coat with the company's insignia on it,
pulled on his ragged jean jacket and walked to where he'd
parked his pickup earlier that morning. His entire body
hurt, from the soles of his feet to the top of his head and
all the way down his back.

All he could think about was a beer and Jesse. If he
was lucky, she'd be in a good mood after he told her that
he'd scoped out Carla's house and then she'd make him
feel better. He realized that he hadn't bought her a present and tomorrow was Christmas. He'd been afraid to use
the money. Not that he would have known what to get her
anyway. She wasn't like the other women he'd known.
She didn't care that much about clothes or jewelry.

When he thought about it, he wasn't sure what she
cared about other than money. Well, he'd gotten her a
ton of cash, hadn't he? Maybe he'd go pick up a bag from
the hiding place in the cave and dump it in the middle
of the living room and they could roll around in it. Jud
smiled at that idea. Jesse had been in such a dark mood
the past few days he was almost afraid of what he would
find when he got home.

He was a few feet from his pickup when one of the
dark shadows moved. He'd been so lost in thought that
he didn't have time to react before the man he knew only
as Wes had him in a beefy-armed headlock.

"What the—"

Wes tightened his hold, cutting off the rest of Jud's words. "Fletch was arrested after he tried to spend one of those twenties you gave us."

Jud closed his eyes. Wasn't this what he'd feared? Jud tried to talk, but couldn't get more than a strangled groan out, and finally Wes loosened his hold. "I don't know what you're talking about," he croaked out.

"Don't lie. I know you pulled the bank job. So where's the money?"

Carla had told herself that she wasn't in the mood for a holiday party. So it surprised her when she slipped into one of her two fancy dresses. She looked in the mirror and felt a rush of excitement. She smoothed the rich silky emerald green fabric down over her hips and felt her mood lighten for the first time in days. She wanted to enjoy this night, to forget about everything but Christmas and…and Davy.

"Carla?" The sound of Davy's voice outside her bedroom door made her swallow and take a final look at herself in the mirror. She'd put her hair up for the party and wore the pearl earrings Davy had bought her for Christmas all those years ago. She hadn't let herself wear them before now because of the painful memories of their breakup.

"Coming!" she called. Pushing back an errant curl, she took a deep breath and had to smile. She was nervous, she realized, because this felt like a date. She quickly reminded herself that Davy was only trying to protect her. He couldn't very well leave her here in the office apartment while he went to his family Christmas Eve celebration.

She warned herself not to make too much of this. It was like any other night. She was only playing dress-up for the occasion.

But then she opened the door and saw Davy. He was dressed in a Western suit, his thick dark hair brushed back to where it curled at his neck. He was wearing his good boots and he held his white Stetson between the fingers of his left hand.

What struck her was that he looked as nervous as she felt. He'd taken her in, his eyes widening in what could only be approval. He let out a low whistle and she felt her cheeks warm.

"Wow," he said, his eyes glowing. "You're *beautiful*."

She felt a little embarrassed. "Is the dress too much?"

Davy chuckled. "Not too much at all."

"I guess I should have asked if this was a casual or formal dinner."

His gaze met hers. "It's perfect. You look…perfect."

She swallowed. If this wasn't a date, she didn't know what was.

Davy had been at a loss for words when Carla stepped out of the bedroom. He was struck by how gorgeous she was. The green dress accentuated her curves, diving at the neck to the swell of her breasts, tucking into her slim waist and skimming down over her hips to fall to midcalf. She'd piled her wild, curly mane of hair up, baring her throat, making him remember the feel of it on his lips. Several locks brushed her high cheekbones, making her blue eyes look wide and liquid.

If he hadn't been enchanted by this woman for years, he would have fallen all over again. He felt that old ache more acutely than ever. James was right—he was in dangerous territory.

"Ready? It's snowing," he said as he helped her with her coat. The faint, sweet scent of her familiar perfume whirled around him for a moment. He took a step back, finally admitting how hard this was. It was hell being this close to her and not being able to take her in his arms and make love to her. He took another step back.

When she turned, she seemed to see the battle going on inside him as if it were etched on his face. "Davy, I—"

He shook his head, stopping whatever she was about to say. "I already loaded the presents in the truck, if that's what you're worried about."

She studied him for a moment, then shook her head. "I guess we should go then."

He readily agreed. The upstairs apartment felt as if it had shrunk and was suddenly too close, too intimate. He was too aware of how bare she was beneath the coat, let alone the dress. He'd once known that body. It had matured in the years since, making it even more lush, more titillating. One more minute in this space with her looking at him like that...

Pushing those thoughts away, he headed down the stairs to his pickup, Carla following. Snow whirled around them, and he remembered another winter night and a stolen kiss. He almost reached for her, his desire to kiss those lips again so strong that he felt powerless over it.

Instead, he opened her door and she climbed inside. Closing the door, he stood for a moment breathing in the cold night air, comforted by the feel of the icy flakes melting on his face. Then, feeling as if he'd been kicked in the gut, he walked around the pickup and climbed behind the wheel.

All he had to do was get through this night without acting on his feelings. *Good luck with that*, he thought as he drove toward Worthington Ranch.

Jud told himself that Wes wasn't going to kill him—not if he thought he had the robbery money. He'd want to know where it was first.

"I don't know what you're talking about," he told the man, once Wes let up the pressure enough on his throat that he could speak clearly. He'd feared that he'd given the men marked money. Now those fears were realized.

What gave him hope was that the men hadn't told their boss where they'd gotten the money. Otherwise, Leon would be here instead of his henchman. Leon wouldn't have had him in a choke hold. Instead, Jud would have battery cables hooked up to parts of his body that would have made him regret being born.

"Where did you really get the money you said your grandmother gave you?" Wes demanded.

"I didn't say she gave it to me. I pawned some of her knickknacks and jewelry hoping she wouldn't miss them," Jud said with enough anger he hoped it would be convincing for Wes.

"What pawnshop?"

Jud told him it had been one in Missoula, where he let Wes believe his grandmother lived. Had she been alive. "Then I bought a few groceries, paid for gas, went home and gave you what I had left. So whoever pulled the heist could have already shopped at one of those places."

Wes eyed him suspiciously. "That's quite a story."

"Would I still be delivering packages if I had that kind

of money?" Jud could see that the man wasn't so sure now. He was glad that Jesse had reminded him to use as many old bills as he could find in the bags. So Wes wouldn't have gotten all marked bills, which would help sell his story.

"If you're lying…" Wes said and let him go. "I'll be back for another installment."

Jud groaned. "I'll have to visit my grandmother again because I don't have it." He could feel Wes studying him. "It's Christmas. Can't you give me until after the holidays? My grandmother's in poor health. Once she crosses over, I'll get everything and can settle my bill in full."

"The boss won't wait that long. I'll be back." With that, the man left.

Jud let himself breathe for a few minutes after Wes drove away. He'd just dodged a bullet. But it didn't leave him much time. They couldn't chance giving Fletch or Wes any more marked money from the robbery. He had to talk to Jesse.

"We need to leave town," he told her when she came home from work. He related his encounter with Wes. "We have all this money. Enough time has gone by. Let's get out of here before another bill turns up from the robbery or Leon comes himself to collect."

"Not until you finish things," she said without looking at him.

"Jesse—"

She spun on him. "If you can't do it, I will. I warned her not to talk and she talked. I can't let that stand."

"Technically, she didn't even know it was you warning her."

"Are you serious right now?" Jesse demanded. "Tell me you aren't taking up for her."

He raised both hands. "I'm not. We're free and rich. Why take a chance getting caught because some dumb fool didn't do what you said?"

"It's about betrayal, standing up for yourself, not letting people disrespect you."

"But no one even knows that she disrespected you."

"I know," Jesse said, giving him a look that seemed to nail him to the floor. "I know and that's all that matters." With that, she turned and stormed into the bedroom.

Jud flinched as she slammed the door. His instincts told him to leave, to go get the money and keep going. Why did he always get involved with domineering women? Before he could move, she came out of the bedroom dressed in all black. He watched her walk into the kitchen and come back out with a butcher's knife.

"Jesse?" His voice cracked.

She stopped to hold the knife up. The blade caught the light. "I'm going to take care of this myself. Be ready to leave when I get back." With that she headed for the door, but stopped with her hand on the knob. "And, Jud, don't even think about leaving me behind. I moved the money." With that, she left.

That magical moment standing outside in the falling snow was lost. All Carla had, along with the ache in her heart, was the memory of what she'd seen in Davy's expression. He'd remembered their kiss that Christmas together—just as she had. The cold, the snow falling around them. Davy had pulled her close for their winter kiss. Wasn't that when they'd both known that they were truly in love—the forever kind?

She closed her eyes now. Carla knew she wasn't wrong. He'd come close to kissing her. Her heart had started to pound, and she'd felt such a yearning… She hadn't realized how badly she'd wanted that kiss until it hadn't happened.

The drive to Worthington Ranch didn't take long. Neither of them spoke. What was there to say? Earlier she had almost brought up the subject of *them*, but Davy had stopped her. Because there was no them. She'd made her choice all those years ago. And he'd made his.

If I'd had my way, we would be married right now.

She'd heard the hurt and pain in his voice. If he'd had his way. She'd tried to imagine what their life would have been like with him on the road all the time, following the rodeo circuit. It wasn't what she'd wanted. It wasn't her idea of marriage and happy-ever-after.

And this is? the little voice at the back of her mind demanded. She hadn't met anyone else she wanted to spend the rest of her life with. Because she'd never gotten over Davy, she admitted to herself now. Being with him and yet not being with him…

She glanced over at him. He looked so handsome in his Western dress suit. She wanted to reach out and touch his arm and tell him—

"We're here," he said, and she looked up to see that he was pulling in front of the Worthington Ranch lodge.

She moved the money? Jud stared after Jesse for several moments, too stunned to move. He didn't have to guess where she was going—or what she planned to do. She was going to get them both arrested. He had to stop her, make her see that she wasn't being rational. How had this become about her and Carla Richmond?

He charged out into the darkness and falling snow in time to see her speeding away. He told himself that she'd come to her senses before she did anything, but he wasn't sure he believed that. He didn't know what to do. Maybe she was lying about moving the money, but somehow he didn't believe that either. Maybe he could find where she hid the money, take it and run. Not unless he wanted that crazed woman with the knife to come after him. Go try to stop her?

With a groan, he realized that he'd set all of this in motion the night he'd gotten involved in that poker game. Once he was in so deep, he'd thought for sure that he could dig his way out with just one more game—double or nothing. He hadn't realized who he was playing against. What had started as a friendly poker game had gotten ugly fast. If Leon hadn't offered to bail him out…

Jud shook his head, trying to clear his thoughts. He couldn't go back and change any of that. That's why he had to end this.

He grabbed his coat. Jesse would go to Carla's house and then the Colt Brothers Investigation office. She didn't know that she wouldn't find Carla at either of those places. Jud wouldn't have either if he hadn't seen Bella Worthington Colt in the grocery store parking lot. He'd overheard the conversation she'd been having with another woman as she'd unloaded her shopping cart into the back of her SUV.

All of the family were coming to her house tonight for Christmas Eve.

Jud started his pickup, his mind clearer than it had been in days. He thought about the day he'd walked into the bank to get a loan. Now he knew that it always had to end this way.

Chapter 18

Carla had been quiet on the drive out to the Worthington Ranch. Davy was glad that she didn't feel the need for small talk. He wasn't sure he could have handled that. But he hated the awkward silence that had filled the cab of the pickup the entire drive. He didn't like leaving things this way between them. What had made him think he could spend this much time together and not get involved again? Being around her and not being able to touch her was pure hell.

He'd come so close to kissing her. He blamed the falling snow and cold for the memory. She'd called it their winter kiss. Like he could ever forget it. Or her.

She had no idea how many times after he'd first left her that he'd thought about quitting the rodeo circuit, coming back to Lonesome and proposing. He'd wanted her that badly. He still did.

It wasn't like he couldn't find a job. He'd recently been offered a position promoting rodeo statewide. Except he wasn't ready to quit the circuit. It was in his blood. Just another year or two, he kept telling himself. But then what? He had some ideas, one in particular he'd been thinking about more since coming home and seeing Carla.

What was a couple more years rodeoing? Like Carla would still be single and waiting for him? He was surprised that some smart man hadn't already snatched her up.

As he pulled in front of the Worthington Ranch lodge, he was relieved that the drive was over. He'd had too much time to think about the almost kiss and his future. *Love shouldn't hurt. It shouldn't demand giving up your dreams*, he told himself as he got out and went around to open Carla's door.

He told himself that they'd chosen their completely different paths years ago. There was no going back, even as he felt his heart ache at the sight of her. Look what his stubborn determination had gotten him, he thought as he saw her avoid his gaze as they headed inside. She couldn't even stand to look at him.

The moment they'd hung up their coats and walked into the main room, James pulled him aside. "Have you heard?" Clearly, he hadn't. "It was just on the news. A man was arrested at the local convenience store trying to buy beer with a twenty-dollar bill from the bank robbery."

Davy couldn't help but get his hopes up. This might be it. The killer might already be behind bars. Then he and Carla would go their separate ways. Isn't that what they both wanted? "What's his name?"

"Fletch. He's a caretaker for that big ranch outside of town that was bought up by that corporation," James said.

Fletch? His disappointment must have shown. "So do they think he had something to do with the robbery?"

James shook his head. "Apparently not. He had an airtight alibi for the day of the robbery, and he's already been released. But the bills are surfacing, Davy. You might be right about the man still being in Lonesome."

Davy groaned as he looked across the room where Carla was visiting with Bella. As James said, if the bills were circulating locally, there was a good chance that the robber hadn't left town. Hadn't his gut told him that Carla was still in danger?

As if sensing him looking at her, she glanced in his direction. She looked so pretty, her cheeks a little flushed from coming in out of the cold into the warm ranch house.

"Please don't say anything tonight about this to Carla," he said.

"She's going to hear about it," James said. "Might be better if it came from you. If the bills are turning up..." James sighed. "I don't know about you, but I could use a drink."

Forty-five minutes and several drinks later, Bella announced that everyone should start heading into the dining room. Davy knew James was right. It would probably be better coming from him. But what he would give if they could just have this one night, he thought as he made a beeline for Carla.

Everyone began to move toward the entrance to the dining room. Bella had invited family and friends, so the huge table inside would be full. Carla had tried to lose herself in the party atmosphere. Everyone was dressed up, tiny Christmas lights twinkled from the log rafters and holiday music formed a background for the laughter and chatter.

She'd wanted to enjoy herself tonight. To let her hair down, so to speak. She needed this. But earlier she'd seen James pull Davy aside. From their expressions it wasn't good news. She'd wanted to go to him and find out what had happened, but Bella had approached her. By the time that conversation ended, Davy had disappeared.

That's why she was startled when he suddenly reappeared beside her. Ahead of her, the crowd was milling toward the dining room. He touched her arm and indicated that he wanted to talk to her. She felt her heart drop. Hadn't they said enough earlier? Or maybe he wanted to tell her what he and James had been discussing. Either way, she feared it was bad news.

Not tonight, she wanted to say. Not tonight in this beautiful home on Christmas Eve. But she also knew that whatever it was, she needed to hear it. Could she even pretend for one night that there wasn't a killer after her?

She turned toward him as the others disappeared into the dining room. "I saw you talking to James. I know something's happened."

"That's not what I wanted to talk about."

"Davy, we can't keep going over the same old grou—"

He touched his finger to her lips to silence her and pointed upward. She frowned since she'd been bracing herself for bad news. When she looked up, she blinked at the sight of mistletoe hanging from one of the log rafters above them.

Her gaze dropped to his. She looked into his amazing blue eyes, fringed with dark lashes. The man was drop-dead gorgeous. But it was that kindness in those eyes, that caring, that love. She felt her heart lean in. What would one kiss hurt?

"Carla, it's Christmas. Could we just enjoy this time together?" he asked as he brushed a lock of her hair back from her eyes. "Can we put our differences aside? We used to be good friends before we became…" He seemed to hesitate. Lovers? "More," he finished. "Can't we just enjoy the holidays together like old friends?" His gaze met hers and practically burned her with its intensity.

Carla wanted that desperately—no matter how dangerous. Davy Colt was a good, loving man. He'd dropped everything to protect her. One night without the past pushing its way between them sounded like heaven. She nodded and he pulled her to him.

The kiss was sweet and soft—at first. But then it changed as he drew her closer, arousing emotions so strong that she found her arms around his neck. He deepened the kiss and she surrendered so willingly that it shocked her. But she couldn't stop herself. She met his tongue with her own, the taste of bourbon and champagne like an accelerant fanning the flames.

They could never be just friends again. They would always be lovers. The thought breezed past as he whispered her name against her lips like an oath. Or a curse. She felt her nipples harden beneath her sheer dress. Her heart took off at a gallop as she pressed the soft swell of her breasts to his rock-hard, solid chest and heard him moan. Her heart drummed in answer.

Wrapped in each other's arms, locked in the passionate kiss, neither of them heard anyone approach.

"Excuse me," Willie said, clearing his throat. "I told Bella it was probably the mistletoe. Guess I was right."

Davy and Carla sprung apart like teenagers caught on

the sofa. But when they looked at each other, the fire still burning inside her, she began to laugh. Davy joined in.

Willie chuckled, shaking his head as he turned to go back to the dining room. "Christmas Eve dinner is being served, in case either of you are interested." He mumbled something under his breath, which only made them laugh harder.

As Willie disappeared, Davy turned toward her. "I guess we should…" He waved a hand toward the dining room.

"Yes, I suppose we should." Carla knew her face was flushed, her lipstick smeared. "I should probably stop in the ladies' room first." She bit her lower lip, the kiss still raging through her veins. But it had felt so good to laugh. To laugh together, like they used to before she'd broken both of their hearts. "You go ahead. Tell them I'll be right in and they shouldn't wait."

He smiled at her. "I'm not sorry."

She knew he meant the kiss and how they'd gotten carried away. She shook her head. "Me neither." She had to clear her voice. "I'll hurry." With that she escaped to the restroom.

Once the door closed behind her, she stepped in front of the mirror. Her cheeks were flushed, her eyes bright. She felt as if she were floating. It was as if all they'd needed was a little Christmas magic like in the movies. A sprinkle of pixie dust and they found their way back together.

The thought made her shake her head. It wasn't pixie dust, but she had to believe that all of this had happened for a reason. The bank robbery right before the holidays had thrown them together. *Maybe it was meant to be*, she told herself, even as that tiny rational killjoy Carla on her shoulder argued that this would only lead to heartbreak. She mentally swatted the pesky voice of reason away. There was no fighting fate, right?

Yet she saw the truth in the mirror as the kiss's effect began to lessen. Nothing had really changed between her and Davy. She would never ask him to choose between rodeo and her again. Had he stayed in Lonesome for her, he would have ended up resenting her. The thought broke her heart.

She'd thought she could forget for one night about what was going on in her life. But that was impossible. Being here with Davy didn't help. He was a constant reminder of how temporary and off-kilter everything was right now—and how it could get so much worse.

As much as she appreciated him being with her, she didn't want him involved. What if the killer did come after her and Davy tried to stop him? She couldn't bear the thought that she might get the man she loved killed when he should be miles from here.

Fate might have thrown them together, but it was temporary. How had she forgotten that in his arms? As she headed for the dining room, she knew in her head and her heart that what fate had given them was a few precious days together—and nothing more.

Davy slipped into the dining room. "Sorry to keep you all waiting. Carla's right behind me. Just had to make a stop." He picked up his wineglass and took a drink. His body vibrated from the kiss, from the rush of desire still thrumming in his veins. Hadn't he known that if he kissed her, all those old feelings would be there? Their chemistry had always been so strong. They'd started as friends long before they'd become lovers years ago.

That foundation was still there. He'd take a bullet for this woman.

"Is there news on the robbery?" Bella asked, drawing him back.

"Apparently one of the marked bills has turned up," he said and put down his empty wineglass.

"That's good, right?" Lori asked. "So they have the man."

James shook his head. "He had an airtight alibi and the police let him go. It appears the bills are circulating in town though. Which could mean the man is a local. Also that he might still be around." Davy felt everyone look to him.

"Why would he still be here?" Bella asked, frowning.

"That we don't know," Davy said and was glad when his wineglass was refilled. He picked it up and turned it in his hands. "He might not be finished with Carla."

Bella let out a cry. "That's horrible. Why?"

Davy shook his head. "We're trying to find that out."

"How is she doing?" Lori asked. Davy was sure she'd quizzed James but she was just being polite by asking.

"She's strong. This is hard for her. She's always been so independent and self-reliant. She's anxious to get back her old life."

"I'm sure you are too," Lori said. "Don't you have a ride coming up right after Christmas?"

They all turned as Carla came into the room. When Davy saw her expression, he knew that she'd heard the last part and was just as keen as everyone else to hear his reply.

"There are other rides," he said and got up to pull out Carla's chair.

The moment he was seated again, she said, "He isn't

going to miss any rides." Carla was smiling as she looked over at him, but he caught the unshed tears glistening in her eyes. "I appreciate how wonderful he's been, but he's a rodeo cowboy. He has to do what he was born to do."

"But what if the killer hasn't been caught by the time he has to leave?" Bella asked, sounding worried.

Davy started to say something, but Carla cut him off. "Neither of us can put our lives on hold until that happens. It might be months, even years or never. Once the investigation is over, I'll be going back to work."

She said it with such ferocity that Davy couldn't help staring at her in surprise before she added, "The bank has put me on administrative leave until then."

He hadn't known. He reached for her hand under the table and squeezed it, but after a moment she pulled it away. He could see her fighting tears. She'd worked so hard to get where she was. This was so wrong. None of this was her fault.

His cell phone rang. He checked the screen, apologizing as he pushed back his chair and stood. "I need to take this. I've been waiting for this call."

Once outside the room, he accepted the call from the delivery company. Earlier, he'd left a message, needing to know which delivery drivers worked in Carla's area. Now he listened as a woman told him. No name that started with *J.*

"Thank you for getting back to me. Merry Christmas." He disconnected. Another dead end. He'd been so sure that there was something strange about the man he'd seen standing on her doorstep with the package. It might have just been a case of a wrong address as the man said.

Davy sighed. He had to question his instincts. He'd also thought for sure that James would find out something suspicious about the nurse, Debra Watney, but he hadn't. Apparently, he'd been wrong about her as well. He'd become so suspicious since the robbery, since there was a killer out there who'd hurt Carla and might still be in town and not finished with her.

But he knew the kiss also had him worked up. The earth had moved for him. But had it for her? If so, then how could she keep denying what the two of them had together? She seemed anxious to get rid of him again.

He felt that old frustration. But he also had to admit that there was some residual anger in him because she hadn't given them a chance ten years ago. He regretted the years they'd spent apart. He looked over at her. Had he really thought anything had changed? He told himself that he couldn't do this again.

She wanted him to leave right after Christmas? Wouldn't that be the smart thing to do? But as he thought it, he knew it was already too late to keep his heart from getting broken all over again.

Davy took his seat again and looked into her eyes. He realized that he wasn't going to let her push him away. Not this time. He reached over and took her hand as he leaned close. "You're not getting rid of me that easily. Not this time."

His words sent a shiver through her. He squeezed her hand. Their gazes locked, stealing her breath. The kiss earlier proved how dangerous it was for them to be together any longer. Why postpone the inevitable? He needed to go back to the rodeo circuit, and she needed to get her job back.

But at the back of her mind, she kept hearing that voice of reason. What if the robber wasn't caught? What if she couldn't go back to her job? For years she'd lost herself in her pursuit of a career. Even with the detour back to Lonesome when her mother got sick and later died, she'd managed to stay in a job using her degree.

Her mother used to joke that her daughter would thrive no matter where she was planted. Often Carla felt like a stubborn weed that fought its way to the sun no matter what she had to overcome. She wasn't one to give up easily.

Yet she'd given up on Davy.

She looked into his eyes and knew that she couldn't again. As painful as it would be when they finally parted again, she wanted this time together. She concentrated on the food as dinner was served by chef Roberto. She'd heard Bella saying what an amazing cook he was. Everything was delicious.

For the rest of the meal, the conversation stayed clear of the robbery. Bella wanted to know if Carla would like to come out and ride horses with her. Carla said she would love that. She hadn't ridden for years but hoped it was like riding a bike.

"You used to love riding," Davy said. "It was something we had in common."

"With any of the Colt brothers you have to love horses," Bella said with a laugh. "Fortunately, I do."

The conversation moved on to babies, with Lori pregnant with a daughter and Bella and Tommy trying to get pregnant. Carla again felt Davy's gaze on her, but she didn't dare look in his direction. Was he thinking that if they'd gotten married right out of high school, or even after she'd finished college, they could have had children of their own now?

The thought made her sad and stirred that desire in

her for a family of her own. But there was only one man she'd wanted to have kids with. Davy Colt. Except with Davy on the rodeo circuit, she would have been a single mother—like her own mother.

That wasn't what she had wanted. That hadn't been part of her dream. But the passion of their kiss still thrumming through her veins demanded to know why she was still hanging on to that old dream, since she'd never been able to fit Davy Colt into it.

The night was black. Low clouds pressed down on the road between the banks of dense pines that lined the road. The pickup's headlights punched a shallow hole in the darkness ahead. Inside the truck cab, Davy felt too close, and yet Carla could feel an ocean between them.

"I know you're angry with me," she said at last, need-ing to break the tense silence. She didn't know what to blame. The kiss? Or what she'd said at dinner?

He glanced over at her, looking surprised. "Is that what I am? Angry?"

"You tell me." She saw his jaw tighten along with his hands on the wheel, but he didn't speak. "I wish we could just be friends again, but I can't see how we can. That kiss proves it, doesn't it?"

"It was just—" he started, then shook his head no. "Like hell it was," he amended quickly, looking over at her. "What that kiss proves is that we're still in love, Carla. Have been for years. When are we going to quit denying it?"

"I'm not denying it. We just want different things."

"Oh, right, that's why we broke up."

"Would you please stop doing that," she snapped.

"And stop pretending that you don't know why I broke up with you."

Davy sighed. "I thought we wanted the same things— marriage, a house, kids, a life together. I thought we were in love."

"We were." Her voice broke. She didn't want to argue, but she couldn't let the past lie between them like a dead body they were both trying to ignore. "What kind of life would that have been with you on the road all the time?"

"I wouldn't have been on the road all the time. Other people make it work—truck drivers, pilots, commercial fishermen. But that wasn't what you wanted, was it?"

"No," she admitted and felt tears sting her eyes. "Breaking up with you was the hardest thing I've ever done. It broke…" Her voice choked again as well and she had to look away. "It broke my heart to walk away from you." She felt him look over at her and swallowed back the tears that threatened to fall.

"You didn't give us a chance," he said quietly, the pain clear in his words.

"You don't know how badly I wanted to." She looked over at him as she was enveloped in the memory of the kiss, of his arms wrapped about her, their bodies molded together in the heat of passion. The worst part was that she still did want to.

The moment their eyes locked she knew she could no longer fight her feelings for him. "Davy." The word came out a plea. She wanted to throw herself into his arms and tell him that she'd never stopped loving him and plead for them to find a way to be together. She opened her mouth, but what came out was a scream as she saw headlights headed right for them.

Chapter 19

At Carla's scream, Davy's gaze returned to the road, only to find himself blinded by the set of headlights bearing down on them. "Hang on!" he cried and jerked the wheel hard to the right. The cab interior filled with light. He braced himself for impact as he caught a flash of the vehicle as it whizzed past his driver's-side window.

To his amazement, the vehicle barely missed the rear of the pickup as he and Carla crashed into the snow-filled ditch. The front tires dropped down into the wind-crusted depths. Snow cascaded over the hood to cover the windshield as the pickup buried itself before coming to a stop.

"Carla," Davy said, glancing over at her. "Are you all right?" Her face had lost all color and she was hanging on tightly if her white knuckles were any indication.

"I thought for sure that car was going to hit us," she said haltingly.

"That was way too close." He glanced over his shoulder and saw a pair of taillights disappearing down the road. "The driver didn't even stop. Must be drunk or…"

She looked over at him then. "It wasn't a drunk driver. It was him, wasn't it?"

Davy wanted to argue but couldn't. The car had been headed unerringly at them. If he hadn't jerked the wheel and put them in the ditch, the vehicle would have hit them head-on. It would have been a suicidal mission—if it was J. He'd caught a glimpse of the pickup as it had sped past. While he hadn't seen the driver, his impression in that split second was that there'd been a man behind the wheel. A man wearing a baseball cap.

As Carla began to cry, he unsnapped his seat belt, then reached over and did the same with hers before pulling her into his arms. She was trembling and fighting tears. His heart was still pounding. He told himself that whoever had run them off the road wouldn't be back to finish them off, but he was glad that his .22 pistol was under the seat. If anyone came down the road from that direction, he would be ready.

"This is killing me," Carla said through sobs against his shoulder.

"I know. I'm so sorry." He knew being a suspect in the bank robbery was added to her pain. That and not being able to get back to her job, her life. She'd always been so independent. She'd always been so strong. He knew how hard this was on her.

"It's going to be all right," he said as he ran his hand over her hair and held her close. "I'm here for you."

At those words she pulled back, her eyes brimming with tears as she shook her head. He could well imagine what she wanted to say. The last thing she wanted was to keep him from going back to his life, the life he'd chosen over her.

"Carla," he said, his heart breaking for her. "I'm sorry this is so hard on you, but I'm not letting you out of my sight until this monster is caught. I'll put the past aside if you can quit worrying about the future. Maybe we could find some common ground because—let's face it—we still feel the same, don't we?"

She nodded, tears filling her eyes. "Yes."

He smiled then and touched her face as he pulled her close. "We're going to get through this." She nodded against his chest, then sat up to wipe her tears. He saw her gather herself, her strength and determination taking over again, before he reached for his phone to call for a tow truck.

Jud looked out the window, angry that Jesse had taken his truck. "What did you do?" he demanded, worry filling him with dread as she walked in the door. He could tell by her flushed face and the brittle brightness in her eyes that she'd done something. He didn't dare guess what.

Jesse shook her head angrily as she swept past him. She took off her coat, kicking off her boots on her way and leaving a trail of snow behind her. "Someone had to do something, and since you don't have the—"

"What did you do?"

She pulled the knife from her coat pocket and tossed it onto the table beside the couch. His gaze shot to it, his heart hammering as he looked to see if there was blood on it. There didn't appear to be.

When Jesse spoke, she spit the words at him. "I tried to kill her." She wiped the spittle at the corner of her mouth. "I drove right at them, but unfortunately, they swerved.

I left them in the ditch. I should have gone back and finished them," she said, shaking her head. "But I wasn't sure he wouldn't be armed."

Jud groaned. "Don't you realize what you've done? The word on the street was that the feds were looking for me in Washington State. Some of the heat was off and now…" He swore. "What was the point of that?"

"It made me feel better." She glared at him, daring him to say that wasn't good enough.

"None of this makes any sense. You do realize that, don't you?" He shook his head. "We should be miles from here. Staying around to make you feel better…" He didn't finish as her eyes narrowed.

"I told you. I'm not leaving until she's dead."

"Then be smart. There is no way to get to her right now. Once she moves back home—"

Jesse's laugh cut him off. "You really want to wait that long? Because I don't. Anyway, how do you know the cowboy won't move in with her and you'll have another excuse not to finish this?" She shook her head. "If you ever want to see that money again, you'd better do something and soon."

When James heard what had happened, he insisted Carla call Agent Grover.

She wasn't surprised when the agent again didn't believe her.

"Probably just someone who had too much to drink on Christmas Eve," the agent said on the phone call. "We have reason to believe that your J might be in Washington State."

The "your J" grated, but she didn't let the agent get to her. When she asked what made him think J was in Washington State, he said he couldn't say but that he would be returning to Lonesome soon for a talk with her, so she'd better have a lawyer.

She hung up more frustrated than ever and repeated what the agent had told her.

"There were several arrested for drunk driving," Willie told them. "It's possible that one of them was responsible for running you off the road."

"The good news is that if they have a lead out in Washington State, then last night was only an accident," James said.

Carla knew that, like her, Davy wanted to believe that's all it had been. She'd made a few calls to attorneys, leaving her number since most were out of the office until the end of the year. But she felt better since making the contact. Hopefully, Agent Grover would find J out in Washington and that would be the end of it.

By Christmas morning, both she and Davy were in better spirits. Davy had picked up a small decorated tree for the upstairs apartment and she woke to Christmas music. They exchanged presents.

"It's just a little something that I saw that reminded me of you," he said when he handed her the tiny wrapped package he'd taken from under the tree.

For a moment, her heart had begun to drum as she remembered another small box he'd given her all those years ago—one with a diamond engagement ring inside.

She quickly unwrapped the box and opened it with trembling fingers, telling herself Davy would never make that mistake again.

"Do you like it?" he asked, sounding worried.

"It's beautiful," she said with relief as she picked up

the silver bracelet from its nest in the box. "I love it." It was delicate, with one tiny star dangling from it.

"For making wishes," he said, seeming a little embarrassed.

She looked up at him, feeling her eyes sting, and asked him to help her with the clasp. Then she handed Davy his present. She'd gotten him a new leather belt for the many buckles he'd won over the years.

He immediately put it on. It fit perfectly, just as she knew it would. "I'll wear it tonight at James and Lori's. You haven't forgotten that we're invited for dinner, right?"

They'd both gone to the small kitchen after that to make a Christmas breakfast. Davy had thought of everything. He seemed determined to make her forget her problems—at least for the holidays. It was almost working, Carla thought.

After their near collision, they'd both gone out of their way to avoid any mention of the past or the future. They both had seemed to adopt a "one day at a time" philosophy.

For Carla, it was strange. She'd seldom taken time off from work, accumulating weeks of vacation time. She realized that it was kind of nice not to have to wake to an alarm clock, not to have to go to work.

The feds were apparently convinced that J had left town with the bank money and gone to Washington State. The focus of their investigation had moved—at least temporarily. Maybe that *had* been a drunk driver last night.

What bothered her was that Agent Grover still believed that it had been an inside job—with her helping the robbers. She'd heard that he was looking at several former employees at the bank—one who now worked at the hospital.

She'd quit fighting Davy about returning to her home—at least for the time being. Instead, she told herself that these days together were a dream, one she didn't ever want to wake up from. For most of her life, she'd spent it looking to the future, planning what it would be like.

When it hadn't turned out anything like she'd planned, she'd been devastated. But now she could see just how different she and Davy were. He lived more day by day, and she was beginning to see the value in that. It was something she'd never done before—not looking to the future, but just enjoying one day at a time.

She'd also come to realize that she'd been living around her job. Without it, she felt adrift. Now with all this time on her hands, she saw that even on her days off work she'd had a list of things to do and would check them off. She'd kept so busy she'd never questioned if she was truly happy.

Being here with Davy without lists and a schedule was truly her first holiday. She tried hard not to remind herself that it had to end. Instead, she couldn't wait to open her door and see Davy every morning. Also, there was usually coffee.

This morning was no different. They finished breakfast. He handed her a cup of coffee before clearing away their dishes. "Remember what we used to do over the holidays?"

She remembered building snowmen, hanging on to the bumpers of cars and sliding down the streets, climbing snow-laden roofs and jumping off into deep drifts. She also remembered making love in his pickup one very cold, starry night.

"You're going to have to be more specific," she said, curious where he was going with this.

"Sledding," he said and grinned as if he'd known where her mind had gone. "Although the thought of getting you in the back of my pickup..." He laughed and she joined him.

"Neither of us want that," she said. They made eye contact for a little too long before she pulled away. They were falling back into their old, easy relationship. She'd forgotten what good friends they'd been. They could tell each other anything and everything. It was nice to be close again.

They'd avoided any more mistletoe though, being close again but not that close. Not that Carla couldn't feel that combination of chemistry bubbling between them. She knew Davy felt it too. When they'd parted last night to go to their separate bedrooms, Carla had had to bite her tongue to keep from calling him back to her.

But this was nice, them being friends again. She told herself that she'd be a fool to let it go further. While they'd agreed to make the best of this time they had together, she knew he'd suggested it to keep her mind off the robbery and the investigation and the killer.

She just hoped the feds were right and the killer was long gone from Lonesome—and her.

Chapter 20

Jud slept in late since he didn't have to work Christmas Day—and he was in no mood to deal with Jesse after last night. By the time he got up, she had left for the hospital. All he could think about was the money. If he found it, he would be in control of his life again. It was his way out.

He tried to think like Jesse, expanding his search and starting with her car, which was now in his driveway because she'd taken his pickup, saying her car was out of gas. Unfortunately, she was too smart to hide the money in such an obvious place. But at the same time, it would be just like her to hide it in front of his nose.

Back in the house, he tore the place apart. Winded and sweating, he stared at the mess he'd made. No money. What if she'd given it to a friend for safekeeping? He immediately discarded that idea. Jesse didn't have any friends that he knew of, especially any she would trust with money.

No, she'd hidden it. He'd start in the rocks up in the mountain near the cave where he'd initially stashed it and work from there.

But when he opened the door, he was shocked to find Cora Brooks standing out by Jesse's car. "Mrs. Brooks?" he asked as he approached her.

"This is her sister's car," Cora said, pointing at the small sedan. "Her sister Debra's car."

He hadn't known that. Jesse had taken her sister's identity right down to her checking and savings accounts—and her car, apparently. How was that possible? Unless...

"They're identical twins, you know," Cora said with distaste. "But only in looks. I'd always hoped that Debra would turn up." She shook her head. "Realizing what Jesse has done... Debra is dead, isn't she?"

He figured it was the reason Jesse had taken not just her car but her life, including the job as an aide at the hospital. "I wouldn't know anything about that," he said.

The old woman sneered. "Thought I'd have a chat with her." Cora tried to see around him inside the house, which he'd just torn apart.

He blocked her view. "She's not here, and I was just going to work."

She gave him a once-over, as if wondering where he went to work dressed like he was, in old jeans and a T-shirt. He was going to tell her it was none of her business, but that had never stopped Cora.

"I'll tell her you stopped by," he said and started back toward the house, hoping she'd take the hint and leave.

"Don't bother," she said and turned to leave. "I'd rather surprise her. Maybe I'll pay her a visit at the hospital. I heard she's working there." Something about Cora's smile chilled him to the bone. He'd heard that she had a bad habit of finding out things about people and then extorting money from them to keep silent. Hadn't she almost gotten killed last year because she'd tried to blackmail the sheriff's brother? Or maybe that was just a small-town rumor.

He watched her head down the street and flag down the senior citizen bus, which pulled up to stop for her. Once she disappeared inside, he went back in for his winter coat and boots. He should probably warn Jesse about Cora. He pushed the thought away. He had bigger fish to fry. He had to find the money and outsmart Jesse.

Once he was rich, this hick town would never see him again—and, he realized with relief, neither would Jesse.

Davy couldn't remember the last time he'd been sledding. He'd had to borrow a sled from old friends in town before driving up into the mountains where he and Carla used to go. They could have gone to the sledding hills around town, but he wanted to be alone with her. He was still worried, even though the feds seemed convinced she was safe. He felt better when they weren't around a lot of other people. Not that it necessarily felt safer.

It had been his idea for them to put the past behind them and just be friends again for the holidays. He'd had good intentions. He'd wanted to keep Carla's mind off the killer. But he'd also wanted this time with her. If this was all they had, then he'd take it.

He just hadn't realized how hard it would be. They'd grown close again, so close that taking her in his arms and kissing her seemed like the most natural thing. Sometimes the way she looked at him… He felt that old firestorm inside him. He wanted her so badly it hurt.

On the drive into the mountains, they fell into a companionable silence. He saw Carla looking out the window, taking in the snowy winter landscape as if seeing it for the first time. He wondered if she hadn't had her head down working for so long that she'd forgotten to look around her—let alone to have fun. He was glad that he'd suggested sledding.

After he parked the pickup, they made the hike up the open mountainside, with him pulling the sled behind him. The sky overhead was cerulean blue without a cloud anywhere, the sun turning the snow into bejeweled waves. The slope was perfect for sledding—and yet not so steep that they had to worry about avalanche danger. Also, they were entirely alone up here. The fresh snow on the narrow road up hadn't been disturbed.

The cold air came out in puffs as they reached the top and caught their breaths. He looked over at Carla. "Ready?"

"I haven't done this in years."

"Me neither. I think it's like riding a bike though," he joked. "Let's find out. Hop on." He held the sled on a flat spot at the top to make sure it didn't take off until he was ready. Once she was situated, he gave the sled a shove and jumped on at the last minute. Putting his legs on each side of her, he wrapped his arms around Carla's waist and pulled her against him as the sled took off.

Snow blew up in an icy wave as they careened down the mountainside. He heard her squeal and then laugh. He pressed his face against her shoulder, feeling the cold and the exhilaration. They'd both needed this, he thought.

The sled slowed and came to a stop. Carla turned to look at him, all grins. Her cheeks were red from the cold, her eyes bright. Snow crystals clung to her lashes and the locks of hair that had escaped her hat.

Davy felt himself grinning as widely as she was.

"Can we do it again?" she cried.

He laughed. "We can do it as many times as you want to."

They both scrambled off and began the trudge back up the mountain. The next few times were as exhilarating as the first one. But this time, when the sled slowed and finally stopped at the bottom of the mountainside, neither of them moved.

"That was amazing," she said and leaned back into him. "Thank you for this." He nodded, unable to speak around the lump that had formed in his throat. She shifted on the sled to face him. Their gazes locked and he felt a rush of heat course through him. Her hat and coat were covered in snow. He brushed one frozen lock of her hair back from her face.

"Carla." He said her name like a plea, an oath, a prayer.

She kissed him. His lips were cool at first—just like her own. She breathed in the scent of him, the pines, the cold. They'd shared other winter kisses that year they were together. But this one—this one was pure joy.

It felt like that first winter kiss of so long ago. Except this one was so filled with pent-up passion it felt like igniting a rocket. Desire swept through her like the sled had careened down the mountainside. The thrill was there along with the heat as she straddled him, cupping his frosty face in her hands.

She heard him unzip her coat and moments later his hand snaked up under her sweater. His ungloved fingers were warm against her naked skin as they moved upward to cup her breast. She felt her nipple harden to an aching peak even before his fingers slipped inside her bra.

A blaze of heat rushed through her veins to her center, and she felt herself go molten.

"I think we should take this to the pickup," Davy said, pulling back from the kiss. His gaze met hers. "Unless you want to stop now."

She shook her head. She could feel his desire pressing into her through her snow pants. She wanted this, needed this, felt as if she would scream if they stopped now. The voice of reason could be heard warning her in the back of her mind, but her need was stronger. "Pickup."

They rose and began stripping off their outer snowy clothes before they reached the truck. Once inside, Davy started the engine and turned on the heater, but Carla knew they didn't need it. Her body felt on fire, and when he touched her again, she groaned with pleasure.

He was easing off her shirt when he saw the tattoo over her heart. It was small and delicate, but when she felt him start, she knew he recognized it. "Carla?"

She felt shy, peeking at him through her lashes. "I know it's silly, but I wanted something that would remind me of you and our dreams. Don't you remember? You gave me your great-grandfather's old branding iron." It had felt like a promise for the future at the time. "That night, you told me about your plans for Colt Ranch. The brand is your family history, your legacy. Now it's part of my history as well."

He shook his head as he gently ran a calloused finger across the tiny brand over her heart before lifting his eyes to hers. "Oh, Carla." He pulled her to him, wrapping her in his arms. "I love you with all my heart. I always have." He drew back to kiss her, and she felt the chemistry between them rocket through her.

When they were teens, their lovemaking had been a

concoction of jacked-up hormones as they raced to a climax. Now Davy took it slow, as if revisiting all her pleasure points, teasing her nipples into rock-hard points and sucking them until she leaned back with a cry of release. It was as if he could make love to her all afternoon and the rest of the night.

When they finally came together, Carla cried out, heart thundering, body quivering as the pleasure roared through her in waves. He reached over and turned off the engine. Then he held her, the two of them catching their breaths, the silence of the winter day around them. Snowflakes fluttered past the steamed-over windows.

"I wish we could just stay right here forever," she whispered.

"Then we have to get a bigger truck," Davy said, his arm around her. He stretched out one long leg, then the other, and they both laughed. They weren't kids anymore, but it was nice revisiting their youth in the cab of his pickup again. The truck began to cool quickly.

"No regrets?" he whispered, and she felt him turn to look at her.

She met his eyes. "None." She leaned up to kiss him on the lips. "None," she repeated. He smiled then and pulled her closer.

Carla could hear the unspoken questions between them as the pickup chilled and Davy started the engine again and they began to dress. Had it been a mistake? How could they not do this again and again until he left? But would they regret it, if not today, then tomorrow or the days ahead?

"I suppose we better get going," Davy said as he climbed out to retrieve the sled. They were going to James and Lori's new house on what was known as the

Colt Ranch. The original homestead cabin was gone and so was the double-wide trailer the boys had used when they were home. But the land was still there, with plenty of room for each of the brothers to build their own lives on.

Years ago, Carla remembered Davy talking about someday building a house for them on the ranch. His great-grandfather had run a few cattle on the land at one time. His grandfather had kept stock in the corrals.

Davy had always said he would come back to the ranch when he quit the rodeo. He'd talked about making it a working ranch again, either raising cattle or horses. Like rodeo, the place was part of the Colt brothers' legacy. At one time the ranch had been part of her dream as well, the blueprint she'd had for her perfect life. But Davy hadn't fit into her perfect plan so neither had Colt Ranch. Still, like Davy, it had a place in her heart.

Carla thought about that as they drove back toward Lonesome.

Carla had grown quiet on the drive out of the mountains. Davy worried that instead of bringing them closer, their earlier lovemaking would drive them even further apart. That was the last thing he wanted.

He was still blown away by Carla's tattoo of his family brand. The chemistry between them had been undeniable. He still wanted her and knew that he would the rest of his days.

But he wasn't fool enough to think it was enough, he told himself as he turned onto a narrow county road that cut through the snow-filled pines. His pickup's headlights punched a hole in the growing darkness, but only yards up the road. This time of the year it got dark by five o'clock. With the weatherman calling for more snow, the night was pitch-black.

"Are you okay?" Davy asked, glancing over at her. He saw her nod. "I'm still planning to come back, you know. I always thought… I hoped…" Their gazes met and he saw that she knew what he'd hoped because she had the same hope.

"Davy."

He heard her unbuckle her seat belt and start to slide across the bench seat toward him. His foot went to the brake.

The cab of the pickup exploded, filling the air with tiny cubes of glass and the shriek of twisted metal. The impact from the right side of the pickup shoved the vehicle into the pines next to the road. He heard wood splintering. A limb struck the windshield, shattering it, as the pickup came to an abrupt stop.

Chapter 21

"Carla!" Davy cried as his brain fought to understand what had happened. They'd been hit. The passenger-side door was caved in, and Carla lay in his lap. If he'd been going any faster… "Carla!"

She sat up, blinking at him in confusion. He could see her in the light from the dash. "Are you hurt?" With relief he saw her shake her head.

"I don't think so. What happened?" she asked.

"I'm not sure." He glanced back and saw what had hit them. A huge truck sat halfway in the old logging road, the headlights shining out at odd angles. He thought he could hear the engine still running.

With a shock, Davy saw that the passenger-side door of the truck hung open.

"I… I think I'm all right," Carla said, then winced. "But I think I might have—"

He didn't hear the rest of her words as he caught movement beyond what was left of her side window. A man dressed in dark clothes, hood up, was looking at them as if to see if they were…hurt? Still alive? Then suddenly, the man turned and ran down the road behind them.

Before that instant, Davy had assumed the crash had been an accident. Like the other night, this hadn't been an accident.

He swore, then grabbed his door handle and shoved his shoulder against it. But the door, wedged tight against the pine trees, didn't budge. He realized that he wasn't getting out that way and quickly smashed the rest of the windshield and climbed out over the hood. "Stay here," he said back at Carla. Once his boots hit the ground, he took off running after the man.

It had begun to snow, visibility dropping quickly. Not that it would have made a difference. He hadn't gone far when he realized that he'd lost him. The figure had cut off into the pines. Davy could see the man's footprints in the snow, but only in the ambient light of the large rig's headlights. Once he stepped into the dark pines, he couldn't see anything.

He turned back, heart pounding. If only he'd thought to grab his flashlight. And his gun from under the seat. He hadn't been prepared. He told himself he would be next time, because just as he'd feared, this wasn't over.

By the time he reached the pickup, he could hear the sound of sirens. Carla must have made the call. Fortunately, they weren't far from town—just like the last crash. He looked into the pickup and saw her cradling her right ankle. "I think it's broken," she said, pain in her voice. He could tell that she was trying hard not to cry.

"I'm so sorry," he said and reached through her side window for her hand and squeezed it as she met his gaze.

"I was so afraid that you would go after him into the woods. It was him, wasn't it?"

"I think so," he said, hating how close they'd come to the killer—how close they'd come to almost catching him. The sound of sirens grew louder. Flashing lights came about the bend in the road. "It's going to be all right," he said to Carla, but neither of them believed that.

The night became a blur of flashing lights and sirens. Carla swam in and out of pain as she was extricated from Davy's wrecked pickup. She still didn't understand what had happened. The EMTs gave her something for the pain once she was on the stretcher and they'd stabilized her ankle. She closed her eyes, welcoming the easing of the pain as the drugs did their job.

It wasn't until she opened her eyes that her terror returned. In alarm, she saw that they were taking her back to the hospital. "No!" she cried and tried to get up.

"As soon as they get a cast on your leg in the ER, I'll get you out of there," Davy said. "I promise."

She closed her eyes, but couldn't shake off the memory of flying broken glass, the sound of metal screaming and looking back to see that a huge truck had T-boned Davy's pickup. Worse was the memory of Davy going after the man while she called 911 because she couldn't help.

True to his word, he stayed by her side even when his brothers rushed down to the hospital to make sure they were both all right. "How are you feeling?" James asked her.

The pain pills had her a little loopy, but unfortunately,

she could still feel her ankle. "I feel like I've been hit by a truck."

"It all happened too fast," Davy said. "I never saw it coming."

"But you're all right?" Tommy asked when he saw Davy favoring his left side. Carla hadn't realized he'd been hurt in the crash. So like Davy to brush it off.

"My body got slammed into the driver's-side door. The EMTs checked me out. I'm fine." He touched the left side of his head. "My head apparently connected with the side window. Dazed me."

"Which explains why you went after the driver of the truck rather than wait for the law," Willie said.

"Aren't you guys wanted somewhere?" Davy asked his brothers, but he smiled when he said it. She loved how close they all were. She'd always wished that she had siblings.

Tommy and Willie started to leave, calling back, "Feel better, Carla."

James had pulled Davy aside. She couldn't hear all of their conversation, but enough of it to know that the driver of the truck that had T-boned Davy's pickup hadn't been found yet.

"This proves that he's still in town and that he's going to continue coming after Carla," she heard Davy say. "He's waiting for her to return to her house, for me to go back to the rodeo circuit and leave her alone."

James said something about him being wrong about Debra Watney. She caught the words "model student" and "excellent work history," then "she left her last job abruptly apparently, because of a family emergency."

Davy shook his head. He'd been so sure there was something off about the woman, Carla thought as he raised his voice. "Well, someone at the hospital put that note on Carla's food tray. The killer wanted her to know he could get to her at any time. The only reason he hasn't is because I've hardly let her out of my sight. But clearly he's not giving up and it looks personal to me."

James nodded. "Apparently he's fine with killing you as well."

"I'm going to find this man if it's the last thing I do."

"You're a rodeo cowboy. No offense, but you have no training for this. Let the feds handle this. Let us see what we can find out. Don't—"

Davy shook his head. "For whatever reason, he wants her dead. Which means he'll come for her again. I plan to be ready this time when he does. Nothing you can say will change my mind."

His brother gave him a hug, whispering something to him before he left.

"How's our patient?" Dr. Hull asked as he came in as James left the room.

"Sore. My ankle hurts."

He nodded. "I'll order you some pain medication. How's the head?"

"It aches some. I think I hit the steering wheel with it."

He shook his head. "At least this time you didn't get another concussion, so that's good. I've ordered you a pair of crutches. Have you ever used crutches before?" She shook her head. "I'll get you into a walking cast as soon as I can. Knowing you, you won't like being immobile, but best to take it easy for a while. No stairs."

"I'll take her home to her house," Davy said. "No stairs."

"I know you'll take good care of her." He winked at Carla and left the room.

She looked over at Davy. "How can you take me home? Your truck—"

"I borrowed a truck. I've got this."

Carla shook her head. "Do I have a say in any of this?"

"I guess it will depend on how well you get around on crutches," Davy joked. "But as long as I can outrun you? Then I guess not."

"Davy." It came out a plea. "Doc said I can get in-home help if necessary. You can't keep taking care of me."

He shook his head. Carla would have argued further if FBI agents Grover and Deeds hadn't come into the room. Grover asked Davy to wait outside.

"Carla?" Davy asked.

She nodded. She'd sworn she wouldn't talk to them again without an attorney present, but she hadn't been able to get one yet. "I'll be fine, since I don't have much I can tell them," she said.

Davy said, "I'll get a wheelchair so you can get out of here. I won't be long." He scowled at the agents as he left the room.

"Did I hear you say you don't remember this any better than the robbery?" Grover glanced around the room. "I don't see your attorney."

"I haven't been able to get an attorney, but we can make this quick. I didn't see anything last night. But it wasn't an accident. The man I call J tried to kill me and Davy as well."

"You know that for a fact?" asked his partner.

"There aren't that many people who want me dead," she snapped.

Grover seemed to consider that. "Why would the same person who robbed the bank steal a truck to run into you? He's got the money. Why would he take the chance of getting caught? Unless there's something more he's afraid you're going to tell us."

She groaned. "I've told you everything I know. I was warned not to talk to you, and someone ran us off the road and now crashed into us. What does that tell you?"

"A falling out among thieves?" Grover said and smiled as if joking. They both knew he wasn't.

Carla shook her head and winced. "It doesn't matter what I tell you. You don't believe me. You're convinced that I'm involved in all this."

"Clearly, you are involved," the agent said.

"Not the way you think." She closed her eyes for a moment. "I told you everything I know."

"You didn't tell us about Samantha Elliot until she was in the hospital in a coma," he said.

"She's still alive?" Carla couldn't help her surprise. Last she'd heard, the woman was in serious condition. Maybe she would make it and give them a name or at least a description of the man who attacked her. Carla couldn't help but believe the man's name started with a *J.* "Did you find J's name in her files?"

"The office was ransacked and a lot of files destroyed," Deeds said. "The Butte police are going through them trying to match the tattoo to the one you told us about. But we suspect the attacker took the file."

"Been to Butte recently?" Grover asked.

"No. Why would we share that information with you if we had anything to do with this?"

"Because you thought she may not have survived. Isn't that right? Now she has a guard outside her hospital room door. Should she regain consciousness and remember her attacker..." He left the rest hanging as a threat.

"I hope she does and remembers not just her attacker but that he is the man she tattooed *J* heart *J* on," she said. "That will be the only way this will ever be over since you aren't looking for this man."

"We are looking for him," Grover said, sounding like he was losing his temper. "But you have to admit. You have given us very little."

"What about the truck that hit us last night?" she demanded. She saw the agents exchange a look. Her heart fell.

"The truck was stolen," Deeds said. "We suspect the driver was wearing gloves. Everything was wiped clean."

"So you have nothing," she said and closed her eyes.

"Ms. Richmond," Deeds said. "We might be able to get you a deal if you tell us the truth. We know you didn't kill those other men. I really doubt you or Davy Colt tried to silence Samantha Elliot. Give us the man's name, turn state's evidence against him and—"

"I can't do that, Agent," she said, opening her eyes with a groan. "If I knew who he was, you would already have his name and he would already be behind bars. Now please, leave. After the holidays I'll get a lawyer before we talk again."

"We're going to keep coming back until you tell us the truth," Grover said. "Think about making a deal, Ms. Richmond. I'd hate to see you spend the rest of your life behind bars. So either hire a lawyer or…"

"Or what?" she snapped.

"Or wait until we arrest you and one will be provided for you." Grover signaled his partner and the two left her room as Davy came in with the wheelchair—and a pair of crutches.

Chapter 22

Jud wasn't surprised to find Jesse waiting for him when he finally got home late the next morning. He figured she'd already heard about what had happened last night. She might have been close enough by that she'd heard the sirens or maybe even seen the flashing lights of the cop cars. She might have even chased the ambulance to the hospital to find out who was inside—and whether or not they were going to survive.

He wouldn't have put it past her.

That's why he half expected her to have the butcher knife within reach as he came through the door. He hesitated as he closed the front door behind him.

She was sitting in the dark waiting for him. He could feel her rage. He stayed where he was as his eyes adjusted and he could see her shape more clearly.

As he decided how to handle this, he watched for any

movement. He might have only an instant between when the blade of the knife caught a slice of sunlight through the crack in the curtains and when she was on him.

"Where have you been?" she asked quietly.

It had been close to daylight before he'd been able to get Jesse's car where he'd left it. He'd been cold and wet. He'd started the engine and turned on the heater and must have fallen asleep. He awoke when the engine died. He'd run out of gas. He'd had to hike into town with the gas can he kept in the back, since this wasn't the first time something like this had happened.

"I think you know where I've been."

She smiled, her teeth shining in the darkness. "While you were messing up my plans, did you also check to make sure the money wasn't where you left it?"

He wanted to turn on a light so he could see her better, but he was afraid of what she might see in his eyes. He would have been home hours ago, but of course she was right—he'd been searching for the money.

"You didn't think I believed that you moved it? By the way, why did you do that? Don't you trust me?"

She made a sound of displeasure before she said, "You know why I moved the money." She waved a hand through the air, as if that covered it. "I told you I would handle things with Carla Richmond if you didn't." Her tone was scarily reasonable. He hadn't seen the butcher's knife out of her reach for a while now.

"I didn't want blood on your hands too," he said. "I did it to protect you."

Her laugh could have shattered crystal. "But you didn't kill her. *Surprise.*"

It was a surprise. He'd T-boned Davy Colt's pickup on the passenger side hard enough to kill her. Now he was even happier that he hadn't turned on a lamp. For sure she would have seen his disappointment that this wasn't over—and right on its heels, his relief that he hadn't killed another person to get out of this mess.

"I had a plan, Jud," Jesse said. "It would have worked too. I was waiting in the alley behind Colt Brothers Investigation. I was waiting for them to come back. She and her cowboy would be dead now. But you had to...*protect* me. I don't think you trust me anymore."

He looked down at the floor, no longer shocked by anything she did. But he didn't want her to know that he'd gone to the spot where he'd hidden the money. She would take that as a betrayal, and he already knew how she reacted when feeling betrayed.

Last night, he'd heard sirens and an ambulance. "She has to be badly injured."

She shook her head. "A broken ankle and a bump on her head. So no, Jud, you failed, and we're not leaving until it's finished."

"It *is* finished," he said, raising his voice. He saw her shift on the couch. He could no longer see both of her hands. "Jesse, I'm begging you. She's not worth it. Let's get the money and leave." He took a wary step toward her, then another. "Staying here will only get us arrested or killed. Please, let this go."

She snapped on the lamp next to the couch, stopping him in his tracks and momentarily blinding him. He blinked and saw that she wouldn't be happy until Carla Richmond was dead.

He wasn't sure he cared about trying to make her happy anymore, but if he wanted the money, he had no choice. He had to kill Carla Richmond—and soon. The problem was that the woman seemed to have nine lives.

Then he would deal with his other problem. Jesse. She was right about one thing. He no longer trusted her. He wasn't all that sure that she wasn't planning to take off with the money without him. Or worse, kill him.

"The good news is that she'll have to go home now to her house—and on crutches," Jesse said. "Even you should be able to handle that."

He watched her get up from the couch. Both of her hands were empty. No butcher's knife. That should have relieved him, except that she was now headed for the kitchen.

"I hope you're hungry," she said over her shoulder. "There's leftover stew."

His first instinct at that moment was to forget about the money, the women, everything and just cut and run. Maybe if he'd had a full tank of gas in the pickup he would have.

"Starved!" he called after her, telling himself that he would outsmart her. "Something smells good," he said, coming up behind Jesse as she pulled a bowl of stew from the microwave and set it on a trivet on the table. He put his arms around her and pulled her against him. At least she didn't have the knife on her. But if he wanted the money and to live to spend it, he'd have to make sure the knife didn't get stuck between his ribs.

Carla looked down at the cast on her leg and wanted to cry. Crutches? She thought her freedom had been taken away before this. Now she really was in trouble. She was a sitting duck. Finding the man should prove easy. She could just sit and wait for him to come. It wasn't like she could run.

Now Davy felt he had no choice but to stay with her.

How could things get worse? They were both trapped. But the worst part was that when J came for her again, Davy would try to stop him. She could get the man she loved killed.

Dr. Hull and Davy helped her into the wheelchair. Her other option was, as Dr. Hull had suggested, getting a nurse. Carla wanted to laugh out loud. Someone from the hospital—a place she was now terrified of? It would just be her luck to bring the killer or his accomplice into her home.

But at the same time, she hated that Davy felt he had to take care of her. She couldn't bear to think of how this was going to end. Davy couldn't stay and protect her forever. Nor would she allow him to.

"Ready?" he asked as he took the wheelchair handles.

"This isn't what I wanted." She sounded close to tears and felt them pool in her eyes.

"You don't always get what you want. Sometimes you get what you need."

She recognized the verse. He'd sung it to her all those years ago—before they'd parted. "Something tells me that we aren't talking about this current situation."

He smiled as he pushed her out of the room and down the hall to the elevator. "I should have fought harder ten years ago. This time, you can't push me away."

Davy drove her home to her house. As he pulled into the drive, she said, "I overheard you talking to your brother. James is right. I'm not your responsibility. I don't want you risking your life for me or putting it on hold any longer." Her voice broke as he parked and turned off the engine. "I'm not going to be responsible for keeping you from what you love." She took hold of her crutches.

"You aren't keeping me from what I love, Carla. Stop

fighting me, because you can't change my mind." His gaze burned into her. "Now let's see how you do on these crutches. I cleaned off the sidewalk of snow earlier, but it will still be icy. You sure you don't want me to carry you to the door?"

She looked at him, aghast, and it made him laugh.

"Just a thought," he said, grinning, and he got out to rush around and open her door.

Carla was determined to make it to the house on the crutches. If she fell… Well, she just wasn't going to fall. She was awkward, but she didn't fall. She felt a rush of pride when she even managed the front steps to the porch. True, Davy was right behind her and would have caught her if she'd even wobbled, but she'd made it on her own.

He reached into her purse, pulled out the keys and opened the front door. She had to prove to him that she would be all right. She had to believe that J would be caught and that she would do fine on crutches until Dr. Hull put her in a walking cast. She had to believe that when Davy left, her heart would somehow survive.

Once inside, she turned to him. She looked into his denim-blue eyes. All of the Colt brothers had the same thick head of dark hair and blue eyes that ranged from faded denim to sky blue. They were all pretty much built alike as well, and all wanted to believe that they were the most handsome of the bunch. Close in age, they spent years confusing their teachers and the town.

But Carla knew that Davy was the most gorgeous of the Colt brothers. He was also the kindest, sweetest and most thoughtful. That she'd let him walk away ten years ago… That she was going to push him away again…

Before she could speak, he said, "Why don't I make

us something to eat?" He moved past her on his way to the kitchen.

"Wait. You cook?" If true, this made him even more irresistible.

He stopped to turn. "You keep underestimating me."

It was true and they both knew it. He would make someone a great husband. She felt it to the tender center of her heart. She almost said that, but knew she couldn't joke about him being with anyone else. She held his look for a few moments, then moved past him on her crutches. "I'm not even sure there is anything to cook in the fridge."

Jud had been called in to work for a few hours and had readily agreed. Anything to get away from Jesse for a while. Not to mention it took the pressure off him to deal with Carla Richmond.

On the way back home that afternoon after cashing his paycheck, Jud realized with everything that had been going on, he'd forgotten that one of Leon's goons would be coming by for a payment. Wes knew what day Jud got paid. He almost turned around—until he saw that Wes was standing by his big black SUV—with a headlock on Jesse. Her hands were bound in front of her with duct tape and so was her mouth.

Heart jumping to his throat, Jud sped up. He couldn't let Wes kill her. Jesse was the only one who knew where the money was. He wheeled in next to the SUV and jumped out.

"Let her go," Jud cried and tried to pull Wes off her. Two men Jud had never seen before tumbled out of the SUV and grabbed him. "What the hell is going on?" he demanded, becoming even more afraid.

"Leon wants all of his money *now*. I'm taking your girlfriend as collateral. You ever hear of collateral damage, Jud?"

Jud tried to break free of the men holding him as Wes shoved Jesse into the back of the SUV. "Wait!" he cried as the two men released him and climbed back in the rig to shove Jesse down on the floorboard and slam the door.

Wes came toward him so quickly that he didn't see the incoming fist. It hit him in the gut, dropping him to his knees on the driveway. He gasped for oxygen, unable to speak.

"Let us know when you have the money," Wes said, crouching down next to him. "Your girlfriend told us that we'd already have our money if you had taken care of things. I suggest you do what has to be done, Jud. You have twenty-four hours. Otherwise, we'll take care of her and come back for you."

"Don't kill her," he managed as Wes climbed into the SUV, started the engine and roared away.

Jud couldn't believe this was happening. Only Jesse knew where the money was. His mind raced. Why hadn't she given them the payment? What the hell was going on? Had she lost her mind?

He watched Wes drive away with Jesse—and his only way to pay the debt before the twenty-four hours were up.

Wes thought that this was about getting the money from his dying grandmother. But Jud had gotten the message loud and clear. Jesse wouldn't pay off Leon—not until Jud took care of Carla Richmond. No matter what he did, the woman wasn't giving up. If he'd had any doubt about her mental state, he no longer did. Cora Brooks was right. There was definitely something wrong with Jesse

Watney, a flaw that he had foolishly overlooked—and now deeply regretted.

His back against the wall, he had twenty-four hours. Otherwise, he could kiss the bank money goodbye. He'd risked his life for it. Not that he didn't realize that even if he did what she wanted, Jesse might still double-cross him.

But he told himself that over his dead body would Jesse get away with all that money as he decided to end this.

Chapter 23

Agent Grover got the call from Butte on his way back to Lonesome.

"Samantha Elliot has regained consciousness," the doctor told him. "She is determined to speak with you. She had me call the number on the card you left for her."

The phone was handed over. He listened as she told him that she'd done some work for a man named Judson Bruckner. "He's the one who attacked me."

Just to clarify, Grover asked, "What did the tattoo look like?"

She described the one that Carla Richmond had said she'd seen during the robbery. *J* heart *J*. He recalled the drawing she'd done of it.

"You're sure he's the man?"

The tattoo artist cursed at him. "I never forget a face—or a tattoo. It just took me a minute to recall his last name.

If he had waited, I would have handed over his paperwork. Stupid fool. When you catch him, I'd be happy to identify him in a lineup and testify against him."

The woman had no idea how lucky she'd been, since if true, Judson Bruckner had already killed three men. He thanked her and quickly did a background check on the suspect. Judson was currently renting a house in Lonesome and temporarily employed by a delivery company for the holidays. He drove an old red pickup. Grover scribbled down the plate number. His rap sheet showed that he'd had a few run-ins with the law, but nothing close to armed robbery and murder.

As he disconnected, he started to call the sheriff's department in Lonesome, but hesitated. He was on his way back from Washington State. He could be in Lonesome in a few hours. He wanted to make this bust himself because he had one very important question for Judson. Who inside the bank had helped him? Because someone had, and he knew that for a fact. He couldn't chance that the local law enforcement would screw up the collar, so he just kept driving, anxious to finally get to the truth.

Carla couldn't imagine how the two of them could live together in her small one-bedroom house. It felt too intimate, Carla thought as she agilely glided across the floor on the crutches past Davy. She stopped to look back at him. "See? I'm fine."

He nodded. "You're better than fine." His gaze was hot and sexy and full of promise.

She felt a rush of desire. How long before the two of them were making love in her double bed as snow fell outside? She shook off the image. It would be fine for a while, but eventually he would resent her for keeping him here. It didn't matter that none of this was her fault—or his either. They'd been thrown together because of an armed bank robbery and a killer who had his own reasons for wanting her dead, apparently.

But how was she going to get Davy to leave if the killer wasn't caught? Because she couldn't keep him. He wasn't hers. Too much of his heart was still taken by the rodeo. If anyone could understand that, it was her. Look how hard she'd worked to succeed, giving up everything but work to prove herself.

Carla leaned on her crutches and opened the refrigerator, surprised to find it stocked. She looked back at Davy, who was lounging against the doorjamb, watching her. "You did this," she said, feeling even guiltier. This man had dropped everything to make sure she was safe, and now this?

"Actually, Lori helped. She thought we might be hungry since we never made it out to their house for dinner."

"And she apparently worried that we might be thirsty," Carla said, pulling out a cold bottle of wine as she balanced on one crutch.

Davy grinned. "Looks like she thought of everything."

Suddenly she wasn't hungry, even though the food stocked in the refrigerator looked delicious. There was only one thing she wanted. She started to close the refrigerator door.

The back door exploded, flying open with the shriek of splintering wood and breaking metal. The first shot was deafening in the small kitchen. Behind her, she heard the bullet hit the wall, burying itself in the Sheetrock. An instant later, the second shot hit the china cabinet in the corner, glass shattering before the bullet made a thwack sound as it burrowed into the wood at the back of the display case.

Carla dropped the bottle of wine in her hand. It hit the tile floor and shattered like a gunshot, sending glass and wine flying. She started to move back, but was shoved into the open refrigerator as Davy dove for the back door. A bullet lodged itself in the refrigerator door she was holding open.

She fell back, dropping one of her crutches as she tried not to come down on her casted leg. She clutched at the refrigerator shelves and screamed, "No!" at Davy. But her cry was drowned out by the fourth shot in the seconds since the back door had been smashed open.

Those terrifying few moments though were nothing compared to the silence that followed. Carla could feel the aching cold of the night coming through the open back door. But over the thumping of her pulse, she heard nothing.

"Davy?" Fear made her voice break and tears rush to her eyes. She reached down and picked up the fallen crutch and awkwardly moved out from behind the refrigerator door, through the spilled wine and glass, terrified of what she would find.

The back door stood open to the night. She could see snow melting just inside it where the man had stood. Past it, she saw two sets of tracks that disappeared into the darkness.

"No!" she cried again and launched herself at the door, only to find that she could see nothing beyond the tracks in the light coming from the kitchen. Nor could she hear anything.

She spun around, searching the floor for a moment,

praying she wouldn't find it. But there it was. Blood. Three drops of it, all leading to the back door.

Stumbling into the living room, she searched frantically for her purse and cell phone. She remembered that Davy had brought it in. She looked around, praying that any moment Davy would come through that back door.

Fighting tears of fear and frustration, she spotted her purse and moved quickly on the crutches toward it. She had to toss them aside to get to her purse and the phone inside.

As she was digging for her cell, she heard a noise and looked up. In that instant, she would have done anything to see Davy standing there. Instead, what she saw turned her insides to liquid. To her horror, the blade of the large knife in the hooded figure's hand caught the light as the hood was thrown back and the blonde aide from the hospital rushed at her.

Davy felt the searing pain in his shoulder—but not until he'd run through the fallen snow, chasing the man who'd shot him. He became aware of the cold along with his ragged breaths as he ran. He followed the sound of branches brushing clothing ahead of him and tried to ignore the pain.

The clouds were low, the night black. He couldn't see movement ahead of him, but he knew he was gaining on the killer. Ahead, he saw a faint light through the pines and realized that the man had veered off to the right—toward the river.

Davy had no idea how far he'd run. It had happened so fast that he hadn't had time to think when he'd rushed the man, only to have him fire a final shot and turn and run. Davy had felt something smack hard into his left shoulder, but hadn't let it stop him. This time, he wouldn't let the bank robber turned killer get away. He was determined to catch this man if it killed him.

He was breathing hard, so at first he didn't realize that he could no longer hear the man crashing through the pines ahead of him. He pulled up for a moment to listen. That's when he heard a cry of surprise, followed by a scream that ended abruptly in silence.

Rushing toward the sound, he came out of the pines into the open and stopped as he saw where he was—standing on the cliff above the river. He listened, hearing nothing but his own blood rushing through his veins. He stepped closer to the edge of the cliff, aware of the trampled snow at his feet.

Even in the darkness he could see the sheen of the water's surface below him and, at its edge, something dark crumpled down there in the rocks. He waited for what he knew was the hooded figure who'd tried to kill them to move as he pulled his cell phone from his pocket and hit 911. The figure didn't move.

As he turned back toward the house, following his own footsteps through the snow, he realized that his shirt was covered in blood. He began to move steadily, anxious to get back to Carla. An engine revved somewhere in the distance. Surely Carla would stay at the house and call the cops.

He began to move quicker, suddenly afraid, suddenly having doubts. J, whoever he was, was dead, lying at the edge of the river. There was no way the man could have doubled back. But what if the man had had an accomplice at the hospital? Davy began to run. He heard an engine rev. He ran harder. Finally, he heard sirens headed this way.

By the time he reached Carla's house, he saw the flashing lights of SUV patrol cars pulling into the drive. The back door still stood open and he charged through it. He could hear the sheriff's deputies knocking on the front door.

Through the doorway, he could see into the living room. His pulse jumped. He saw evidence of a struggle. A lamp lay broken on the floor next to one of Carla's crutches.

"Carla!" He was calling her name, his voice cracking with fear, as he rushed through the house. "Carla!" Her purse was on the floor by the couch, the contents—including her cell phone—scattered across the floor. The deputies were pounding harder at the front door. He rushed to it, facing his greatest fear.

Carla was gone.

Someone had taken her.

J? But if true, then who was that lying dead at the edge of the river?

The second *J*.

Chapter 24

Davy felt as if he were in shock—from the loss of blood, from the loss of so much more. He'd been taken to the hospital, where the bullet had been removed from his upper arm and the wound bandaged.

He was anxious to be released. While his brothers and most of the sheriff's department were looking for Carla, he had to get out of the hospital so he could find her. Not that he had any idea where to look.

But right now there was a sheriff's deputy outside his hospital room door, apparently to keep him there. Federal agents were on the way to question him.

The moment Grover walked in, Davy could tell he was angry, demanding to hear what had happened in detail from the beginning.

"This is a waste of time," Davy had snapped after he told the agents everything that had occurred. "Now can we please find Carla?"

"I'm sure she's long gone," Grover said and seemed surprised that Davy was still anxious to leave to look for her. "You don't get it, do you? The robbery? Judson Bruckner had inside information from someone working at the bank. We know that for a fact. We believe that information came from your girlfriend."

"You're wrong. From the very beginning she told you she had nothing to do with it," Davy snapped. "We were almost killed by that man. You found his body lying down on the edge of the river, right?"

Grover nodded. "Which is unfortunate. I really wanted to ask him about the missing money. But apparently, it and Carla Richmond are gone."

"How can you think that? There were obvious signs of a struggle when I got back to the house," Davy said.

"Maybe too obvious," Grover said.

Davy shook his head in irritation. "Someone took her."

"Who do you think that was?" Deeds asked. "You said that you were chasing a man in a hoodie. Was there someone else with him?"

"Just because I didn't see anyone else…" Davy raked a hand through his hair. He felt sick to his stomach. His brothers had warned him, and he hadn't listened. He should never have gone after the man. He should never have left Carla alone. Now someone had her.

"So, who is he, the man at the bottom of the cliff? Have you been able to ID him?" The moment he asked the question, he saw the answer on the agent's face. "You know already?"

"Samantha Elliot, the tattoo artist who inked him, regained consciousness and gave us his name. I was on my way back here to question him."

"But if you know who he is, then you should be able

to find out who he was working with," Davy said. "The note on Carla's tray at the hospital… Does he work at the hospital?"

Grover shook his head. "His name is Judson Bruckner. He worked temporarily for a delivery company."

"I saw him," Davy cried. "He was looking in the window of her house. He had a package, but he said it was the wrong address and left before I could question him further." Davy couldn't believe he'd been that close to the killer, that close to catching him. If only he had, Carla would be safe now.

The agent looked at the small notebook in his hand. "You and Ms. Richmond, you hadn't had any contact for how long before the robbery?"

Davy shook his head, confused for a moment as to why the agent was asking him this. "I told you, I saw her the day before—"

"Before the robbery. I'm asking about before that. Had you had any contact with Ms. Richmond?"

"No. I stopped by the bank the day before the robbery to see her. Before that, I hadn't seen her in months. But what does this have to do with—"

"You have to understand my skepticism, Mr. Colt," Grover said. "You said Ms. Richmond wasn't injured during the shooting at the house, but you were."

"She had the refrigerator open. I shoved her against it, the door blocking any bullets, as I lunged at the shooter." He groaned. "Agent Grover, could we please quit wasting time? Carla is in trouble. If this Judson Bruckner didn't work at the hospital, then someone he knew does."

"Doesn't this remind you of the truck that hit you? Haven't you asked yourself how it was that neither of you were hurt?"

"One of us *was* hurt," he said through gritted teeth. He could feel time running out. They were wasting precious moments here while Carla… Who knew where or what was happening with her? "Carla's ankle was broken."

"Still, the way the side of your pickup was crushed, I'm surprised she wasn't killed."

"I was slowing down. She'd unbuckled her seat belt and was moving toward me."

"So she's what? Making a move on you, and out of the blue a big truck just happens to crash into your pickup on Ms. Richmond's side at that exact moment? How lucky that she slid over by you just before that happened."

"You can't still think she had anything to do with this," Davy cried.

"Why not? Tell me…now that you've had time to think about this. Doesn't it seem strange that the shooter fired shots all over the place—except for the one that winged you, Mr. Colt?"

Davy swore. "You didn't see his face. I did. His eyes were wild and his hand was shaking. But all that aside, I've had enough of this. You're wrong. Carla's been taken. By someone connected to the killer. Maybe someone even more dangerous. Instead of talking nonsense, you should be trying to find her before it's too late." His voice broke at the fear that it might already be too late.

Grover shook his head. "Ms. Richmond knew I was onto her. She needed to disappear. Now she has." The agent got to his feet. "I'm sorry, Mr. Colt. I can tell that you care about this woman, but you're kidding yourself if you think she isn't involved. Why do you think the robber stayed in town this long? He couldn't leave without her. And he would have—if you hadn't run him over a cliff."

He started toward the door only to turn back. "Carla

Richmond's gone and so is the money. She staged it so you'd think someone took her, struggled with her. But don't worry, we'll find her. However, you'd be smart to put this little…episode behind you. She used you." With that he turned and walked out.

Davy could practically hear the clock ticking as he was finally allowed to leave the hospital. Now at least he knew J's name. Judson Bruckner. Apparently, he'd been living in Lonesome for a few years.

But who had taken Carla? All he knew was that she had put up a fight. His gut instinct told him whoever it was had been working with Jud Bruckner. The other *J*? Someone who worked at the hospital?

But when James had gotten the list of employees, that had been a dead end.

Davy thought of the blonde nurse. He still thought there was something about her that bothered him. What if he wasn't wrong? The answer was here, he told himself as he went down to the hospital's main office.

"Can I help?" the woman at the desk asked.

"I'm looking for an aide who works here. Debra Watney?"

"I'm sorry, she isn't working tonight. Is there someone else who can help you?"

"Did you say Debra Watney?"

He turned at the deep, coarse female voice, recognizing the sound of it at once. It was the same one that had yelled at him and his brothers for stealing her apples from the tree near both of their properties. Davy groaned inwardly. Cora Brooks had been the bane of their existences for years and the worst neighbor a bunch of wild

Colt boys could have. She'd threatened numerous times to shoot them with her shotgun loaded with rock salt.

Cora stood not even five feet tall, but she was a force to be reckoned with. He saw that her right wrist had been bandaged, which he realized might explain what she was doing here. "Why are you asking about Debra Watney?" Cora demanded.

He had to bite his tongue for a moment. Nosy old busybody. "She's an aide who works here."

"Not likely," Cora said with a scoff. "She's dead."

Davy didn't have time for this. He started past her, but she grabbed his arm with her free hand. "Cora, I have to find this woman—"

"You aren't looking for Debra Watney," Cora said, dropping her voice and pulling him away from the nurse's station. "Her name's Jesse. Jesse Watney. I knew she was back in town, but I had no idea that she'd stolen her twin's name and profession." She clucked in disgust.

He'd frozen at the name—*Jesse*. Cora had to be wrong, and yet hadn't he been suspicious of the aide from the get-go? "How can you be sure her name is Jesse and not Debra?"

"I know, so just leave it at that. Debra disappeared a while back and hasn't been seen since getting into a car with Jesse. Jesse's the devil incarnate."

"Where can I find her?" he asked, telling himself that if he was right about the blonde aide, then what Cora was telling him just might be true.

"She's been living with Judson Bruckner in a house they rent on the edge of town."

He felt his heart kick up and then drop. Maybe Cora did know what she was talking about—but the aide wouldn't take Carla there. Too obvious. "Is there some-where she'd go if she didn't want anyone to find her?"

"Probably back to the family hovel in the mountains."

"Around here?" he asked in surprise, and Cora nodded. "Can you draw me a map of how to get there?"

"I can do you one better. I'll show you." She must have seen him hesitate. "That's the deal. I go with you, or you don't get the information. I want to see her face when retribution comes knocking."

"Cora, it's going to be dangerous. You don't want to—"

"Of course it's going to be dangerous," the elderly woman snapped. "Jesse would just as soon kill you as spit in your eye. You underestimate her evil and you'll be dead as a doornail. I'm going." She started for the door. "We'll take my rig. I keep my stinger in it."

Davy wanted to argue, but he'd left the pickup he'd borrowed out at Carla's. He climbed into Cora's small pickup, as she pulled her shotgun off the rack on the rear window.

"Let's go get her," Cora said with obvious delight. "On the way, you can tell me why Jesse has your girlfriend." He started to tell her that Carla wasn't his girlfriend, but of course she didn't give him a chance. "What were you thinking not marrying her a long time ago anyway?"

Carla surfaced as if from the bottom of a lake. She opened her eyes slowly, fighting to focus. Her brain felt foggy. For a moment, all she wanted to do was close her eyes and go back to the darkness.

But then her brain snapped in. Her eyes flew open, and she bolted upright to quickly take in her surround-ings. The smelly, lumpy mattress she'd been lying on.

The worn wooden floor. The log walls. The cloudy dust-coated old window. The snowy pines beyond it.

At the sound of something popping and cracking, she turned her head and saw the ancient rock fireplace, its face dark with layers of soot. A small fire burned at the back of it, sending out puffs of heat into the cold room.

"You're finally awake."

She started at the female voice, her head swiveling around to see the woman standing in the doorway. It all came back in a flash at the sight of the blonde aide. A gun dangled from the woman's right hand as she moved into the room and dragged over what was left of an old cloth recliner. She sat and leaned forward, balancing the gun on one thigh.

"Where are we?" Carla asked, her mouth dry and her tongue feeling too large for her mouth. Their conversation earlier tonight had been short, punctuated by the needle the woman had jammed into her arm as they'd struggled on the couch. Carla had been at a distinct disadvantage, given the cast on her leg. She vaguely remembered being half dragged out to the woman's vehicle. After that, nothing.

"Does it matter where we are?" the blonde asked.

She guessed not and tried to clear the fog still drifting around in her head. "You're the aide from the hospital." Carla frowned as she tried to remember the name James had told her. "Debra."

"You can call me Jesse," she said with a smile.

"Jesse?" She felt her pulse jump. "The other *J.* Of course."

"Jud and that stupid tattoo," Jesse said with a rueful shake of her head. "He's had his uses, I'll give him that, but let's face it—he's a dim bulb."

Carla gathered that Jud, the other *J*, wasn't here with them. She supposed that was something. "Why have you brought me here?"

"Why?" Jesse laughed. "You don't like the place? I grew up here." She glanced around, all humor erased from her face. "I swore I'd never come back here." Her gaze returned to Carla. "Because of you, here I am and here you are." Her face hardened. "You shouldn't have told the feds about the tattoo. I told you not to talk to them. You should have listened."

"You wrote the note." Her mind was taking its time clearing. Not that it helped. She had a cast on her leg and Jesse had a gun. The odds of getting out of here alive weren't good.

Jesse rose and began to pace the small room. "I spent my life being disrespected because of my family, my perfect twin, everyone—" She spun to face her. "People just like you who thought they were better than me."

"I don't even know you."

"You should have given Jud a loan."

She blinked. "He never applied for one." At least, not under the name Jud.

Jesse let out a rude sound. "Don't pretend you would have given him one if he had."

"I guess we'll never know." Carla looked around the room, afraid to ask what happened next. She had a bad feeling she already knew. But a small bubble of hope rose in her as she wondered why she was still alive. Jesse could have killed her back at the house. So why hadn't she?

The thought of the house brought a heart-dropping memory. "The last I saw my friend Davy, he was chasing a man out the back door of my house. I assume it was Jud." Since Jud wasn't here, Carla hoped that meant that Davy had caught up to him and was fine. "Do you know what—"

"Happened? Your guess is as good as mine. They might both be dead." Jesse shrugged. "It doesn't matter."

It did to Carla. She felt her eyes burn with tears. Wasn't this what she'd feared? That Davy would get injured or killed trying to protect her? But Jud could have gotten away, she realized. He could be headed up to this cabin right now. And Davy…? He had to be alive.

She realized Jesse was studying her intently, frowning as she did, as if surprised that she wasn't more terrified. If the woman only knew. But Carla was doing her best not to panic. It was her nature to keep control over her emotions. Except for when she thought of Davy.

"What? You aren't going to ask?" Jesse smiled as she sat back down on the edge of the recliner. Carla shook her head, pretending she didn't know what it was the woman was getting at. "Come on, don't you want to know what I'm going to do with you?"

"I would imagine you plan to kill me."

Jesse smiled, then cocked her head as if to listen before sending a glance toward the window and the darkness outside.

Carla realized that she was expecting someone. Jud? Of course. Her heart sank. She was waiting for Jud before she killed her. Or was it Jud who would be pulling the trigger?

Listening, she didn't hear anything. The deep snow was like thick cotton insulation, swallowing up sound. She was on her own with a gun-toting Jesse and possibly her even more dangerous boyfriend. If she had any hope of getting away from the Js, she had better come up with a plan.

She thought of Davy and her heart ached. Her life couldn't end here in this cabin deep in the mountains. If he was alive, he would blame himself. She couldn't bear the thought.

Over against the fireplace she saw an old branding iron that was apparently being used as a poker. How ironic, she thought, that the one weapon in the room other than Jesse's gun was a branding iron.

As Davy rode shotgun, Cora filled him in on what she knew about Jesse Watney and he told her what had happened back at the cabin. If Carla was in Jesse Watney's hands, then she was in worse trouble than if she'd been taken by Jud. Jesse had threatened her at the hospital, but that was mild compared to the stories Cora told him about the woman.

He was wishing he didn't know, fearing that he would be too late, that Carla was already dead. That is, if this woman named Jesse Watney had her.

When his cell rang, he quickly picked up, seeing that it was James.

"I just spoke with Agent Grover. What a… Where are you?"

"Probably on a wild-goose chase." He heard Cora grunt in the driver's seat. "Judson Bruckner was living with a woman named Jesse Watney. We're on our way to Jesse's family cabin in the mountains right now."

"We're?"

"Cora's with me." The road was getting worse. "Got to go."

After he disconnected, he could feel the elderly woman's gaze on him. "You didn't ask how I hurt my wrist," Cora said as they left the county road and headed up into the mountains.

He glanced over at her. His first thought was that she'd been spying on someone. Everyone in the county knew that she kept binoculars handy and had even bought herself some night-vision ones. If the grapevine could be believed, she loved learning people's secrets and then cashing in on them. That highly illegal quirk had almost gotten her killed last year, but Davy doubted it had stopped her.

"Gardening?" he asked, clearly joking.

She cackled. "Yep, winter gardening." She was still chuckling when she said, "The road is going to get a lot worse, I'll warn you right now. Best hang on. The cabin's all hell and gone back in here. Place has been empty for years. I figure she'll go there like an animal returns to its den."

Even though she'd been right about Jesse working as Debra Watney at the hospital, he still wasn't sure that she wasn't leading him on a fool's errand back up here in the mountains. He could feel time slipping away.

"It's not far now," Cora said, sitting up to strain to see into the glow of the headlights.

At first he didn't even see the road. But then he saw the fresh tire tracks in the snow. Only one set. Pine trees stood like towering snow-covered walls on each side as the road narrowed to a Jeep trail.

"I'm trying to decide if we should walk the last part or drive right up to the cabin," Cora said as she shifted into four-wheel drive. "Not sure it makes a difference, since if I know Jesse, she'll be expecting us."

He shot her a look. "What are you saying?"

"If she wants your girlfriend dead…" Again he thought about correcting her. They weren't boyfriend and girlfriend. He wasn't sure what they were. "Then she would have killed her at your house. Why bring her up here unless she was waiting for someone?"

"Jud isn't going to show up, but she might not know that," Davy said. He could feel Cora's gaze swing to him.

"Probably won't make a difference to Jesse which man shows up. I suspect she was planning to kill that boyfriend of hers anyway. He was the kind she would eventually squish beneath her boot. She'd much rather you see her kill Carla."

Davy felt his stomach roil. He was beginning to wonder about Cora and if she even knew what she was talking about, when a cabin came into view in the headlights.

Chapter 25

Carla realized that Jesse had heard something. She had her head cocked, listening, and didn't seem surprised when headlights cut through the grime-coated glass of the front window. "Stay here!" she ordered and moved to the door.

Carla knew she didn't have long. She slid across the mattress, then reached over to grab the branding iron from the edge of the fireplace. She had just enough time to hide the iron next to her before Jesse turned.

The blonde's face hardened to stone. "You moved."

"I'm freezing. I moved closer to the fire."

Jesse studied her for a moment before glancing at the fire.

Carla held her breath, afraid she would see that the branding iron was no longer leaning against the soot-coated rocks.

At the sound of boots on the porch, both of their gazes were drawn toward the front door. Jesse quickly came back over to her to point the gun at Carla's head.

"I figured someone would come looking for you," Jesse said. "Hope it's your cowboy. If his PI brothers are worth their salt, then they know about me by now—and that I had family up here in the mountains. Thing is," she said, frowning, "the place isn't that easy to find."

Cora parked and turned off the engine. There was no sneaking up on the cabin. Anyone inside would know that they had company. The headlights went off, pitching them into darkness.

The only light that flickered inside the structure was from a fire. Davy couldn't see anyone through the grime-covered window, but he felt as if they were being watched. No one, however, had come to the door.

He wondered if Carla was here with the woman Cora called Jesse. If so, who was Jesse expecting to come driving up? Jud? "You should stay in the truck," he said to Cora.

The elderly woman harrumphed and was out the pickup door before he could stop her, taking her shotgun with her. He hurried after her. As they reached the porch, he stopped to listen, afraid he'd hear a gunshot.

Cora scaled the rickety porch steps and was almost to the door when Davy heard a female voice call, "Come in!"

Davy recognized it as that of the blonde aide from the hospital, the same one Cora swore was actually Jesse Watney—an alleged killer, and the woman who he knew in his gut had Carla. He reached past Cora, grabbed the door handle, turned it and pushed. The old door groaned and creaked as it swung slowly open.

The fire in the room illuminated the scene before him. Carla sat on an old mattress a few feet from the fireplace, and the blonde stood over her with a gun pointed at Carla's head.

He met Carla's gaze and saw strength and determination in those blue eyes. He hadn't expected anything less. He gave her a small nod—not sure how to get her out of this unharmed, but willing to risk his own life to make it happen.

Cora set her shotgun aside and pushed past him and into the room. Davy could feel his gun where he'd tucked it into the back waistband of his jeans as he was getting out of the pickup. Cora was a loose cannon, but if not for her, he wouldn't have known where to find this place. He just worried about what she would do next and knew he had to be ready.

"Hope you aren't planning to go back to your job at the hospital," Cora was saying, taking obvious delight in the news she was about to impart. "They know you lied about who you are. I would imagine they have already called the sheriff."

"What did you bring this old bat for?" Jesse demanded, seemingly unfazed by the news. "I wasn't going back to that job anyway." Her gaze moved to Davy. "Where's Jud?"

"He had an accident."

"Dead?" she asked. He nodded and she smiled. "One thing less to take care of before I leave town."

"You actually think you're going to get away this time?" Cora demanded, hands on her skinny hips. "The feds are involved. This time you're going down for your crimes. Finally, Debra is going to get what she deserves. Payback for what you did to her."

Jesse frowned, tilting her head as she stared at the older woman. "Why do you care so much?"

"I knew your grandfather and I remember your sister as a child. She was good to her soul," Cora said, her voice breaking. "She deserved better than she got, especially from her twin sister."

Jesse's eyes blazed for a moment and Davy feared she might start shooting—starting with Carla. He swore under his breath, wishing he had insisted on Cora staying in the pickup. He knew he would have had to hogtie her though.

To his relief, Jesse seemed to tamp down her anger. She shook her head, dismissing Cora as she shifted her gaze to him. "Let's get this over with. I know you have a weapon on you. Toss it over by the fire."

"You need to let Carla go, and we'll all walk out of here," he said. "Carla has nothing to do with this."

Jesse laughed. "She has *everything* to do with this. If it wasn't for her…" She shook her head. "She should have kept her mouth shut about what she saw during the robbery. I warned her. She didn't listen. Her mistake. Now yours for coming up here to try to save her—and worse for bringing this old hag with you."

Cora moved with surprising quickness for her age. She charged like a small tank going into battle. Davy had only an instant to react. He half expected Jesse to pull the trigger and kill Carla before turning the gun on Cora. He drew his weapon, knowing he would probably have only one chance for a clear shot.

For years, he and his brothers had competed against

each other firing at tin cans. Davy had always been the better shot. He prayed he still was.

As he raised his gun to aim and fire, he saw Carla reach beside her. As Cora charged Jesse, Carla lifted what looked like an old branding iron. In one fluid movement, she swung it high across her body, striking Jesse's arm with the gun.

The sound of the gunshot was deafening in the small room. Davy had thought the blow with the branding iron would dislodge the gun from Jesse's hand, but he was wrong. He heard her cry of pain, then one like a war cry as she swung the gun at Cora, who was inches away from tackling her. The blow to the side of Cora's head sent her headlong into the floor next to Jesse.

Davy saw it all happen in what felt like an instant before he was looking down the barrel of Jesse's gun, the black hole taking aim at his heart. He fired first. But she still got off a shot before his bullet hit her in the throat. He felt the bullet whiz past his head to lodge in the door behind him.

Blood was spurting from Jesse's throat, but she was still standing, the gun still in her hand. Worse, she was starting to turn, to swing the barrel toward Carla, who'd gotten to her knees on the mattress. As he started to fire again, he saw Carla swing the branding iron in both hands like a batter going for a home run.

The makeshift weapon caught Jesse in the knees. She opened her mouth as if to scream, but only emitted a gurgling sound as she crumpled to the floor next to Cora.

Davy lowered his gun as Carla pried the gun from Jesse's grip and tossed it aside. Davy rushed to her and dropped down next to her to take her in his arms. He'd never been more relieved in his life. This could have gone so much worse. Carla clung to him so tightly that he hoped she'd never let him go.

"Cora?" she asked after a few moments.

"I'm too mean to die" came the answer from the floor as the older woman pushed herself up into a sitting position and flinched as she touched the knot on the side of her head. "Is she dead?" Cora asked of Jesse, before prodding her with a boot toe.

The worn wooden floor was bright red with blood. He could see Jesse's eyes, wide open, lifeless. "She's gone."

"Thank goodness," Cora said and sighed.

"I can't believe you found me," Carla said against his chest.

"It was all Cora's doing. If I hadn't run into her at the hospital…" Davy pulled back a little to look at Carla. Her gaze went to his shoulder and his blood-soaked coat sleeve.

"You're shot," she cried.

"That was from Jud back at the house. That's what I was doing at the hospital—getting it bandaged up."

"He'll live," Cora said. "I just texted the cops. Told them to send a wagon for the body and an ambulance for one of the Colt boys who's been winged."

"Davy," he said. "I'm Davy Colt."

The elderly woman shrugged as if it was all the same to her. "I'm just glad you're a decent shot. I used to listen to the lot of you shooting tin cans by the hour." She shook her head. "All you Colt boys, you're all the same to me. Wild and incorrigible." But there was a twinkle in her eye.

Chapter 26

Carla's emotions veered off in every direction. She was so thankful to be alive. So thankful that Davy was alive. She would be forever grateful to Cora for helping them. The bank's money had been recovered—at least most of it—from the cabin where Jesse had taken her. Both Jud and Jesse were dead. She didn't know how to feel about that—guilty for being relieved that they were gone, angry that they'd done what they had, guilty for not being sorry that two people were dead and that she might have played a part in it.

She'd met with Agents Grover and Deeds one final time. Grover didn't quite apologize, but at least he'd told her that she was no longer a suspect. A former employee at the bank had finally confessed that she'd given Jesse information while she'd been in labor at the hospital. She said that the woman she knew as Debra Watney had asked a lot of questions after learning that she had worked there. The woman said she had thought the aide was just trying to keep her mind off the labor. She had had no idea she was giving away information that would be used in the robbery—and key the agents to an inside job.

While Carla felt for the woman, she was grateful that she herself was no longer a suspect. Her boss had called to say that her job was waiting for her whenever she felt up to coming back.

For days all she'd wanted was for her life, and Davy's, to return to normal. Normal meant she would go back to the bank, back to her house alone each night, back to spending her days crossing items off her to-do lists.

For Davy it would mean catching up on the rodeo circuit. The holiday was winding down. It was time. Yet neither of them mentioned it. Since coming out of the mountains, they'd spent every minute of the past few days together at her house. One of Davy's brothers fixed the back door with a better lock and dead bolt and cleaned up the place.

If they ignored the bullet holes in the kitchen wall and refrigerator, they could almost pretend that none of it had happened.

But Carla couldn't pretend that things were going to change. Doc Hull had put her in a walking cast and given her a scooter that she could use at work. She was able to get around by herself with little trouble, and it wouldn't be all that long before even the walking cast would come off.

They'd fallen into a pattern over the days. Lying in bed in the morning until they felt like getting up. Having a breakfast one or both of them prepared. Making love. Cooking and going back to bed to make love again. She loved lying with Davy in her double bed together, her head on his shoulder, her cheek pressed against his skin.

"I love you, Carla. I've always loved you." It was the day before he was to leave. He turned to kiss her deeply. "I was so afraid that I'd lost you. I never want to let you go again." His blue gaze met hers and she felt that fire ignite at her center again.

"I love you, Davy. Always you."

"Come with me," he said, his expression brightening as if the idea had just come to him. He leaned on one elbow so he could look at her face. "We're both still young. We have plenty of time to settle down. We can spend the next few years traveling around the country."

She stared at him, unable to believe what he was suggesting—again. He'd suggested this ten years ago. Didn't he remember how that had ended? "Davy, I have a job. A house. A—" She'd almost said *life*. "A…house that's paid for." These days living in this house, the two of them acting like a real married couple, had she let herself dream that he might see the life they could have here? That he might want it?

But from the look on his face, it was the last thing he wanted. He rose from the bed, his face suddenly stiff, his expression cold. "You thought that I would quit the rodeo." He shook his head, the look ripping apart her heart. "I told you. I'm not ready to quit. I thought…"

"I thought since you were talking about only a couple more years…"

"That I would change my mind."

There was no reason to lie. He knew from her disappointed expression that she'd hoped he would change his mind. She should have known better. One last night after making love ten years ago, they'd lain in bed talking.

He'd romanticized about the two of them on the rodeo circuit going places she'd never been, seeing country she might never see again, eating food that she would never have in Lonesome, meeting people, being together.

At the time, she'd been tempted to chuck her life here and hit the road with him. But she wasn't that girl from ten years ago and she certainly wasn't going to chuck it all now, she told herself.

"You never considered coming with me, did you?"

She met his gaze and felt her heart shatter. When she spoke, her voice broke with emotion. "My job, my house... I can't just pick up and leave like you can. I have *responsibilities*." She rose from the bed to go to him, snatching up her shirt and pulling it on as she did. "Please." How could he not see how much this was killing her? How could he walk away from her now? She tried to cup his cheek, but he took a step back. "Davy, I love you."

"You love me?" he asked as he grabbed up his jeans and pulled them on. "How is that possible, since you want me to be someone I'm not? Or do you love the idea of me? Rodeo cowboy Davy Colt. Because if you loved me, you'd love all of me, whether you agreed with it or not. Hasn't it always been about you trying to change me, so I fit into this perfect picture you have of marriage and our lives together?"

"I could say the same about you," she said, drawing back from him. "You want me to give up everything for you. What's the difference?"

"You're not your job, Carla. Or are you going to tell me that your dream is to work as an executive loan officer in a bank in Lonesome, Montana?"

She took a step back as if he'd slapped her. "You know

how I ended up in Lonesome working at the bank. I had to change my plans because it was the right thing to do."

He nodded and took a step toward her, taking her shoulders in his hands. "You had to change your plans. How about changing them for us?"

She'd never wanted to say yes more than she did at that moment. "I'm not like you, footloose and fancy-free to go and do whatever you please."

He shook his head and let go of her to pull on his boots. "You can't blame your mother, Carla. She's been gone now for over five years. But you're still here. Why?"

He made it sound as if she'd chosen the path of least resistance. As if she lacked courage. "I'm not like you."

"You're right about that," he said. "I've spent my life taking chances, drawing rank bucking horses that will either put me in the money or the dirt or the hospital. Betting on myself, fighting the odds, testing myself over and over again against eighteen-hundred-pound animals. In all that time, you've never taken a chance. Not one. Not on me," he said. "Not even on yourself."

She watched him snatch up his Stetson. Their gazes met and held for a moment. She could see him waiting for her to say something. To ask him to stay. But she couldn't do that any more than she could ten years ago, she told herself.

"I swore I wouldn't let you break my heart again," he said, his voice cracking. "This time, it is all on me. Goodbye, Carla."

She stood there, shaken to her core. Only minutes ago they'd been locked in each other's arms, promising to love each other forever. What had happened? She heard him drive away in his new pickup, furious with him and what he'd said, furious with herself and how much of what he said might be true. Either way, her heart was breaking all over again.

It wasn't until the sound of his pickup engine died off in the distance that she let herself break down and cry.

Davy went down to the office the next morning. He'd smelled coffee and knew he'd find someone there working.

James was behind their father's large old desk. He looked up, not seeming surprised. "Packing up to go?" he asked.

Davy helped himself to a cup of coffee from the pot that was usually going—except when something happened that called for them to dip into their father's blackberry brandy. "You were right."

James put aside his work to give Davy his full attention. "I'm always right, but you'll have to enlighten me why this time." Then he seemed to see his brother's face. "You and Carla. She didn't take it well, you returning to the circuit?"

He shook his head. "I actually thought I could talk her into going with me. Just for even a year, and if she hated it, I would have quit and come back here."

"Did you tell her that?"

"What would be the point? She's settled. My life isn't for her even if I quit the rodeo. There was nothing I could say."

"I'm sorry," James said. "I know how you feel about her."

All Davy could do was nod, his chest aching from the heartbreak when he thought about how much he loved her. "These days together… So tell me about Dad's case," he said, wanting to change the subject. "Willie thought he could get a copy of the file—or at least get a look at it."

James shook his head. "It's missing."

"You know it's those Osterman brothers' doing. Both Osterman sheriffs were crooked as a dog's hind leg. So there's nothing we can do?"

"There's a good chance there wouldn't have been anything helpful in the file anyway," James said.

"Or there could be something someone wanted to stay hidden," Davy argued. "Why get rid of it otherwise?"

Before James could respond, Willie came in the door, followed quickly by their brother Tommy. One look at Davy and Willie said, "Sorry, bro. I get it, I do. But if after all this you still can't find a way to be together—"

"You've never been in love," Davy said to Willie as his brothers came in the door on a gust of winter-cold air and snow.

Willie looked as if he wanted to argue, but conceded the point since they all knew it was true. Their older brother guarded his heart closely when it came to women. "If it hurts as bad as you look, then I never want to fall in love."

"How's this sheriff's deputy gig going?" Davy asked him, again anxious to change the subject.

"Good," Willie said, sounding almost surprised himself. "I like it. I have a lot to learn and I'm definitely a rookie at this point, but..." He smiled. "I'm a fast learner."

"We were just talking about Dad's case," James told them.

"I guess James told you that the file on the accident is missing," Willie said. "But I did find out something interesting. I think Dad's pickup might still be in Evidence. I just need to find out where if that's the case."

"I'm not sure I want to see his pickup if you find it," Tommy said with a shudder. "I don't even want to think about the kind of damage the train did. Anyway, what could you hope to find in it after all this time?"

Willie shook his head. "I don't know, but if I can find the pickup, I'm definitely going to. So, you're leaving," he said to Davy, clasping his brother's shoulder. "Hope they give you some decent broncs. Do you know who's supplying the stock for your first ride?"

Davy was grateful that the conversation didn't return to Carla and his broken heart. Not that he could stop thinking about her. He could still smell her on his skin and ached at the thought that he might never hold her again.

Chapter 27

A few days after Davy walked out of her life, Carla got up, showered, dressed and headed for the bank. She'd cried until there were no more tears. She'd also had a lot of time to think about the robbery and the times she'd escaped death. Mostly she thought about Davy and what he'd said to her before he'd left her house.

Before driving to the bank, she'd looked around her house. She loved what she'd done with the place since she'd moved in. But having Davy live with her there made it feel too empty now. A friend had suggested she get a cat. Carla had laughed, even though she loved cats.

"Life is about choices and consequences," her mother used to say. Carla couldn't agree more as she walked into the bank and went straight toward her office. But she didn't enter it at first. Instead, she stopped in the doorway, taking in the space as if seeing it for the first time.

She'd been proud of this accomplishment because it was a symbol of her hard work and what she'd given up to get here. Back then her office had been a place of comfort and safety. She knew her job and did it efficiently. She'd always thought that one day she might move up and be a branch manager. Maybe it wasn't what she'd set out to do, but she'd accepted it.

Just as she'd accepted that she and Davy Colt would never be together.

Shoving away the thought, she stepped in to walk behind her desk, but she didn't sit down. Instead, she stared at the open doorway, remembering Judson Bruckner standing there the first time he'd come to the bank for money. He'd looked so nervous, so unsure of himself, so scared.

And then him later in the Santa costume.

Her boss suddenly filled the doorway, startling her for a moment.

Appearing uncomfortable, he stepped in and closed the door behind him. "I know I've already tried to talk you out of this, but I have to try one last time," he said. "We have trauma experts you can talk to about your fears."

Carla chuckled. "I'm not afraid of working in the bank or of another robbery." She shook her head. "It's personal, like I told you. All the robbery did was make me realize what I really want out of life."

"If you're sure I can't talk you out of this," he said.

"No, I've made up my mind. It's definitely out of my comfort zone and it will be the first time that I don't have a plan or know what the future holds. But I'm not scared anymore and that's a really good feeling." She smiled. "I've never felt so free."

"Well, if you change your mind or need a job in the future…" He turned to walk toward the door.

"Thank you. I appreciate that." But she didn't see herself coming back here. She'd put away money for years. With the sale of her house, she would have plenty to live on for a long while, since she'd never lived extravagantly and she didn't really see that changing.

As her boss opened the door to leave, she dragged her gaze to the box she'd brought to clean out her desk. Before Christmas, she couldn't wait to get back here to this job, to the routine, to the comfortable life she'd managed to make for herself here in Lonesome. A safe, secure life. She realized the past few days that keeping Davy in her heart had also been part of her protection from moving on with her life. He'd been safe there, just under the branding iron tattoo. And she'd been happy enough with that.

Then Judson Bruckner had walked into the bank, and everything had changed. He brought Davy—the real live cowboy—back into her life. How had she thought that after everything she could just walk back into her old life that easily? She'd almost been killed—not once, but numerous times—since she'd left this office. But oddly, that wasn't what had jolted her into making a decision about that life.

She'd lived in fear, she'd realized, long before the bank robbery. She'd feared disappointing her mother, feared becoming like her, feared veering off the path she'd set for herself. She'd feared what it would mean loving the rodeo cowboy part of Davy, who would always get on the back of a rank horse and try to ride it.

Her biggest fear had been taking a risk and following her heart.

Carla opened a drawer and began to take out her personal items and put them into the box.

"I'll leave you to it then," her boss said, having stopped in the open doorway. "I wish you all the luck in the world."

Luck? She smiled and thanked him. She was lucky to be alive, but it would take more than luck to get what she wanted. It would take true love, the kind that compromised, that changed dreams, that didn't always give you what you thought you wanted. But gave a woman what she needed soul deep. While that scared her, nothing could hold her back. Not anymore.

Davy couldn't count how many times he'd almost turned around and gone back to Lonesome. He hated the way he'd left. He regretted the things he'd said to Carla. He felt as if he'd burned their last bridge. There was no going back because they'd reached an impasse—*just like ten years ago*, he told himself as he drove toward Arlington, Texas.

So he'd kept going, even though his heart wasn't in it—even when he'd drawn a horse he'd been wanting to ride for a long time. He told himself that Carla loved the idea of him—but not the man he was. She needed a man who wore a suit to work, who got off every night at five and mowed the lawn on the weekends.

But even as he thought it, his heart broke even worse to think of her with another man. He asked himself if this really had anything to do with the rodeo. Was he being unreasonable? What was another two years on the circuit? What if he didn't want to quit even after that?

He stopped in Cheyenne, Wyoming, for gas. The sun was starting to set. He found himself looking back up the highway toward Montana. Regret seemed to weigh him down even more. He was weary from the miles pulling his horse trailer across the country. Why had he fought so hard to do this? He'd always planned that one day he'd quit rodeo and raise rough stock. He had the land and had saved enough money to make it happen.

But it had always been down the road. He'd wanted a few more years riding bucking horses that were determined to toss him into the dirt more often than not. Man against beast. It was something that, whether Carla liked it or not, was in his genes, he told himself.

So why wasn't he excited like he usually was when he hit the road? He needed these Texas-sanctioned rodeos. He had to earn enough wins to count toward circuit standings. He had wanted desperately to draw a horse named Pearl that weighed close to fifteen hundred pounds and was said to send cowboys to the Pearly Gates. Pearl had never been successfully ridden. He'd told himself he had to try to change that if he got the chance.

Gas tank full, he climbed behind the wheel, determined to make it to Dodge City, Kansas, before he pulled over and climbed into his horse-trailer camper to sleep.

Carla was packing her car for the trip to Arlington, Texas, before the next snowstorm hit. A light dusting of flakes drifted down. She planned to be there when Davy rode and was hurrying to finish when she heard a vehicle pull into her drive. Turning, she blinked.

Through the falling snow, she couldn't see the driver behind the wheel. She didn't have to. She knew this shiny new truck intimately. Carla felt goose bumps race over her. Davy? Her mind whirled. What was he doing back here? Had something happened?

The pickup door swung open, and he stepped out. He adjusted his Stetson and seemed to hesitate, but only for a moment as he started toward her.

Carla realized that she hadn't moved, that she'd barely taken a breath.

"Going somewhere?" he asked. Snow was beginning to collect on his Stetson.

She glanced back at her SUV, now loaded with only what she'd thought she'd need on the road. When she turned back, he was almost to her.

"Thought I'd see what life was like on the open road," she said, surprised that her voice sounded almost normal around the lump in her throat. What was he doing here? "I was going to start in Arlington. Don't you have a ride there?"

He took a step closer. The love she saw in his blue eyes was her undoing. She felt tears rush to her eyes even as snowflakes caught on her lashes. All she got out was his name before she was in his arms. He kissed her like there was no tomorrow.

When he finally drew back, he asked, "You really quit your job?"

"It was just a job." He grinned at that. "Davy—"

He touched a finger to her lips. "There's something I need to say to you first. I got down the road. Almost made it to Dodge City when I realized my heart was no longer in rodeo. I'd left it in Montana with you. Carla, I love you, have for years, always thinking that one day I'd come back and we'd be together."

"But I was coming to you."

He laughed. "I see that." His smile broadened even as he shook his head. "Coming so close to almost losing you made me realize what I really want. What I've always wanted. I said you were afraid to live life? Well, I was the one who was hanging on to what had become familiar as well. So I turned around and I came home. I want a life with you."

"But you can have that and rodeo too," she said, motioning toward her packed car as snow began to fall harder. "I've already talked to a Realtor about selling the house—"

Davy shook his head. "You can't sell it. We're going to need somewhere to live until our house is built on the ranch. I'm not going back, Carla. This is where I belong. It's what I've always wanted." His gaze met hers. "You. This isn't how probably either of us pictured this…" He dropped down into the snow on one knee. "Will you marry me?"

"Davy." She was laughing as she dropped down next to him. "Are you sure?"

"I've never been more sure of anything in my life," he said and kissed her. As far as winter kisses went, this was the best one yet.

"Was that a yes?" Davy asked, pulling back from the kiss.

"No, this is a yes," she said, and cupping his handsome face, she drew him to her for another kiss.

That's where his brothers found the two of them after James got a call from someone who'd just seen Davy drive past pulling his horse trailer. It didn't take them long to figure out where Davy was headed—if true.

"What are you two kids doing?" James demanded as he and his brothers climbed out of their rig and walked toward where the two were kneeling in the snow. Snowflakes whirled around them all as Davy and Carla got to their feet, laughing.

"We're getting married," Davy announced and put a protective arm around her. "Anyone have a problem with that?"

"About damned time," James said. The Colt brothers all laughed.

"No problem at all," Willie said.

"I think this calls for blackberry brandy down at Dad's office," Tommy said. It had become a celebration ritual, and now Carla was part of it—and part of this big, rowdy family. She couldn't believe this was happening, especially since she'd always planned her life down to the minute.

She looked over at Davy. For so long she'd pictured their perfect life together. She laughed now, realizing she had no idea what was ahead for the two of them. More surprising, she'd never felt more free or more excited. All she knew was that with Davy—and this family of his—it would be a wild ride.

* * * * *

CARDWELL RANCH
TRESPASSER

Chapter 1

Just inside the door, she stopped to take a look around the apartment to make sure she hadn't forgotten anything. This place, like all the others she'd lived in, held no special sentimental value for her. Neither would the next one, she thought. She'd learned a long time ago not to get too attached to anything.

The knock on the other side of the door startled her. She froze, careful not to make a sound. The building super, Mr. McNally, again, wanting the back rent? She should have left earlier.

Another knock. She thought about waiting him out, but her taxi was already downstairs. She would have to talk her way out of the building. It wasn't as if this was the first time she'd found herself in a spot like this.

She opened the door, ready to do whatever it took to reach her taxi.

It wasn't Mr. McNally.

A courier stood holding a manila envelope, a clip-board and a pen.

"Dee Anna Justice?" he asked.

She looked from him to the envelope in his hand. It looked legal. Maybe some rich uncle had died and left Dee Anna a fortune.

"Yes?"

He glanced past her into the empty apartment. She'd sold all the furniture and anything else that wasn't nailed down. Seeing him judging her living conditions, she pulled the door closed behind her. He didn't know her. How dare he? He had no idea what kind of woman she was, and he certainly wasn't going to judge her by the mess she'd left in the apartment.

She cocked a brow at him, waiting.

"I need to see some identification," he said.

Of course he did. It was all she could do not to smile. Well, sneer, as she produced a driver's license in the name of Dee Anna Justice. She'd known where to get a fake ID since she was fourteen.

He shifted on his feet and finally held the pen out to her and showed her where to sign.

She wrote *Dee Anna Justice* the way she'd seen her former roommate do it dozens of times, and held out her hand impatiently for the envelope, hoping there was money inside. She was due for some good news. Otherwise the envelope and its contents would end up with the rest of the trash inside the apartment.

"Thanks a lot," she said sarcastically, as the courier finally handed it over. She was anxious to rip into it right there, but she really needed to get out of here.

It wasn't until she was in the backseat of the cab,

headed for the train, that she finally tore open the envelope and pulled out the contents. At first she was a little disappointed. There was only a single one-page letter inside.

As she read the letter through, though, she began to laugh. No rich uncle had died. But it was almost as good. Apparently Dee Anna had a cousin who lived on a ranch in Montana. She ran her finger over the telephone number. According to the letter, all she had to do was call and she would be on her way to Montana. With a sob story, she figured she could get her "cousin" to foot most if not all of her expenses.

She had the cabdriver stop so she could buy a cell phone in the name of Dee Anna Justice. After she made her purchase she instructed the driver to take her to the airport, where she bought a first-class ticket. She couldn't wait to get to Montana and meet her cousin Dana Cardwell.

Chapter 2

"You're never going to believe this."

Hilde Jacobson looked up from behind the counter at Needles and Pins, her sewing shop at Big Sky, Montana, and smiled as her best friend came rushing in, face flushed, dark eyes bright. Her dark hair was pulled back, and she even had on earrings and makeup.

"You escaped?" Hilde said. "I don't believe it." Dana didn't get out much since the birth of her twin boys last fall. Now she had her hands full with four children, all under the age of six.

Her friend dropped a packet of what appeared to be old letters on the counter. "I have family I didn't know I had," she said.

Hilde had to laugh. It wasn't that long ago that Dana was at odds with her siblings over the ranch. *Family* had been a word that had set her off in an entirely different direction than happy excitement.

Last year she'd reunited with her siblings. Her sister, Stacy, and baby daughter, Ella; and brother Jordan and his wife, Deputy Marshal Liza Turner Cardwell, were now all living here in Big Sky. Her other brother, Clay, was still in California helping make movies.

"A cousin is on her way to Montana," Dana announced. "We have to pick her up at the airport."

"We?" Hilde asked, looking out the window at the Suburban parked at the curb. Normally the car seats were full and either Dana's husband, Hud, or Stacy would now be wrestling a stroller from the back.

"Tell me you'll go with me. I can't do this alone."

"Because you're so shy," Hilde joked.

"I'm serious. I'm meeting a cousin who is a complete stranger. I need you there for moral support and to kick me if I say something stupid."

"Why would you say something stupid?"

Dana leaned in closer and, although there was just the two of them in the shop, whispered, "This branch of the family comes with quite the sordid story."

"How sordid?" Hilde asked, intrigued but at the same time worried. Who had Dana invited to the ranch?

"I was going through some of my mother's things when I found these," Dana said, picking up the letters she'd plunked down on the counter and turning them in her fingers.

"That sounds positive," Hilde said, "you going through your mother's things." Mary Justice Cardwell had died nearly six years ago. Because it had been so unexpected and because it had hit Dana so hard, she hadn't been able to go through her mother's things—let alone get rid of anything. Not to mention the fact that her siblings had tried to force her to sell the ranch after their mother's death because Mary's most recent will had gone missing for a while.

"About time I dealt with her things, wouldn't you say?" Dana asked with a sad smile.

"So you found something in one of these letters?" Hilde asked, getting her friend back on track.

Dana brightened. "A family *secret!*"

Hilde laughed. "It must be on the Cardwell side of the family. Do tell."

"Actually, that is what's so shocking. It's on the *Justice* side." Climbing up on a stool at the counter, her friend pulled out one of the letters. "My mother had a brother named Walter who I knew nothing about. Apparently he left home at seventeen and married some woman of ill repute, and my grandparents disinherited him and refused to have his name spoken again."

"*Seriously?* That is so medieval," she said, stepping around the counter so she could read over Dana's shoulder.

"This is a letter from him asking for their forgiveness."

"Did they forgive him?"

"Apparently not. Otherwise, wouldn't I have known about him?"

"So you tracked him down on the internet and found out you have a cousin and now she is on her way to Montana."

"Walter died, but he left behind a family. I found one cousin, but there are apparently several others on that side of the family. Isn't that amazing?"

"Amazing that you were able to find this cousin you know nothing about." Hilde couldn't imagine doing such a thing—let alone inviting this stranger to come visit—and said as much.

"It's not like she's a *complete* stranger. She's my *cousin*. You know, since I had my own children, I realize how important family is. I want my kids to know all of their family."

"Right," Hilde said, thinking of the six years Dana had been at odds with her siblings. She'd missed them a lot more than she suspected they'd missed her. "I'm sure it will be fine."

Dana laughed. "If you're so worried, then you absolutely must come to the airport with me to pick her up."

"How did you get out alone?" Hilde asked, glancing toward the street and the empty Suburban again.

"Stacy is babysitting the twins, and Hud has Mary and Hank," Dana said, still sounding breathless. It was great to see her so happy.

"How are you holding up?" Hilde asked. "You must be worn out."

Hilde babysat occasionally, but with Stacy, Jordan and Liza around, and Hud with a flexible schedule, Dana had been able to recruit help—until lately. Jordan and Liza were building their house on the ranch and Stacy had a part-time job at Needles and Pins and another one working as a part-time nanny in Bozeman. Mary was almost five and Hank nearly six. The twins were seven months.

"I'm fine, but I am looking forward to some adult conversation," Dana admitted. "With Stacy spending more time in Bozeman, I hardly ever see her. Jordan and Liza are almost finished with their house, but Jordan has also been busy with the ranch, and Liza is still working as a deputy."

"And I haven't been around much," Hilde added, seeing where this was going. "I'm sorry."

"We knew expanding the shop was going to be time-consuming," Dana said. "I'm not blaming you. But it is one reason I'm so excited my cousin is coming. Her name is Dee Anna Justice. She's just a little younger than me—and guess what?" Dana didn't give Hilde a chance to guess. "She didn't know about us, either. I can't wait to find out what my uncle Walter and the woman he married were like. You know there is more to the story."

"I'm sure there is, but let's not ask her as she gets off the plane, all right?"

Dana laughed. "You know me so well. That's why you have to come along. Dee Anna is in between jobs, so that's good. There was no reason she couldn't come and stay for a while. I offered to help pay her way since she is out of work. I couldn't ask her to come all the way from New York City to the wilds of Montana without helping her."

"Of course not," Hilde said, trying to tamp down her concern. She was a natural worrier, though—unlike Dana. It was amazing that they'd become such close friends. Hilde thought things out before she acted. Dana, who wasn't afraid of anything, jumped right in feetfirst without a second thought. Not to mention her insatiable curiosity. Both her impulsiveness and her curiosity had gotten Dana into trouble, so it was good her husband was the local marshal.

For so long Dana had had the entire responsibility of running Cardwell Ranch on her shoulders. Not that she couldn't handle it and two kids. But now with the twins, it was good that Jordan was taking over more of the actual day-to-day operations. Dana could really start to enjoy her family.

"I'll get Ronnie to come in," Hilde said. "She won't mind watching the shop while I'm gone with you to pick up your cousin."

"I have another favor," Dana said, and looked sheepish. "Please say you'll help show my cousin a good time while she's here. Being from New York City, she'll be bored to tears hanging around the ranch with me and four little kids."

"How long is she staying?" Hilde asked.

Dana shrugged. "As long as she wants to, I guess."

Hilde wondered if it was wise to leave something like this open-ended, but she kept her concerns to herself. It was good to see Dana so excited and getting a break from the kids that she said, "Don't worry, you can count on me, but I'm sure your cousin will love being on the ranch. Did she say whether or not she rides?"

"She's a true city girl, but Hud can teach anyone to ride if she's up for it."

"I'm sure she will be. Did she tell you anything about her family?"

Dana shook her head. "I still can't believe my grandparents had a son they never mentioned. Or, for that matter, that my mother kept it a secret. It all seems very odd."

"I'm sure you'll get to the bottom of it. When is she arriving?" Hilde asked, as she picked up the phone to call Ronnie.

"In an hour. I thought we could have lunch in Bozeman, after we pick her up."

Fortunately, Ronnie didn't mind coming in with only a few minutes' notice, Hilde thought as she hung up. Hilde suddenly couldn't wait to meet this mysterious Justice cousin.

Deputy Marshal Colt Dawson watched Hilde Jacobson and Dana Savage come out of the sewing shop from his spot by the window of the deli across the street. Hilde, he noticed, was dressed in tan khakis and a coral print top she'd probably sewn herself. Her long golden hair was bound up in some kind of twist. Silver shone at her throat and ears.

Colt couldn't have put into words what it was about the woman that had him sitting in the coffee shop across the street, just hoping to get a glimpse of her. Most of the time, it made him angry with himself to be this besotted with the darned woman since the feeling was far from mutual.

As she glanced in his direction, he quickly pretended more interest in his untouched coffee. He'd begun taking his breaks and even having lunch at the new deli across from Needles and Pins. It was something he was going to have to stop doing since Hilde had apparently started to notice.

"She's going to think you're stalking her," he said under his breath, and took a sip of his coffee. When he looked again she and Dana had driven away.

"I figured I'd find you here," Marshal Hud Savage said, as he joined him. Colt saw Hud glance across the street and then try to hide a grin as he pulled up a chair and sat down.

He realized it was no secret that he'd asked Hilde out—and that she'd turned him down. Of course Hilde told her best friend, Dana, and Dana told her husband. Great—by now everyone in the canyon probably knew.

The "canyon," as it was known, ran from the mouth just south of Gallatin Gateway almost to West Yellowstone, miles of winding road along the Gallatin River that cut deep through the mountains.

Forty miles from Bozeman was the relatively new town of Big Sky. It had sprung up when Chet Huntley and a group of men started Big Sky Ski Resort up on Lone Mountain.

Hud ordered coffee, then seemed to study him. Colt bristled at the thought of his boss feeling sorry for him, even though he was definitely pitiful. He just hoped the marshal didn't bring up Hilde. Or mention the word *crush*.

Hilde had laughed when he'd asked her out as if she thought he was joking. Realizing that he wasn't, she'd said, "Colt, I'm flattered, but I'm not your type."

"What type is that?" he'd asked, even though he had a feeling he knew.

She'd studied him for a moment as if again trying to decide if he was serious. "Let's just say I'm a little too old, too serious, too...not fun for you."

He knew he had a reputation around the canyon because when he'd taken the job, he'd found there were a lot of young women who were definitely looking for a good time. He'd been blessed with his Native American father's black hair and his Irish mother's blue eyes. Also, he'd sowed more than a few oats after his divorce. But he was tired of that lifestyle. More than that, he was tired of the kind of women he'd been dating.

Not to mention the fact that he'd become fascinated with Hilde.

Hilde was different, no doubt about it. He'd run into her a few times at gatherings at Hud and Dana's house. She *was* serious. Serious about her business, serious about the life she'd made for herself. He'd heard that she had been in corporate America for a while, then her father had died and she'd realized she wasn't happy. That was when she'd opened her small sewing shop in Big Sky, Montana.

Other than that, he knew little about her. She was Dana's best friend, and they had started out as partners in the shop. Now Dana was a silent investor. Hilde also had her own house. Not one of the ostentatious ones dotting the mountainsides, but a small two-bedroom with a view of Lone Mountain. She'd dated some in the area, but had never been serious about anyone. At least that's what he'd heard.

Some people talked behind her back, saying that she thought she was too good for most of the men around the area. Colt would agree she probably *was* too good for most of them.

"Maybe I've changed," he'd suggested the day he'd asked her out.

Hilde had smiled at that.

It had been three weeks since she'd turned him down. He'd had numerous opportunities to date other women, but he hadn't. He was starting to worry about himself. He figured Hud probably was, too, since the canyon was such a small community, everyone knew everyone else's business.

"I thought I'd let you know I might be taking off some more time," Hud said after the waitress brought him a cup of coffee. Neither of them had gotten into the fancy coffees that so many places served now in Big Sky. Hud had taken off some time when the twins were born and a few days now and then to help Dana.

"Things are still plenty slow," Colt said, glad his boss wanted to talk about work. He and Hud had gotten close since he took the job last fall, but they weren't so close that they could talk about anything as personal as women.

"Dana discovered she has a cousin she's never met. She and Hilde have gone to pick her up. Stacy's babysitting all the kids right now, so I have to get back. I'll be in and out of the office, but available if needed. Dana wants me to teach her cousin to ride a horse. She's going to try to talk Hilde into taking her cousin on one of the river raft trips down through the Mad Mile. I told her I'd do whatever she wants. As long as Dana is happy, I'm happy to go along with it," he added with a grin.

"Wait, Hilde is going on a raft trip?" Colt couldn't help but laugh. "Good luck with that."

"I think there's a side to Hilde you haven't seen yet. You might be surprised." Hud finished his coffee and stood. "Might be a good idea for you to go along on that raft trip," he added with a grin.

As the plane flew over the mountains surrounding the Gallatin Valley, the now Dee Anna Justice prepared herself for when she met her cousin.

She'd been repeating the name in her head, the same way she used to get into character in the many high school plays she'd performed in. She'd always loved being anyone but herself.

"Dee Anna Justice," she repeated silently as the plane made its descent. The moment the plane touched down, she took out her compact, studying herself in the mirror.

She'd always been a good student despite her lack of interest in school. So she knew how to do her homework. It hadn't taken much research on her laptop to find out everything she could about her "cousin" Dana Cardwell Savage.

The photos she'd found on Facebook had been very enlightening. Surprisingly, she and her "cuz" shared a startling resemblance, which she'd made a point of capitalizing on by tying back her dark hair in the plane bathroom.

"Dee Anna Justice," she had said into the mirror. "Just call me Dee."

The man in the seat beside her in first class had tried to make conversation on the flight, but after a few pleasantries, she'd dissuaded him by pretending to read the book she'd picked up at the airport. He was nice-looking and clearly had money, and she could tell he was interested.

But she'd needed to go over her story a few more times, to get into her role, because once she stepped off this plane, she had to be Dee.

"Hope you enjoy your stay at your cousin's ranch," he said, as the plane taxied toward the incredibly small terminal. Everything out the window seemed small—except for the snowcapped mountain ranges that rose into a blinding blue sky.

"I'm sure I will," she said, and refreshed her lipstick, going with a pale pink. Her cousin Dana, she'd noticed, didn't wear much—if any—makeup. Imitation was the best form of flattery, she'd learned.

"Is this your first time in Montana?"

She nodded as she put her compact away.

"Staying long?" he asked.

"I'm not sure. How about you?" He'd already told her he was flying in for a fly-fishing trip on the Yellowstone River.

"A short visit, unfortunately."

"Dee Anna Justice," she said extending her hand, trying out the name on him. "My friends call me Dee."

"Lance Allen," he said, his gaze meeting hers approvingly.

Any other time, she would have taken advantage of this handsome business executive. She recognized his expensive suit as well as the watch on his wrist. He'd spent most of the flight on his computer, working—his nails, she noted, recently manicured.

She'd known her share of men like him and hated passing this one up. It didn't slip her mind that she could be spending the week with him on the Yellowstone rather than visiting some no-doubt-boring cousin on a ranch miles from town. But the payoff might be greater with the cousin, she reminded herself.

The plane taxied to a stop. "You don't happen to have a business card where I could reach you if I can't take any more of home on the range?" she asked with a breathy laugh.

He smiled, clearly pleased, dug out his card and wrote his cell phone number on the back. "I hope you get bored soon."

Pocketing his card, she stood to get down her carry-on, giving him one final smile before she sashayed off the plane to see if her luck had changed.

Hilde wasn't surprised that Dana was questioning her impulsive invitation as the plane landed. "What if she doesn't like us? What if we don't like her?"

"I'm sure it will be fine," Hilde said, not for the first time, even though she was feeling as anxious as her friend.

"Oh, my gosh," Dana exclaimed, as her cousin came off the plane. "She looks like me!"

Hilde was equally shocked when she saw the young woman. The resemblance between Dana and her cousin was startling at a distance. Both had dark hair and eyes. The ever-casual ranch woman, Dana had her long hair pulled up in a ponytail. Her cousin had hers pulled back, as well, though in a clip.

All doubts apparently forgotten, Dana couldn't contain her excitement. She rushed forward. "Dee Anna?"

The woman looked startled but only for a moment, then began to laugh as if she, too, saw the resemblance. Dana hugged her cousin.

Hilde had warned her friend that Easterners were often less demonstrative and that it might be a good idea not to come on too strong. So much for that advice, she thought with a smile. Dana didn't do subtle well, and that was one of the many things she loved about her friend.

"This is my best friend in the world, Hilde Jacobson," Dana said, motioning Hilde closer. "She and I started a sewing shop, even though I don't sew, but now I'm a silent partner and Hilde does all the work. She always did all the real work since she's the one with the business degrees."

"Hi," Hilde said, and shook the woman's hand. Dana took a breath. The woman's hand was cold as ice. She must be nervous about meeting a cousin she didn't know existed. It made Hilde wonder if Dee Anna Justice was ready for Cardwell Ranch and the rest of this boisterous family.

"Let's get some lunch," Hilde suggested. "Give Dee Anna a chance to get acclimated before we go to the ranch."

"Good idea," Dana chimed in. "But first we need to pick up Dee Anna's bags."

"Please call me Dee, and this is my only bag. I travel light."

The three of them walked outside and across the street to where Dana had left the Suburban parked.

"So how far is the ranch?" Dee asked after they'd finished lunch at a small café near the airport.

"Not that far," Dana said. "Just forty miles."

Dee lifted a brow. "*Just* forty miles?"

"We're used to driving long distances in Montana," Dana said. "Forty miles is nothing to us."

"I already feel as if I'm in the middle of nowhere," Dee said with a laugh. "Where are all the people?"

"Bozeman is getting too big for most people," Dana said, laughing as well. "You should see the eastern part of the state. There's only .03 people per square mile in a lot of it. Less in other parts."

Dee shook her head. "I can't imagine living in such an isolated place."

Dana shot Hilde a worried look. "I think you'll enjoy the ride to the ranch, though. It's beautiful this time of year, and we have all kinds of fun things planned for you to do while you're here. Isn't that right, Hilde?"

Hilde smiled, wondering what Dana was getting her into. "Yes, all kinds of fun things."

Dee stared out the window as they left civilization behind and headed toward the mountains to the south. They passed some huge, beautiful homes owned by people who obviously had money.

She tried to relax, telling herself that fate had gotten her here. The timing of the letter was too perfect. But luck had never been on her side, so this made her a little nervous. Not to mention the thought of being trapped on a ranch in the middle of nowhere. She fingered the business card in her pocket. At least she had other options if this didn't pan out.

She considered her cousin. Dana, while dressed in jeans, boots and a Western shirt, didn't look as if she had money, but she drove a nice new vehicle. And was a partner in a sewing shop—as well as owned a ranch. Maybe her prospects were good, Dee thought, as Dana drove across a bridge spanning a blue-green river, then slipped through an opening in the mountains into a narrow canyon. Dee had never liked narrow roads, let alone one through the mountains with a river next to it.

"That's the Gallatin River," Dana said, pointing to the rushing, clear green water. Dana had been giving a running commentary about the area since lunch. Dee had done her best to tune out most of it while nodding and appearing to show interest.

The canyon narrowed even more, the road winding through towering rock faces on both sides of the river and highway. Dee was getting claustrophobic, but fortunately the land opened a little farther down the road, and she again saw more promising homes and businesses.

"That's Big Sky," Dana said finally, pointing at a cluster of buildings. "And that is Lone Mountain." A snow-capped peak came into view. "Isn't it beautiful?"

Dee agreed, although she felt once she'd seen one mountain, she'd seen them all—and she'd seen more than her fair share today.

"Is the ranch far?" She was tiring of the tour and the drive and anxious to find out if this had been a complete waste of time. Lance Allen was looking awfully good right now.

"Almost there," Dana said, and turned off the highway to cross the river on a narrow bridge.

The land opened up, and for a moment she had great expectations. Then she saw an old two-story house and groaned inwardly.

So much for fate and her luck finally changing. She wondered how quickly she would escape. Maybe she would have to use the sick-sister or even the dying-mother excuse, if it came to that.

Just then a man rode up on a horse. She did a double take and tried to remember the last time she'd seen anyone as handsome as this cowboy astride the horse.

"That's Hud, my husband," Dana said with obvious pride in her voice.

Hello, Hud Savage, Dee said to herself. Things were beginning to look up considerably.

Chapter 3

Deputy Marshal Colt Dawson got the call as he was driving down from Big Sky's Mountain Village.

"Black bear problem up Antler Ridge Road," the dispatcher told him. "The Collins place."

"I'll take care of it." He swung off Lone Mountain Trail onto Antler Ridge Road and drove along until he saw the massive house set against the side of the mountain. Like many of the large homes around Big Sky, this one was only used for a week or so at Christmas and a month or so in the summer at most.

George Collins was some computer component magnate who'd become a millionaire by the time he was thirty.

Colt swung his patrol SUV onto the paved drive that led him through the timber to the circular driveway.

He'd barely stopped and gotten out before the nanny

came running out to tell him that the bear was behind the house on the deck.

Colt took out his can of pepper spray, attached it to his belt and then unsnapped his shotgun. The maid led the way, before quickly disappearing back into the house.

The small yearling black bear was just finishing a huge bowl of dog food when Colt came around the corner.

It saw him and took off, stopping ten yards away in the pines. Colt lifted the shotgun and fired into the air. The bear hightailed it up the mountain and over a rise.

After replacing the shotgun and bear spray in his vehicle, he went to the front door and knocked. The nanny answered the door and he asked to see Mr. or Mrs. Collins. As she disappeared back into the cool darkness of the house, Colt looked around.

Living in Big Sky, he was used to extravagance: heated driveways, gold-finished fixtures, massive homes with lots of rock and wood and antlers. The Collins home was much like the others that had sprouted up around Big Sky.

"Yes?" The woman who appeared was young and pretty except for the frown on her face. "Is there a problem?"

"You called about a bear on your back deck," he reminded her.

"Yes, but I heard you shoot it."

"I didn't *shoot* it. I scared it off. We don't shoot them, but we may have to if you keep feeding them. You need to make sure you don't leave dog food on the deck. Or birdseed in your feeders. Or garbage where the bears can get to it." Montana residents were warned of this—but to little avail. "You can be fined if you continue to disregard these safety measures."

The woman bristled. "I'll tell my housekeeper to feed

the dog inside. But you can't be serious about the bird-seed."

"It's the bears that are serious about birdseed," Colt said. "They'll tear down your feeders to get to it and keep coming back as long as there is something to eat."

"Fine. I'll tell my husband."

He tipped his Stetson and left, annoyed that people often moved to Montana for the scenery and wildlife. But they wanted both at a distance so they didn't have to deal with it.

As he drove back toward Meadow Village, the lower part of Big Sky, he thought about what Hud had said about a raft trip down the river. No way would Hilde go. Would she?

Hilde had been watching Dee Anna Justice on the ride from the airport to Cardwell Ranch and fighting a nagging feeling.

What was it about the woman that was bothering her? She couldn't put her finger on it even now that she was back in the sewing shop—her favorite place to be.

"So what is she like?" Ronnie asked. The thirtysomething Veronica "Ronnie" Tate was an employee and a friend. Hilde loved that she could always depend on Ronnie to hold down the fort while she was away from the shop.

"Dee Anna Justice? It's eerie. She looks like Dana. But she doesn't act like her."

Ronnie seemed to be waiting for Hilde to continue.

Hilde weighed her words. Dana was her best friend. She didn't want to talk about Dana's cousin behind Dana's back.

"More subdued than Dana, but then who isn't? She's from New York City and all this is new to her."

Ronnie laughed. "Okay, what is wrong with her? I can tell you don't like her."

"No, that's not true. I don't *know* her."

"But?"

What *was* bothering her about the woman? Something. "I just hope she doesn't take advantage of Dana's hospitality, that's all." Dana had flown her out here and was paying all her expenses, and Dee was letting her. That seemed wrong.

Ronnie was still waiting.

"I don't want her to be a hardship. Dana is stretched thin as it is with four kids, two still in diapers."

"How long is she staying?" Ronnie asked.

"That's just it—Dana doesn't know." Hilde had always thought visitors were like fish: three days and it was time for them to go. But then again, she enjoyed being alone to read or sew or just look out the window and daydream. Dana was more social, even though she'd deny it.

"I'm sure Dana will show her a good time," Ronnie said.

"I'm sure she will since she has already drafted me to help."

After Ronnie left, she was still wondering what it was about Dee Anna Justice that bothered her. She started to lock up for the day when she recalled Dee's reaction to Hud as he'd ridden up on his horse.

Dee had suddenly come alive—after showing little interest in Montana, the canyon or the ranch before that moment.

Dee moved restlessly around the living room of the old ranch house this morning, running her finger along the horns of some kind of dead animal hanging on the wall. Hud had told her, but she'd forgotten what kind.

Last night, while Dana had seen to the kids, Hud had shown her around the ranch. Dee hadn't been impressed with the corrals, barn, outbuildings or even the view. But Hud, who was drop-dead gorgeous and so wonderfully manly, was very impressive. She'd never met a real live cowboy before. It made him all the more interesting because he was also the marshal.

When the tour of the ranch ended, Hud had excused himself and she'd been forced to stay up late talking with her "cousin." Dana had shared stories of growing up here on the ranch.

Dee had made up a sad childhood of being raised by nannies, attending boarding schools and hardly ever seeing either of her wealthy parents. The stories had evoked the kind of sympathy she'd hoped to get from Dana. By the time they'd gone to bed, Dana had been apologizing for not knowing about Dee and saving her from that lonely childhood.

"Ready?"

Dee turned to smile at Hud. He had offered to teach her to ride a horse this morning. Her first instinct had been to decline. She'd never been on a horse in her life and she really didn't want to now. But she loved the idea of Hud teaching her anything.

"Ready," she said past the lump in her throat.

Hud must have seen her reluctance. "I'm going to put you on one of the kids' horses. Very gentle. There is nothing to worry about."

"If you say so," she said with a laugh. "Let's do it."

Hud led the way outside. He had two horses tied up

to the porch railing. She felt as if she was in Dodge City. This was all so… Western.

"Just grab the saddle horn and put your foot in my hands and I'll help you up," Hud said. She did as he instructed, wobbled a little and fell back. He caught her, just as she knew he would. The man was as strong as he looked.

"Let's try that again," he said with a laugh. Behind them, she heard Dana come out on the porch with the two oldest of their children. Dee had forgotten their names.

"Is she going to ride my horse, Mommy?" the little girl asked.

"Yes, Mary, she needs a nice horse since she has never ridden before," Dana answered.

"Really?" The kid sounded shocked that anyone could reach Dee's age and have never ridden a horse.

This time Dee let Hud lift her up and onto the horse. She gripped the saddle horn as the horse seemed to shiver and stomp its feet. "I don't think it likes me," she said.

"Star likes everyone," the girl said.

Dee was glad when they rode away from the house. She'd always found children annoying. It was beyond her why anyone would want four of them.

Once she got used to the horse's movement, she began to relax. The day was beautiful, not a cloud in the sky. A cool breeze blew through the pine trees, bringing with it a scent like none she'd ever smelled before.

"So this is what fresh air smells like," she joked.

"A little different from New York City?"

She laughed at that. "It's so…quiet."

"You'll get used to it. Did you have trouble getting to sleep last night? People often complain it's too quiet to sleep."

She hadn't been able to sleep last night, but she doubted it was from the quiet. Dana had put her in a large bedroom upstairs at the front of the house. When she'd tested the bed, she found it to be like lying down on a cloud. It was covered with what appeared to be a handmade patchwork quilt, the mattress on a white iron frame that forced her to actually climb up to get into it.

The sheets had smelled like sunshine and were soft. There was no reason she shouldn't have drifted right off to sleep. Except for one.

She found herself reviewing the day in small snapshots, weighing each thing that happened, evaluating how she'd done as Dee Anna Justice. She was much more critical of herself than anyone else could possibly be. But she'd learned the hard way that any little slipup could give her away.

"Dana tells me you grew up back East?" Hud asked, clearly just making conversation as their horses walked down a narrow dirt road side by side.

The real Dee Anna Justice had never been exactly forthcoming about her life growing up. But she'd always gotten the feeling that something had happened, some secret that made Dee Anna not want to talk about her life.

She'd found that amusing, since she would put her childhood secrets up against the real Dee Anna Justice's any day—and win hands down, she was sure.

"It wasn't like *this*," Dee said now in answer to his question. Then she quickly asked, "Did you grow up here? I get the feeling that you and Dana have always known each other."

"My father was the marshal," Hud said. "I grew up just down the road from here. Dana and I go way back." Something in his tone told her that there had been some problem before they'd gotten together. Another woman? Or another man?

Dee made a mental note to see what she could find out from the sister, Stacy. She'd only seen her for a few minutes, but Dee could tell at once that Stacy and Dana were nothing alike. And while the two seemed close, she got the feeling there was some sort of old friction there.

She'd spent her life reading people to survive. Some people were literally an open book. If they didn't tell you their life story, you could pretty well guess it.

Glancing over at the cowboy beside her, she knew he was honorable, loyal and trustworthy. She considered what it would take to corrupt a man like that.

Hilde put the Open sign in her shop window. As she did, she glanced at the deli across the street. She'd gotten used to seeing Deputy Marshal Colt Dawson sitting in that front window and was a little surprised to find someone else sitting there this morning.

It surprised her also that she was disappointed.

She shook it off, chastising herself.

"Colt has a crush on you," Dana had said a few days before. "Hud says he hasn't dated a single woman since he asked you out and you turned him down."

"I'm sure he'll snap out of it soon," Hilde had said. Colt Dawson could have any woman he wanted—and had. The man was too handsome for his own good. He'd gotten his straight, thick black hair from his father, who was Native American, and his startling blue eyes from his Irish mother. On top of that, he was tall, broad-shouldered with slim hips and long legs, and he had this grin that...

Hilde shook herself again, shocked that she'd let her thoughts go down that particular trail. It was flattering that Colt had asked her out, but she was his age, and he hadn't dated a woman his own age since he'd come to Big Sky, let alone one who was looking for something more than a good time.

As she started to turn away from the front window of her store, she saw the man at the deli's front table get up and leave. Colt Dawson quickly took his place, his blue-eyed gaze coming up suddenly as if he knew she would be standing there.

Hilde quickly stepped back, but she couldn't help smiling as she hurried to the counter at the back of the store.

A moment later the bell jangled as someone came in the front door. Her heart took off like a shot as she turned, half expecting to see Colt.

"Just need some black thread," said one of her older patrons. "It's amazing how hard it is to keep black thread in the house."

Hilde hurried to help the woman. When she looked out the window again, the front table at the deli was empty, Colt long gone.

"Why didn't you go out with him?" Dana had asked her. "What would it have hurt?"

She hadn't had an answer at that moment. But she did now. A man like Colt Dawson was capable of breaking her heart.

Dee hated it when the horseback ride ended, even though she could definitely feel her muscles rebelling. She'd insisted on helping as Hud unsaddled the horses and put them in the corral. *Helping* might have been inaccurate. She'd stood around, asked questions without listening to the answers and studied the man, considering.

Back at the house, Dana announced that Hud was

going to take care of the kids while she and her cousin went for a hike and picnic at the falls. That is, if Dee wasn't too tired.

She would much rather have taken a nap than go on a hike since she hadn't gotten much sleep last night, but she couldn't disappoint Dana, especially in front of Hud. So she'd helped pack the lunch to the pickup and the two of them had driven out of the ranch and toward what Dana called Lone Mountain.

"So this is the town of Big Sky?" Dee asked a few minutes later. "I thought it would be bigger."

"It's spread out. There is the upper mountain where the ski lifts are, and the lower mountain where the golf course is. Plus a bunch of houses you can't see from the road," Dana told her. "We'll have to take the gondola to Lone Mountain, if you're here long enough. I think you'll like that—the view is nice. And tomorrow I've set up a rafting trip for the three of us."

"Oh, Hud is going?" Dee asked.

"No, he's taking care of the kids. Hilde is going with us. In fact, she's joining us for the picnic today." She turned onto a narrow road that went past a cluster of houses and businesses before climbing up through the pines. "Yep, there's Hilde's SUV already parked at the trailhead. Hilde is so punctual." Dana laughed. "It's amazing we're best friends since we are opposites on so many things."

Hilde. The best friend. Dee recalled yesterday feeling Hilde watching her a little too closely. Dana was so trusting, so open. Hilde was more reserved and definitely not trusting, Dee thought. Dana parked next to Hilde's SUV, and Dee glimpsed the woman behind the wheel, her brown eyes so watchful.

* * *

Dana chattered away on the hike up to Ousel Falls. Hilde dropped behind her friend and Dee. She hadn't been up to the falls in several years and was enjoying the gentle hike through the pines. She could hear the roar of the creek. It was early in the year, so snow was still melting in the shade and the creek was running fast and high.

The cool air felt good. Hilde was wondering why Dana had insisted she come along. She felt like a third wheel. Not that Dee and Dana seemed to be hitting it off. Dee was quiet, nodding and speaking only to say, "Really?" "Oh, that's interesting." And "Huh." Clearly she wasn't finding anything all that interesting in the information Dana was imparting about the area and its history.

Dana stopped to wait for her in a sunny spot not too far from the falls.

At the falls, Dana opened the cooler she'd brought, and they sat on rocks overlooking the falls to drink iced tea and eat roasted elk sandwiches.

"It's…interesting," Dee said of the sandwich. "I thought you raised beef?"

Dana laughed. "Wild meat will grow on you," she promised. "Hud always gets an elk and a deer each year. We both really like it."

"I'm not sure I'll be here long enough for it to grow on *me*," Dee said.

This gave Hilde an opening. "So how long *will* you be staying?" she asked.

"I'm not sure," Dee said, and looked to Dana, who appeared shocked that Hilde would ask such a thing.

"As long as she wants to," Dana said.

Dee smiled. "That could definitely wear out my welcome. The more I see of this place, the more I love it here and never want to leave."

"Montana does that to people," Dana said.

"At least this time of year," Hilde said. "You might not find it as hospitable come winter."

"Oh, I don't know." Dee stretched out on the ground and stared up at the blue sky. "I can see myself sitting in front of that huge rock fireplace at the house with a mug of spiked cider, being pretty content."

"A woman after my own heart," Dana said.

Hilde began to clean up the picnic, putting everything back in the cooler before she got up and wandered over to the edge of the falls.

"What has gotten into you?" Dana whispered next to her a few moments later.

"Sorry. I was just curious how long she's planning to stay," she whispered back. "I didn't mean to be rude." When Dana said nothing more, she glanced over at her. *"What?"*

"You're jealous of my cousin."

"No, that's not it at all." But Hilde could tell there was no convincing her friend otherwise. "Fine, I'm jealous."

"Don't be," Dana said with a laugh. "You're my *best* friend and always will be." She lowered her voice. "Not only that, Dee has had a really rough life."

"She told you that?" Hilde asked, unable to keep the skepticism out of her voice.

"She didn't have to," Dana said. "I could tell. So be nice to her for me. Please?" Hilde could only nod. "I'm going to get my camera and take a photo."

Hilde turned back to the falls, thinking maybe Dana was right. Maybe she *was* jealous, and that was all it was. The roar of the water was so loud she didn't hear Dee come up behind her. She barely felt the hand on her back before she felt the shove.

She flailed wildly as she felt herself falling forward toward the edge of the roaring falls, nothing between her and the raging water but air and mist.

Dee grabbed her arm and pulled her back at the last second.

"I found my camera," Dana called from over in the trees, and turned in their direction. "Look this way so I can get a picture of the two of you." A beat, then: "Is everything all right?"

"Hilde got a little too close to the edge," Dee said. "You really should be careful, Hilde. Dana was just saying earlier how dangerous it can be around here." She put her arm around Hilde's shoulders. "Say cheese."

Dana snapped the photo.

Chapter 4

"I don't think your friend likes me," Dee said once they were in the pickup and headed back to the ranch.

"Hilde likes you," Dana said, not sounding all that convinced. "But I think she might be a little jealous."

"I suppose that's it," Dee agreed. "Well, I hope she accepts me. I feel so close to you. It's almost like we're sisters instead of cousins, you know what I mean?"

Dana readily agreed, just as Dee had known she would. "Hilde is just a little protective."

"A *little?*" Dee said with a laugh. "I think she's worried I will take advantage of you, stay too long."

"Put that right out of your mind," Dana said, as she parked in front of the house. "You're family. You can stay as long as you'd like."

"Hilde has nothing to be jealous of me about," Dee said. "She's beautiful and smart and self-assured and has her own business. She's what I always wanted to be."

"Me, too," Dana said with a laugh.

"Oh, you have even more going on for you," Dee said. "You have Hud. And the kids," she added a little belatedly, but Dana didn't seem to notice. "And the ranch. I bet you were practically born on a horse."

"I have been riding since the time I could walk," Dana said, then fell silent for a moment. "Do you want to talk about your childhood? I don't mean to pry."

Dee realized that she'd sounded jealous of both Dana and Hilde. The truth had a way of coming out sometimes, didn't it? She would have to be more careful about that around both women.

"There isn't much more to tell." Only because the real Dee Anna Justice hadn't been forthcoming about her family. There had definitely been something in her background she hadn't wanted to talk about. But it could have just been that some wealthy people didn't like talking about themselves or their wealthy families.

So now Dee had to wing it, hoping to give Dana enough to make her feel even more sorry for her. "As I told you last night, when I wasn't away at school, my parents were never around. My father traveled a lot. My mother was involved in a lot of charity and social events. I grew up feeling alone and unloved, yearning for what everyone else had." At least the last part was true.

"I'm sorry, Dee. I wish I had known about you. Maybe you wouldn't have felt so alone," Dana said, as she parked in front of the house. "I would have shared the ranch with you."

Dee watched Hud come out onto the porch and thought about Dana's generous offer to share what she had. "Hud mentioned some high country back behind the ranch that has a great view. I'd love to see it. But this is probably a bad time."

As Dana got out, she suggested it to Hud, who said the kids were napping and he'd be happy to take her if that was what she wanted to do.

"You sure it's not an inconvenience," Dee said.

"Not at all," he said.

She watched as he gave his wife a kiss and felt that small ache in her stomach at the sight.

"I'll help with dinner when I get back," he said to Dana.

"I'll help, too," Dee said, even though she'd never cooked in her life. In New York City it was too easy to get takeout.

She followed Hud to the four-wheeler parked by the barn and climbed on behind him, putting her arms around his waist. He started the motor and they were off. It didn't take long before the house disappeared behind them and they were completely alone.

Dee watched dark pines blur past. The air got cooler as they climbed, the road twisting and turning as it wound farther and farther back into the mountains. She laid her cheek against the soft fabric of his jean jacket and breathed in the scent of him and the mountains.

There were few times in her life that she'd ever felt safe. It surprised her that now was one of them. Hud was the kind of man she'd always dreamed would come along and sweep her off her feet. How could she still believe in happy ever after after what she'd lived through?

Her parents had hated each other to the point where they'd tried to kill each other. Her father… She didn't even want to think about the role model he'd been to his daughter.

And the men she'd met since then? She let out a choked

laugh, muffling it against Hud's jacket. They'd hurt her in ways she'd thought she could never be hurt.

She'd been waiting her whole life for a hero to come along. When she'd seen Hud Savage come riding up, her heart had filled with helium at the sight of him. He looked bigger than life, strong, brave, the first real man she'd ever known.

She held on a little tighter, wishing Hud was hers.

When they reached the summit, Hud stopped the four-wheeler and shut off the engine.

Dee let go of his waist, stretched and climbed off to look out across the tops of the mountains. "This is amazing," she said, actually meaning it. "You can see forever."

"It is pretty spectacular up here, isn't it?"

She tried to imagine living in country like this. It seemed so far away from the noise and filth of the big cities she'd wandered through so far in her life. What must it be like to wake up to this every morning?

Hud began to point out the mountain peaks, calling each by name with an intimacy that plucked at her heart-strings. She could hear his love for this land in his voice. There was nothing sexier than a man who loved something with such passion.

It took all her self-control not to touch him.

"So what are those mountains over there?" she asked, wanting this moment to last forever. She didn't listen to his answer. She just liked the sound of his deep and melodious voice. Desire spiked through her, making her weak with a need like none she'd known. She wanted this man.

"You have a wonderful life here," she said, realizing she'd never been so jealous of anyone as she was Dana Savage. "It's so peaceful. I can't imagine having the tie to the land that you do. I've moved around a lot. I've never felt at home anywhere." *Until now,* she thought, but she didn't dare voice it.

Like Hilde, she was sure Hud was wondering how long she was going to stay. But she'd never met a man she couldn't charm. Hud Savage would be no exception.

She moved to the edge of the mountaintop and breathed in the day. She'd been telling the truth about her family moving around a lot. Her father couldn't bear to stay long in any one place—even if he wasn't forced to flee town before the law caught up to him. A small-time con man, he worked harder at not working than he would have had he just gotten an honest job.

"I feel as if I could just fly out over the tops of all these mountains," she said, as she freed her hair to let it blow back in the wind. She stuck out her arms, laughing as she laid her head back. The wind felt good. She felt alive. Free.

"I wouldn't get too close to the edge," Hud said, stepping to her. "I don't want to have to explain to Dana how I lost her cousin."

"No, we don't want that," she agreed, as she met his gaze.

"We should get back. The kids will be waking up and Dana will need help with dinner," he said.

Disappointed, she pulled her hair up again and turned to walk back to the four-wheeler. For a moment, she had felt as if he was responding to her.

She hadn't gone but a few feet when she stepped on a rock, twisting her ankle as she fell. Hud rushed to her as she dropped to the ground with a groan.

"How bad is it hurt?" he asked, frowning with concern.

"I think I just twisted it, but I can't seem to put any pressure on it," Dee said, wincing in pain as she held her ankle. "I've spent my life walking on sidewalks. I don't know how to walk on anything that isn't flat. I'm sorry."

"Don't be sorry. It happens. Can you get to the four-wheeler?"

She made an attempt to put weight on her ankle and cried out in pain. "I don't mean to be such a big baby."

"I'm just sorry you hurt yourself. Here, I can carry you over to the four-wheeler. If it's still hurting when we reach the ranch, Dana will take you over to the medical center."

"Are you sure you can carry me?" she asked. "I'm so embarrassed."

"Don't be. I can certainly carry someone as light as you," he said, lifting her into his arms.

She was quite a bit slimmer than Dana since her *cousin* had delivered twin sons not that long ago. Nice that he'd noticed, she thought. She put her arms around his neck, and he carried her with little effort over to the four-wheeler. She hated to let go when he set her down on the seat.

"How's that?" he asked.

She lifted her leg over the side, wincing again in pain but being incredibly brave. "Fine. Thank you."

"No problem." He got on and started the motor. "Dana is going to have my hide, though."

"I'm sure it will be fine by the time we reach the house. I don't want to upset Dana or get you into trouble with her. It's already starting to feel better."

Dee wrapped her arms around Hud's waist, leaning against him again as they descended the mountain. She breathed in the scent of him. She would have him. One way or the other.

After the hike to the falls, Hilde was still trembling an hour later back at the shop. The worst part was that there was no one she could tell. The shove had happened so quickly, even now she couldn't be sure she'd actually felt it. And yet, she knew that Dee had pushed her. Was she trying to scare her?

Or to warn her to back off? The shove had come right after Hilde had asked how long Dee would be staying.

The shop phone rang, making her jump. She really was getting paranoid, she thought as she answered. "Needles and Pins."

"Hi," Dana said. "I just wanted to call and tell you what time we're floating the Gallatin tomorrow."

"Dana, I—"

"Do. Not. Try. To. Get. Out. Of. This."

"You don't need me," Hilde said, and realized she *was* sounding jealous. "I really should work."

"I know business is slow right now. Remember? I'm your silent partner. So don't tell me you have to work. Come on. When was the last time you floated the river?"

"I've never floated it."

"*What?* You've never been down the Mad Mile?"

"No, and I really don't think I want to do it now when the river is so high. Dana, are you sure this is a good idea?"

"I've already talked to Dee. She's excited. She was trying to get Hud to go with us. Stacy said she'd watch the kids, since Hud said he had something he had to do. Dee was excited to hear you were going with us."

I'll just bet she was.

"Come on. It's going to be fun. You need a thrill or two in your life."

"Don't I, though." What could she say? That there was something not quite right about Dee Anna Justice? That the woman had shoved her at the top of the falls? But then grabbed her to "save" her?

"Great," Dana was saying. "We'll pick you up tomorrow at your place so we can all ride together."

"Great," Hilde said. By the time she hung up, she'd almost convinced herself that Dee hadn't pushed her. That there was nothing to worry about. That she was just jealous. Or crazy.

More likely crazy, she thought, glancing out the front window of the shop hoping to see Colt Dawson. His usual table was empty.

Colt was at the marshal's office filling out paperwork when Hud walked in.

"I would really appreciate it if you would go on this rafting trip with Dana and her cousin this afternoon," Hud said. "Dana's cousin is a little clumsy. Hell, a whole lot clumsy. I don't want her falling off the raft and taking Dana with her."

Colt looked at his boss. "You aren't really asking me to babysit your wife and her cousin, are you? Why don't you go?"

"I have to take care of a few things at the station. Oh, and I did mention Hilde is going, right?"

Colt swore under his breath. "You think that's going to make me change my mind?"

Hud grinned. "I could make it an order if that would make you feel better."

"You should be worried about Hilde drowning *me*."

His boss laughed. "You'll grow on her over time. Look how you've grown on all of us around here."

"Yeah. What time do I have to be there?"

"You probably better go change." He told him the name of the raft company and where they would be loading in about an hour. "Good luck."

Colt ignored him as he left to head to his cabin. When he'd taken the job, he'd lucked out and gotten a five-year lease on a small cabin in the woods outside of Big Sky. One of the biggest problems with working in the area was finding a reasonable place to live.

At the cabin, he changed into shorts, a T-shirt and river sandals. As he did he wondered what Hilde would have to say when she saw him. He'd never been tongue-tied around women—until Hilde. What was it about her? She seemed unfazed by him. He really didn't know what to do when he was around her.

He knew what he wanted to do. Carry her off and make mad passionate love to her. Just the thought stirred the banked fire inside him.

Colt shook his head, realizing how inappropriate his thoughts were under the circumstances. Hilde hadn't looked twice at him. His chances of getting her to go out on a date with him didn't even look good.

Well, he'd make this float with her and Dana and Dana's cousin because Hud had asked him to keep an eye on them. But he would give Hilde a wide berth. She'd made it clear she wasn't interested. The best thing he could do was move on. Maybe there'd be some young woman on the raft who'd want to go out to dinner later tonight. Best advice he had was to get back on that horse that had thrown him.

With that in mind, he drove down the canyon to where the rafting company was loading the rafts. Dana waved him over as he got out of his pickup. Her cousin stood next to her. He did a double take. The two looked a lot like each other, especially since they were both wearing their hair back. Her cousin was a little slimmer and not as pretty as Dana. There was a hardness to the woman that Dana lacked.

Hilde was standing off to the side, her arms crossed over her chest. He got the feeling she didn't want to be here any more than he did. She wore white shorts and a bright blue print sleeveless top. Her honey-colored hair was pulled up in a way that made her look even more uptight.

He gave her a nod and turned his attention to Dana and her cousin.

"This is my cousin Dee Anna Justice," Dana said.

"Just call me Dee." The woman shook his hand, her gaze locking with his, clearly flirting with him.

"Colt Dawson."

"Colt is a deputy marshal. He works with Hud."

"How interesting," Dee said, still holding his hand.

He didn't pull away. He knew Hilde was probably watching him. Impulsively, he said, "Maybe you'd like to hear more about crime in the canyon at dinner tonight."

"Maybe I would," Dee agreed and looked to Dana.

"Oh, remember? My family is coming tonight for dinner at the ranch so they can meet you," Dana said. "Colt, why don't you come?"

"No, I couldn't. I—"

"I know you don't have other plans," Dana pointed out.

She had him there.

"Hilde's coming, too," Dana said.

He glanced at Hilde. She was studying the ground at her feet, poking one sandaled foot almost angrily at the dirt.

Minutes later, they were all dressed in wet suits and life jackets provided by the rafting company. Dee latched onto his arm as they started to load the rafts, riders sitting three across.

Their guide, though, had him move to a spot on the outside next to an older woman and her husband. In the row directly in front of him, Dee was forced to sit in the middle with Dana on one side and Hilde on the other. Both Hilde and Dana were given paddles.

From where he sat, he could catch only glimpses of Hilde. As their guide shoved the raft off from the shore, everyone on the sides paddled as they'd been instructed. The raft went around in circles for a few minutes before everyone got the hang of it.

Hilde took to paddling as if she'd done it before. The woman was right about one thing. She was serious in most everything she did. He liked that about her and felt like a jackass for having asked Dee out in front of her.

Now they would all be at some family dinner tonight at Cardwell Ranch. He couldn't imagine anything more uncomfortable—unless it was this raft ride.

The river swept them slowly downstream past huge, round boulders and through glistening, clear green water. A cool breeze stirred the trees along the bank. Overhead, white puffy clouds bobbed along. It was the perfect day for a raft trip.

Hilde tried to relax and enjoy herself, but the memory of what had happened up at the falls made her edgy. She was only too aware of Dee in the seat next to her. She could feel the woman watching her as if measuring her for a coffin. Who was Dee Anna Justice? Not the woman Dana thought she was, that much was clear.

But how was Hilde going to convince Dana of that?

Maybe it was better to keep it to herself; after all, Dee would be leaving soon and probably never coming back.

Out of the corner of her eye, she could hear Dana and Dee talking and laughing as the raft picked up speed. Behind her, she was aware of Colt. She'd heard him ask Dee out. Not very subtle, she thought, realizing that she'd hurt him when she'd turned him down for a date. That surprised her.

She tried to concentrate on the river and her paddling. But it was hard with Dee so close and Colt probably watching everything she did. He probably hoped she'd end up in the river.

The Gallatin was known as one of the premiere rafting rivers in the West. The river wound through the narrow canyon with both leisurely waters as well as white-water rapids.

Most of the raft trip so far had been through fairly calm waters, the navigation easy. They'd passed through a few sets of rapids here and there that had had most everyone on the raft screaming as they'd roared through them, water splashing over the raft, Hilde and the other paddlers paddling furiously to keep the raft from turning or capsizing.

But Hilde knew that the rough part was ahead, where they would have to run technical rapids past House Rock for the Mad Mile in the lower canyon.

The Mad Mile was a mile of continuous rapids. The cold water ran fast with huge waves, holes and a lot of adrenaline paddling in the Class IV water. That stretch of river required more precise maneuvering, especially this time of year when the river was higher, and she wasn't looking forward to that.

Hilde noticed that Dee and Dana seemed to be having a great time. She was glad she'd decided not to say anything to Dana. She could almost talk herself into believing that Dee hadn't pushed her at the falls. Almost.

She didn't dare sneak a look back at Colt. She concentrated on her paddling. Not telling Dana was the right thing. It wasn't like Dee was…dangerous.

That thought hit her as the raft made the curve in the river just before the Mad Mile. She could hear Dana explaining about the next stretch of river ahead. Dee actually seemed interested.

They made it through the first few rapids, and the raft passed under the bridge. House Rock was ahead, a huge rock that sat in the middle of the river, forcing the fast water to go around it on each side.

The ride became rougher and wetter with spray coming up and over the raft. There were shrieks and screams and laughter as the raft dipped down into a deep hole and shot up again.

Hilde could see House Rock ahead. It was the other rocks they had to maneuver through that were the problem. The guide picked a line down through the rocks and shouted instructions to the paddlers.

The standing waves were huge. The raft went into the first one, buckling under them. The front of the raft shot down into the huge swell, then quickly upward, stalling for a moment.

Hilde reached with her paddle to grab the top of the wave and help the raft slip over it when suddenly her side of the raft swamped. She tried to lean to the middle of the boat, but Dee was pushing against her. Before she knew what was happening, she was in the water, the top of the wave crashing down on her, the current pulling her under.

As she struggled to reach the surface, Hilde realized

she wasn't alone. Dee had fallen out of the raft as well—and she had ahold of Hilde's life jacket. She was dragging her under.

She fought to get away, but something was wrong. She couldn't see light above her. Was she trapped against House Rock? She'd heard about kayakers getting caught against the rock and almost drowning.

But she wasn't against a rock. She was rushing downriver through the huge rapids—trapped under the raft. Somehow, her life jacket had gotten hooked onto a line under the raft. As she struggled to get it off, she realized Dee still had hold of her. She kicked out at the woman, struck something hard, then worked again to free herself.

She couldn't hold her breath any longer. The weight of the raft was holding her down. If she didn't breathe soon—

Arms grabbed her from behind. She flailed at them, trying to free herself from the life jacket and Dee's grip on her. The life jacket finally came off. She had to free herself from Dee's hold and swim out from under the raft before she drowned.

The darkness began to close in. She could no longer go without air. She felt her body give in to the strong grip on her.

Chapter 5

Hilde came to lying on a large flat rock with Colt Dawson kissing her. At least that was her first impression as she felt his mouth on hers. She coughed and had to sit up, gasping for breath.

She could see where the raft had pulled over downstream. The guide was leaning over Dee, who was lying on the side of the raft. "Dee." It was all she could get out before she started coughing again.

"Dee's all right," he said.

Hilde shook her head and let out a snort. "She tried to drown me." Her voice sounded hoarse and hurt like the devil.

Colt looked at her for a full minute before he said, "She tried to save you and almost drowned."

She shook her head more adamantly. "She was the one who hooked my life jacket on the rope under the raft." Hilde could see he didn't believe her. "It's not the first time she's tried to hurt me. When we were up at the falls, she pushed me."

He seemed to be waiting.

"Then she grabbed me just before I fell."

Colt nodded and she realized how crazy she must sound. But if he had been under that raft with her...

"Is Dana all right?" she asked, looking downriver.

"She's just worried about you."

"And *Dee*," Hilde said, seeing how her friend was clutching Dee's hand.

"She's probably worried about Dee because her cousin almost drowned, and this raft trip was her idea," Colt said. "You apparently kicked Dee in the face."

"Because she was trying to hold me down while she hooked my life jacket to that rope." She could see that he didn't believe her and felt her eyes burn hot with tears. "Colt, you have to believe me—there is something wrong with her cousin. I was under that raft with her. She wouldn't let go of me. She hooked my life jacket onto that rope. If you find my jacket..." She was trying to get to her feet.

"Hilde, I'm not sure what you think happened under the raft—"

"I don't know why I expected you to believe me," she said angrily. "Especially about someone you have a date with tonight." He reached for her as she stumbled to her feet, but she brushed off his hand. Stepping down through the rocks, she found a place to cross that wasn't too swift. She could hear him behind her.

All she could think about was getting to Dana, telling her the truth about Dee. Dee was dangerous. Dana had to be warned.

She still felt woozy and should have known better, but

she made her way downstream toward the raft. Dana was still holding Dee's hand as she approached. The sight angered her even more.

Hilde remembered right before she'd gone into the river. She'd tried to lean back, but Dee was pushing on her, pushing her out of the boat and going with her. There was no doubt in her mind that the woman had tried to drown her.

"She tried to kill me," Hilde cried, pointing a trembling finger at Dee, who lay on the edge of the raft clearly enjoying all the attention she was getting.

"Are you all right?" the guide asked, sounding scared.

"Did you hear what I said?" she demanded of Dana. "Your cousin tried to kill me."

Everyone on the raft went deathly quiet. "She pushed me off the raft, then she pulled me under and hooked my life jacket on the rope underneath the boat. If Colt hadn't pulled me out of there…" Hilde realized she was crying and near hysteria. Everyone was looking at her as if she was out of her mind.

"I tried to help you," Dee said in a small, tearful voice. She touched her cheek, which Hilde saw was black-and-blue. "If you hadn't kicked me I would have gotten you free from under the raft."

"She almost drowned trying to save you," Dana said.

Hilde let out a lunatic's laugh. "*Save* me? I'm telling you she tried to kill me, and it wasn't the first time." She felt someone touch her arm and turned her head to see Colt standing beside her.

"Let me get you off the river and into some dry clothes," he said, his gaze locking with hers. She saw the pleading in his eyes. He thought she was making a fool of herself. No one believed her. Everyone believed

Dee. "I'll take care of Hilde," Colt said to Dana. "You make sure your cousin is okay."

Crying harder, she looked at Dana, saw the shock and disbelief and pity in her eyes. Through the haze of tears she saw all the others staring at her with a mixture of pity and gratitude that it hadn't been them under the raft.

Her gaze settled on Dee. A whisper of a smile touched her lips, before she, too, began to cry. As Dana tried to assure her cousin that Hilde was just upset, that she hadn't meant what she'd said, Colt urged Hilde toward the edge of the river and the vehicles waiting on the highway above it. The guide had apparently called for EMTs and a rescue crew.

"I don't need a doctor," she said to Colt, as he drew her away from the raft. She could feel everyone watching her and tried to stem the flow of her tears. "I don't need you to take care of me."

"But you do need to get into some dry clothes," he said. "My place is close by."

She looked over at him, ready to tell him she had no intention of going to his house with him.

"You can tell me again what happened under the raft," he said.

"What would be the point? You don't believe me." She stumbled on one of the rocks. He caught her arm to keep her from falling. His hand felt warm and strong on her skin.

"How about this? I believe you more than I believe Dee."

She stopped, having reached the edge of the highway, and glared at him. "Then why didn't you speak up back there?"

"Because it's your word against hers, and as upset as

you are, she is more believable right now. That's why I stopped you from telling them about what happened at the falls. Come on, I know this EMT. He'll give us a ride."

"I am so sorry," Dana said for the hundredth time since the raft trip.

Dee planned to milk the incident for all it was worth but was getting tired of hearing Dana apologize. Almost drowning had gotten her out of helping with the huge family meal Dana had cooked. It also had Hud hovering protectively over her.

Dana had told all the family members about the mishap on the river as each arrived. Dee noticed that she'd left out the part about her best friend accusing her cousin of trying to kill her.

It would have been amusing except for the fact that Hilde had almost drowned *her*. Hilde had kicked her hard. For a moment, she'd seen stars. She really could have drowned under that raft. She was lucky she hadn't died today.

She'd had to meet all the family before dinner. There was the sister, Stacy, a smaller version of Dana, whom she'd met only briefly before. She had a pretty, green-eyed baby girl named Ella. Dee remembered that because she got the feeling Stacy might be a good resource—even an ally in the future.

Jordan and his wife, Deputy Marshal Liza Cardwell, were nice enough, but both were wrapped up in each other. Newlyweds, Dana had said. Then there was their father, Angus, and their uncle, Harlan. The talk at that end of the table was about the house Jordan and Liza were building somewhere on the ranch. Far enough away that they hadn't been a problem, Dee thought.

Apparently Dana had another brother, Clay. He worked in the movies in Hollywood and seldom came up to the ranch. Another positive. Hud's father, Brick, wasn't well. He lived in West Yellowstone and seldom got down the canyon. That was also good since he was an ex-marshal.

At the sound of a knock at the front door, Dee looked through the open dining room door into the living room. She could make out a dark shadow through the window.

Probably not Hilde or Deputy Colt Dawson, she thought with no small amount of relief. Hilde had come off as crazy on the river earlier. Dana had been shocked by her friend's accusations and torn in her loyalties. Dee had pretended to be hurt, which only made Dana more protective of her.

Hopefully that would be the last they saw of the woman, she thought, rubbing her jaw. It didn't surprise her that Hilde was turning out to be a problem. That first day Hilde had asked too many questions and was too protective of Dana. Not only that, she paid too much attention.

She suspects something is wrong.

Dee had run across a few intuitive people in her life. Best thing to do was get them out of your life as quickly as possible. After what happened on the river today, she didn't think she would have to worry about Hilde again.

She'd seen the moment when Hilde had realized there was nothing she could say to convince Dana that cousin Dee had been responsible for her almost drowning. Blood was thicker than water—didn't Hilde know that? Dee almost laughed at the thought since she and Dana shared none in common. But it didn't matter as long as Dana believed they did.

All the others on the raft had felt sorry for Dee. Everyone agreed Hilde was just upset and confused. They had tried to comfort Dee, telling her she shouldn't feel bad. The bruise on her cheek from where Hilde had kicked her was now like a badge of honor. She'd tried to save the woman—but there was no saving Hilde from Hilde, she thought now with a silent chuckle.

But apparently Deputy Marshal Colt Dawson was determined to try. Nice that he forgot he'd asked her for a dinner date tonight. She hoped she wasn't wrong about him not being at the door. No, he was probably home taking care of poor Hilde.

She'd seen Dana on the phone earlier. No doubt checking on her friend. Dana was so sure that once Hilde calmed down she would realize that Dee hadn't tried to drown her. So far Dana hadn't seemed to have any doubts to the contrary. Dee had to make sure she stayed that way.

Hud got up from the table to go answer the second knock at the door. Dee got the impression that most anyone who stopped by just walked in and didn't bother knocking.

As the door swung open, she felt her heart drop. She stumbled out of her chair and into the living room. "Rick?"

He saw her and smiled. Anyone watching would have thought everything was fine. Dee knew better.

"Rick, what a surprise." She hurried to the door, belatedly remembering to limp only the last few steps. She'd managed to hurt herself again in the river—at least that was her story. It would get her out of helping Dana with the dishes and the kids.

"I had to come after I got your phone call," he said smoothly. "Are you all right?"

"It's just a sprain," she said, and realized Hud was

watching and waiting for an introduction. Before Dee could, Dana joined them.

"Rick, this is my cousin Dana I told you about and her husband, Hud. Rick... Cameron, a friend of mine from back East." She gave Rick a warning look. "We were just sitting down to a family dinner. Tell me where you're staying and I'll—"

"We always have room for one more," Dana said quickly. "Please join us. Any friend of Dee's is welcome."

Rick stepped in, letting the door close behind him as he looked around, amused at her discomfort. "*Dee,* are you sure you're all right? I've been worried about you."

"I'm fine. You really didn't need to come all this way just to check on me." She bit the words off, angry with him for showing up here and even angrier that he didn't take the hint and leave. She hung back with him as Hud and Dana returned to the large family dining room, where everyone else was waiting.

"What are you doing here?" she demanded under her breath so no one else could hear.

"Is that any way to greet an old friend, *Dee?*"

Her mind whirled. How had he found her? Then with a curse, she realized what she'd done. She'd left a change of address so she could get Dee Anna Justice's mail in care of the ranch. That way she'd know quickly if her cover was blown—as well as collect at least one of Dee Anna's trust fund checks.

In retrospect that had been a mistake. She should have known Rick would come looking for her once he realized she'd bailed on him and the apartment. He'd know the real Dee Anna hadn't gone to a ranch in Montana.

"You can't stay," she whispered. "You'll mess up everything."

He smiled at her. "I can't tell you how good it is to see you, *Dee*."

"Stop doing that."

"I set another place for you, Rick," Dana called from the dining room doorway. "Come join us and I'll introduce you to everyone."

Dee had indigestion by the time the meal wound down. Dana had introduced Rick, and he'd seemed to be enjoying himself, which made it worse. She couldn't wait until dinner was over so she could get him out of here. The trick would be getting him out of town.

Rick could smell a con a mile off. The fact that she was going by Dee Anna Justice had been a dead giveaway. He knew she was up to something. He would want something out of this.

She couldn't have been more relieved when dinner was finally over. Fortunately, because of her re-"sprained" ankle, she didn't have to help with the dishes. Rick helped clear the table. She heard him chatting in the kitchen with Hud and Dana.

She was going to kill him.

Finally, Rick said he was leaving and asked Dee if she felt up to walking him out to his rental car. She wouldn't have missed it for the world.

"You have to leave," she told him outside.

He glanced at the stars sparkling in the velvet canopy overhead and took a deep breath. "This is nice here. A little too hick for me, but the food was good," he said, finally looking at her. "I've missed you. I thought you would have at least left me a note."

"What do you want?"

"You always were good at cutting right to the heart of it. Isn't it possible I really did miss you?"

"No." He hadn't come here for a reunion. If anything, he'd come to blackmail her.

"Look," she said. "I will cut you in, but I need time. I don't even know what there is here yet."

He laughed. "You can call yourself Dee or anything else you like, but remember, I *know* you. You've staked out something here or you would be gone by now. Is it the land? Is it worth something? Or is there family money I'm just not seeing?"

"There isn't any hidden wealth," she said. "I'm just spending a few days here like a tourist while my cousin shows me a good time. She's picking up my little vacation. That's it."

"You're such a good liar. Usually. But I don't get what you could possibly be thinking here. Does Hud have a rich brother I haven't met yet?"

"Rick—"

"You'd better get back into the house," he said, glancing past her. "You really shouldn't be on that bad ankle too long." He chuckled. "Don't forget to limp or you're going to be doing dishes with the women in the kitchen the rest of your little vacation."

With that, he climbed into his rental car and slammed the door. She slapped the window, trying to get him to roll it down, but he merely made a face at her, started the engine and drove off.

She stood in the faint moonlight mentally kicking herself. Rick was going to ruin everything.

"Are you feeling better?" Colt asked, as Hilde came out of his bathroom dressed in the sweatpants and T-shirt he'd given her.

She nodded. He'd changed into jeans and a T-shirt

that molded his muscled body. She'd never seen him in anything but his uniform before. No wonder he was so popular with women.

He handed her a mug of hot chocolate with tiny marshmallows floating in it. He must have seen her surprise.

"My mother used to always make me hot chocolate when I had a hard day in school," Colt said, and grinned shyly. "I thought it might help."

She curled her fingers around the mug, soaking in the warmth, and took a sip. She couldn't help smiling. "It's perfect." She was touched at his thoughtfulness. "I don't believe I thanked you for saving my life earlier."

He waved her apology away. "I'm just glad you're okay. Would you like to sit down?" he asked, motioning to his couch.

She glanced around his cabin. It was simply but comfortably furnished. He'd made a fire in the small fireplace. This time of year it cooled down quickly in the canyon.

The fire crackled invitingly as she took a seat at one end of the couch, curling her feet under her. She'd finally quit shaking. Now she just felt scared. Scared that she was right about Dee. Even more scared that she wasn't. Had she wrongly accused the woman?

Colt seemed to relax as he joined her at the opposite end of the couch. "Why don't you tell me about Dee?"

She hesitated, upset with herself for the scene she'd made earlier. It was so unlike her. No wonder Dana had looked so shocked. She shouldn't have confronted Dee in front of everyone, but she'd been so upset, so scared. She'd almost drowned. If Colt hadn't pulled her out when he had…

"You can tell me how you really feel," he said quietly.

She took a breath. "I don't know anymore."

"Sure you do," he said and smiled. "Follow your instincts. I have a feeling your instincts are pretty good."

Hilde laughed. "After seeing that hysterical woman on the river a while ago?"

"Almost drowning does that to a person."

She studied him for a moment. He was way too handsome, but he was also very nice. He'd saved her life and now he was willing to listen to her side of it. "What if my instincts are wrong?"

"You know they aren't."

Did she? She took another sip of the hot chocolate. It *did* help. Bracing herself, she said, "There's something… off about Dee."

He nodded, urging her to continue.

"I admit I was worried when Dana told me that she'd asked a cousin she'd never met to come visit. She's paying for all Dee's expenses. That seemed odd to me. But according to Dana, Dee recently quit her job. Add to that, no one knows how long she plans to stay."

"So you thought right away she might be taking advantage of your friend."

Hilde nodded. "After we picked her up at the airport, Dana was telling her all about this area. I noticed that she didn't seem interested. It wasn't until we reached the ranch and she met Hud that Dee perked up."

He nodded but said nothing.

"I know this all sounds so…small and petty."

"Tell me about the day at the falls."

She finished the hot chocolate and put her mug on the table next to her elbow, noticing the bestseller lying open, his place marked halfway through the book. It was one she'd been wanting to read, and she was momentarily distracted to know that Colt was a reader.

"I didn't want to go on the hike, but Dana insisted. I was probably rude. I asked how long Dee planned to stay. Shortly after that I was standing at the edge of the falls. Dana had gone over to the picnic spot to look for her camera, and all of a sudden I felt a hand on my back and a hard shove. Then Dee grabbed me and warned me to be careful, that it was dangerous around here."

"You believed it was a threat."

"I did."

"But you didn't say anything to Dana."

"I was too shocked and—"

"You talked yourself out of believing it."

She nodded. "Also, Dana was enjoying her cousin so much, I didn't have the heart to tell her."

"You feared she wouldn't believe you."

Hilde let out a laugh. "With good reason. She didn't believe that Dee tried to drown me today."

"But you do."

She swallowed, then slowly nodded. "She wasn't trying to save me. I know you find that hard to believe because I tried to fight you off moments later, when you were only trying to save me."

"Why do you think she pushed you at the falls and yet saved you, then today tried to drown you and maybe really did try to save you?"

"I don't know. It makes one of us seem crazy, doesn't it?"

He smiled. "What is it you think she wants? Dana and Hud don't have a lot money. She can't possibly think she can get her hands on the ranch. She's going to wear out her welcome within a week or so."

"That's just it, I don't know. I just can't get over the feeling that she wants something from Dana. But the more I think about it, the more I feel I must be wrong. What if I'm overreacting? Maybe she *was* trying to save me in the river today."

"Maybe she didn't push you at the falls?"

She looked away. "Dana thinks I'm jealous." She turned to meet his gaze. "Maybe I am." She got to her feet. "I should go home."

Colt rose, too. "What are you going to do?"

"Stay away from Dee," she said with a laugh. "Like you said, she'll wear out her welcome and leave."

"Hud called while you were changing clothes. He's taking Dee up to Elkhorn Lake on a horseback ride tomorrow. Dana's idea. I think we should go."

"*What?* And give her another chance at me?"

He grinned. "That's what I thought. You don't think you imagined any of this. Dee's dangerous, isn't she?"

"Yes. But you're the only person who believes me. Dee always comes away looking like a hero."

"Almost as if she planned it that way. If you really think Hud and Dana are in danger, then I think we need to keep an eye on Dee. Meanwhile, I'll be keeping an eye on you."

Hilde couldn't help but feel a small thrill at the last part. She liked the idea of Colt keeping an eye on her. She told herself not to make anything of it.

"The last thing I want to do is go on a long horseback ride with Dee Anna Justice. What makes you so sure she won't try to kill me again?"

"I can't promise that. But it will look more than a little odd if you meet with yet another accident. I have a plan. But you probably won't like it."

She didn't, but she was so thankful that Colt believed her, she would have gone along with anything he asked.

"Right now, she's won," he said. "You need to throw her off balance and stay close to Dana. There's only one way to do that."

"He's a boyfriend, isn't he?" Dana said excitedly when Dee returned to the house after walking Rick out. Hud had apparently gone up to bed. Everyone else had left as she was coming back into the house.

"No, he's…" She saw the sympathy in Dana's expression. Her "cousin" was waiting for some heartbreaking love story. How could she disappoint her with so much at stake?

"Your ex, isn't he." Her cousin drew her over to the couch and patted the cushion, indicating she should sit and spill all. Dee was thankful she had only Dana to deal with now. Dana saw what she wanted to and clearly loved finding a cousin she'd never known she had. Hilde wouldn't have been fooled by her relationship with Rick.

"I can tell he still cares about you," Dana was saying. "He followed you all the way to Montana to make sure you were all right."

Maybe it would be better for everyone to think Rick was a boyfriend, then when she broke up with him and sent him packing, it would play well with the family. It could buy her more time here. She wouldn't want to go back East right away after such a traumatic breakup.

"That's why you quit your job," Dana said. "Did you work with him?"

Why not give her what she wanted and then some? "He was my boss."

"Oh, those kinds of things are so…sticky."

"I knew better, but he was unrelenting."

"I can see that in him. To fly all the way out here."

"I should never have called him and told him where I was. But I knew he'd worry and I certainly shouldn't have mentioned that I sprained my ankle."

"You couldn't know that he'd follow you," Dana said. "He seems nice, though. Is there no chance for the two of you?"

No chance in hell. "He's married," she lied.

Dana looked worried. "Children?"

Dee shook her head. "He and his wife are separated. He's always wanted children, but his wife didn't. She says she doesn't like kids."

Her cousin looked shocked. "Oh, how awful for him."

"Yes. I feel sorry for him, but he needs to try to work things out with his wife."

Dana agreed.

Dee realized she was painting too sympathetic a picture of Rick. "He's been so despondent since I broke it off and…" She lowered her voice. "He's been taking… pills. I'm worried sick he might do something…crazy, between the depression and the drugs. Still I shouldn't have called him to check on him." Like she would have ever called him, but she was grateful that Rick was quick on his feet when it came to lying.

"You did the right thing. Just imagine how you would have felt if you hadn't called and something had happened to him."

"Hmm," she said. "You're right. But maybe I should go back home. I hate bringing my problems to your door."

"Don't be silly." Dana reached out and squeezed her hand. "That's what family is for."

She'd always wondered what family was for. A part

of her felt sorry for Dana. The woman was so caring. It must be exhausting.

"You're tired and you've had such an emotional day," her cousin said, glancing at her watch. The fact that Dana still wore a watch and didn't always carry a cell phone told Dee how far from civilization she now was.

"I hope Hilde is all right." She watched Dana's expression out of the corner of her eye, trying to calculate whether or not Dana would call her friend to patch things up or not.

"It's just a good thing Colt was there," Dana said. "He'll take care of her. I'll give her a call later to make sure."

"I feel badly about what she said."

"Don't let it bother you. She was just talking crazy because she was scared. Still, it wasn't like the Hilde I know at all."

She could tell Dana was worried about her friend. "Almost drowning would do that to anyone. I just don't want to come between the two of you."

"You won't. I shouldn't have insisted Hilde come on the raft trip. It really isn't her thing. And anyone would have panicked if they'd been trapped under the raft like that."

"It was just such a freak accident," she agreed.

"I'm sure Hilde realized that, once she had a chance to calm down. I wouldn't be surprised if she shows up tomorrow to apologize."

Don't hold your breath on that one. "I hate to even ask what you have planned for tomorrow," Dee said with a small laugh. She hoped Dana would come up with something away from the ranch with Hud and as far away as possible from Big Sky and Hilde and Rick. "You really are showing me such a great time. How will I ever be able to repay you?"

"It's my pleasure. I thought you'd like to ride up to Elk-horn Lake."

"So you'll be able to go?" she asked.

"No, I have to stay here. Hud is going to take you by horseback, if you're up to it. The lake is beautiful and the trip is really wonderful."

Oh, yes. She couldn't wait.

"I think his deputy Colt is going along."

Dee swore silently. Colt? The man who'd saved Hilde.

"It sounds like fun," she said, although it had sounded much more fun when it was just going to be her and Hud. "I just wish you could go. Maybe next time?"

Dana nodded. "You must come back every year."

Or never leave. "Oh, I would love that."

"Well, sleep tight and don't worry about Rick."

Easy for Dana to say.

Chapter 6

The next morning, Dee got up early and borrowed Dana's pickup to drive into Meadow Village. She still didn't get the town of Big Sky. Everything was so spread out, but it was all close enough that it didn't take her long to find Rick's rental car parked in front of an older motor court motel.

Rick had always been cheap, usually out of necessity because he was broke. She could only guess that that was the case this time.

She had to knock three times before he finally opened the door wearing nothing but a towel wrapped around his waist.

"I wondered when you'd show up," he said with a grin.

She shoved past him into the room. It was pretty much what she expected: bed, television, bathroom. A discount-store piece of so-called art of a mountain from some other state hung on the wall over the unmade bed. Rick's clothes were strewn on the floor and there were a half-dozen empty beer cans next to the bed.

"You always were a slob," she said, turning to look at him. "You have to leave. Now."

"I wish I could, but I spent every dime I had just to get here to see you."

How had she known that was the case? She reached into her shoulder bag. "Here's enough to get you back home and a little extra so you won't starve on the way. The next flight is this afternoon. Be on it." With that she started to leave. "And Rick. No drugs."

"Come on, you know I'm clean. Anyway, you need my help."

She stopped next to him. "No, I don't. I know what I'm doing."

"You and I used to make a pretty good team, as I recall. I'm probably the only person you can truly trust."

"Unless you get drunk or high and shoot your mouth off."

"I've kept your secrets all these years, drunk or sober. Come on, there's a bond between us that not even you can deny." He touched her shoulder.

She pulled away. "I mean it. Don't buy drugs with that money."

"Don't try to kill that blonde woman again."

"I don't know what you're talking about."

"Remember when you and I were little more than kids and I almost drowned? I know you, remember?"

"Then you know to stay out of my business, don't you."

By the time she returned to the ranch, Hud was busy saddling horses. She drove into the yard, but didn't get out of the truck right away. She liked watching him, watching the muscles in his arms and back, imagining being in those arms. Desire hit her like a sucker punch. She wanted him, and she'd always made a habit of getting what she wanted, any way she had to.

"Best get dressed," Hud called to her, as she climbed out of the truck. "Dana's put out some clothes for you to wear in your room."

She smiled. "Thanks." Inside she went right to her upstairs room. She could hear Dana in the kitchen with the kids. How could the woman stand that noise all the time?

She quickly dressed in the Western attire her cousin had so thoughtfully put out for her, right down to the cowboy boots. Fortunately or unfortunately they were close enough in size that all the clothes fit.

"They're my prebaby clothes," Dana said when Dee came downstairs in them. "I knew they would fit you."

They did, she thought, as she caught a glimpse of herself in the front window reflection. At a glance, she could pass for Dana. A slightly skinnier version, but still…

Dana had made her a breakfast sandwich since she'd apparently missed the usual ranch breakfast. She couldn't believe how these people ate. It was no wonder Dana hadn't gotten back to her pretwins weight.

Breakfast often consisted of pounded and floured fried deer steaks, hash browns, milk gravy, biscuits and eggs. She'd never seen anything like it in her life. There would be changes if she were running this house.

There would have to be a lot of changes. She realized with a start that she hadn't thought this through. Getting Hud would be hard enough. But what to do with Dana and the kids? Dana would have to go. So would the kids.

She wasn't interested in having them even come visit on weekends or summers.

She thought of Rick. Maybe he could be helpful after all. She was debating calling him to tell him they should talk, when she looked out and saw with a groan that Hud was saddling *five* horses.

"I see Hud has saddled a bunch of horses," she said nonchalantly to her cousin over the screaming of the children. "Did you decide you could go on the ride with us after all?"

Dana smiled but shook her head. "I need to spend some time with my babies."

"Then Mary and Hank are going?" She was amazed that she finally remembered their names. They were cute kids. If you liked kids.

"No," Dana said with a laugh. "They're too young for this ride."

Just then the front door opened. She turned and was unable to hide her shock as Hilde came in duded out in Western attire. "Hilde?"

"Dee," the young woman said. She hurried to Dee and took both her hands. "I am so sorry about yesterday. Can you ever forgive me?"

Even if she hadn't been good at reading people, she would have seen through *this* apology. But out of the corner of her eye, she saw that Dana was smiling, buying into every word of it. The only gracious thing to do was pretend it was real.

"Hilde, you don't need to apologize, really. I was so scared for you. I'm just glad you're all right. It was such a freak accident."

"Wasn't it, though?" Hilde agreed. "Thank you for being so understanding. I told Dana I couldn't wait until

I saw you to tell you how sorry I was for thinking you had anything to do with my almost drowning."

I'll just bet. "Well, it's good to see you looking so well today. Thanks for coming by."

"Hilde's going on the ride up to the lake with all of you," Dana said.

It took all her effort not to show how that news really made her feel. Hilde was smiling as if she knew exactly what Dee was feeling right now. Apparently such a close call with death hadn't taught Hilde anything.

"That's great," Dee said. "But I would think you'd want to stay home and rest today after what you've been through."

"That's what I told her," Dana said. "But Hilde is tougher than she looks." She smiled and gave Hilde's arm a squeeze.

"I'm not so tough," Hilde said to her friend. "Look at your cousin. She almost drowned yesterday, too, and look how *she's* bounced back." Hilde turned back to her. "Oh, Dee, that bruise on your cheek looks like it hurts. Did I do that?"

"I know you didn't mean to," Dana said quickly.

Ha, Dee thought. "So who else is going with us?" she asked just an instant before Hud came in the door with Colt Dawson right behind him and Rick bringing up the tail end. "Is anyone protecting Big Sky?" Dee asked. "It seems the entire force is right here."

"The other two deputies are holding down the fort," Colt said. "So don't worry about the canyon being safe while we're here with you."

Dee swore silently as Hud asked if they were ready to go. "I can't wait," she said. Rick was more of a dude than she was. She hoped he got saddle sores.

As they all filed out to the saddled horses, she wondered what the trail was like to this Elkhorn Lake. Hopefully it wasn't too dangerous. She would hate to see anything happen to Hilde. Let alone Rick. Horses were so unpredictable.

Before she mounted her horse, she surreptitiously picked up several nice-sized rocks and stuck them in her pocket.

Colt made sure that he and Hilde stayed behind the others as they rode away from the ranch. He liked riding next to her. It was a beautiful Montana spring day. The air smelled of new green grass, sunshine and water as they followed the creek up into the mountains. Sun dappled the ground as it fingered through the pine branches.

"So tell me about Hilde Jacobson," he said, as their horses ambled along. The others had ridden on ahead, but Colt kept them in sight in case anything happened.

"There isn't much to tell," she said. Then, as if realizing he really was interested, she added, "I grew up in Chicago. My father was a janitor, my mother worked as a housekeeper. I was an only child. My father was determined that I would be the first in his family to go to college."

"And you were?"

She nodded. "I went into business. My father had worked around corporate America and decided that would be the world that I should conquer. I gave it my best shot at least for a while."

"How did you end up in Big Sky owning a fabric store?"

"My father died. My mother told me to follow my

heart. I hated big business. I came up here skiing, met Dana and Hud, and the rest is history."

"You and Dana are close, aren't you?"

"We *were*."

He heard the catch in her throat.

"Your turn," she said after a moment. "Tell me your life story."

"I grew up north of here. I married young. It didn't work out. I went into law enforcement and got the job here."

"You like Big Sky?"

He looked back at the country they'd just left behind and nodded. "It's not as open as I'm used to—the mountains are so much larger—but it grows on you living in the canyon."

"Doesn't it?" she said. "Some people think its paradise and hate to leave."

He saw that she was looking at the two riders ahead of them. Dee was in a deep conversation with Hud. Rick was nowhere to be seen.

Dee was leaning toward Hud and pretending to be fascinated by the different types of rock faces ahead when Hilde and Colt came riding up. Colt cut Hud away from her as slick as the ranch cow dog she'd seen herding calves in the pasture.

A few moments later she found herself riding next to Hilde, also not a coincidence.

"Where's Rick?" Hilde asked, looking behind her. "We seem to have lost him."

"I think he needed to see a tree about a dog. Isn't that what you locals say out here?"

"I'm not a local," Hilde said. "I'm actually from Chicago, and I think it's a dog about a tree."

"Really? I just assumed you were like Hud and Dana, born and raised out West."

"So is Rick from New York City, too? Is that where the two of you met?"

Dee smiled over at her to let her know she knew what she was doing and it wasn't going to work. "I'm still surprised you were up for this ride today after your near-death experience yesterday." She touched the bruise on her cheek. "I know I was still feeling the aftereffects this morning. I didn't realize Montana was such a dangerous place."

"It sure *is*—when you're around." With that, Hilde spurred her horse and rode on up to join Colt and Hud.

So much for that earlier apology, Dee thought with a curse.

She hadn't planned to actually drown Hilde yesterday, but at some point it hadn't seemed like such a bad idea. Dana would have eventually gotten over losing her friend. In fact, she would have needed her cousin even more.

But Dana would have had to lean even more on her husband. Dee had hoped to avoid all of that and just get Hilde to keep her distance. Apparently her plan hadn't worked after the incident at the waterfalls or on the raft trip.

Hilde needed stronger encouragement to get out of her way. Dee stuck her hand into her pocket, closed her fingers around one of the rocks, hefting it in her hand. Ahead, the trail narrowed as it cut across the side of a rocky mountain face. The horses with Hud, Colt and Hilde fell into single file as they started across the narrow trail.

Dee looked down at the drop-off. Nothing but large boulders all the way down to the creek far below. She let Hilde and her horse get a little farther ahead. She didn't want to be nearby when things went awry.

Poor Hilde. She was having such a bad week. First almost falling off Ousel Falls, then almost drowning in the Gallatin River. Clearly she shouldn't have come along on this ride after what had happened yesterday. She really wasn't up to it.

Dee lifted the rock, measuring the distance. The trail was narrow. If a horse bucked off its rider right now, the rider could be badly hurt—if not killed.

She told herself she had no choice. Hilde had managed to get back in Dana's good graces. Dana was more apt to believe whatever Hilde came up with now. And there was no doubt Hilde would be trying to find out everything she could about cousin Dee.

Reining in her horse at the edge of the pines, she pulled back her arm to throw the rock. All she had to do was hit the back of Hilde's horse. If it spooked even a little, it might buck or lose its footing, and both woman and horse could fall.

Just as she was about to hurl the stone, a hand grabbed her arm and twisted the rock from her grip. She let out a cry of both surprise and pain. Turning in her saddle, she swore when she saw it was Rick.

"Don't be a fool," he said under his breath. "If she has another accident this early, it will only make everyone more suspicious."

"I have to stop her. She's onto me."

Rick shook his head. "I'll help you, but not here. Not today. Be nice to her but watch yourself." He dug into her pocket to pull out the other rocks. "Just in case you get another smart idea while looking at *my* horse's backside," he said, and rode on up the trail to catch up with Hilde.

Hilde kept her eye on Dee during the ride to the lake. But the woman seemed almost subdued after their little talk.

Rick spent most of the time talking with Hud on the last part of the ride up and even when they'd reached Elkhorn Lake. Hilde saw Dee watching the two of them. She got the impression Dee didn't like her boyfriend talking with Hud.

When Hud broke out the lunch Dana had packed, Colt brought her over a sandwich and sat down with her on the rocks at the edge of the lake away from the others.

"Have you noticed the way she is with Hud?" she asked quietly before taking a bite of her sandwich. They'd both been watching Dee.

"Yep."

Hilde locked gazes with him. "I think I know what she's after. She wants Hud."

Colt let out a laugh. *"Hud?"*

"I've been trying to figure out what she wants other than a Montana vacation, all expenses paid."

"She likes to flirt."

"Did she flirt with you?"

He admitted she hadn't except for a few minutes at the river before the raft trip and he suspected that little bit of flirting with him had been for Dana's benefit only. "If Hud's what she's after, then she's wasting her time. He's crazy in love with Dana, not to mention they have four kids together. Hud would never be interested in Dee."

"She wouldn't be the first woman who went after another woman's man."

"Or vice versa," Colt said.

Hilde glanced at him. She knew Colt was divorced. Earlier he'd said he'd married young and that it hadn't worked out. Had another man come after his wife? Or had Colt been seduced away from his marriage?

"But I don't believe any woman can get a man to leave his marriage unless he's willing," Colt added, keeping her from asking him about his marriage. "As they say, it takes two to tango."

"I agree," she said. "Hud would never jeopardize his marriage for a fling with someone like Dee." But had Colt?

"So what's Dee's plan, do you think?" Colt asked quietly. They both watched Dee, who was sitting in a tight circle with Hud and Rick. She was taking tiny bites of her sandwich, clearly not interested in food. Rick had Hud talking, and Dee appeared to be hanging on Hud's every word.

"I wish I knew," Hilde said, feeling a growing desperation as she watched the woman. Dee had wormed her way into Dana's and Hud's lives and she wasn't finished yet. "Now that I know what she's capable of, if I'm right and she is after Hud and she can't get him through seduction, then she will do something more drastic. That's what has me scared."

Colt looked up from his lunch to study Hilde. She was breathtaking: the sun on her face, her hair as golden as autumn leaves. He was surprised when he'd first come to Big Sky and learned that Hilde and Dana were best friends. They were so different.

Dana was all tomboy. She could ride and rope and shoot as well as any man. Being a mother had toned her down some, but she was a ranch girl born and bred, and she was at home in the great outdoors.

Hilde was all girl, from the clothes she wore to the way she presented herself. He didn't doubt for a moment that she was smart or that she was strong. She could get tough, too, if she had to. He'd seen that the way she'd gone after Dee on the river, but there was something so wonderfully feminine about her. Clearly she enjoyed being a woman.

The combination of smart, strong and ultra-feminine was more powerful than she knew. He suspected it scared away most men.

Dana had told him that Hilde didn't date much. "She must know the kind of man she wants. I just hope she finds him. Hilde deserves someone special."

Colt looked away. He was far from anyone special, but he did wonder what kind of man she was looking for. Or if she was even looking. He thought of his short marriage and the heartbreak it had caused. He'd told himself he would never marry again. But that was before he met Hilde.

They had just finished their sandwiches when there was a splash followed instantly by a scream. He and Hilde turned to look across the lake in the direction the sound had come from and there was Dee swimming in the clear, cold water.

She was laughing and shrieking, but clearly enjoying herself.

Colt noticed that even Hud was smiling at the crazy Easterner.

When it became apparent that she was nude, the men turned around and let her rush out of the water without them watching.

"Did you see that?" Hilde asked.

"I didn't peek."

"Not Dee. Did you see that even Rick turned around? Doesn't that seem odd if the two were boyfriend and girlfriend?"

Colt shrugged. Everything about Rick Cameron seemed odd to him. Add Dee to the mix and you had a rodeo. "She does like attention," he said.

"And she's getting it. Hud isn't completely immune to her. If for some reason Dana wasn't around…"

Colt frowned as Dee came out of the trees dressed again, her hair wet, her face aglow from her swim.

Hud laughed and shook his head when Dee suggested he should have come into the water. No man was completely immune to a woman's attention, especially one who, on the surface, seemed so much like his wife.

Colt had learned that the hard way.

Chapter 7

After the horseback ride up to the lake, Hilde couldn't wait to get home, shower and curl up in her bed. She hadn't gotten much sleep last night. Add to that everything that had happened to her in the past forty-eight hours and she knew she had good reason to be exhausted.

"Are you sure you don't want to stay and have dinner with us?" Dana had asked. "Hud is going to broil some steaks. I'm making a big salad."

"I would love to, really, but the ride took a lot out of me," Hilde said. She could see that her friend was disappointed, but Hilde had had all the Dee she could take for one day.

She gave Dana a hug, hugging her more tightly than she normally did, afraid for her friend. "Thank you for the offer, though," she said when she let go.

"Once you get to know Dee you'll see how vulnerable

and sweet she…" Dana's words died off as she must have seen something in her friend's expression that stopped her.

"Be careful," Hilde said. "I don't want anything to happen to you."

Dana gave her a sympathetic look, and Hilde sensed that things had changed between them. It made her sad, but she couldn't blame her friend. Dee was like a slow but deadly poison.

"Oh, Hilde, aren't you staying for dinner?" Dee said all cheery, as she came down the stairs. She'd showered and now wore a sundress that accentuated all her assets—which were no small thing. "I know Dana has missed you. I'm afraid she's getting bored with me. I'm not much fun."

"You are plenty fun," Dana said to her cousin. "I could never get bored with you."

"Am I the luckiest woman in the world to have such an amazing cousin?" Dee asked with a too-bright smile. "I'm so glad she found me and invited me to Montana. I'm having a terrific time. I've missed having family so much."

"I know that feeling, so I'm glad," Dana said to her cousin, then turned to Hilde. "Change your mind about dinner."

"Another time." Hilde held Dana's gaze. "Take care of yourself." And she was out the door and headed for her SUV. It was all she could do not to run. She saw Colt glance up from where he and Hud were talking by the corrals. Concern crossed his expression, then his gaze went to the porch where Dee was standing, backlit by the light coming from inside the house.

Dee said something to the two men. Hud laughed and

Dee started to come off the porch toward them. Dana called from the kitchen for her cousin. Dee hesitated, clearly disappointed, but went back inside to help Dana.

On the drive to her house, Hilde felt sick to her stomach. She'd never been violent. She was a forget-and-forgive kind of person. At least she thought she was. But for a few moments back there at the house, she'd wanted to walk back to the porch and punch Dee in the face.

"I really need some rest," she told herself, as she parked in front of her house. Once inside, she showered and changed into her favorite silk robe before padding into the kitchen for a glass of warm milk. She knew she couldn't eat anything the way she felt right now.

Back in the bedroom, she finished the milk and crawled into bed with a book she'd been wanting to read—the same one Colt was reading. A book would be the only thing that could get her mind off Dee and her fears for Dana and her family.

She'd read only a few pages, though, when she must have fallen asleep. When the ringing of the phone woke her, she was lying on the open pages of the book, her cheek creased and damp. It took her a moment to realize what had awakened her.

"Hello?" she said, snatching up the phone. Her first thought was that something had happened out at the ranch. Her heart took off like a shot.

"I was afraid you were out with your boyfriend."

She didn't recognize the voice, but her heart was still pounding. "I beg your pardon? I think you have the wrong number." She recognized the laugh, though, and sat up in the bed, trying to shake off sleep. "Rick?"

"One and the same," he said with another laugh. "I've been sitting here having a few drinks, thinking about you."

Hilde groaned inwardly, afraid where this was headed.

"I know your type," he continued. "You like nice things but you try to hide the fact that you come from money."

She was momentarily surprised by his insight.

"I like nice things, too, but I'm afraid I don't come from money. Far from it." Another laugh. "I'll make you a deal. You want to know the scoop on *Dee?* If you can get your hands on ten thousand dollars, which I have a feeling you can without much trouble, then I will tell you things about dear *Dee* that will make your hair stand on end."

"You sound drunk."

"Not yet."

"Why should I believe you?"

"Because I know she tried to kill you on the river. I'm betting it wasn't the first time she put a scare into you."

"You would sell out your own girlfriend?"

He chuckled. "That's the other thing. *Dee* and I have a complicated relationship. I'll tell you all about it when you get here. How she sold my soul to the devil a long time ago. You'd better hurry before I get too drunk, though. I'm starting to feel the effects of this whiskey." With that he hung up.

Colt was at the marshal's office when the call came in. He saw the dispatcher look in his direction then said she would put the call through to Deputy Marshal Colt Dawson.

The woman on the other end of the line sounded hysterical, and for a moment he didn't recognize Hilde's voice. "Where are you?" he broke in, hoping she would take a breath.

"At the Lazy T Motel, room 9. It's Rick Cameron. He's

dead. She killed him, Colt. She killed him because she knew I was coming here tonight."

Colt wondered why Hilde was going to Rick's motel room, but he didn't dare ask right now. "Step outside the room. Take some deep breaths. I'm on my way." The moment he put down the phone he called Marshal Hud Savage, then he headed for the Lazy T, siren blaring and lights flashing.

Hilde was standing outside, just as he'd told her to. She wore a pair of jeans, a blue-and-tan-print blouse and nice sandals. Her hair was piled on top of her head. Had this been a date?

Jealousy bit into him like the bite of a rattlesnake, filling him with its venom. "What are you doing here, Hilde?" he asked the moment he reached her.

"Rick called. He said he'd tell me about Dee for ten thousand dollars. She killed him. You know she did." The words came flying out, tumbling all over each other.

"Easy," he said and drew her to the side, away from the motel room doors. They had opened, and guests were looking out to see what was going on. "You were going to pay him ten thousand dollars?"

She nodded. "I was asleep when he called. I dressed as quickly as I could."

He had to smile. Only Hilde would grab a matching outfit to come pay off a con man. She'd even taken the time to pull up her long hair into a do that made her look like a model on a runway.

"Stay here, okay?" he said, holding her at arm's length to look into her face. She'd been crying, but she still looked great. As he stepped to the door of the motel, he heard Hud's patrol pickup siren in the distance.

Several more guests stuck their heads out to see what was going on.

"Please go back inside," Colt told them. Inside the motel room he found Rick Cameron sprawled on the bed. There was an empty bottle of whiskey on the floor and an empty bottle of prescription pills under the edge of the bedspread.

He checked for a pulse. Hilde was right. The man was dead. Still when the EMTs arrived seconds later, they attempted to revive him without any luck.

"Looks like an overdose," one of the EMTs told Hud as he came in the door.

Colt stepped out to Hilde, but she'd already heard. "No," she cried, trying to get past him to talk to Hud. "This wasn't an accident. He knew I was on my way over."

The EMTs brought out the body and loaded it into the ambulance. Hud came out after them and walked over to Hilde, clearly unhappy to see her there.

"Dee killed him," Hilde said before the marshal could speak.

Hud raised a brow but didn't respond to the accusation. "I'm going to have to ask you a few questions. Why don't we go down to the office?" He turned to Colt. "Stay here and talk to the motel owner when he gets here."

Colt nodded and didn't look at Hilde as she and the marshal left. The lines had been clearly drawn now. Hud had made that point by telling him to stay there and wait for the motel owner.

He and Hilde were alone on their side of that line, and from Hud's disappointed look as he left, they were on the *wrong* side.

* * *

Hilde followed Hud in her SUV the few blocks to the marshal's office, her mind racing.

Rick had been ready to tell her the truth about Dee. Surely Hud would realize it was too much of a coincidence for him to overdose right before she got there. She said as much as she followed him into his office.

"I've seen enough of these where the victim mixed alcohol and heavy-duty pain pills. It looks to me like an accidental drug overdose," Hud told her.

"Well, you're wrong." She hated the way her voice broke. Even to her own ears, she sounded close to hysteria. Why wouldn't he believe her?

"Hilde, you're upset. You've been under a lot of strain lately—"

Of course Dana would have told him about her breakdown on the river. "Are you telling me you can't see that people have a lot of accidents around Dee?" she snapped.

"Why don't you tell me how it is that you're the one who found the victim," Hud said, as he settled into his chair behind his desk.

She'd known Hud for years, ever since she'd moved to Big Sky and met Dana. He was like a brother to her. But when he'd sat down behind his desk just then, she saw him become the marshal, all business. She felt the wall come up between them and had to fight tears of frustration and regret.

Taking a breath, she tried to calm down. But she was at war with herself. She knew he wasn't going to believe her, but at the same time she had to try to make him see the truth.

"I was asleep. Rick called me." She told him about the conversation, recalling as much as she could of it.

Hud nodded when she finished. "You said he sounded as if he'd been drinking. He said he would give you 'the scoop' on Dee. His words?"

"Yes and the way he said 'Dee,' I got the impression she might not really be Dee Anna Justice." She instantly saw skepticism in Hud's expression. No doubt Dana had also told him that she thought Hilde was jealous of her cousin. "There is something wrong with Dee. I feel it."

She quickly regretted blurting it out when Hud said "Hilde" in a tone that made it clear she was too biased against the woman to be credible.

Thank goodness Colt believed her.

"Hud, you have to admit it's suspicious that he calls, ready to tell me about her, and ends up dead."

"You said he sounded drunk. He might have already taken enough drugs to kill him. Which would explain why by the time you got there, he was already dead. Also, you have no idea what 'the scoop' on her might have been. He was a disgruntled ex-boyfriend."

"Was he?" she asked. "All we have is Dee's word on that. I assume she has an alibi?"

"She was at the house. Hilde, she was there all evening."

She knew Dee was behind it. Maybe she'd put something in the bottle of bourbon that was beside the bed. Or hired someone to kill him. But there was no doubt in Hilde's mind that she'd killed him.

"Rick was addicted to prescription drugs," Hud said with a sigh. "Dee said it was one reason she'd broken up with him. She was also worried that he might hurt himself because of the breakup. Apparently she told him after the horseback ride to the lake that they wouldn't be getting back together."

Hilde smiled, not surprised that Dee had covered her bases. Again. "She set that up nicely, didn't she?" she asked, unable to keep the amusement out of her tone.

"Hilde." His voice reeked with impatience.

She got to her feet, giving up. She'd cried wolf too many times without any proof to back it up. No one believed her. Except Colt. If he was telling the truth. She groaned inwardly at the thought that he might just be indulging her because he liked her. Liked her? Or just wanted to get her into his bed because she was a challenge?

"If those are all your questions…"

"Did you see anyone leaving the motel when you drove up?" Hud asked with a sigh.

She shook her head.

"The motel room door was unlocked?"

She nodded.

"Did you hear anyone going out the back as you entered?"

Why was he doing this? He believed it was an accidental overdose. Was he just trying to get her to see that she was wrong? "I didn't see anyone. I really can't tell you any more."

Hud gave her a regretful look. He knew she was angry that he didn't believe her, but there was nothing she could do about that.

"She's after you, Hud."

"Who?" he asked, frowning.

"Dee. She wants *you*."

He got to his feet, angrier now. "Hilde, I don't know what's gotten into you. You of all people know how I feel about Dana, about our family." He shook his head. "Go home and get some rest."

She nodded, seeing that there was nothing more she could say. "If you have any more questions, you know where I live." With that she left.

Colt had a pretty good idea how things had gone the moment Hilde answered the door. He'd thought about waiting until morning, but he was worried about her. If things had gone as he suspected they had, she would be upset and might welcome company.

"I just wanted to be sure you were all right."

She shook her head and motioned him inside. "Dee had an alibi. Not that she needs it. No one believes me anyway. She set this up so perfectly, telling Hud and Dana about Rick's drug problem and that she was worried he would do something terrible to himself."

"I'm sorry," he said. "*I* believe you."

"Do you?" She met his gaze with a fiery one of her own. She was good and mad, and she'd never looked more beautiful. He'd only glimpsed this kind of passion in her before tonight. "Or are you just trying to get into my pants?"

He laughed. "As tempting as that offer is, I like to think I have a shot without being forced to lie to you. I believe you, Hilde. It's too much of a coincidence that he should overdose when you're on the way to his motel room. She got to him. I'm not sure how, but she got to him."

Tears filled her eyes. "Why can't Hud see that?"

"Because Dee's good at hiding her true self and Hud operates on proof."

"Colt, I don't even think she *is* Dee Anna Justice."

He raised a brow.

"It's the way Rick called her 'Dee.' I heard him do it

on the horseback ride up to the lake. Is there any way to find out if she's even the woman she says she is?"

Colt gave that some thought. He wasn't sure he believed Dee was pretending to be Dana's cousin. He wasn't sure how she could have pulled that off, but he was willing to put Hilde's mind at rest and his own.

"I'll see if I can get her fingerprints. I might need your help."

"You know you have it," she said. "Would you like something to drink? I have some wine."

"You're tired. I should go."

"I could use the company. Just one drink."

He smiled. "If you had a beer…"

"I do."

He followed her through the house to the kitchen. Her house was neat as a pin and nicely furnished. But not overdone. He realized they had that in common: a minimalistic view of the world.

She handed him a beer, poured herself a glass of wine and led him into the living room.

"Dee already told Dana that Rick had been depressed and she was worried about him, since she told him it was over after the horseback ride," Hilde said. "I swear she must have been planning to drug him right from the moment he showed up."

"It's proving it that's the problem," he said. Sitting here in Hilde's house seemed the most natural thing in the world. "I want you to stay away from her unless I am there to make sure she doesn't try to kill you again."

Hilde looked up in surprise. "You can't believe she would try again. She couldn't get away with *another* murder."

"Rick's death will probably be ruled an accidental overdose," he reminded her. "Consider how it would look if something happened to you now. You've been having a streak of bad luck. Plus you've been…overwrought." She started to object, but he held up his hand. "I'm just saying how Dee would spin it. You got careless, you haven't been yourself. You get the idea. That's why I want you to give the woman a wide berth until she leaves."

"She's not leaving."

"Well, she can't stay forever."

"She can if she finds a way to get Hud all to herself," Hilde said. "I told Hud that Dee was after him."

Colt groaned. "I can imagine how he took that."

"He needed to be warned."

Colt couldn't argue that. He just hoped it wouldn't have the opposite effect and make Hud more sympathetic to Dee.

"She knows we're onto her." Hilde drained her wineglass. "What scares me is what she'll do next. I'm afraid for Dana and her family. If she makes a play for Hud… I have a feeling Dee doesn't take rejection well."

Colt agreed that the whole family could be in danger. "I wish there was some way to get her out of that house."

"I doubt dynamite would work, even if Dana would let you blast her out. Dee has completely snowed Dana."

He could hear her disappointment. "I know it's frustrating seeing Dana and even Hud taken in like this. But you have to admit, Dee is good."

"She's playing this perfectly, too perfectly," Hilde said. "Which makes me think this isn't her first time she's done this."

"Whatever *this* is," Colt said. "I'll see what I can find

out about her. Meanwhile, I'll see what we can do about getting her fingerprints." He'd have to be careful. He couldn't let Hud find out that he was investigating his wife's cousin. If Dana wasn't so happy having found a cousin she never knew she had, then Colt was sure Hud would be suspicious of Dee by now.

"I want to help."

"You are going to stay clear of the ranch unless I'm with you. Promise me."

She promised, but he could tell her concern for her friend was weighing heavily on her. What worried him was that if Dee decided to make a move against her, she would use that concern and Hilde would fall right into the trap.

He finished his beer, saw how late it was and got up to leave. Hilde walked him to the door. As he opened it, a cool breeze blew in, ruffling her hair. He reached to tuck an errant golden strand behind her ear like he'd seen her do the few times she'd worn her hair down.

But the moment he did, his hand slid around to the back of her slim neck. His eyes locked with hers. Her skin felt cool to his touch as he drew her to him.

The kiss was gentle and sweet and so unexpected. Just the touch of his lips sent a jolt through her. Colt must have felt her tremble because he pulled her closer. She could feel his heart hammering under the hard muscles of his chest.

Her lips parted and she felt a rush of heat as he enclosed her in his arms and deepened the kiss.

She felt light-headed. No one had ever kissed her like

this. She leaned into him, into the kiss. For the first time in days, Dee Anna Justice was the last thing on her mind.

Colt pressed her against the wall. She could feel the passion in his kiss, in his body. She wouldn't have been surprised if they had made love right there.

Headlights washed over them. Dana pulled in behind Hilde's SUV. They both drew back as if the lights were ice water thrown on them.

"I should go," Colt said. He touched her hand, his gaze locking with hers for a moment. Then he sauntered out to his patrol pickup and drove off.

"Are you all right?" Dana cried. "Hud told me what happened." She turned to look after Colt. "Did I interrupt something?"

"No, it…" She waved a hand through the air. "I'm just glad to see you. Did you want to come in?"

"Just for a moment. I know it's late, but we were out of milk and I couldn't sleep without making sure you were all right," Dana said as she stepped inside. "You've been through so much lately."

"Haven't I," Hilde said.

"You found his body? That must have been horrible."

"You have no idea." She realized she couldn't confide in her once best friend.

"Dee is a basket case."

Hilde tried to hide a smile. "I'm sure she is," she said.

But Dana knew her too well. "Hilde, the man was her *boyfriend.*"

"Was he? Or is that just what she told you? Dana, the only thing you know about her is what she's told you. How can you be sure any of it is true?"

Dana stood in the middle of the living room, suddenly looking uncomfortable. "I know you don't like her, but to be this suspicious about everything she says or does—"

"She's playing you, Dana. You told her about the past six years that you didn't have your family because of the fight over the ranch, didn't you?" She saw the answer in her friend's face. "You are so desperate to have family that you're blinded by this woman."

"I don't understand why you're acting like this," Dana said, sounding close to tears.

Hilde tried to stop herself, but she couldn't. She had to tell Dana everything, had to try to reason with her, to warn her.

"She tried to kill me, Dana. At the falls? She pushed me while you were getting your camera, only grabbing me at the last second before I fell."

"Why would she—"

"Because she doesn't want me around you."

"That's crazy," Dana said.

"Yes, it is. And she's living with you and your husband and your children."

They stood only inches apart staring at each other, but Hilde felt as if there was a mountain range between them, one neither of them might be able to climb.

"I'm worried about you, Hilde."

"Really? Because I'm scared to death for you. She killed Rick to keep him from telling me the truth tonight. He'd called me and said he'd tell me Dee's secrets, but I got there too late."

Dana was shaking her head and Hilde saw that her friend was never going to believe her. Until it was too late. "I should go."

Hilde nodded. "Watch her, Dana. I think she's after Hud."

Dana gave her a disbelieving look as if Hilde had finally lost her mind, then she turned and left.

Hilde closed the door behind her and leaned against it. She hadn't even realized she was crying until she tasted the salty tears.

Chapter 8

"You can't blame yourself for Rick's overdose," Dana said the next morning at breakfast. Hud had left early, called in on some new case. Her "cousin" had been trying to console her. "There are just some people who can't be helped no matter how hard we try."

Dee heard something in Dana's voice. "Like Hilde? I feel responsible for this rift between the two of you as much as I do for what Rick did."

"Don't. Hilde has just been under a lot of strain lately. I didn't realize how much. Then to find Rick like that…"

"So Hilde was the one who found him?" Dee felt her blood pressure rise like a rocket. That bastard. After their horseback ride, he'd threatened to blow her plans out of the water if she didn't include him. "Why would she go over to Rick's?"

Dana looked away to tend to one of the kids. "Apparently he was upset after you broke things off with him again. He called Hilde, wanted ten thousand dollars to tell her things about you."

If she could have killed him again, she would have made this time much more painful. "Why would he do that?" she wailed. "It must have been the drugs talking."

"I'm sure it was."

"So what did he say when she got to his motel room?" Dee asked, trying hard not to let her fear show.

"He was already dead."

Dee tried not to breathe a sigh of relief. "I'm sure he just wanted a shoulder to cry on."

"But to ask her for ten thousand dollars for information about you…" Dana said, and looked at her.

Dee saw the doubt beginning to bloom and knew she had to nip it in the bud and quickly. "I told you Rick had turned to pills," she said, and began to cry again. She'd learned to cry on cue so this was the easy part. "Well, the truth is… Rick had a drug habit. I'm so ashamed."

"You have nothing to be ashamed of," Dana said, quickly coming to her side.

"How could I have fallen in love with a man like him? I didn't know for a long time. Once I realized… I tried to help him. But it was too late. He'd blown all his savings on his habit. It wasn't love that brought him all the way to Montana or me. I was too ashamed to tell you this, but the real reason was to ask me for money. When I turned him down, both for money and his feeble attempt to get me back, I guess he was desperate. He knew Hilde didn't like me…. She was probably ready to give him the money for any kind of dirt on me she could dig up. Oh, Dana, I'm sorry. I know she's your best friend…. See why I feel so badly about all this?"

"But you shouldn't. You haven't done anything. We can't control the way other people react." Dana sounded sad.

"We need to do something to cheer us both up. I would love to go into Bozeman. We could have lunch, maybe do some shopping. What do you say?" She held her breath. She'd seen Hud go off to work this morning and had a pretty good idea that Dana didn't have anyone to take care of the kids. Couldn't really call Hilde, could she? Also, she'd heard Dana promise to make pies with the kids today.

"That sounds wonderful," Dana said. "But I'm afraid it will have to wait." Mary and Hank came running into the room, as if on cue.

"We're making pies with Mommy today," Mary announced.

Dee smiled, but did her best to look disappointed. "As fun as that sounds, Dana, would you mind if I borrowed your truck and went into Bozeman? You probably could use some time alone, and I need to do some shopping."

"Of course. The keys are in the truck. Please help yourself. And when you come back, there will be pie!" Dana laughed as the kids began to cheer noisily.

Dee couldn't wait to leave. "I might take the whole day, then," she said, as she hurried upstairs to get her purse.

Colt called the shop the next morning right after Hilde opened. "How are you doing?"

She glanced across the street to the deli, half expecting to see him sitting in his usual place. She was disappointed to see that the table was empty. "I'm okay."

"Did you get some sleep?"

"Yes. The wine and you stopping by helped," she admitted.

"Good, I'm glad to hear that. I wanted you to know that I have to go up to West Yellowstone today on a burglary case."

She could hear the smile in his voice and laughed. "And you thought you'd better remind me that I'm not to go near Dee?"

"Yeah," he said. "Too subtle?"

"I appreciate you thinking of me."

He was silent for a moment before he said, "I've been thinking of you for a long while."

She didn't know what to say, especially since a lump had formed in her throat.

"I wish that kiss hadn't gotten interrupted."

"Me, too."

"How did things go with Dana, or shouldn't I ask?"

"Not well. I know I should have kept my mouth shut, but Colt, I had to warn her. If I put even a little doubt in her mind…"

"You did what you had to. Listen, I probably shouldn't be telling you this. Hell, I *know* I shouldn't. I meant to tell you last night. When we searched Rick, we found three different forms of identification in three different names. We sent his fingerprints to the crime lab in Missoula and we're waiting to see if we get a hit. Right now, we don't know who the guy is."

Hilde felt her heart take off at a gallop. "So there is more to the story. Just like there has got to be with Dee."

"It sure looks that way."

"We have to get her fingerprints."

"Hilde, promise me you won't do anything while I'm in West. You know how dangerous she is. Also…"

She heard him hesitate. "What?"

"She's gone into Bozeman today to do some shopping. She stopped by the office to ask Hud where there was a good place to have lunch. When she heard he's going to be testifying in a trial down there this afternoon, she talked him into having lunch with her."

Hilde never swore so she was as shocked as anyone when a cuss word escaped her mouth. "Even after I told Hud she was after him?"

"You had to be there," Colt said. "She's playing Rick's death to the hilt. She said she needs someone to talk to and has questions that only Hud can answer…. You get the idea."

Unfortunately she did. "We have to get her fingerprints soon."

"I promise you we will. Just be patient. I'll be back tonight. I was wondering if we could have dinner?"

Was he asking her on a date? Or was he just worried about her? "I'd like that."

He sounded relieved. "Good. I could pick you up by seven. I thought we'd go up to Mountain Village, get away for a while."

She felt a shiver of excitement race through her. "I look forward to it." She hung up feeling like a schoolgirl. It was all she could do not to dance around the shop.

Hilde might have let herself go and danced, but the bell over the door jangled and she turned to see Dana's cousin step inside. As Dee entered, she flipped the sign from Open to Closed and locked the door before turning to face Hilde.

"Don't make a fool of yourself," Dee snapped, as she saw Hilde fumble for her cell phone. Hilde looked so much like a deer in the headlights that Dee had to laugh. "What are you going to tell the marshal? That I came into your shop to try to kill you again? Really, Hilde. You must realize how tiresome you've become."

"Don't come any closer," Hilde said, holding up the phone.

"You're wasting your time. Hud is in Bozeman, Colt is on his way to West Yellowstone—and what's that other deputy's name?"

"Liza."

"Right. She just got a call and is headed up the mountain. By the time any of them get here, I will have unlocked the door and left you safe and as sound as you can be under the circumstances and you'll only look all the more foolish."

"What do you want?" Hilde demanded. But she lowered the cell phone as she stepped behind the counter.

Dee couldn't help being amused as Hilde snatched up a pair of deadly-looking scissors from behind the counter. "You aren't going to use those. Even if you had it in you, everyone would just assume you went off the deep end. You've been teetering on the brink for several days now."

"What. Do. You. Want?" Hilde repeated.

Dee had to hand it to the woman. She was tougher than she looked. "I want you to leave me alone."

"Don't you mean you want me to leave Dana alone?"

"Just let me enjoy this vacation with my family."

"Are they really your family? Rick didn't seem to think so."

Finally. She'd known Rick had shot off his mouth on the phone with Hilde. She'd just needed to know what he'd told her, and apparently Hilde was more than ready to tell anyone who'd listen.

"Rick was on drugs."

"How convenient," Hilde snapped. "He was going to tell me all about you and I have a feeling he knew plenty."

"But ten thousand dollars' worth?" Dee shook her head as she moved closer to the counter and Hilde.

"Dana told you about that?" Hilde didn't sound so sure of herself suddenly.

"She told me everything—how you were convinced that I'd killed Rick—and right before you were finally going to learn all my deep, dark secrets. How frustrating that must have been for you."

Hilde brandished the scissors. "You really don't want to come any closer."

Dee smiled, but stopped moving. "So if I'm not Dee Anna Justice, then who did Rick say I was?" She saw the answer at once on Hilde's face. The woman wasn't good at hiding her emotions. She would never survive in Dee's world. "So he didn't say. You just got the *feeling* I wasn't Dee?" She shook her head. "Yep, you're teetering on the brink. One little push and I'm afraid you're going over the edge. It's going to break Dana's heart. She really does care for you, her *best* friend."

"But you'll be there to pick up the pieces, right?"

"That's what I came here today to tell you," Dee said. "I'm not going anywhere. Accept it. If you don't, I'm afraid of what it will do to you mentally. You seem so fragile as it is."

"You're wrong," Hilde said. "I'm a lot stronger than I look."

Dee didn't expect Hilde to lunge at her with the scissors. It wasn't much of a lunge. Her reaction was to grab Hilde's arm and twist it. The scissors clattered to the floor to the sound of Hilde crying out in pain.

As the shop owner stumbled back, rubbing her wrist and looking scared, Dee bent down and picked up the scissors from the floor by the blades.

"If you're going to try to kill someone, it works better if they don't see you coming at them," Dee said in disgust. As she placed the scissors on the counter, she studied Hilde, realizing she was much closer to the edge of insanity than she'd thought. It wouldn't take hardly anything to push her over.

"I need to get to Bozeman," Dee said. "I have a lunch date with Hud. I suggest you close up shop and get some rest. You might want to see someone about that wrist. I hope it's not sprained. How will you ever explain what happened?" She laughed as she turned toward the door. She almost wished that Hilde would grab up the scissors and come for her again.

At the door, she flipped the sign to Open, unlocked the door and let herself out. When she looked back, Hilde was still standing with her back against the wall, rubbing her wrist. The look in her eyes, though, wasn't one of fear. It was…triumph.

Dee stopped to look again, surprised and worried by what she'd glimpsed in Hilde's eyes just then. Was it just a trick of the light through the window? She couldn't shake the feeling that there was something she was missing. Hilde kept throwing her off balance. The woman was impossible. Anyone else would have taken the hint long before now.

But when she glanced into the shop again, she saw Hilde rush to the door to lock it and put up the Closed sign. Apparently the woman *had* taken her advice and was going to get some rest.

* * *

Hilde waited until she saw Dee drive away before she carefully slid the scissors into a clean plastic bag. She was positive she'd gotten the woman's fingerprints because Dee had picked up the scissors by the blades, holding them out as if she wanted to seem nonthreatening.

What a joke. Everything about Dee was threatening.

Once she had the scissors put away, it was all she could do not to call Colt and tell him, but he was working. She would have to wait until dinner tonight since in order for him to run Dee's prints, he would have to do it under Hud's radar. Hilde realized what a chance he would be taking.

Just the thought of Colt made her heart beat a little harder.

He would have a fit when she told him how she'd managed to get Dee's prints. She'd been pretty sure that Dee would take the scissors away from her. She had hoped that Dee wouldn't use them on her, had bet that Dee wasn't ready to kill again. Not yet, anyway. Even if Dee would have claimed self-defense, few people would have believed it.

Well, they wouldn't have believed it before the past few days. Now Hilde wasn't sure what her friends thought of her. That she was mentally unbalanced? That like Dee said, she was teetering on the edge?

Wait until Dee's prints came back. She'd see what they thought then.

What if she is *Dee Anna Justice?* Hilde tried to remember what Dana had told her about Dee Anna and her family. Maybe Dana's grandparents had had a good reason for disinheriting Walter Justice and demanding that his name never be spoken again.

The thought gave her a chill. If there had been something wrong with Walter, wasn't it possible Dee Anna had inherited it?

"No, she's not Dee Ana Justice," she said to herself now. "And I'm going to prove it." If she had a good set of Dee's prints on the scissors. Now she was worried that she might not have.

Hilde started to open her shop when a thought struck her. Dee had gone into Bozeman to have lunch with Hud. That meant Dana would be at the house alone with the kids.

"You promised Colt you wouldn't go near the ranch," she reminded herself, as she went into the back to stuff several plastic bags into her purse. "Colt meant don't go near Dee, not the ranch, and I might not have this opportunity again."

As she started for the door, she realized she was talking to herself. Dee was right. She was teetering on the edge. She was starting to scare herself.

Locking up behind herself and leaving the Closed sign in the window of the sewing shop—something she never did—Hilde headed for Cardwell Ranch.

Chapter 9

"Dee," Hud said the moment there was a lull in the conversation.

She'd chosen a private booth at the back of the local bistro and had been doing her best to entertain him with fabricated stories about her life.

He'd laughed at the appropriate times and even blushed a little when she'd told him how she'd lost her virginity. Well, how she *could* have lost it if it wasn't for her real life. Her fabricated story was cute and sad and wistful, just enough to pluck at his heartstrings, she hoped. She had Dana where she wanted her. Hud was another story.

She'd noticed that he'd seemed a little distracted when he'd sat down, but she'd thought she'd charmed away whatever was bothering him.

"Dee," he repeated when she'd finished one of her stories. "I have to ask you. How much do you know about Rick?"

The bastard was dead, but not forgotten. She'd been relieved earlier when she'd stopped by Needles and Pins to learn that Rick hadn't had a chance to tell Hilde anything of importance. Had he lived much longer, though, he would have spoiled everything.

"What do you mean?" she asked, letting him know he'd ruined her good mood—and her lunch—by bringing up Rick.

"I found three different forms of identification on him in three different names."

The fool. Why had he taken a chance like that? Because it was the way they'd always done it. So she knew he was planning to start over somewhere else—once he got money from her. If she could have sent him straight to hell at that moment, she'd have bought him a first-class ticket.

"I don't understand." It was the best she could do. Now the marshal would look into Rick's past. It was bound to come out who he really was. Damn him for doing this to her. He really was going to ruin everything.

"Did you suspect he might not be who he said he was?"

She let out a nervous laugh. "He's Rick Cameron. I met his friends. He even had me talk to his mother one time on the phone. She sounded nice."

"I think he lied to you," Hud said gently.

She let him take her hand. His hands were large and strong. She imagined what they might feel like on the rest of her bare skin, and she did her best to look broken-hearted. She even worked up a few tears and was pleased when Hud pulled out a handkerchief and handed it to her.

"Thank you. I don't know what I would have done if this had happened in New York. I have friends there, but at a time like this it is so good to be around *family*." She gave him a hug, but not too long since she felt him tense.

Hilde. The blasted woman had warned him. Of course she had.

"You are so lucky to have such a wonderful family," she said. "Dana is amazing and the kids...what can I say?"

He nodded and relaxed again. "I *am* lucky. And Dana is so happy to have found a cousin she didn't know she had."

"I feel as if I'm wearing out my welcome, though." He started to say something. Not to really disagree, but to try to be polite. "I'll be taking off Saturday. Dana's invited me back for a week next year. I hope she and Hilde regain their friendship. I know it's not my fault, but still..."

Hud smiled. "They'll work it out. I'm just glad you came out to the ranch. You'll have to keep in touch."

"I'll try," she said, furious that between Rick and Hilde, they'd managed to ruin her lunch with Hud and force her to move up her plan—because she wasn't leaving Cardwell Ranch.

When Dana opened the door, Hilde saw her expression and felt her heart drop. She thought of all the times she'd stopped by and her best friend had been delighted to see her. Today wasn't one of those days.

"Hilde?" She looked leery, almost afraid. How ironic.

Hilde wanted to scream, *I'm not the one you should fear!* Instead she said, "I bought those ice cream sandwiches the kids like."

Dana glanced at the bag in her hand, but didn't move.

"I won't stay long. I just haven't seen the kids for a few days now. I've missed them."

"Auntie Hilde?" Mary cried and came running to the door. She squeezed past her mother and into Hilde's arms.

She held the adorable little girl close. Mary looked just like the pictures Hilde had seen of Dana at that same age. Was that another reason Dee had been able to fool Dana? Because there was a resemblance between Dana and Dee, one no doubt Dee had played on?

"We're making pies!" Mary announced, as Hilde let her go. "Come on, I'll show you."

Hilde took the child's hand and followed her through the house. Dana had been forced to move out of the doorway, but she looked worried as Hilde entered. What did she think Hilde was going to do? Flip out in front of the kids?

"These are beautiful," Hilde said when she saw the pies. The kitchen looked like a flour bomb had gone off in it. Dana was so good at letting the kids make as big a mess as they had to. She was a great mother, Hilde thought as she looked up at her friend and smiled.

Dana seemed to soften. "Would you like a pie?"

Hilde shook her head. Only a few days ago, Dana would have asked her to stay for dinner and have pie then. Now she seemed anxious that Hilde not stay too long. Dee would be returning.

"We'd better put these in the freezer," Hilde said, handing Dana the bag with the ice cream sandwiches.

"What do you say to Auntie Hilde?"

"Thank you, Auntie Hilde," Mary and Hank chimed in. Dana stepped out on the old back porch to put the ice cream in the freezer.

"I'm taking off now," Hilde called. She said good-bye to the kids, then hurried back into the living room and up the stairs. She assumed Dana had put Dee in the guest bedroom. Hilde had stayed over enough; she almost thought of it as her own.

The door was closed. She opened it quickly and stepped inside. The curtain was drawn so it took her a moment before her eyes adjusted. She knew she had to move quickly.

Dee's cosmetic bag was on the antique vanity. She hurried to it, trying not to step on the floorboards that creaked. Taking the plastic bags out of her purse, she used them like gloves. They were awkward, but she managed to pick up a bottle of makeup, then spied Dee's toothbrush. DNA. She grabbed it, stuffed both into her purse again and hurriedly moved to the door.

Opening it, she stepped out and was partway down the hall headed for the stairs when Dana came up them.

"Hilde?"

"I'm sorry, I just needed to use your bathroom. I hope you don't mind. I drank too much coffee this morning."

Dana relaxed a little. She, of all people, knew about Hilde's coffee habit.

"Thank you for letting me see the kids."

Tears filled her friend's eyes. "I hate this," Dana whispered.

"Me, too. But we'll figure it out. We have to."

Dana nodded, looking skeptical. Who could blame her?

Hilde smiled and touched her shoulder as they passed. She practically ran down the stairs. Dee would realize her makeup and toothbrush were missing. And knowing Dee, she would figure it out.

As Hilde climbed into her SUV, she saw Dana watching her leave. Colt would be furious. He'd realize what was just sinking in for her. Dee had warned her numerous times. The next time they crossed paths, Dee would make sure Hilde Jacobson was no longer a problem.

Hilde just hoped before that time came that she would have the proof she needed to stop Dee Anna Justice—or whoever the woman was.

Dee called Stacy after her unsuccessful lunch with Hud. Dana had told her that Stacy had a part-time job as a nanny. Dee was hoping that meant Stacy could get away long enough to talk.

"I was just in town and thought maybe we could have a cup of coffee somewhere," she said when Stacy answered. Dee had gotten her number from the little book Dana kept by the downstairs phone. She'd gotten Hilde's cell phone number out of the book as well.

"Coffee, huh?" Stacy asked.

"Okay, you found me out. I do have some questions about the family."

Stacy laughed. "So you called me. Sure, I know where all the bodies are buried. Do you know where the Greasy Spoon is, off Main Street?"

"No, but I can find it. Ten minutes?"

"I'll have to bring the kids, but they have a play area at the café."

Dee was waiting when Stacy came in with two toddlers: Ella, who she said was now over a year old, and Ralph, the two-year-old she babysat. Stacy deposited the two kids in the play area and came back to sit down with Dee. She could watch the children from where they sat.

"Who names their kid *Ralph?*" Dee asked.

Stacy shrugged and helped herself to the coffee and mini-turnovers Dee had ordered for them. "Named after his wealthy grandfather."

"Then I can see why they love the name," she said and laughed. "I hope I'm not putting you on the spot."

Stacy's laugh was more cutting. "You want to know about me and Dana and Hud, right?"

Dee lifted a brow before she could stop herself. "You and Hud?"

"Dana didn't tell you?"

She lied. "She hinted at something, but I never thought—"

"To make a long story short, Hud and Dana were engaged. I was strapped for money, and truthfully, I was always jealous of Dana. Someone offered me money to drug Hud and get him into my bed so Dana would find him there. It was during a really stupid part of my life. Thankfully my sister forgave me, but it split Hud and Dana up for five years—until the truth came out."

"Wow." Dee hadn't expected this. "Dana mentioned a rift with you and her brothers after your mother died?"

Stacy's laugh held no humor. "We were all desperate for money. Or at least we thought we were. So we wanted to sell off the ranch and split the money. Since our mother's old will divided the ranch between us…"

"But then the new will turned up."

Stacy nodded. "We treated Dana really badly. Family had always meant so much to her… It broke her heart when we turned against her. I will never forgive myself."

"Families are like that sometimes," she said, thinking of her own. "I'm just so glad that Dana found me and I get to be part of yours. I can't tell you how much it means to me."

"Okay, now tell me the big secret with your side of the family." Stacy helped herself to another mini-turnover. "Dana said the family disinherited your father, Walter, because they didn't like who he married? There has to be more to it."

Dee had known Stacy might be more outspoken than her sister. She was a little taken aback by how much. Also, the real Dee Anna Justice had never told her about her father, so Dee was in the dark here.

"I had no idea I had other family," she said. "My father led me to believe my grandparents were dead. Clearly he'd never been close to them."

"And your mother?"

"She's a socialite and philanthropist."

"What?" Stacy cried. "She's not a tramp?"

"Far from it. The woman was born with a silver spoon in her mouth, can trace her ancestry to the *Mayflower* and has more money than she knows what to do with." Dee was offended the family had thought Dee Anna's mother was a skank, even though it wasn't her mother and she didn't like Marietta Justice. The woman was an uptight snob, colder than the marble entry at her mansion. But thanks to her, Dee would be getting her daughter's trust fund check soon.

"So why did the Montana Justice family disinherit his son for marrying wealth?" Stacy asked. "That makes no sense."

No, it didn't. As Stacy said, there had to be more to the story. Dee could only guess. "It's a mystery, isn't it?"

Colt couldn't wait to get back to Big Sky. He'd been anxious all day and having trouble concentrating on his investigation. It wasn't like him. He took his job seriously. Just like Hilde.

When he'd finally gotten a chance, he'd called Needles and Pins. The phone rang four times and went to voice mail. He doubted she was so busy waiting on a customer that she couldn't answer the phone.

So he waited ten minutes and tried again. Still no answer. He'd never known Hilde not to open the shop. His concern grew even more when he tried later in the afternoon.

He'd finally called Dana and asked for Hilde's cell phone number. "I tried the shop and couldn't reach her."

"That *is* odd," Dana agreed after she'd given him the number. "She stopped out earlier and brought the kids ice cream sandwiches."

Colt swore silently. "How did that go?"

"Okay. But she was acting…strange. Is she all right?"

"She's been through a lot the past few days," he said. "So she didn't stay long?"

"No."

"I'll give her a call and make sure she's all right," he said.

"You'll let me know if…if there is anything I can do?"

"Sure." He quickly dialed Hilde's cell and felt a wave of relief when she answered on the third ring. "You went out to the ranch." He hadn't meant for those to be the first words out of his mouth.

"Don't be mad. I got her fingerprints."

He bit back a curse. "Hilde."

"I know. But she stopped by the shop right after I opened this morning."

If he'd been scared before, he was petrified now. "What did she want?"

"To threaten me. Again. She made it clear that if I didn't back off—"

"So you went out to the ranch and got her fingerprints. I hate to even ask."

"I feel like we are racing against the clock," she said. "I had to do something. She's more dangerous than even I thought."

He agreed. "Okay, just do me a favor. Where are you now?"

"I'm at home. I was too antsy to work today."

"You have the items with her fingerprints on them at the house, right?"

"Yes."

"Okay, just stay there, lock the doors, don't open them for anyone but me. I'm on my way from West. I should be there in an hour. You don't happen to own a gun, do you? Sorry, of course you don't."

"You think you know me that well?" she demanded.

"Yep. Are you going to tell me you do own a gun and know how to shoot it?"

"No."

He laughed. "Go lock your doors. I'm on my way."

Dee was disappointed when she reached the ranch and found out that Hud was working late at the office. He was the only bright spot in a dreary day.

"I see your ankle is better. That's good," Dana said when Dee came in with the small presents she'd brought the kids. She hadn't wanted to spend much, so she'd found some cheap toys. Mary and Hank thanked her, but she could tell she'd bought the wrong things.

Dinner was just the four of them. Dana had fed the twins and put them to bed. The house was deathly quiet since Mary and Hank were practically falling asleep in their dinner plates.

Dee walked around the ranch while Dana bathed the kids and got them to bed. The night was cool and dark.

As she walked, something kept nagging at her about earlier at the sewing shop.

She hadn't been surprised when Hilde had picked up the scissors and lunged at her. Just as she wasn't surprised the woman was slow and uncoordinated, so much so that it had been child's play to take the scissors away from her. Often anger made a person less precise, even clumsy, right?

Coming at her with scissors had seemed a fool thing to do, but Dee hadn't questioned it. Until now.

She recalled how easily it had been to get Hilde to drop the scissors and how surprised she'd been when Hilde had stood there rubbing her wrist as if Dee had broken it.

Hilde hadn't been trying to stab her. Far from it. Then why—

The truth hit her like a ton of bricks.

The scissors.

She swore, stopping in her tracks, to let out her anger in a roar aimed at the night sky. All the pieces fell into place in an instant. The triumphant look in Hilde's eyes.

The woman had gotten her fingerprints!

All the implications of that also fell into place. Once she had her boyfriend Colt run the prints…

Dee slapped herself hard. The force of it stung her cheek. She slapped herself again and again until both cheeks burned as she chanted, "You fool. You fool. You fool." Just as her mother had done.

By the time she stopped, her face was on fire, but she knew what she had to do.

Hilde couldn't remember the last time she was this excited about a date. Well, not exactly a date, she supposed. Dinner. Still she wore an emerald-green dress she'd bought and saved for a special occasion.

Colt's eyes lit when he saw her. "You look beautiful."

She *felt* beautiful.

"I don't think you have any idea what you do to me," he said, his voice sounding rough with emotion. "You make me tongue-tied."

"I really doubt that," she said with a small nervous laugh. The desire in his gaze set her blood aflame.

He took a step to her, ran his fingers along one bare arm. She felt her heart jump. Goose bumps skittered across her skin. His gaze moved over her face like a caress before it settled on her mouth. If he kissed her now—

"We had better go to dinner," he said, letting out a breath as he stepped back from her. "Otherwise..." He met her gaze. "I want to do this right, you know."

She smiled. "I do, too."

"Then we'd better go. I made reservations up on the mountain. It's such a nice night...."

She grabbed her wrap. Montana in the mountains was often cold, even in the summer after the sun went down. She doubted she would need it, though. Being this close to Colt had her blood simmering quite nicely.

They didn't talk about Dee Anna Justice or the scissors and other evidence locked up back at the house. Colt asked her about growing up in Chicago. She told him about her idyllic childhood and her loving parents.

"I had a very normal childhood," she concluded. "Most people would say it was boring. How about you?"

"Mine was much the same. It sounds like we were both lucky."

"So your parents are professors at the University of Montana."

"My mother teaches business," he said. "My father teaches math. They'd hoped I would follow in their footsteps, but as much as I enjoyed college, I had no interest in teaching at it. I always wanted to go into law enforcement, especially in a small town. I couldn't have been happier when I got the job here at Big Sky."

He had driven up the winding road that climbed to the Mountain Village. There weren't a lot of businesses open this time of year, but more stayed open all year than in the old days, when there really were only two seasons at Big Sky.

The air was cold up here but crystal clear. Colt was the perfect gentleman, opening her door after he parked. Hilde stood for a moment and admired the stars. With so few other lights, the sky was a dark canopy glittering with white stars. A sliver of moon hung just over the mountains.

"Could this night be more perfect?" she whispered.

When she looked at Colt, he grinned and said, "Let's see." His kiss was soft and gentle, a brush across the lips as light as the breeze that stirred the loose tendrils of her hair. And then he drew her to him and deepened the kiss, breaking it off as the door of the restaurant opened and a group of four came out laughing and talking.

"We just keep getting interrupted," Colt said with a laugh. He put his arm around her waist and they entered the restaurant.

Hilde had never felt so alive. The night seemed to hold its breath in expectation. She could smell adventure on the air, feel it in her every nerve ending. She had a feeling that tonight would be one she would never forget.

Over dinner, they talked about movies and books, laughed about the crazy things they did when they were kids, and Colt found himself completely enthralled by his date.

Hilde was, as his grandfather used to say, the whole ball of wax. She was smart and ambitious, a hard worker, and yet she volunteered for several organizations in her spare time. She loved nature, cared about the environment and made him laugh.

On top of that, she was beautiful, sexy and a good dancer. After dinner, they'd danced out in the starlight until he thought he would go crazy if he didn't get her alone and naked.

"Is it just me, or do you want to get out of here?" Colt said after they took a break from the dance floor.

"I thought you'd never ask."

He laughed and they left. It was all he could do not to race down the mountain, but the switchback curves kept him in check.

Once out of the vehicle, though, all bets were off. They were in each other's arms, kissing as they stumbled toward her front door. Once inside, they practically tore each other's clothes off, dropping articles of clothing in a crooked path before making it only to the rug in front of the fireplace.

"Hilde," Colt said, cupping her face in his hands as he leaned over her. He couldn't find words to tell her how beautiful she was or how much he wanted her. Or that he had fallen in love with her. He couldn't even tell her the exact moment. He just knew that he had.

Fortunately, he didn't have to put any of that into words. Not tonight. He saw that she understood. It was in her amazing brown eyes and in the one word she uttered as he entered her. "Colt."

* * *

Later, Colt carried her to her bed and made love to her slowly. The urgency of their first lovemaking had cooled. He took his time letting his gaze and his fingers and his tongue graze her body as he took full possession of her.

Hilde cried out with a passion she'd never known existed as he cupped her breasts and lathed her nipples with his tongue until she felt her whole body quake. She surrendered to him in a way she'd never given herself to another man. His demanding kisses took her to new heights.

And when he finished, his gaze locked with hers, she felt a release that left her sated and happier than she'd ever known.

As he lay curled against her, one arm thrown protectively over her, she closed her eyes and drifted off to sleep feeling…loved.

Chapter 10

Dee woke from the nightmare in a cold sweat. For a few moments, she couldn't catch her breath. She swung her legs out of bed and stumbled to the window, gulping for air. Her heart felt as if it would pound its way out of her chest.

It was the same nightmare she'd had since she was a girl. She was in a coffin. It was pitch-black. There was no air. She was trapped, and even though she'd screamed herself hoarse, no one had come to save her.

She shoved open the screenless window all the way and leaned out to breathe in the night air. A sliver of moon hung over the top of the mountain. A million stars twinkled against the midnight-blue sky. She shivered as the cold mountain air quickly dried her perspiration and sent goose bumps skittering over her skin.

The nightmare was coming more frequently—just as the doctor had told her it would.

"Do night terrors run in your family?" he'd asked, studying her over the top of his glasses.

"I don't know. I never asked."

"How old did you say you were?"

She'd been in her early twenties at the time.

He'd frowned. "What about sleepwalking?"

"Sometimes I wake up in a strange place and I don't know how I've gotten there."

He nodded, his frown deepening as he tossed her file on his desk. "I'm going to give you a referral to a neurologist."

"You're saying there's something wrong with me?"

"Just a precaution. Sleepwalking and night terrors at your age are fairly uncommon and could be the result of a neurological disorder."

She'd laughed after she left his office. "He thinks I'm crazy." She'd been amused at the time.

But back then she was sleepwalking and having the nightmare only every so often.

Now...

She looked out at the peaceful night. "This is all I need. This place and Hud and I will be fine," she whispered. "Once I get rid of the stumbling blocks, I'll be fine for the first time in my life."

But that was the problem, wasn't it? There were more stumbling blocks than she'd ever run into before. More chances to get caught.

"It would be worth it, though," she said as she heard a horse whinny out in the corrals. All this could be hers. *Would* be hers. She deserved Dana's happiness. She deserved Dana's life—minus the kids.

After getting dressed, she sneaked out and made the walk into town. It was only a couple of miles and she'd walked it before and gotten away with it. If anyone discovered her missing, she'd say she'd gone out to the corral to check the horses. She wasn't worried. So far, they'd believed everything she told them.

The next morning, Colt tried to talk Hilde out of opening the shop. "Can't you have someone else man Needles and Pins for a few weeks?"

Hilde touched his handsome face, cupping his strong jaw, and smiled into those blue eyes of his. He'd been so gentle, so loving, last night when they'd made love. At least the second time. Before that, he'd let his passion run as wild as horses in a windstorm.

Her skin still tingled from the memory. She'd never known that kind of wild abandon. Just the thought thrilled her. She'd awakened feeling as if she could conquer the world. Hadn't she always known that she could be anything she wanted with the right man—in or out of bed?

"I am not going to let Dee or whoever she is keep me from doing what I love," she said, as she felt the rough stubble along his strong jawline. "Especially this morning when I'm feeling so…"

He laughed. "So…?"

"Invincible."

Colt pulled her to him and kissed her. As he drew back, he said, "I love seeing you like this, but Dee will figure out that you have her fingerprints and DNA. She isn't going to take this lying down. You have to know that."

She nodded. "Remember? I know what she's capable of. And I know she isn't finished. How long before we know who she is?" Colt had left for a while before daylight to go to the office to run Dee's fingerprints. He had a friend at the crime lab he'd called.

"You're counting on her fingerprints being on file. She might not have a record. Also, she might actually be Dee Anna Justice."

Hilde knew Dee was slippery. She might have avoided getting arrested. Might never have had a job that required she be fingerprinted. She might even be who she said she was. But all Hilde could do was hope that not only was she right about Dee being an impostor—but also that the woman had had at least one run-in with the law so her prints would come up. The sooner Dee was exposed, the sooner she would be gone from the ranch.

"I just don't want you getting your hopes up. The toothbrush was a good idea. We might be able to compare Dee's DNA to Dana's."

"I should have thought to get Dana's DNA while I was at it."

"Don't even think about," he said, holding her away from him so she couldn't avoid his gaze. "I'm serious. You have to stay away from Cardwell Ranch."

Hilde nodded. By now Dee would have realized that her makeup and toothbrush were missing. Hopefully she was running scared.

Colt hated that he had to go back down to West Yellowstone on the burglary case today. He didn't like leaving Hilde alone.

"Can I see you for a minute?" the marshal asked, as he was getting ready to leave the office later that morning.

Colt stepped into Hud's office.

"Close the door, please."

He turned to close the door, worry making him anxious. Hud had always run the station in a rather informal way. Not that they all weren't serious about their jobs. But Hud had never seen the need to throw around his weight.

"Have a sit," he said now.

"Is something wrong?" Colt asked, afraid Hud had somehow found out that he'd sent Dee's prints to his friend who worked at the crime lab.

"I wanted to talk to you about Hilde." Hud shook his head. "I know, it's not my place as your boss. Or even as your friend. But I feel I have to. Did you see her last night?"

Colt almost laughed. He figured Hud already knew that his patrol pickup had been parked in front of her house all night. News traveled fast in such a small, isolated community. Gossip was about the only excitement this time of year. It was too early for most tourists or seasonal homeowners, so things were more than a little quiet.

"Yes, I saw her," he said, keeping his face straight.

"I've known Hilde for a long time. I'm concerned about her."

"She's been a little distraught," Colt said. "She truly believes that Dee might be dangerous and is concerned about you and your family."

"I gathered that," Hud said with a curse, then studied him for a long moment. "I get the feeling you agree with her."

"I think there is cause for concern." He hurried on, before Hud could argue differently, knowing he was in dangerous territory. "You never laid eyes on this woman before she showed up at your door. You can't even be sure she is who she says she is."

"Dana sent her a certified letter that she had to sign for at her current address. And I've seen her identification."

That surprised Colt. "Then you *were* suspicious."

Hud sighed. "I had to be after the allegations Hilde was making. But she checks out, and Dana is enjoying her visit. She thinks Hilde is jealous. I can see that you don't agree."

"I'm just saying, you might want to keep an eye on her, that's all."

His boss looked as if there was more he wanted to say. Or more he was hoping his deputy would. But Colt held his tongue. His friend at the crime lab had promised to run the prints as quickly as he could.

Whatever the outcome, he hadn't figured out what to do after that. Until then, there was little he *could* do.

"We finally got a positive identification on Rick Cameron," Hud said, and tossed the man's file across his desk to Colt.

He opened it, glanced at the latest entry and jerked his head up in surprise. "Richard Northland?" So he hadn't been using his real name at all?

Hud nodded. "And before you ask, Dee had no idea he was lying about his name."

Colt let out a laugh as he tossed the file back. "As your friend? Get Dee out of your house. As your deputy? I really should get to work."

Hilde was lost in the memory of last night with Colt as she unlocked Needles and Pins. Dinner had been magical. The lovemaking had been beyond anything she'd ever experienced. She'd been lost in a dream state all morning.

That's why it took her a moment to realize what she was seeing.

The shop had been vandalized.

Bolts of fabric were now scattered over the floor. Displays had been toppled, and spools of thread littered the areas of the floor that weren't covered by fabric bolts.

She fumbled her phone from her purse, her heart pounding as she realized whoever had done this could still be in the shop. That was when she noticed the back door standing open. The vandal had left a large roll of yellow rickrack trailing out the back door like the equivalent of a bread trail through the shop.

"911. What is your emergency?" she heard an operator say.

"My shop has been vandalized," Hilde said.

"You're calling from Big Sky?"

"Yes. Needles and Pins."

"Is the vandal still there?"

"No. I don't believe so."

"Please wait outside until the marshal or one of his deputies arrive. Do you need to stay on the phone with me?"

"No. I just can't imagine who would—" That's when Hilde saw the scissors. Six of them. All stabbed into the top of her counter just inches from where she'd pretended to attack Dee to get the woman's fingerprints.

"You look tired," Dana said when Dee came downstairs. "Did you sleep all right?"

"Like a baby." Once she got into bed again. Last night's exploits had left her exhausted. Clearly just what she'd needed since once she'd hit the sheets, she hadn't had the nightmare again.

Dana was busy with the kids as usual. "It might be just as well that I don't have anything planned for you today. Maybe a day just resting would do us all good."

Dee didn't know how the woman managed with four kids. She'd apparently just finished feeding the two oldest because she was only now clearing away their plates. She sent them off to the bathroom to wash up.

The two youngest were in some kind of contraptions that allowed them to roll around the kitchen. They'd gotten caught in a corner and one of them was hollering his head off.

Dana saved him, kneeling down to cajole him before she asked, "I made Mary and Hank pancakes, Dee. Would you like some?"

The kitchen smelled of pancakes and maple syrup. Dee heard her stomach growl. She was starved, also probably because of all the exercise she'd gotten last night. She'd been careful to stay away from any streetlights, and she was sure no one had seen her leaving and returning to the ranch.

"I'd love pancakes, but let me make them," Dee offered, knowing Dana wouldn't take her up on it.

"It's no trouble. Anyway, you're my guest."

Dee could hear something in Dana's voice, though. Her hostess was tiring of her guest. Probably all the drama. Dana would be glad when Dee left.

Well, there was nothing she could do about that, because the drama was far from over. Forced to move up her plan, she said, "I'm thinking I've stayed too long."

Dana turned from the stove. "No. I don't want you to feel that way at all. I'm just sorry. I really wanted you to have a good time."

"I *am* having a good time." Dee went over and gave Dana a hug. "But I need to get back home and look for a job. I can't be off work for too long." Sometimes she couldn't believe how easy lying came to her. She was more amazed by people who couldn't tell a lie. Maybe it was a talent you were born with.

Or maybe you had to learn it at your daddy's knee, she thought bitterly.

"I checked this morning about a flight," she said with equal effortlessness. "I'm booked for Saturday on a nonstop flight to LaGuardia." She knew Dana and Hud wouldn't check to see if it was true or not. But Colt might.

Dana didn't try to get her to change her mind. *Yep, it's time.* She just said, "Well, I hate to see you cut your trip short, but you know best."

"This isn't my only trip to Cardwell Ranch," Dee said.

"Well, I insist on paying for your flight." Dana held up her hand even though Dee hadn't protested. "No arguments. I want this trip to be my treat."

"That is so sweet of you. I'm going to pay you back, though, and then some." By booking the nonstop flight that was available only on Saturday, she had bought herself a little more time. It wasn't perfect timing, but she'd have to make it work, especially after finding her toothbrush and makeup missing. She'd already put the wheels in motion. *Hang on,* she thought, because she knew what was about to hit the fan.

Dana looked visibly relaxed now that she knew her guest was leaving. Dee hated Hilde at that moment. The woman had been a thorn in her side from the beginning. If she had just backed off… But it was too late for regrets, she thought, and checked her watch.

Any minute poor Hilde would be crying on the marshal's shoulder and no doubt blaming her.

Marshal Hud Savage stopped in the doorway of Needles and Pins and demanded, "What are you doing?"

"I'm cleaning up my shop," Hilde said, as she placed another bolt of fabric back where it went. She was thankful that most of the fabrics hadn't gotten soiled or ruined. Dee could have torn up the place much worse. Hilde knew she should be thankful for that.

She'd started cleaning up the moment she'd realized who'd done this. At that same moment, she'd known there was no reason to wait for the marshal. Hud wasn't going to believe Dee had done this. And the only way to try to change his mind would be to show him the scissors and explain why they were a message from Dee.

Hilde couldn't do that without telling what she'd done to get Dee's fingerprints and Colt's involvement. She wasn't about to drag him into this any more than he already was.

"You shouldn't have touched anything until I got here," Hud said behind her. "Hilde—"

She stopped working to look at him. Fueled by anger, she'd accomplished a lot in a short time. "The person broke in through the back. I haven't touched anything back there."

He looked toward the back of the shop, where she had a small kitchen she and her staff used as a break and storage room. She'd found a chair moved over against the wall under the open window. There appeared to be marks on the window frame where someone had pried it open.

When she'd stepped outside in the alley, she'd discovered the large trash container pulled over under the window.

Hud went back in the break room, then outside. "Is anything missing?" he asked when he came back in.

"I don't believe so. I don't leave money down here. I think it was just a malicious act of vandalism."

"Looks like it might have been kids, then," Hud said.

Hilde had stopped to look at him, after restoring almost all of the bolts of fabric to their correct places. She saw him staring at the countertop where the half-dozen new scissors had been stuck in the wood.

"Kids resort to this sort of thing just for something to do, I guess," he said.

"It wasn't kids." She crossed her arms because she was trembling and she didn't want him to see it. She thought that if she kept calm and didn't get upset or cry, he might believe her.

"Don't tell me Dee did this." He looked as resolute as she felt.

"Okay, I won't. You don't want to hear the truth, fine. Kids did it."

"Hilde," Hud said in that tone she was getting used to. "Dee went to bed last night before we did. If she had driven into town, I would have known it."

"Maybe she walked."

"It's a couple of miles. She can barely walk around the yard without twisting an ankle. You think she climbed up into that window back there?" He was shaking his head. "I'm sorry this happened. I'll file a report and you can turn it over to your insurance. I'm glad nothing was destroyed."

She laughed at that. Dee had destroyed so much—the shop was the least of it.

"Are you going to be okay?"

The concern and kindness she heard in his tone was her undoing. The tears broke loose as if they had been walled up, waiting for the least bit of provocation to burst out.

He patted her shoulder. "Take the rest of the day off. Go home. Get some rest."

As if rest would make her world right again.

* * *

Fortunately, the rest of the day was busy at the shop. All the women who'd come in to sign up for quilting classes buoyed Hilde's spirits.

Dana called midmorning. "Just wanted to say hi."

Hilde figured she'd heard about the vandalism from Hud. He must not have told her about the allegations against her cousin.

"Fourteen women have signed up for the quilting classes so far," she told her silent partner in the shop.

"Oh, that's great. You must be excited to get them started."

"I am. It's going to be a good summer." Hilde said the last like a mantra, praying it was true.

"Dee's leaving Saturday," Dana said.

The words should have made her heart soar, but she heard sadness in her friend's voice. "I'm sorry her visit didn't go like you had hoped."

The bell over the door jangled as another customer came in.

Dana must have heard it. "You're busy. I'll let you go. I just wanted you to know I was thinking about you."

"Thank you for calling." It was the best she could do before Dana hung up.

The rest of the day slipped by. Hilde had moments when she would forget about the break-in. She knew she would have to replace the top of the counter. The scissor holes were a gut-wrenching reminder each time she saw them that it wasn't over with Dee.

Colt must have called when she was helping a customer by carrying her fabric purchases out to her car. He'd left a message that he hoped he could see her tonight.

She texted back that she was looking forward to it.

And suddenly it was time to close up shop. She gathered her things, trying hard not to look at the top of the counter. Thinking about Dee only made her blood boil.

A gust of wind caught the door as she started to lock up. She hadn't realized the wind had come up or that a storm was blowing in.

As she turned, she saw that her SUV parked across the street was sitting at a funny angle. Then she noticed the right back tire. Flat.

All she'd been thinking about the past few minutes was going home, taking a nice hot bath and getting ready for when Colt got back from West Yellowstone.

After finding her store vandalized first thing in the morning, she wasn't going to let a flat tire ruin her mood now, she thought. For a moment, she considered changing the tire herself, but she wasn't dressed for it, and her house was only a short walk from the shop.

As she started down the street, she saw that the storm was closer than she'd thought. Dark clouds rolled in, dimming the remainder of the day's light. She'd be lucky to get home before it started to rain, and in April the rain could easily turn to snow.

Hilde laughed, surprised that even the storm didn't bother her. She was seeing Colt again tonight and she couldn't wait. The only real dark cloud right now was Dee Anna Justice, and apparently there wasn't a darned thing she could do about her.

When she looked up and saw Dee coming down the dark street toward her, she feared she'd conjured her. Because of the upcoming storm and the time of the year, the streets were deserted—something she hadn't noticed until that moment.

Stopping, she considered what to do. Dee had realized

that she had her fingerprints and DNA. That was probably why she'd torn up the shop. Did that mean she'd realized whatever she'd been up to was about to come to a screeching halt? Or would the prints only prove that the woman really was Dee Anna Justice, a psychopath who would be able to keep fooling Dana unless Hilde and Colt could prove otherwise?

More to the immediate point, what was she doing here now? Hilde considered whether she should make a run for it. She didn't have that many options. Calling the marshal's office for help would be a waste of time.

"You don't have to look so scared," Dee called to her. "I came to give you some news that I think will make you happy."

Hilde let the woman get within a few feet of her. "That's close enough. What is it?"

"You win."

"You're the one who made it into a competition."

Dee chuckled as she took another step closer. "I've known women like you my whole life. Everything comes so easy to you. You've never had to fight for anything. You wouldn't have lasted two seconds in my world."

"I'm sorry you had a rough life, Dee, if that is really your name. But that doesn't give you the right to take someone else's—literally."

"You're right," Dee said, not even bothering to deny anything. "I'm leaving. I just wanted you to know. That, and I'm sorry. I don't expect you to understand. I don't even understand why I'm like I am sometimes." She put her head down, actually sounding as if she meant it.

Hilde wondered what kind of life this woman really *had* lived through. Dee was right that her own had been cushy. As much as she hated it, she felt some sympathy for the woman. "You should try to get some help."

Dee slowly raised her head. It took Hilde an instant to realize Dee had stepped closer during all this. When she met her gaze, Hilde saw that something had changed in her eyes. It was an instant too long.

Before Hilde could react, Dee grabbed her right hand and raked Hilde's nails down her own left cheek.

Hilde let out a cry of shock and jerked her hand back.

Dee was smiling as she touched the four angry scratches down her face. Laughing at Hilde's reaction, she reached down and picked up a chunk of broken sidewalk at the edge of the street.

Hilde took a step back as Dee said, "You think I need help? Maybe I *should* see someone." She hit herself in the face with the piece of concrete and for a moment, Hilde thought Dee would buckle under the savage blow. But she straightened, dropped the chunk of sidewalk and, in the next instant, began to tear at her clothes.

"What are you doing?" Hilde cried. "Have you lost your mind?"

"Isn't this what you wish you were able to do to me?" Dee asked, smiling again. Her left eye was already swelling shut from where she'd hit herself. There was blood at the corner of her mouth and her lip was split and bleeding. The scratches down the left side of her face were bleeding now as well.

"No, I would never—" The rest of Hilde's words died on her lips as she realized exactly what Dee *was* doing. "No one will believe I did that to you!"

"Won't they?" Dee asked with a smirk. "Wanna bet?" With that she turned and ran screaming down the street.

Chapter 11

Hilde rushed back to Needles and Pins, fumbled the key in the lock and, once inside, relocked the door behind her. She was in shock, never having witnessed anything like that in her life.

Her hands shook as she took out her cell phone. She tried to call Colt but only got his voice mail. She left a message that it was urgent she talk to him. Only after she hung up did she remember he had to go back to West Yellowstone today.

She'd barely hung up when she saw Marshal Hud Savage pull up in his patrol pickup in front of the shop. Past him, across the street, she spotted her SUV with the flat tire. She hadn't had a flat in years. Why hadn't she realized it was a trap?

Because that wasn't how her mind worked. She'd never had to read evil into everything—until Dee arrived in town.

Hilde felt like a fool. She'd played right into the woman's hands, not once, but time and again. The more she protested, the worse it got. She knew that even if she hadn't started to walk home, Dee would have found an opportunity to make this happen.

Lightning cut a zigzagged line across the sky behind Hud as he headed for her front door. Thunder followed on its heels. Large drops of rain pelted the sidewalk as she put her cell phone back in her purse and hurried to unlock the shop door. "Hud, I—"

"I need you to come with me down to the station," he said, his voice hard as the sidewalk Dee had hit herself with.

"I didn't do any of that to her," Hilde cried. "Hud, you have to believe me."

He grabbed her right hand, holding it up. "Hilde, her skin is still under your fingernails."

"Hud, I know this sounds crazy, but that's the problem. Dee, or whatever her name is, *is* crazy. She's insane. She did all of that to herself."

He shook his head looking as sad as she had ever seen him. "Are you telling me you didn't attack her previously with a pair of scissors right here in your shop?"

Of course Dee would have told him about that, too. "No. I mean, yes, but—"

He began to read her rights to her. "Let's go," he said when he finished.

"You're really arresting me?" She couldn't believe any of this was happening. "You know me, Hud—"

"I thought I did. Dee Anna is pressing assault charges against you. Hilde, what is going on with you?"

She swallowed and shook her head. Even if she told him about the scissors incident, it wouldn't help her. Nor help Colt. She just had to put her faith in Colt to find out the truth about the woman—and soon.

Colt tried to reach Hilde the moment he got her message. Her phone went straight to voice mail. He called the shop, just in case she was working late. She did that a lot, especially since she'd recently taken over the space next to Needles and Pins and expanded the business.

She was buying a line of sewing machines and would be starting quilting lessons, now that she had the room. He loved her work ethic. Loved a lot of things about her, he thought, reminded of last night.

With growing concern when she didn't answer at the shop, he realized he didn't know whom else to call. Not that long ago, he could have called Dana. She would have known where Hilde was. Dana and Hilde had been that close.

But not now. Thanks to Dee.

He was holding his phone, trying to decide what to do, when it rang. It was one of the dispatchers, Annie Wagner, a cute twentysomething redhead who was dating a Bozeman police officer he knew.

"I thought you'd want to know," Annie said in a hushed voice. "Hilde has been arrested."

"What?" His mind whirled. Hilde?

"Dee Anna Justice came screaming into the office thirty minutes ago saying Hilde had attacked her."

Colt groaned. He'd understood Hilde's thinking with the scissors, but—

"Dee was a mess. She looked like she'd gotten into a cat fight. Black eye, scratched up, bleeding."

He couldn't imagine Hilde doing that to anyone even

if she was provoked. But if she was defending herself—

"Where is Hilde now?"

"Hud has her in his office. I just put through a call from Dee Anna Justice. Do you want me to call you if anything changes?"

"Thanks, Annie. I appreciate it. I'm on my way back from West Yellowstone. I should be there within the hour."

What had happened? He couldn't even imagine.

He'd told himself that Hud would see through Dee soon. Or Dee would give up once she realized Hud loved Dana and would never fall for her. He'd told himself that as long as Hilde stayed away from the ranch and Dee, this wouldn't escalate.

He'd been wrong. He also realized that until that moment, he hadn't really thought Dee had tried to kill Hilde. The scare at the falls had been just that. The incident under the raft? He thought Dee had probably pulled the same thing. Held Hilde under the raft then tried to save her, only this time Hilde had fought her off.

Now he was angry with himself for not truly believing what Hilde had known in her heart. Dee was capable of horrendous things. Even murder. Maybe she'd drugged Rick. What had she done to get Hilde arrested? Tried to kill her only to have Hilde fight back?

His heart was pounding as he switched on his lights and siren and raced toward Big Sky.

Hilde knew she was lucky that Hud hadn't brought her into jail in handcuffs. She figured that might be Dana's doing. Dana would go to bat for her even if she believed that her once best friend had attacked her cousin.

It still amazed her that anyone would believe Dee.

But look at the extremes the woman would go to. She *was* insane. How else could Hilde explain it? Insane and desperate. This was a ploy to keep Hilde from getting her fingerprints run. Which had to mean that Dee really wasn't Dee Anna Justice—just as the now deceased Rick had insinuated.

But none of that helped Hilde right now, she thought, as she looked across the marshal's big desk. He was on the phone and had been for several minutes. From his tone of voice, she suspected it had been Dana who'd called, but Hilde now thought that Dana had put Dee on the line.

"I do understand," Hud was saying. "But I'd prefer that you came down here and we discussed this before you made any—" He listened for a moment, his gaze going to Hilde, before he said, "If you're sure. I would strongly advise you against this." More listening, then he said, "Fine," and hung up.

Hilde hadn't realized that she'd been holding her breath toward the end of his conversation until she let it out as he hung up.

Hud sat for a moment before he turned to her. "Dee is dropping the charges. I can still hold you, if I want to, and I'm certainly considering it."

She could tell that Dana had fought for her. Why else would Dee have dropped the charges? She felt tears sting her eyes. She knew better than to argue that she hadn't done anything to Dee. She'd already tried the truth and that had gotten her arrested, so she waited.

"Dee is filing a temporary restraining order that is good for twenty days. I assume you know what that is," he said.

A restraining order? It was all she could do not to

scream. "It means I can't go near her." Which meant she couldn't go near the ranch or Dana. Her tears now were of frustration. Dee kept maneuvering her into impossible situations where Hilde always came out looking like the villain.

"That's going to be hard to do in Big Sky. Hilde," he said with a sigh. "Think about taking a vacation. Go see your mother in Chicago. Or go lay on a beach for a couple of weeks. Get out of here."

"For twenty days?" Wouldn't Dee love that. "Or maybe she'll make it a permanent restraining order, since she doesn't seem to be leaving, does she?"

"Hilde, I'm trying to help. I'd think you'd want to get out of here for a while."

"You don't know how tempting that is, Hud." She felt as beat-up as Dee was. She'd lost control of her life. She'd certainly lost her friends, her shop had been vandalized and she was losing faith that she would ever be able to fix any of this before things got worse.

"Dana is worried about you," he said, and she heard some of that old caring in his voice.

"And I'm worried about her. I wish I *could* leave, but I can't, Hud. I can't leave Dana knowing what's living in your house right now. I'm sorry," she said when she saw his expression harden. "So can I go now?"

He nodded. "Hilde? Stay away from Dee."

"Believe me, I'm doing my best. For the record, do you want to actually hear the truth?" She didn't wait for him to answer. "I came out of the shop after locking up to find I had a flat tire. I should have suspected something then, but I've never been a suspicious person. I started to walk home, no big deal, that's when I saw Dee. She called to me, said she had some news. When she got close, she told me she was leaving. She said she was sorry for what she'd done to me."

Hilde stopped for a moment, smiled and said, "You know I actually believed her. She is that good. And then she grabbed my hand, raked my fingernails down her face. I was so shocked I couldn't move. I jerked my hand back. That's when she picked up a chunk of broken sidewalk from the side of the street and hit herself in the face. I know," she said, seeing his disbelieving expression. "I had the same reaction. Right after that was when she began to rip her clothing. She said no one would believe me. So far, she's been dead-on, hasn't she?"

With that she turned and walked out, leaving Hud frowning after her.

Only a few miles out of Big Sky, Colt got the call that Dee was refusing to press charges, deciding to take out a temporary restraining order instead. He swore, anxious to get to Hilde and find out what had happened.

He found her at her house. She hadn't been home long when she opened the door. He saw that she had a stunned look on her face. Stunned and devastated. It was heartbreaking.

Without a word, he took her in his arms. She was trembling. He took her over to the couch, then went to her liquor cabinet and found some bourbon. He poured her a couple fingers' worth.

"Drink this," he said.

"Aren't you afraid what I might do liquored up?" she asked sarcastically.

"Terrified," he said and stood over her until she'd downed every drop. "You want to talk about it?" he asked, taking the empty glass from her and joining her on the couch.

She let out a laugh. "*I* hardly believe what happened. Why would I expect anyone else to?"

"I believe you. I believe everything you've told me."

Tears welled in her brown eyes. He drew her to him and kissed her, holding her tightly. "I'm sorry you had to go through this alone."

She nodded and wiped hastily at the tears as she drew back to look at him. "You're my only hope right now. We have to find out whatever we can about this woman." And then she told him everything, from finding the shop vandalized to what led up to her being nearly arrested.

When she finished, he said, "We shouldn't be surprised."

"Surprised? I'm still in shock. To do something like that to yourself…"

"You knew Dee was sick."

Hilde nodded. "What will she do next? That's what worries me."

Colt didn't want to say it, but that worried him, too. "Maybe Hud has the right idea. Isn't there somewhere—"

"I'm not leaving. Dee told me that I've never had to fight for anything. Well, I'm fighting now. I'm bringing her down. One way or another."

"Hilde—"

"She has to be stopped."

"I agree. But we have to be careful. She's dangerous." He felt his phone vibrate, checked it and saw that his boss had sent him a text. "Hud wants to see me ASAP." Not good. "I don't want to leave you here alone."

"I'll be fine. Dee won this round. She won't do anything for a while, and I'm not going to give her another chance to use me like she did today."

He heard the courage as well as the determination in her voice. Hilde was strong and, no matter what Dee had told her, she *was* a fighter.

"Would you mind if I came by later?"

Her kiss answered that question quite nicely.

Hud was waiting when Colt arrived. He motioned him into his office. "What the hell do you think you're doing?" he said the moment Colt closed the door and sat down.

"I beg your pardon?" He had a pretty good idea what the problem was, but he wasn't about to hand him the rope to hang him.

"Tell me about the unauthorized request to run fingerprints you sent to the crime lab," the marshal said.

That's what Colt figured. Someone had caught his friend. He hated that he'd gotten the man into trouble. Sticking out his own neck was one thing. Sticking out someone else's was a whole other story.

"They're the woman's now staying at your house, the one you call Dee Anna Justice," he said.

Hud swore and slammed a hand down on his desk as he sat forward. "What the hell were you thinking sending an unauthorized request to the crime lab?"

"I was trying to protect you and your family."

"That isn't going to wash and you know it. Well, let me give you the news. There are no prints on file." Hud let that sink in. "That's right. Dee has no record. Satisfied?"

So she'd never been arrested. That didn't surprise him given what he'd seen of her maneuvers so far.

"This is about Hilde, isn't it?" Hud demanded. "You did this for her. This is so you can get closer to her."

Colt got to his feet. "If that's what you think—"

"You're suspended."

This, too, didn't come as a surprise. He met Hud's gaze. "If you really think I would use law enforcement resources to try to get a woman in bed, then I think you should fire me."

"Damn it, Colt, you're a fine deputy marshal and I don't want to lose you. Two weeks without pay. Get out of here."

He left Hud's office, knowing there was nothing he could say. He'd taken a risk. It had cost him. Worse, it had only made Dee look more innocent.

"Colt," Annie whispered, as he started for the door out of the station. He could tell that she'd probably heard everything. The department was small, the walls thin. She motioned him over and secretly slipped him a folded sheet of paper. "I think you'll want to see this."

They both heard Hud come out of his office. Colt mouthed *Thank you* and quickly left. It wasn't until he reached home that he finally unfolded the sheet and saw what was written on it.

He went straight to his computer. It didn't take long before he found what he was looking for—and then some.

Chapter 12

Hilde knew things hadn't gone well at the marshal's office the moment she opened the door and saw Colt's face.

"What happened?" she asked, as she let him in.

"Nothing to worry about."

"He found out that you sent Dee's fingerprints to the crime lab."

"I knew there was a chance that might happen."

"Tell me he didn't fire you," she cried.

"He didn't. Suspended for two weeks. As it turns out, the suspension couldn't come at a better time. I've got some news."

They moved into the kitchen, where Hilde got him a beer and poured a glass of wine for herself. She had a feeling she was going to need it. "I hate getting you into trouble."

"You didn't. I'm in this just as deep as you are," he

said, and kissed her as he took the cold bottle of beer she offered him. He took a sip. She watched him, desire making her legs weak as water.

She dropped into a chair in front of the fireplace, curling her legs under her and taking a drink of her wine. She'd built a small fire since he'd said he would be back. She'd tried not to count the minutes.

Colt didn't sit but stood in front of the fire. She could tell he was worked up, too antsy to sit.

"You have news?" she asked, afraid what he was about to tell her.

"Rick Cameron's real name was Richard Northland. Cameron was apparently one of a number of aliases he has used. He was a small-time con artist, been arrested a couple of times, but nothing that got him more than a little jail time. The person he cheated tended to drop the charges."

Hilde felt her eyes widen. "So he and Dee had a lot in common."

"I'm sure Dee was shocked by the news when Hud told her."

Hilde let out a humorless laugh. "I'm sure she was."

"There's more. Her fingerprints weren't on file. But when I did some digging online, I found a story about Richard and his sister, Camilla Northland."

"His *sister?*"

Colt nodded. "The two of them were the only survivors of a fire at their home in Tuttle, Oklahoma. Both parents were killed. Apparently there was some suspicion that one or both might have purposely started the fire. Richard was fourteen at the time, Camilla sixteen."

"Are you saying what I think you are?" Hilde asked.

"I'm trying hard not to jump to any conclusions. All

we know for sure is that the man lying in the morgue is Richard Northland from Tuttle, Oklahoma. I'll know more once I get there."

"Get there?"

"I'm flying to Oklahoma tomorrow on the first flight out."

Hilde got up from her chair and moved to the fire as a sudden chill skittered across her skin like spider legs. "You think there's a possibility that Dee is his sister?"

"A possibility based on nothing more than a feeling that the two of them knew each other longer than Dee said."

She recalled how Rick had turned around when the naked Dee had gotten out of the lake. "Dana thought Rick was Dee's boyfriend."

"Probably because that's what she told her. I haven't been able to find out much of anything about Camilla because she dropped off radar right after the fire. According to a newspaper account, the two were going to live with an aunt since their parents were the only family they had."

"She dropped off the radar because she's not using her real name?"

"That would be my guess. While I'm gone I want you to stay clear of Dee."

"If she finds out where you've gone…"

"She won't. I'll tell someone at the station that I'm going to Denver to see my brother. I'm sure by now they all know I've been suspended."

"Colt," she said, touching his strong shoulder. "I don't want to see you lose your job."

"I won't. I think whatever I find out in Oklahoma will change things drastically."

Hilde couldn't help being nervous. "Be careful. I'm just afraid what Dee might do if she thinks you're onto her. So far it's just me she's after."

"Yeah, that's what worries me. Look what happened to Rick," Colt said.

Hilde shivered and he took her in his arms. "I just don't want her moving up her plan, whatever it is."

"I'm more worried about you. I wish you were going with me."

"If we both went, it would look even more suspicious. Anyway, she's accomplished what she set out to do. Dana and I are hardly speaking."

"I hate seeing you like this," he said, and kissed her. "It's going to be all right. I know you're worried about Dana. But we're going to get this resolved."

She nodded. "Hopefully before something horrible happens."

"Hilde, I don't think Dee is through with you, so be careful."

"I will."

"Promise?"

She smiled and leaned up to kiss him. "I'll be careful."

"I'll call you from Oklahoma as soon as I know something. I won't be gone any longer than I have to. I'm going home to pack, but first…" He swung her up in his arms. "I don't want you to forget about me while I'm gone."

"Like that could happen," she said with a laugh, as he carried her into the bedroom.

Colt tried to get on standby, but the earliest flight he could get on was that afternoon. He hated leaving Hilde. Last night he'd managed to talk her into letting Ronnie open the shop and man it until he got back. It had taken some talking, though. Hilde was one determined woman.

He tried not to speculate on what Dee might do. When he'd called Annie at the office, he'd told her he was flying to Denver to visit his brother. Of course, she knew he'd been suspended.

"Mrs. Savage was in earlier," Annie told him in a hushed whisper. "She and the boss had a row over your suspension. Seems her cousin has booked a flight to New York City for Saturday."

That had been news. Saturday was only two days away. If Dee was telling the truth. "I suppose there is no way to find out if she really did book that flight," he said to Annie.

She chuckled. "I'll see what I can do."

After he hung up, he wondered if this meant Dee was giving up. Maybe she'd realized that Hilde had her fingerprints and DNA, so it wouldn't be long before they knew who she really was. *Best to leave town before that happened, huh, Dee?*

His plane landed in Salt Lake City with a short layover before he flew into Oklahoma City, where he rented a car. It was too late to drive to Tuttle, so he got a motel. When he called Hilde, she sounded fine, anxious, but staying in the house. He breathed a sigh of relief.

"Try to get some sleep," he told her. "I won't know anything until tomorrow at the soonest." He didn't sleep well at all and early the next morning set off for Tuttle.

The town had once been a tiny suburb. Now the buildings along the former main street were boarded up. It was one of many small, dying towns across the country.

Colt stopped at the combination grocery and gas station and wandered inside. A fan whirred in the window near the counter behind an elderly woman who sat thumbing through a movie magazine.

"Can you believe all the divorces they have out in Hollywood?" She looked up at him over her glasses as if actually expecting an answer.

"No, I can't."

She closed the magazine, studying him. "You aren't from around here."

He shook his head. "But I'm looking for someone *from* around here."

Her eyes widened a little. "I figured you were just lost. Who are you looking for? I know most everyone since I was born and raised right here."

That had been his hope. "Maybe you know them, then. Richard and Camilla Northland?

The woman's expression soured in a heartbeat. She leaned back as if trying to distance herself from his words. "Well, you won't find them around here."

"Actually, I'm looking for their aunt, the one who raised them after their parents died."

"Didn't die. Were murdered." She shook her head. "What do you want with Thelma?"

"I have some news about her nephew."

"There isn't any news she'd want to hear except that he's six feet under," the woman snapped.

"Then I guess I have some good news for her."

Hilde tried not to go down to the shop the next day, but Ronnie called to say there was a problem with the new sewing machine invoice and the deliveryman wasn't sure what she wanted him to do.

"I'll be right there." She was thankful for the call. Sitting around waiting to hear from Colt was making her all the more anxious. She was also thankful that the sewing machines hadn't arrived before Dee vandalized the shop.

Once at the shop after taking care of the problem, Hilde showed Ronnie some of the ideas she had for quilting classes, and they began to work on a wall hanging for the sewing room.

Hilde loved the way the shop was coming together. She'd long dreamed of a place where anyone who wanted to learn to quilt could come and sew with others of like mind. Quilting was a restful and yet creative hobby at any age. She had great plans for the future and was so excited about them that she'd almost picked up the phone and called Dana to tell her.

Dana still had money invested in Needles and Pins. Hilde realized that might change now. She should consider buying her out if their friendship went any further south. The thought made her sad. If only they could prove that Dee wasn't her cousin.

She was mentally kicking herself for not thinking to take Dana's toothbrush as well as Dee's, when the bell over the door jangled and she turned to see Dana walk into the shop.

Hilde felt her face light up—until she saw Dana's expression. Her stomach fell with the memory of what had happened yesterday. Dana must be horrified. But how could her once best friend not realize that Hilde could never beat up anyone?

She felt a spark of anger, which she quickly tamped down as Dana stepped into the shop. Letting her temper flare was a surefire way to make herself look more guilty.

"Could we talk alone?" Dana asked quietly.

"Ronnie, would you mind watching the counter for a few minutes?" Hilde called. Ronnie said she'd be happy to. Hilde led Dana into the break room and closed the door. She didn't want Ronnie hearing this. But the news was probably all over town anyway. The shop had been unusually slow today.

"I don't know what to say to you," Dana said.

Hilde stepped to the coffeepot, fingers trembling as she took two clean glass cups and filled each with coffee. She handed one to Dana, then sat down, ready for a lecture.

Dana seemed to hesitate before she sat down. Hilde didn't help her by denying anything. Instead she waited, relieved when Dana finally took a drink of the coffee and seemed to calm down some.

"How long have we known each other?" Hilde asked.

Dana looked up from her cup in surprise. "Since you came to town about…six years ago. But you know that."

"So for six years we've been close friends. Some might even have said best friends."

Dana's eyes suddenly shone with tears.

"Would you have said you knew me well?" She didn't wait for an answer. "Remember that spider in my kitchen that time? I couldn't squish it. You had to do it."

"You can't compare killing a spider to—"

"Dana, what if Dee wasn't your cousin?"

"That's ridiculous because she *is* my cousin."

Hilde wasn't going to argue that. Not right now anyway. "What if she was just some stranger who ended up on your doorstep and things began happening and the next thing you knew you and I were…" She couldn't bring herself to say where they were. "Would you take a stranger's word over mine?"

Dana put down her cup. "She said you would say you didn't attack her."

Hilde sighed and put down her own cup. "That you came here today makes me believe that there is some doubt in your mind. I hope that's true, because it might save your life."

"It's talk like that, Hilde, that makes me think you've lost your mind," Dana said, getting to her feet. "Why would Dee want to hurt me?"

"So she could have Hud."

Dana shook her head. "Hud loves *me*."

"But if you were gone…"

Dana reached into her jeans pocket and took out a piece of paper. Hilde recognized it as a sheet from the notepad Dana kept by the phone. "I called around. This is the name of a doctor everyone said was very good." When Hilde didn't reach for the note, Dana laid it on the table. "I think you need help, Hilde." Her voice broke with emotion.

"She doesn't just want you out of the way, Dana. Your children will have to go, too."

Dana's gaze came up to meet hers.

Hilde saw fear. "Trust me. Trust the friendship we had. You're in trouble. So are your babies."

A tear trailed down Dana's cheek. She brushed at it. "I have to go." She hurried out, leaving Hilde alone in the break room.

The moment she heard the bell jangle, Hilde got up, took a plastic bag from the drawer and carefully bagged Dana's coffee cup.

"What are you doing?"

She turned in surprise to find Dana standing in the doorway. She must have started to leave, but then changed her mind.

"I asked you what you were doing."

Hilde knew there was no reason to lie even if she could have thought of one Dana might believe. "I need your DNA to check it against Dee's."

The shocked look on Dana's face said it all. That and what she said before turning and really leaving this time: "Oh, Hilde."

Colt drove out of Tuttle, took the third right and pulled down a narrow two-track toward a stand of live oak. He hadn't been in the South in years. Oklahoma wasn't considered the South to people from Georgia or Alabama, but anywhere that cotton grew along the road was the South to him.

He followed the directions the woman at the grocery and gas station had given him until the road played out, ending in front of a weathered, stooped old house that was much like the elderly woman who came out on the porch.

He parked and climbed out. Thelma Peters was Richard and Camilla Northland's aunt on their mother's side of the family, PJ Harris had told him.

"Everyone's called me PJ since I was a girl," the elderly woman at the store had told him. "Not because it has anything to do with my name, which by the way is Charlotte Elizabeth. No, I got PJ because that's what I was usually wearing when I would come down here, to this very store, in the morning so my father could make me breakfast. My mother had died when I was a baby, you see. He'd pour me a bowl of cereal, ask me if I wanted berries. I always said no, then he'd pour on some thick cream." Her eyes had lit at the memory. "I can still taste that cream. Can't buy anything like it anymore."

He'd finally managed to turn her back to Richard and Camilla's aunt.

"Thelma Peters. She's an old maid. I can see where having those two in her house turned her against ever having any of her own children." PJ had studied him again then. "Don't be surprised if she comes out on her porch with a shotgun. Don't take it personally. Just make sure she knows you aren't that no-count nephew of hers. I'd hate to see you get shot."

"I'll keep that in mind," he'd promised.

"I'm here with some good news," Colt called out now to the elderly old maid holding the shotgun.

"If you're preaching the Gospel, I've already found the Lord. You wasted your gas coming out here," she called back.

"I'm a deputy marshal from Montana," he called to her. A slight exaggeration at the moment. He saw the change in her as if she was bracing herself for whatever bad news he was bringing. "Your nephew Richard has been killed."

Thelma Peters nodded, then took a step back and sat down hard in an old wooden chair on her porch. The barrel end of the shotgun banged against the worn wood flooring at her feet, but she held on to the gun as she motioned him to come closer.

Colt walked up to the house, shielding his eyes against the sun. The yard was a dust bowl. The weeds that had survived were baked dead. "I'm sorry to bring you the news."

She looked up then and, from rheumy but intelligent blue eyes, considered him for a long moment. "You certainly came a long way to give it to me."

"I need to ask you about Camilla."

Thelma let out a cough of a laugh. "You cross her path, too? Best say your prayers."

"I don't know if I've crossed her path or not. Do you happen to have a picture of her?"

The woman looked at him as if he was crazy. "Not one I keep out, I can tell you that."

"I sure would appreciate it if you could find one for me. I'm worried about a family in Montana that this woman has moved in with."

She grunted and pushed herself to her feet, using the shotgun like a crutch. "Better step inside. This could take a while."

When Dana came back from town, she was clearly upset.

"You didn't go see Hilde," Dee said, wanting to wring her neck. She'd begged her to stay away from her former friend. "Dana, what were you thinking?"

Hud, who'd come home to watch the kids while she ran to the store, seconded Dee's concern.

"I had to see her," Dana cried, then shook her head.

Dee had been so excited when Dana had told her that Hud was coming home to help her watch the children. She knew that neither of them wanted to leave the little darlings with her. She'd made it clear she knew nothing about kids, especially babies.

But all the time Hud had been home, he'd been so involved with the children that he wasn't even aware Dee was in the room.

"I hope you didn't listen to Hilde's crazy talk," Dee said, worried that that was exactly what Dana had done. She'd felt Dana pulling away from her. Worse, Hud was doing the same thing, she feared.

If only Hilde had just drowned that day under the raft.

Dee touched her sore black eye. "You're just lucky you didn't end up like me."

Dana glanced at her, wincing at the sight. Dee had to admit she looked like she'd been run over by a truck. But she'd wanted to make a statement and she had. Dana had been so thankful when she'd dropped the charges against Hilde. Even Hud had seemed relieved when he'd come home that night.

"It's worse than I thought," Dana said and looked at Hud. "I sat down and had a cup of coffee with her at the shop…"

Dee gritted her teeth in anger. How could Dana do that after seeing what Hilde had done to her cousin?

"She seemed calm, even rational…" Dana glanced at Dee then back at Hud.

Dee felt her heart begin to race. Hilde had gotten to Dana. She'd started believing her.

"Then I got ready to leave, made it as far as the door, thought of something and went back." She stopped and took a breath. "Hud, she was bagging my coffee cup."

Dee let out a silent curse that was like a roar in her ears.

"I demanded to know what she was doing," Dana continued now in tears. "She told me she was going to check my DNA against Dee's. I'm sorry, Dee," Dana said, turning to her again. "I'm so sorry."

"Don't be. Clearly Hilde has had some sort of psychotic episode. How can she think I'm not your cousin? We look so much alike."

Dana nodded, still obviously upset.

"I'd ask who she thought she was going to get to run

the tests, but I'm sure Colt is helping her," Hud said. "I can't imagine what he's thinking."

"I thought you said he went to Denver to see his brother?" Dee asked.

"That's what I heard, but I have my doubts. I can't see him leaving Hilde alone now. He must be as worried about her as we are."

Thelma Peters's house was small and cramped. She left him in a threadbare chair in the living room and disappeared into a room at the back. Periodically he would hear a bump or bang.

He looked around, noticing a picture of Jesus on one wall and a cross on another. A Bible lay open on the table next to his chair. He picked it up, curious what part she'd been reading. She had a passage underlined—Acts 3:19. *Repent therefore, and turn again, that your sins may be blotted out.*

"Here is the only one I could find." Thelma came back into the room with a snapshot clutched in her fingers. "I haven't seen Camilla in years, so I don't know what she looks like now. But this is what she looked like at sixteen."

Chapter 13

Colt looked down at the photo. His heart sank. The photo was of two people, a young man and a girl with long dark hair. The young man was the same man still at the morgue in Montana—Rick Cameron, aka Richard Northland.

The girl—was definitely not Dee.

He told himself it had been a long shot, but now realized how much he'd been counting on Dee being Camilla Northland. Maybe Rick really was her boyfriend. Maybe she didn't even kill him.

"This isn't the woman in Montana," he told Thelma.

"Like I said, she was only sixteen. I have no idea what she looks like now." She took the photograph back. "You look disappointed. You should be thankful the woman in Montana isn't Camilla. You should be very thankful."

"Were she and her brother really that bad?" he had to ask.

The old woman scoffed. "They killed their parents. Burned them to a crisp. That bad enough for you? They tried to poison me. Camilla pushed me down the stairs once no doubt hoping I would break my neck. I hate to think what they would have done if I'd broken a leg and needed the two of them to take care of me. I finally ran them off." Still clutching the photo, she sat down in a chair across from him and patted her shotgun. "I've always felt guilty about that." Her gaze came up to meet his. "But I couldn't have killed them even knowing what I was releasing on the world."

He felt a chill at her words as she looked from him to the photograph and seemed startled by what she saw.

"I grabbed the wrong photograph. This isn't Camilla. This is that awful girlfriend of Richard's." She pushed to her feet, padded out of the room and returned a moment later.

This time she handed him a photo of Richard and a girl standing on the porch outside. The girl's face was in shadow, but there was no doubt it was the woman who called herself Dee Anna Justice.

At sixteen, she already had those dark, soulless eyes.

Dee had been waiting, so she wasn't surprised when Dana finally asked.

"I know nothing about your father," Dana said, as she was making dinner. "Do you have any idea why our families separated all those years ago?"

Mary and Hank were making a huge mess building a fort in the living room. The twins were in dual high chairs spreading some awful-looking food all over themselves and anything else within reach.

Dee moved so she wasn't in their line of fire. Dana had

put her to work chopping vegetables for the salad. Now she stopped to look at the small paring knife in her hand. She tried to remember exactly what she'd told Stacy.

"I really have no idea," she said, thinking that if she had to cut up one more cucumber she might start screaming. Hud hadn't been around all day. Spending "free" time with Dana and the kids was mind-numbing.

"Can you tell me what your father was like?" Dana asked as she fried chicken in a huge cast-iron skillet on the stove. The hot kitchen smelled of grease. It turned Dee's stomach.

"He was secretive," Dee said, thinking of his daughter. The real Dee Anna had never talked about her family, her father in particular, which had been fine with her because she wasn't really interested. She liked her roommates to keep to themselves, just share an apartment, not their life stories.

"Secretive?" Dana said with interest. "And your mother?"

Dee gave her the same story she'd given Stacy. She had actually met Marietta Justice, so that made it easy.

"That surprises me. I can't imagine why my family wouldn't have been delighted to have Walter marry so well," Dana said.

"Maybe they didn't want him leaving here and they knew that was exactly what was going to happen," Dee said, as she chopped the last cucumber and dumped it into the salad. The entire topic of Dee Anna's family bored her. If Dana wanted to hear about an interesting family, Dee could tell her about hers.

"Tell me more about your side of the family," Dee said, knowing Dana would jump at the chance. She tuned her out as she ripped up the lettuce the way Dana had showed her and thought about her plan. She felt rushed, but she had no choice. In order to make this happen, she had to move fast.

Hilde had done a lot of damage, but Dee was sure that after Dana and the kids were gone, Hud would lean on her. Eventually.

She thought of the man she'd met on the airplane. He was still over on the Yellowstone River for a few more days. All she had to do was pick up the phone and call him. She could walk away from here and never look back. All her instincts told her that was the thing to do.

Dee heard the kids start screaming in the other room, then the front door slam. A moment later Hud Savage came into the kitchen with Mary and Hank hanging off him like monkeys. All three were laughing.

"What smells so good?" he asked. Even the two babies got excited to see him and joined in the melee.

Dee watched him give Dana a kiss. She felt her heart swell. She'd never wanted anything more in her life than what Dana had. No matter how long it took, she would have this with Hud Savage. Only he would love her more than he'd ever loved Dana.

"So Camilla is the woman you mentioned back in Montana," Thelma Peters said, and added under her breath, "God help you all."

Colt's heart was pounding. "If you know for certain that she and her brother killed their parents, why weren't they arrested?"

"No proof. Those two were cagey, way beyond their years. She was far worse than her brother. Smarter and colder. She made it look like an accident. Anyone who knew Camilla knew what had really happened out at that house the night of the fire. She fooled everyone else, making them feel sorry for her."

He thought about the way she'd worked Hud and Dana. Even himself that day on the river. Camilla Northland was a great actor. "And yet, you let them move in here."

"They were so young. I thought I could turn them around. I dragged the two of them to church." She shook her head. "It was a waste of time. The evil was too deep in her, and Richard was too dependent on her."

"Would you mind if I took this photograph?" he asked.

"Please do. For years, I've prayed never to see that face again. I've always worried that when I got old, she would come back here."

Thelma didn't have to say any more. He had a pretty good idea now of what Camilla might do to the aunt who had taken her in all those years ago.

"Do you believe in evil, Marshal?"

He didn't correct her. "I do now."

She nodded. "I assume she's already hurt people or you wouldn't be here."

He nodded, reminded that she'd gotten away with it, too. And might continue to get away with it because there was never any proof and she was very good at her lies.

"I pray you can stop her," Thelma said. "I couldn't. But maybe you can."

Hilde was at the shop when Colt called. After Dana had left, she'd been so upset she'd thought about going home. But she couldn't stand the thought of her empty house. So she'd stayed and helped set up the new sewing machines with Ronnie.

When her cell phone rang, she jumped as if she'd been electrocuted. Ronnie shot her a worried look. Hilde saw that it was Colt calling and, heart racing, hurried into the break room and closed the door.

"Where are you?" she asked.

"On my way to the airport. I was able to get a flight out this afternoon. If I can make the tight connections, I'll be home tonight."

Home tonight. She thrilled at his words. "It is *so* good to hear your voice."

"Rough day?" he asked. "Hilde—"

"Don't worry, I haven't seen Dee. Dana stopped by. I'll tell you about it when you get back." She braced herself. "What did you find out?"

"First, I need you to remain calm. I almost didn't call you because I was afraid you'd go charging out to the ranch."

"She's this Camilla person who they think killed her own parents," Hilde said.

"Yes."

She closed her eyes, gripping the phone, emotions bombarding her from every direction. Relief that she'd been right about the woman. Terror since a killer was still out at the ranch with her best friend and her kids.

"Listen to me, Hilde. If you go charging out there or even call, they aren't going to believe you—and you could force Dee to do something drastic and jeopardize everyone, okay?"

She nodded to herself, knowing what he was saying was true. Dana wouldn't believe Colt any more than she had Hilde. "You've told Hud, though, right? So he's going to take care of everything."

"I've been trying to reach him. I've left him a message. He'll know how to handle this. I need your word that you'll sit tight. I'll be there by tonight and this will all be over."

She wished it were that simple. She prayed he was right. "Okay. I know what you're saying. I won't do anything."

"Where are you?"

"At the shop. I couldn't stay at the house."

"I wish you would go home and wait for me. Lock the doors. Don't leave for any reason."

She smiled, touched by his concern.

"Hilde, I… I love you."

His words brought tears of joy to her eyes. For years she'd waited for the right man to come along. Dana had been her biggest supporter.

"I want you to find someone like Hud so badly," Dana would say.

Hilde had wanted that, too, but she'd thought it could never happen.

"Are you crying?" he asked.

She gulped back a sob. This was the happiest moment of her life and she couldn't share it with her best friend. "I love you, too, Colt."

"Okay, baby," he said. "I have to go. I'll call you the moment I land. Be safe."

She hung up and let the tears fall that she'd been fighting to hold back all day.

A moment later, Ronnie opened the door a crack. "Are you all right?"

Hilde almost laughed. Dana and Hud weren't the only people looking at her strangely lately. "Colt Dawson just told me that he loves me."

Ronnie started to laugh, clearly relieved. "That's wonderful. I guess you must be one of those people who cries when they're happy?"

Hilde nodded, although some of the tears were out of a deep sadness. In a matter of days, her life had changed so drastically it made her head spin.

"Do you want me to stay with you?" Ronnie asked. "If you don't feel like locking up tonight by yourself—"

Hilde hadn't realized it was so late. "No, I'm fine."

Ronnie hesitated. Of course she'd heard about Dee's alleged attack and probably even the restraining order.

"I don't think there will be any trouble tonight," Hilde said, thinking she should have gotten a restraining order against Dee. As if a restraining order would stop someone like her.

As Ronnie left, Hilde locked up behind her. She wasn't quite ready to go home yet. A part of her was still chilled by the news that the woman posing as Dee Anna Justice was actually Camilla Northland, sister of Richard Northland, both of them believed to be cold-blooded killers.

It was easy for Hilde to believe that of Dee. She knew firsthand what the woman was capable of. The fact that Dee was probably out on the ranch right now having dinner with Dana and Hud and the kids…

Colt was right, of course. Calling out there to warn Dana was a waste of breath. It could even make matters worse.

Hilde turned out the lights in the front of the store and walked to the break room. Closing the door, she pulled out her cell phone. At the touch of one button she could get Dana on the line.

She thought about what she could say. She hit the button. The phone rang three times. They were eating dinner. Dana wasn't going to answer the call.

Hilde had just started to hang up when it stopped ringing. "Dana?" She could hear breathing. "Dana, I just called to tell you that Colt just told me he loved me."

"I'm sorry, but you have the wrong number." The line went dead.

For just an instant, Hilde thought she had gotten the wrong number because that hadn't been Dana's voice.

Then her mind kicked into gear.

It had been Dee's voice. She'd answered Dana's cell phone.

Colt couldn't believe he'd blurted it out like that. *I love you.* He'd said it without thinking. He let out a chuckle. He'd just said what was in his heart.

He considered calling her back to warn her again about doing anything crazy. He had debated telling her about Dee to start with, afraid of what Hilde would do. For a woman who he suspected had never been impulsive in her life, she had been doing a lot of things on the spur of the moment lately.

Like telling him she loved him, too.

He felt his heart soar at the memory of her words. He couldn't wait to get home for so many reasons.

The moment he walked into the airport terminal, though, he felt his heart drop. Something was wrong. He could feel it in the air as he hurried to the airline counter and saw that his flight had been canceled.

"What's going on?" he asked of a man waiting in line. He could hear a woman arguing that she had to get to Salt Lake.

"All flights into Salt Lake City have been canceled for today because of a bad spring snowstorm," the man said. "Snow's falling at a rate of six inches an hour. I just saw it on the weather channel. Doesn't look good even for in the morning."

Colt felt like the woman arguing with the airline clerk. He desperately needed to get home. But unlike that woman, he realized he wasn't going to be flying.

He'd just reached the car rental agency when Annie called from the marshal's office in Big Sky. "Ready to be surprised? Dee Anna Justice *did* book a flight to New York City for tomorrow."

He *was* surprised. "You're sure?"

"I had the airline executive double-check. Because I called concerned about Dee Anna Justice, I figure they'll take her into one of those little rooms and do an entire cavity search," she said with a satisfied chuckle.

Colt was trying to make sense of this. Dee was really leaving tomorrow? Maybe she was just covering her bets.

"Not only that, Hud announced that he plans to take Dana on a trip to Jackson Hole beginning Sunday. Jordan and Liza are going to stay at the house for a couple of days and watch the kids."

"You're sure Dee isn't going with them?" he asked.

"Definitely not. He said he hoped things calmed down once Dana put Dee on the plane."

Colt bet he did. "Thanks for doing this, Annie. One more thing. I left a message for Hud—"

"There's been a break in the burglary case in West Yellowstone. He was up there today and he's coming back tomorrow. That's probably why he hasn't returned your call."

Either that or he'd seen who'd called and didn't want to deal with his suspended deputy right now. While Hud had to be having his own misgivings about Dee, Colt knew that the marshal would be skeptical even if Colt gave him the information he'd gathered in Tuttle—until he saw the photograph of Camilla Northland and her brother.

"You're in luck," the woman behind the counter told him. "I have one vehicle left. I'm afraid it's our most expensive SUV."

"I'll take it," he said, and pulled out his credit card. Getting the paperwork done seemed to take forever. He glanced at his watch. Not quite noon. While he was waiting for the woman to finish the paperwork, he'd checked.

It was twenty-two hours to Big Sky. That didn't take into account the bad weather ahead of him. He knew he wouldn't be able to make good time once he reached the snow. He would have to make up for it when he had dry roads.

But he could reach Big Sky by late morning. He just prayed that wouldn't be too late.

Finally, she handed him the keys. A few minutes later, he was in the leather, heated-seat lap of luxury and headed north.

Hilde had sounded disappointed when he'd called to tell her the news. "But I'm glad you're on your way. Just be careful. I checked the weather before you called. It looks like that storm is going to stay to the south of us."

Neither of them had mentioned what they had said to each other earlier.

"I can't wait to see you," he said.

"Me, too."

"I'd better get off and pay attention to my driving." He'd hung up feeling all the more frustrated that he couldn't get to her more quickly. Hud still hadn't returned his call.

He pushed down on the gas pedal, hoping he didn't get pulled over.

Dee saw how disappointed Dana was at dinner when Hud told her he had to go up to West Yellowstone the next day. Any other time, Dee would have felt the same way.

She touched the small vial in her pocket. Hud didn't realize how lucky he was. Now she could implement her plan without involving him. This was so much better.

"I should be back by late afternoon," Hud was saying. "What do you and Dee have planned?"

"She flies out tomorrow afternoon, so it's up to her," Dana said. She and Hud looked at Dee.

"I just want to spend the morning here on the ranch with Dana and the kids," Dee said. "I don't know when I'll get to see them again, so I want to make it last. If it's nice, I'd love to take the kids on a walk. I saw those tandem strollers you have out there. I thought we could hike up the road, pick wildflowers..."

"That's a wonderful idea," Dana said. "I could pack a lunch."

"You're not going," Dee said. "You are going to stay here and put your feet up and relax. You have been waiting on me for days. It's my turn to give you a break. The kids and I can pack the lunch, can't we?"

Mary and Hank quickly agreed. "I want peanut butter and jelly," Mary said.

"Mommy's strawberry jelly," Hank added, and Mary clapped excitedly.

"Good, it's decided," Dee said. "You aren't allowed to do any work while we're gone. When was the last time you had a chance to just relax and, say, read a book or take a nap?"

Dana smiled down the table at her, then reached to take her hand to squeeze it. "Thank you. I really am glad you came all this way to visit us. I'm just sorry—" Her eyes darkened with sadness.

"None of that," Dee said, giving her hand a squeeze back. "I can't tell you how thankful I am that you invited me."

As she sat picking at her food, the rest of the family noisily enjoying the meal, Dee counted down the hours. She could feel time slipping through her fingers, but she was relatively calm. Once she'd decided what she was going to have to do, she'd just accepted it.

She'd learned as a child to just accept things the way they were—until she could change them. There was nothing worse than feeling trapped in a situation where you felt there was nothing you could do.

That had been her childhood—feeling defenseless. She'd sworn that the day would come when she would never feel like that again. It took a steely, blind determination that some might have thought cold.

But the moment she'd lit that match so many years ago, she'd sworn she was never going to be a victim again.

Chapter 14

Hud had been in such a good mood after dinner that he'd suggested one last horseback ride.

Dee couldn't contain her excitement once she'd heard that it would be just the two of them. Dana had considered calling Liza to see if she would babysit, but one of the twins was teething and cranky, so she'd told Hud and Dee to go and have a good time.

"Oh, here," Hud had said. "I picked up the mail on my way in. You had something, Dee." Mail was delivered to a large box with Cardwell Ranch stenciled on the side. The box sat at the edge of Highway 191, a good quarter mile from the ranch house.

She took the envelope with the name Dee Anna Justice typed on it. The trust fund check. She hoped she would never have to use it. But it was always good to have money tucked away—just in case she had reason to leave town in a hurry.

Hud watched her open it, peek inside, then stuff the folded envelope into the hip pocket of her jeans. Having mail come to her in Dee Anna Justice's name seemed to seal the deal as far as who she was. At least for Hud.

While he went out to saddle two horses, Dee insisted on staying in the house and helping Dana with the dishes. She could tell Hud had liked that.

Hud smiled at her now as she walked out to the corral where he was waiting. She smiled back, warmed to her toes. He seemed comfortable and at ease with her. She wouldn't let herself think that his good mood had to do with her plans to fly out the next day.

It was the perfect evening, the weather cool but not cold. The sky was still bright over the canyon, the sun not yet set.

Dee let him help her into the saddle, loving being this close to him. She felt comfortable in the saddle. Hud could never love a woman who didn't ride.

"I think I could get into horseback riding," she said, as the two of them left the ranch behind and headed up into the mountains.

"You should check into riding lessons when you get home," he suggested. "I'm sure they're offered in New York."

"Yes," she agreed, reminded again that there was nothing waiting for her back in the city. She'd given up the apartment. Given up that life.

She considered what the real Dee Anna Justice would do once she realized Dee had borrowed her name. The best thing to do was send the check back. Put "Wrong Address" on the envelope. Dee Anna would never have to know.

That decided, Dee began to relax and enjoy the ride

and the man riding along next to her. At that moment she was so content, so sure that everything was going to work out the way she'd planned it, that she couldn't have foreseen the mistake she would make just minutes later on top of the mountain.

Colt made good time, and by seven that night he wasn't far outside Denver. He stopped for gas and coffee, figuring he had at least another fourteen hours minimum to go.

Hilde answered on the second ring as if she'd been waiting by the phone. "Where are you?"

He told her. "The roads haven't been bad. I expect they will be worse the closer I get. I should be there by nine or ten in the morning. Get some sleep."

"What about you?" she asked.

"I'm okay. When I first got into law enforcement I had to work some double shifts. I learned how to stay awake. Anyway, I'll be thinking of you the whole time."

He could hear the smile in her voice when she said, "Same here."

He stretched his legs and got back into the SUV. He tried Hud again. His call went straight to voice mail. Cussing under his breath, he headed for the interstate.

His thoughts were with Hilde. What Camilla's aunt had told him had him scared.

"Even when she was a little girl, if another child had a toy she wanted, she'd take it from her," Thelma Peters had said. "If that child got hurt in the process, Camilla was all the more happy for it. I remember one time scolding her for that behavior. She must have been four or five at the time. She and her family had come for a visit. Her father was often out of work. I'll never forget the way she turned to look at me. I remember my heart lurching in my chest. I was actually frightened."

Thelma had taken a moment, as if the memory had been too strong, before she continued. "That child looked at me and said, 'She should have given the toy to me when I told her to. If she got hurt, it's her own fault. Next time, she'll give it to me when I ask for it.'"

"What about her mother and father? They must have seen this kind of behavior and tried to do something about it."

Thelma had shook her head sadly. "I mentioned what I'd seen to my sister. Cynthia wasn't a strong woman. She said to me, 'Leave her be. Camilla's just a child.' Herbert? He smacked her around, then would hold her on his lap and pet her like she was a dog." The aunt had wrinkled her mouth in disgust. "That child worked him. Cynthia was too weak to stand up to her husband or her daughter."

"And Richard?"

"He idolized his sister, did whatever she wanted. The two were inseparable. I'm not surprised they were together in Montana when he died."

"There's a chance she killed him," he'd told her.

Thelma's hand had gone to her heart. "It is as if something is missing in her DNA. A caring gene. Camilla has no compassion for anyone but herself. I always wondered what she would do with Richard when she got tired of him."

"If she was responsible, why did she want her parents dead?"

Thelma had looked away. "I have my suspicions, ones I've never voiced to anyone."

"You think Herbert was abusing her?"

Her face had filled with shame. "I tried to talk to my

sister. I even called Social Services. Herbert swore it wasn't true. So did Camilla."

"You think your sister knew and just turned a blind eye."

"That's why Camilla killed them both," Thelma had said. "I saw that girl right after the police called and told me about the fire and that my sister and brother-in-law were dead. Richard? He's crying his eyes out. Camilla? Cool as a cucumber. She waltzes into the house and asks me what I have to eat, that she's starving. She sat there eating, smiling to herself. I tried to tell myself that we all grieve in our own way. But it was enough to turn my blood to ice."

As the sun sank lower behind the adjacent mountains, Dee and Hud reached a spot where aspens grew thick and green.

They reined in and climbed off their horses to walk to the edge of the mountain. This view was even more spectacular than the one she'd seen on the four-wheeler ride into the mountains.

"It's so peaceful here," Dee said, as she breathed in the evening. The air was scented with pine and the smell of spring. She hugged herself against the cool breeze that whispered through the trees. Shadows had puddled under them.

Unconsciously, she stepped closer to Hud as she thought of the bears and mountain lions that lived in these mountains. Hud seemed so unafraid of anything. She loved his quiet strength and wondered what her life would have been like if she'd had a father like him. Or even a brother like him.

As she glanced at him, she told herself that life had given her another chance to have such a man to protect her.

"Hud." Just saying his name sent a shiver through her.

He looked over at her expectantly as if he thought she was about to say something.

She didn't think. At that moment, she felt as if she would die if she didn't kiss him. No matter what happened, it was all she told herself she would ever want.

The kiss took him by such surprise that he didn't react at first. She felt his warm lips on hers as she pressed her chest into his hard, strong one.

One of his arms came around her as if he thought she'd stumbled into him and was about to fall off the edge of the mountain.

Several seconds passed, no more, before he pushed her away, holding her at arm's length. "What the—" His eyes darkened with anger. "What was that, Dee?" he demanded.

"I… I just—" She saw the change in his expression and knew that Hilde had warned him that she was after him. He hadn't believed her—until this moment.

Hud shoved her away from him.

She felt tears burn her eyes and anger begin to boil deep in her belly. She wanted to scream at him, *Why not me? What is so wrong with me?*

Instead, she said, "I'm so sorry," and pretended to be horrified by what she'd done when, in truth, she was furious with him.

"It was all of this," she said, motioning to the view. "I just got swept up in it and, standing next to you…" She looked away, hating him for making her feel like this.

"We should get back," he said, and turned to walk

toward the horses where he'd left them ground tied by the aspens.

She tried to breathe out her fury, to act chastised, to pretend to be remorseful. It was the hardest role she'd ever played.

They rode in silence down the mountain through the now dark pines.

Dee thought about the kiss. She'd been anticipating it for days and now felt deeply disappointed. Hud had cut her to the quick. She could never forgive him.

Worse, he would now suspect that everything Hilde had said was true. Good thing she'd made that plane reservation for tomorrow. She couldn't wait to get away from here.

Hilde got the text from Dana the next morning as she was starting to open the shop.

u r rght abt D Im so—

She hurriedly tried to call her friend. The phone went straight to voice mail. "Dana, call me the moment you get this."

Hilde stood inside the shop for a moment. The apparently interrupted text scared her more than she wanted to admit.

She called the sheriff's office. If Hud was home… But she was told that Hud had been called away on a case in West Yellowstone.

So Dana was alone out at the ranch with the kids… and Dee.

Colt was on his way, but she couldn't wait for him. She had to make sure Dana was all right.

Locking the shop, she headed for her vehicle, thankful Colt had changed her flat and retrieved it for her. Her mind was racing. The text had her terrified that something had happened. She drove as fast as she could to the ranch, jumping out of the SUV and running inside the house without knocking.

"Dana!" she screamed, realizing belatedly that she should have at least thought to bring a weapon. But she didn't have a gun, let alone anything close to a weapon at the house or shop other than a pair of scissors. She shuddered at the thought.

Dana appeared in the kitchen doorway looking startled. She was wearing an apron and had flour all over her hands. "What in the—"

"Are you all right?" Hilde said, rushing to her.

"I'm fine. What's wrong?"

"I got your text."

"My *text?* I didn't send you a text. In fact, I haven't been able to find my cell phone all morning."

Belatedly, Hilde remembered who'd answered Dana's cell just the afternoon before. She looked around the kitchen as that slowly sank in. Dee must still have the cell phone. Dana hadn't sent the text. But why would Dee send her a text that said she was right unless... *"Where are the kids?"*

"Hilde, you're scaring me. The kids just left with Dee for a walk up the road."

Hilde glanced around, didn't see Angus and Brick. "The twins, too?"

"She took them in the stroller to give me some time to myself this morning."

"No one is with her?" She saw the answer in her friend's face. "We have to find them. *Now.*"

"Hilde, Dee might have her problems but—"

"Colt called me from Oklahoma."

"Oklahoma? I thought he went to Denver?"

"He went down there to find out what he could about Rick. The woman you thought was Dee is his *sister,* Dana. When they were teenagers, the two of them were suspected of torching their house and killing their parents, but it could never be proven."

Dana paled. "Dee is Rick's *sister?*"

"Her name isn't Dee Anna Justice. It's Camilla Northland. Or at least it was."

"Then where is Dee Anna Justice?"

"I have no idea, but right now we have to get the kids." For all Hilde knew, the woman calling herself Dee had killed Dana's cousin and taken over her life.

"You can't really believe she'd hurt my—"

"*She wants Hud, Dana.* She's been after your life since the moment she saw Hud. Do you really think she wants the kids as well?"

Dana seemed to come out of the trance Dee'd had her in since arriving in Montana. Surely she'd seen the way Dee fawned over her husband.

"Hud told me she has a crush on him, but… You *have* to be wrong about her," Dana cried. But she grabbed the shotgun she kept high on the wall by the back door.

As they ran outside, Hilde prayed the babies were all right. She told herself that if Dee stood any chance of getting away with this, then she couldn't have hurt them. But the woman had apparently already gotten away with murdering her own parents—and her brother. Possibly Dana's cousin as well. Who knew what she'd do to get what she wanted.

Dee and the kids were nowhere in sight.

"She must have gone up the road," Dana said.

"There!" Hilde cried as she spotted the stroller lying

on its side in front of the barn. Dana rushed into the barn first, Hilde right behind her. They both stopped, both breathing hard.

"Mary! Hank!" Dana called, her voice breaking. Silence. She called again, her voice more frantic.

A faint cry came from one of the stalls.

Rushing toward it, they found Mary and Hank holding the twins in the back of the stall. Hilde heard the relief rush from Dana as she dropped to the straw.

"What are you two doing?" Hilde asked, fear making her voice tight.

"We're playing a game," Hank said.

"Auntie Dee told us to stay here and not make a sound," Mary said in a conspiratorial whisper.

"But Mary made a sound when she heard you calling for her," Hank said. "Now Auntie Dee is going to be mad, and when she's mad she's kind of scary."

"Where is Auntie Dee?" Hilde asked.

Hank shook his head and seemed to see the shotgun his mother had rushed in with. "Are you and Auntie Hilde going hunting?"

"We are," Hilde said. "That's why we need you and your sister to stay here and keep playing the game for just a little longer. Can you do that?"

Dana shot her friend a look, then picked up the shotgun. "Be very quiet. We'll be back in just a minute, okay?" Both children nodded and touched fingers to their lips.

Hilde stepped out of the stall and looked down the line of stalls. The light was dim and cool in the huge barn. Dee could be anywhere.

As they moved away from the stall with the children inside, Dana whispered, "Maybe it *is* just a game."

Hilde bit back a curse. Dana was determined to see the best in everyone—especially this cousin who'd ingratiated herself into their lives. But Hilde had to admit whatever game Camilla Northland was playing, it didn't make any sense.

They both jumped when they heard the barn door they'd come through slam shut. An instant later, they heard the board that locked it closed come down with a heart-stopping thud.

"She just locked us in," Hilde said, her voice breaking.

Dana had already turned and was racing toward the back door of the barn. Hilde knew before she saw Dana reach it that she would find it locked.

Only moments later did she smell the smoke.

Chapter 15

"I'm about ten minutes outside of Big Sky," Colt said when he'd called Hilde's phone and gotten voice mail. "I don't know where you are or why you aren't picking up." He didn't know what else to say so he disconnected and tried to call her at the shop.

His anxiety grew when the recording came on giving the shop's hours. He glanced at his watch. Hilde was a stickler for punctuality. If she'd gone to the shop, there was no way she would be thirty minutes late for work unless something was wrong.

When his phone rang, he thought it was Hilde. Prayed it was. He didn't even look to see who was calling and was surprised when he heard Hud's voice.

"I can't get into all of it right now," he told Hud, "but I have proof the woman at the ranch isn't Dee Anna Justice, and I can't reach Hilde at the shop or on her cell. I can't reach the ranch, either."

"I'm on my way home from West Yellowstone," Hud said. "I haven't been able to reach Dana, either. I was hoping you had heard something."

"I'm five minutes out," Colt said. "I'm going straight to the ranch."

"I'm twenty minutes out. Call me as soon as you know something."

He hung up and called the office, asked if there was any backup, but Deputy Liza Turner Cardwell was in Bozeman testifying in a court case and Deputy Jake Thorton was up in the mountains fishing on his day off.

"Liza should be back soon," Annie had told him.

Not soon enough, he feared. He tried Dana's brother Jordan. No answer. No surprise. Jordan was busy building his house and probably out peeling logs.

He disconnected as he came up behind a semi, laid on his horn and swore. The driver slowed, but couldn't find a place to pull over and the road had too many blind curves to pass.

Colt felt a growing sense of urgency. He needed to get to Cardwell Ranch. *Now.* All his instincts told him that Hilde was there and in trouble. Which meant so were Dana and the kids.

Mentally, he kicked himself as the vehicles in both lanes finally pulled over enough to let him through. He shouldn't have told Hilde what he found out in Oklahoma. She must have gone out to the ranch to warn Dana. He wouldn't let himself imagine what the woman calling herself Dee Anna Justice would do if cornered.

Along with the smell of smoke, Hilde caught the sharp scent of fuel oil. She could hear the crackling of flames.

The barn was old, the wood dry. Past the sound of fire they heard an engine start up.

For just an instant Hilde thought Dee might be planning to save them—the way she had her at the falls and possibly the way she had tried on the river.

But they heard the pickup leave, the sound dying off as the flames grew louder.

They rushed back to the children. Hilde dug in her pocket for her cell phone, belatedly realizing she'd left it in the SUV when she'd jumped out. She looked up at Dana. "You said you haven't been able to find your cell phone?"

Dana shook her head. The smoke was getting thicker inside the barn. Hilde could see flames blackening the kindling dry wood on all sides. It wouldn't be long before the whole barn was ablaze.

"Let's try to break through the side of the barn," Hilde said, grabbing up a shovel. She began to pound at the old wood. It splintered but the boards held.

Dana joined her with another shovel.

Hilde couldn't believe Dee thought she could get away with this. But at the back of her mind, she feared Dee would. Somehow, she would slip out of this, the same way she had as a kid. The same way she had killed her brother and gone free. And it would be too late for Hilde and Dana and the kids.

"I can't believe she would hurt innocent children," Dana said, tears in her eyes.

"What's wrong, Mommy?" Mary asked.

"Is the barn on fire?" Hank asked.

Hilde and Dana kept pounding at the wood at the back of the stall. If she could just make a hole large enough for the kids to climb out.

The wood finally gave way. She and Dana grabbed hold of the board and were able to break it off to form a small hole. Not large enough for them, but definitely large enough to get the children out.

What would happen to them if Dee saw them, though? They'd heard the sound of the pickup engine, but what if she hadn't really left? The question passed silently between the two friends.

"We're going to play another game," Dana said, crouching down next to Mary and Hank. "You and your sister are going to crawl out. I am going to hand you Angus and Brick. Then you're going to go hide in that outbuilding where we keep the old tractor. You can't let Dee see you, okay?"

Hank nodded. "We'll sneak along the haystack. No one will see us."

"Good boy," Dana said, her voice breaking with emotion. "Take care of the babies until either me or Daddy calls you. Don't make a sound if Dee calls you, okay? Now hurry."

Hilde looked out through the hole. No sign of Dee. She helped Hank out and Dana handed him Angus. Mary crawled out next and took Brick. They quickly disappeared from sight.

The smoke was thick now, the flames licking closer and closer as the whole barn went up in flames.

"Oh, Hilde, I'm so sorry for not trusting you," Dana cried, and hugged her.

"Right now, we have to find a way out of here."

The two of them tried to find another spot along the wall where they could get out. The barn was old but sturdily built, and the smoke was so thick now that staying

low wasn't helping. They could hear the flames growing closer and closer.

With a *whoosh* the back of the barn began to cave in.

The rest of the structure groaned and creaked. But
over the roar of the flames and the falling boards, Hilde
heard another sound. A vehicle headed in their direction.

Dee had left Dana a note. "I couldn't find you and the
kids when I got ready to leave for the airport, so I borrowed your pickup. Thank you for everything. I'll leave
the truck in long-term parking. Dee."

Then she'd taken the keys from where she'd seen Dana
hang them on a hook by the door and left.

After they'd finished their horseback ride yesterday,
Hud had unsaddled the horses and put everything away.
Then she'd heard him go upstairs, his boots heavy on the
steps, as if he dreaded telling his wife about her cousin.

She'd listened hard but hadn't heard a sound once he
entered his and Dana's bedroom, confirming what she'd
suspected. That he hadn't awakened Dana last night to
tell her.

Earlier this morning when Dee had come downstairs,
she'd seen Hud and Dana with their heads together. He
had definitely told her something. She'd seen how reluc-
tant he was to leave his wife. They'd done their best to
act normal. But she could tell they were counting down
the hours until she left.

She'd helped herself to a cup of coffee. Dana had made
French toast and sausage for breakfast and offered her a
plate. Dee ate heartily as Dana took care of the kids and
nibbled at the food on her plate. "You should eat more
breakfast," Dee told her.

"I'm fine. Anyway, I still need to lose a few pounds after the twins."

But this is your last breakfast, Dee had wanted to say. She hoped on her last day on earth she ate a good breakfast, since she would never be eating again.

As she drove away from the ranch, she glanced at the barn. Flames were licking up the sides. She looked away, thinking how sad it was that things hadn't worked out differently.

She looked back only once more as she drove past Big Sky. Smoke billowed up into the air across the river, an orange glow behind the pines. She gave the pickup more gas. She had a plane to catch, and there was no going back and changing things now.

She turned on the radio and began to sing along. She had no idea where she was going or what she would do when she got there, but she had Dee Anna Justice's trust fund check and options. She would find another identity and disappear.

What amazed her as she left the canyon was that she'd ever thought she could be happy living on Cardwell Ranch with Hud.

Colt saw the smoke and flames in the distance the moment he came out of the narrow part of the canyon. He felt his heart drop. He raced up the highway, calling the fire department as he went, and turned onto the ranch road.

At first he thought it was the house on fire, but as he came up over a rise, he saw that it was the barn. For a moment he felt a wave of relief. Then he saw Hilde's SUV parked in front of the house. Dana's ranch pickup was gone. Maybe they'd all left to take Dee to the airport. Maybe they were all fine.

But his gut told him differently.

When he saw the stroller lying on its side in front of the barn and the door barred, he knew. Holding his hand down on the horn, he hit the gas and raced toward the burning front door of the barn.

The bumper smashed through the burning wood as the expensive rental SUV burst into the barn. Pieces of burning wood hit the windshield, sparks flew all around him and then there was nothing but dark thick smoke.

The moment the SUV broke through the door, he hit his brakes. *It's too late,* he thought when he saw the entire shell of the barn in flames, the smoke so thick he couldn't see his hand in front of his face. He leaped from the rig, screaming Hilde's name. The heat was so intense he felt as if his face were burning. He feared the vehicle's gas tank would explode any moment.

Then he heard her answer.

She and Dana came out of the smoky darkness silhouetted against the walls of flames.

"Where are the babies?" he yelled over the roar of the flames.

"They got out!" Hilde yelled back.

He shoved them both into the SUV and threw it in Reverse. The heat was unbearable. He knew if he didn't get the rig out now…

The hood of the SUV, the paint peeling and blackened, had just cleared the edge of the barn when he heard the loud crash, and the barn began to collapse.

If he'd been just a few minutes later…

He wouldn't let himself even imagine that as he slammed on the brakes back from the inferno. Hilde and Dana were coughing and choking, but he could hear fire trucks and the ambulance on its way.

"My babies," Dana choked out.

"They're in that outbuilding," Hilde said, pointing a good ways from the burning remains of the barn.

"Where's Dee?" he asked them.

"She left after she started the fire," Hilde said.

"I heard her take my truck," Dana added. She was already getting out of the SUV to go after her children, Hilde at her heels. Colt ran ahead and found the children all safe, huddled together in a back corner of the outbuilding.

Later, as the fire department and EMTs took care of Hilde and Dana and the kids, he told Hilde, "I have to go after Dee. I can't let her get on that plane."

"I'm fine," she told him. "Go!"

Chapter 16

The ride to the airport outside of Bozeman was the longest one of Colt's life. He called ahead and asked that Dee Anna Justice be detained, but he was told that she'd already gone through security. Two airport officials were looking for her, but so far they hadn't found anyone matching the description he'd given them.

Camilla's plane was scheduled to board within twenty minutes.

"Don't let her get on that plane," Colt ordered. "Hold her there until I get there. Consider her armed and dangerous."

"Armed? She just went through security. I'm sure if she was—"

"You don't know this woman. She's dangerous. Have your officers approach her with extreme caution."

He was just outside of Belgrade when Hud called.

"I'm on my way to the airport," Hud said. "Make sure that woman doesn't get away, Deputy."

"I'm doing my best," Colt said. "But I'm on suspension."

"Your suspension was lifted hours ago," Hud said. "About the time you saved my wife's life. We'll talk about that later. Where are you?"

Colt told him he was turning onto the airport road. He was only minutes away from confronting Camilla Northland.

Dee looked into the women's restroom mirror, appraising herself. She'd brushed out her hair. Since it was naturally curly, it flowed around her head like a dark halo.

She'd applied makeup, especially eye shadow, mascara and blush, sculpting her face. It amazed her how different she looked from the woman who'd been staying at Cardwell Ranch.

As she studied herself in the mirror, she liked what she saw. She'd been able to cover most of the damage she'd done to herself. But maybe when she got wherever she was going, she'd change her hair. Something short and blond. Yes, she liked that idea. A whole new her.

That thought made her laugh. When she'd first left Oklahoma, she'd believed in her heart that she could put the past behind her, become whoever and whatever she wanted.

She hadn't realized then how deep the past had embedded itself in her. It ate at her like a parasite, a constant reminder that she was broken and while she might be able to put back the pieces, she would never be whole.

One of the female security guards stuck her head in the restroom door. Camilla saw her out of the corner of her eye but continued to carefully apply another coat of bright red lipstick.

"Excuse me," the woman said. "We're checking boarding passes. May I see yours?"

"Of course," Camilla said. She took her time putting the lipstick back into her purse. "Here it is."

The woman started to take it, her attention on the slip of paper. More important the *name* on the paper. No Dee Anna Justice but Amy Matthews.

Dee Anna's boarding pass was buried at the botton of the trash container.

The security officer looked from the boarding pass to Camilla, then handed the paper back. "Have a nice flight, Ms. Matthews. I believe your flight is boarding now," the woman said.

"Thank you." Camilla walked out and got into line for the flight to Seattle. In a few minutes she would be on board.

She had hoped to catch an earlier flight, but it hadn't worked out. Fortunately, she'd planned for this, making several flights in three different names. One in the name of Dee Anna Justice to New York. Another as Amy Matthews to Seattle. And a third flight earlier that day to Las Vegas under the name Patricia Barnes.

Like Rick, she had three different identities ready. She'd just been smart enough not to get caught with them on her, though.

She'd missed the flight to Vegas by only minutes. Finishing up her business at the ranch had taken longer than she'd hoped.

Not that it mattered now. Within minutes she would be on her way to Seattle. No one was looking for Amy Matthews.

She figured Hud must have come home sooner than expected. Or that deputy, Colt Dawson, had showed up. Either way, it would be too late.

It wasn't as if she'd thought for a moment they wouldn't suspect her given everything that had happened. But they had no proof.

Anyway, she would be long gone before they could get to the airport. Even if they should somehow track her down, they still couldn't do anything except get her for using an alias. Or yes, and pretending to be Dee Anna Justice.

She'd cried her way out of more of those situations than she could remember. If tears didn't work, then her life story definitely did. Of course she was messed up. Imagine living your life with such suspicions hanging over you.

It had worked every other time. It would now, too, because without proof, they couldn't touch her. With Dana, Hilde and the kids gone…

She left the restroom and walked to her gate. The woman taking her boarding pass told her to hurry, her flight was about to leave.

She hurried down the ramp and into the plane just moments before the flight attendant was about to shut the door. She'd timed it close, but she hadn't wanted to risk sitting at the gate in case anyone she knew was looking for her.

As she slipped into her first-class seat next to a businessman in a nice suit, she told herself her luck might be changing.

"Hello," she said and extended her hand. "I'm Amy Matthews."

"Clark Evans."

The flight attendant asked her what she would like to drink.

"I'd love a vodka Collins," she said. "I'm celebrating. Today's my birthday. Join me?" she asked the business executive, taking in his gold cuff links, the cut of his suit and the expensive wristwatch.

"How can I say no?" he said, already flirting with her.

"Yes, how can you?" she asked, flirting back. "I have a feeling that this could be a very interesting flight."

Colt ran into the airport. The head of security met him the moment he came through the door.

"Dee Anna Justice hasn't checked in for her flight. It was supposed to leave ten minutes ago," the man told him. "We've held it as long as we can. So far, she's a no-show."

"Dee Anna Justice definitely isn't on the flight? You checked all the passengers?"

"No one matching her description is on the flight, and everyone is accounted for," he assured Colt.

Colt had been so sure she would make her flight. As gutsy as the woman was and as bulletproof as she'd been, she would think she had nothing to fear.

She'd already gone through security, so she'd been here. But that didn't mean she didn't change her mind and leave.

Maybe she was running scared, though he highly doubted it. Camilla had an arrogance born of getting away with murder.

"What other flights have left in the last hour?" he asked.

"Only one, but it's to Seattle. The plane is taxiing down the runway right now."

"Stop that plane."

"I'm not sure—"

"This woman just tried to kill six people, four of them children, by burning them alive. Stop the plane. *Now.*"

Camilla was sipping her drink, smiling at her companion, when the pilot announced they would be returning to the terminal because of an instrument malfunction.

She looked past the man next to her out his window. Sunlight ricocheted off the windows of the terminal, reminding her of the day she'd flown in here. If she'd gone fishing on the Yellowstone River with Lance...

Still, even though she knew there was nothing wrong with the instruments, she wasn't worried. The barn had been burning so quickly, the boards locking the doors would be ashes—all evidence gone.

Even the spilled fuel oil she'd used to get the barn burning fast would look like nothing more than an accident—at first. She'd started the fire with several candles she'd found in the back of Hilde's sewing shop, complete with the cute little quilted mats that went with them.

Everyone knew that Hilde had been losing her mind lately. But to do something this horrible because Dana turned against her? It was almost unthinkable—unless her behavior had been so out of character lately that everyone feared she was having a nervous breakdown. But taking her own life and her friend's along with Dana's four children? This story would make headlines across the country.

The plane taxied back to the small terminal. It wasn't but a few minutes after she'd heard the door being opened that Deputy Colt Dawson appeared.

She turned to the man next to her and asked him a

question. Out of the corner of her eye, she saw Colt start to move through the plane. He was almost past her when he stopped and took a step back until he was right at her elbow. "Camilla," he said.

She looked up at him, frowned and said, "I'm sorry. You're mistaken. My name is Amy Matthews."

"Miss... Matthews. I'd like you to come with me. *Now*," he said when she hesitated. "You won't be taking this flight today."

She sighed and, picking up her bag, got to her feet. "We'll have to celebrate another time," she told the businessman. Colt took her bag from her and quickly frisked her, which made her smile as if she was amused.

"I never noticed how cute you are," she said, as he escorted her off the plane to four waiting security guards. He insisted on cuffing her once she was out of sight of the passengers.

"Is that really necessary?" she asked. "What is this about, anyway? So I didn't use my real name. I have an old boyfriend who I don't want to find me. So sue me."

"This is about the attempted murder of six individuals, four of them children." Colt appeared to be fighting to keep his emotions in check.

Camilla was silent for a moment, then she frowned and said, "Attempted?"

"That's right. They're all alive. Hilde and Dana will be testifying against you in court."

Camilla let out a little laugh. "I suppose you're the one I should thank for this?"

"Be my guest," Colt said, as he led her up the ramp. They were almost to the boarding area when Marshal Hud Savage appeared.

Colt felt Camilla tense. They all did at the look in the

marshal's eyes. Colt knew exactly how he felt. In the old West she would have been strung up from the nearest tree.

But this wasn't the old West, and he and Hud didn't mete out justice. All they could do was hope and pray that this woman never saw the outside of a cell for the rest of her life.

Once at the law enforcement center, Camilla Northland's story was that she'd left the ranch right after Hilde arrived. Dana was with the kids on the front porch as she drove away and had asked Hilde if she wanted to go on a walk with them. That was the last she said that she saw of them.

She'd seemed surprised that Dana and Hilde had told another story. "I don't know why they would lie, except that Hilde has been telling lies about me ever since I came to Montana, and Dana must be confused."

"It's over, Camilla," Colt said, as they all sat in the interrogation room. He tossed the photo of her as a teenager on the table. "Your aunt told me everything. She said she would fly up here if need be."

She stared at the photo of herself and her brother. When she looked up, she suddenly looked tired—and almost relieved.

"It would appear I'm going to need a lawyer," she said.

"Just tell me this. How was it that you ended up here pretending to be Dee Anna Justice?"

For a moment, she didn't look as if she would answer. "Dee Anna was my roommate in New York City for a while," she said with a shrug. "The letter came after she'd moved out."

"And you decided to take her identity?"

"I'd never been to Montana," she said. "I liked the idea of having a cousin I'd never met." She looked unapologetic as her gaze locked with Hud's. "And I'd never met a real cowboy."

"Where is Dee Anna Justice?" Hud demanded, clearly not amused by her flirting with him.

She looked away for a moment, and Colt felt his heart drop. He now knew what extremes this woman would go to and feared for the real Dee Anna Justice.

"She's in Spain visiting some friend of hers. Her mother, Marietta, probably knows how to contact her."

"Marietta's family is from Spain?"

"Italy." Camilla smiled. "No one told you that Dee Anna is half-Italian?" She laughed. "Dana asked me why her grandparents disinherited their son. He married a *foreigner.* Apparently a woman who spoke Italian and wanted to live in the big city wasn't what they wanted for their son. But you'd have to ask Dee Anna if that is really why they disinherited him." She shrugged. "Dee Anna and I were never close. She was a lot like Hilde. For some reason, she didn't like me." Camilla laughed at that. "I'll take that lawyer now."

Epilogue

Hilde held it all together until a few weeks after Camilla's arrest. Suddenly she was bombarded with so many emotions that she finally let herself cry as the ramifications of what had happened—and what had almost happened—finally hit her.

Over it all was a prevailing sadness. She and Dana were trying to repair their relationship, but Hilde knew it would take time—and never be the same. She felt as if someone had died and that made her all the sadder.

"Hilde, can you ever forgive me?" Dana had cried that day, as they'd watched the rest of the barn burn from the back of the ambulance. "I should have listened to you. I'm so sorry. I'm just so sorry."

"There is nothing to forgive," she'd told Dana, as they'd hugged. But in her heart, she knew that something was broken. Only time would tell if it could be fixed.

Hud was going through something even worse, Colt had told her. He blamed himself for not seeing what was right in front of his eyes.

"I was just so happy that Dana was enjoying her cousin, I made excuses for Dee's behavior just like Dana did. I didn't want to see it," he kept saying. "I almost lost my family because of it. And what I did to Hilde—"

She'd told him and Dana both that she understood. Camilla had been too good at hiding her true self. Hilde didn't blame them. But a part of her was disappointed in them that they hadn't believed her—the friend they'd both known for years. That was going to be the hard part to repair in the friendship.

Colt was wonderful throughout it all. He'd saved her life and Dana's. Neither of them would ever forget that.

Hilde, who'd always thought of herself as strong, had leaned on him, needing his quiet strength to see her through. Both she and Dana had recovered from the smoke inhalation. It was the trauma of being trapped in a burning barn with a psychopath trying to kill them that had residual effects.

Jordan and Liza had a housewarming a few months after everything settled down. Their new home was beautiful, and Hilde could see the pride they shared with all the work they'd done themselves. Hilde gave them a quilt as a housewarming present.

"I'd like to take your beginner quilting class," Liza said, making both Hilde and Dana look at her in surprise. She was a tomboy like Dana and had never sewn a thing in her life.

Liza grinned and looked over at Jordan, who nodded. "We're going to have a baby! I want to make her a baby quilt."

Cheers went up all around, and Hilde said she would be delighted to teach her to quilt, and she also had some adorable baby quilt patterns for girls.

"Stop by the shop and I'll show you," she said.

At the party, Dana told Hilde that she'd called Marietta Justice, only to receive a return call from the woman's assistant confirming that the real Dee Anna Justice was alive and well in Spain traveling with friends.

Hilde could tell that Dana had been disappointed the woman hadn't even bothered to talk to her herself. But fortunately, Dana hadn't taken it any further. Whatever was going on in that part of the Justice family, it would remain a mystery.

At least for now, since Hilde knew her friend too well. Dana had a cousin she'd never met. Maybe more than one. She wouldn't forget about the very real and mysterious Dee Anna Justice and family. One of these days, Dana wouldn't be able to help herself and she would contact her cousin.

Hilde hated to think what might happen—but then again, she wasn't as trusting as Dana, was she?

The party was fun, even though things were still awkward between all of them.

"They'll get better," Colt promised her. "You and the Savages were too good of friends before this happened. Right now everyone is a little bruised and battered, especially you. I can see how badly they both feel when they're around you."

That was what was making things so awkward. They wore their regrets on their sleeves.

"Are you still worried about Hud?" she asked him on their way back to her house.

"He's really beating himself up. I think he's questioning whether he should remain marshal. He's afraid he can't trust his judgment."

"That's crazy. He's a great marshal."

"He let a psychopath not only live with them, but also take his children for a walk the morning of the fire."

"He didn't know she was a psychopath."

"Yeah. I think that's the point. He overlooked so much because he wanted Dana to have a good time with her cousin. You told me how excited she was about finding a cousin she'd never met."

Hilde nodded. "They both tried to make the woman he thought was Dee Anna Justice fit into their family. Dana was at odds with her siblings for years, so I understand her need for family."

Colt looked over at her. "What about you?"

"Me?"

"How do you feel about a large family?"

She laughed. "As an only child, I've always yearned for one."

"Good," he said with a smile. "Because I have a large family up north, and they're all anxious to meet you."

She looked at him. "You want me to meet your family?"

He slowed the truck, stopping on a small rise. In the distance, Lone Mountain was silhouetted against Montana's Big Sky. Stars glittered over it. A cool breeze came in through his open window, smelling of the river and the dense pines. The summer night was perfect.

Colt cut the engine and turned toward her. "I can't wait for my family to meet you. I'm just hoping I can introduce you as my fiancée."

Hilde caught her breath as he reached into his pocket and pulled out a small black jewelry box.

"Hilde Jacobson? Will you marry me?" He opened the box, and the perfect emerald-cut diamond caught in the starlight.

For a moment she couldn't speak. So much had happened, and yet they'd all come out of the ashes alive with their futures ahead of them.

"I know this is sudden, but we can have a long engagement if that's what you want," Colt added when she didn't answer him.

She shook her head. She'd always been a woman who never acted impulsively. Until recently. She believed in taking her time on any decision she made. Especially the huge ones.

But if she'd learned anything from all this, it was that she had to follow her instincts—and her heart. "I would love to marry you, Colt Dawson. I can't wait to be your bride."

He let out a relieved laugh and slipped the ring on her finger. It fit perfectly. As he pulled her into his arms and kissed her, Lone Mountain glowed in the starlight.

"I was so hoping you would say that," he whispered.

Wrapped in his arms, she knew whatever the future held, they would face it together. Time and love were powerful healers. With Colt by her side, she could do anything, she thought, as her heart filled to overflowing.

* * * * *

THE 2022 ROMANCE CHRISTMAS COLLECTION

6 FREE TRADE-SIZE BOOKS IN ALL!

In this loveliest of seasons may you find many reasons for happiness, magic and love, and what better way to fill your heart with the magic of Christmas than with an unforgettable romance from our specially curated holiday collection.

YES! Please send me the first shipment of **The 2022 Romance Christmas Collection**. This collection begins with 1 FREE TRADE SIZE BOOK and 2 FREE gifts in the first shipment. Along with my free book, I'll also get 2 additional mass-market paperback books. If I do not cancel, I will continue to receive three books a month for five additional months. My first four shipments will be billed at the discount price of $19.98 U.S./$25.98 CAN., plus $1.99 U.S./$3.99 CAN. for shipping and handling*. My last two shipments will be billed at the discount price of $17.98 U.S./$23.98 CAN., plus $1.99 U.S./$3.99 CAN. for shipping and handling*. I understand that accepting the free books and gifts places me under no obligation to buy anything. I can always return a shipment and cancel at any time. My free books and gifts are mine to keep no matter what I decide.

☐ 269 HCK 1875   ☐ 469 HCK 1875

Name (please print)

Address   Apt. #

City   State/Province   Zip/Postal Code

Mail to the **Harlequin Reader Service:**
IN U.S.A.: P.O. Box 1341, Buffalo, NY 14240-8531
IN CANADA: P.O. Box 603, Fort Erie, ON L2A 5X3

HARLEQUIN
PLUS

Announcing a **BRAND-NEW** multimedia subscription service for romance fans like you!

Read, Watch and Play.

Experience the easiest way to get the romance content you crave.

Start your **FREE 7 DAY TRIAL** at <u>www.harlequinplus.com/freetrial</u>.